Island Going

Island Going

Robert Atkinson

This edition published 1995 by
Birlinn Limited
13 Roseneath Street
Edinburgh EH9 1JH

First published by Collins 1949

ISBN 1 874744 31 9

A CIP record of this book is available
from the British Library

Detail from a photograph of
Isle if Rhum from Cleadale, Isle of Eigg
by John MacPherson

Designed by Gourlay Graphics Glasgow

Made and printed in Finland by
Werner Söderström OY

AUTHOR'S NOTE

I AM grateful to too many of the kind people of the Hebrides to name all of them here ; some are in this book and my indebtedness to them will be plain. But I must begin by saying a formal thank you to Kenneth MacIver of Stornoway, for the help and influence which so smoothed the way in pre-war days ; and for his great generosity since, without which Hebridean voyagings (still unexhausted) could hardly have been resumed.

A three weeks' stay on the island of St. Kilda was with the generous permission of the owner, now Marquess of Bute. A later visit was with the assistance of James Fisher. The kindnesses of Alec MacFarquhar, grazing tenant of the island of North Rona, are unforgotten.

Certain facsimile illustrations are reproduced by permission of : the Editor, *The Illustrated London News* ; the executors of the late Cherry Kearton ; and the Controller of H.M. Stationery Office. Various quotations are printed by permission of : Malcolm Stewart ; D. M. Reid and the publishers of *The Cornhill Magazine* ; the executors of the late Richard Kearton ; the Editor, the *Stornoway Gazette* ; The Moray Press ; Hugh MacDiarmid and B. T. Batsford, Ltd. ; Messrs. Douglas and Foulis (extracts from J. A. Harvie-Brown's *Vertebrate Fauna of the Outer Hebrides*). As well as those already acknowledged to him on the plates, John Ainslie took the following photographs : the kittiwakes and arctic tern among the sea-fowl of Plate VIII, the top left-hand photograph of Plate X, the skyline of Plate XIV, the top right-hand photograph of Plate XXIV, and the gannetry cliffs of Plate XLIII. The rest are my own.

R. A.

CONTENTS

Contents

Contents

SIXTH YEAR

The Hebrides Regained

LIST OF ILLUSTRATIONS

ILLUSTRATIONS IN THE TEXT

At first it seem'd a little speck,
And then it seemed a mist. . . .
A speck, a mist, a shape, I wist!
And still it near'd and near'd. . . .

The Outliers

A SMALL unheard-of sea-bird, chance-found in the index of a bird book, was called—Leach's Fork-tailed Petrel. It sounded like a true ornithologists' child, cumbrously museum-named, and not far removed from the class of lesser yellow-bellied fire-eater. It was just what we were looking for, in January or February of 1935.

> The only known European stations are in the British Isles—on St. Kilda, the Flannans, North Rona, and a few islands off the west coast of Ireland.

Admirable! Leach's petrel was allied to the much more familiar storm petrel, " Mother Carey's Chicken," whose habits its own appeared to resemble, but "Information is scanty." We, John Ainslie and myself, soon had *Oceanodroma leucorrhoa leucorrhoa* on a short list. We wanted some far place and outlandish, little known bird ; we wished to join the searchers after rarity, who went on expeditions to skim the cream from new places.

The Flannan Isles were disqualified by a lighthouse ; St. Kilda was well known and long ago the Kearton brothers had taken their pioneering camera there, followed by very many others. We had never heard of North Rona before, but the tiny island seemed sufficiently remote and inaccessible when we found it marked as a dot some forty miles to seaward from Cape Wrath, the very north-westward corner of Scotland. We plumped for Rona and Leach's petrel. The next land beyond was the Faroes, and then Iceland. It did seem a thing that in Britain there should be ground, a decent-sized desert island, where you would be parted from the nearest other Man by forty miles of grey northern sea—this was something to imagine from the south of England. But how on earth to get to North Rona and what was to be found behind the name?

Gradually during the early months of 1935 we came to find out a little about the history and resources of the island. It lay roughly equidistant from the lighthouses of Cape Wrath and Butt of Lewis, pertaining to the Outer Hebrides but making, along with St. Kilda and the Flannans, a line of ultimate outliers from twenty to forty miles beyond them. The island was a bare grassy hump, about 350 feet at its best elevation and of about 300 acres extent. Once it had had its own natives, " a skiff their navy, and a rock their wealth," but for nearly a hundred years now it had lain uninhabited and deserted. There were the remains of a village, derelict overgrown stones ; this was where the Leach's petrels were found. Some sort of hermit, whether of history or mythology, had built a cell there in the Dark Ages. A flock of gone-wild sheep roamed over the island. The coast was entirely rock-bound with no beach of any sort ; landing was " difficult."

How to make a start, with Rona empty and far away and the people and resources of the north-west corner of its parent Scotland foreign and unknown? We wrote to any one we could think of who might conceivably know something of Rona and of a way of getting there, to harbour-masters, lighthouse-keepers, yachtsmen, fishermen, trawler owners, curators of museums, naturalists. The stamped addressed envelopes came back with kindly but unadvancing replies until between us we had a sheaf of contradictory information, suggestion and bafflement :

It is so many years ago (1894) that I visited North Rona that I do not know in the least the present circumstances. I was becalmed in my yacht in the neighbourhood of the island when returning to Stornoway from the Faroes. . . . I have no note of seeing any fork-tailed petrels. At that time the island was uninhabited. . . . The weather of course would be a great gamble.

Or this :

I have just received your letter re information about the Island of North Rona but I'm sorry I cannot give you very much. North Rona belongs to Lewis and the crofters about the Port of Ness have sheep grazing on it and I understand they usually go out to clip their sheep either this month or next month. I expect some of them will have motor boats now. You will have to go either to Mallaig or Kyle of Lochalsh to get a steamer for Stornoway and then Motor Bus to the Port of Ness. I would advise you to communicate with The Principle Lightkeeper, Butt of Lewis Lighthouse, Port of Ness, Stornoway, Scotland.

"Just a short note along with the information about North Rona," wrote the Principal Lightkeeper from the Butt of Lewis.

A Drifter is leaving here at the end of June or early in July, to go out for sheep. They will probably be ashore for 12 hours or so. A. MacFarquhar, Mill House, Dell, Ness, Lewis, rents the place, and he arranges for the time of sailing, as the sheep belong to him. If this will suit you, communicate with him, and I have no doubt he will be pleased to take you. Another alternative route would be via Aberdeen, if any trawlers from that port were using the Rona ground. . . . Then the Fishery Cruiser often goes out there, and if you communicate with the Secretary, Fishery Board, Edinburgh, and state your requirements, he may land you and call again for you later in the season. I am afraid these are the only routes to get to North Rona. I hope some of the routes will suit you. . . . This is all the information I can gather meantime so will close hoping you will manage to get a landing.

This helpful letter turned out to be largely accurate but unfortunately neither drifter nor trawler (not that we knew the difference between them) would do. Hours or days on North Rona were no use, we wanted weeks on the island to investigate the nocturnal, subterranean and probably obscure habits of our chosen petrel. The drifter for the sheep went for only one day once a year. There was a vague possibility of chartering a Stornoway drifter but at such immense cost it was out of the question. And even if an east coast trawler rounding the north of Scotland to the Atlantic fishing grounds should land us on her outward trip, we would have to return on her homeward voyage within a few days ; or be stranded. We were much too unofficial for the Fishery Board.

At this stage—" Dear John, Somebody's even written a book about Rona, did you ever—I've just been sent a copy. Very exciting but actually it doesn't get us much forrarder," etc., etc. The book was Malcolm Stewart's invaluable *Ronay*, describing Rona, its companion rock Sula Sgeir and also the Flannan Islands. The author had been an undergraduate reading geology at Oxford, and during the long vacations of 1930 and 1931 had twice managed to get a landing on North Rona. He had pieced together old travellers' accounts and quoted from them in a handbook which would surely be ever blessed by hopeful followers to these isles, which, so he claimed, " have even disappeared from the modern map of Scotland." His first visit had been with D. M. Reid, science master at Harrow, his second with T. H. Harrisson. They had worked the east coast route by trawler from Aberdeen :

> With the cold grey light of breaking dawn land was clearly discernible some few miles off the starboard bow. . . . As the ship approached, so the land grew and grew until it was easily possible to make out the shape of the island. . . .

The thrill that Fig. 2 communicated !—a fuzzy snapshot of " North Rona from the East," a choppy sea and a dark hump of land across the horizon. Or Fig. 3, " The S.W. Extremity from the Village," some heaps of overgrown stones and a coast sprawling into mist beyond.

> A boat was lowered. Though so easily said, this operation required many minutes to perform, since it had not been lowered in many years, a point of honour amongst trawlermen. The best place for getting ashore appeared to be in a small inlet towards the centre of the east side. But even here landing was by no means easy, for the swell lifted and lowered the small boat ceaselessly. A quick jump ashore while the boat rose and a desperate grab at the rock was the only possible course to adopt, while the gear had to be thrown ashore piecemeal. . . .
>
> As the trawler steamed on its way two men were left over

forty miles from the nearest soul, with a great expanse of sea between, but with an unknown island at their feet to explore. (*Ronay*, 1933).

" Our Loneliest Isle " by D. M. Reid in the *Cornhill Magazine* for September, 1931 (which we turned up) also described that visit. Leach's fork-tailed petrels were there all right.

This scourge lives in burrows in the roofs of the houses and remains quiet all day. Once you have got yourself comfortably tucked in for the night and have at last really got to sleep, these birds begin to take a hand in things. First of all they sit round in a circle and talk to each other in an extremely loud voice which sounds something like this—Pui-e-e-e brrrrrrrrr—the later part like a very bad and very prolonged gear-change. This ultimately, after a series of nightmares, wakes you up. While you are still trying to adjust your ideas to account for it all, something walks unhurriedly across your face and reaching' your forehead says " Pui-e-e brrrr——" and all your returning senses fly to pieces and you make a wild grab and catch nothing. And so the night goes on. . . .

But our own prospects of reaching Rona seemed increasingly remote. " I have to confess that you have set me a difficult job ! " wrote D. M. Reid himself. " It used to be easy to get from Aberdeen on a trawler to N. Rona. That method, however, is no longer possible. . . ."

" I was lucky enough to have the loan of my father's yacht when I was on N. Ronay," wrote A. B. Duncan whom we had traced as a visitor in July, 1929. The last word did seem to be yacht, but indeed whose ? And who would not only land us but come back to take us off a month or so later ? Time was getting short ; correspondence certainly pointed out the difficulties but could not solve the problem. " Years had passed in vain attempts, and still we had not reached North Rona," wrote a visitor of a hundred and more years before ; " nothing seemed to have been attained while that remained to be done." We too began to think of trying again next year. Perhaps this summer we could at least discover some base from which Rona could be reached, and then knowing more of the circumstances could make plans for a year ahead.

It was already well into July when we met D. M. Reid in person. We had to agree when he could only suggest as alternative the north-west corner of the mainland. Some off-lying isles there with queer names were little known and would be worth looking into. He himself kept a boat up there, his boatman might be able to take us out. At least Sutherland was the nearest mainland to Rona. Possibly there might be some sizable fishing boats thereabouts. And once from the tower of Cape Wrath lighthouse Malcolm Stewart had made out an ultimate speck on the horizon. " For all the accuracy of the map can this be land ? " he had asked. North Rona seen from the mainland !

> *Some unsuspected isle in the far seas !*
> *Some unsuspected isle in far-off seas !*

FIRST YEAR

HANDA ISLAND

*

1935

I

The Sailors' Home

IN his mother's car, on July 25th, 1935, John Ainslie and myself set out from Oxfordshire for the north-west corner of Sutherland. It was a fine morning with heat to come, and when that was over, and the day nearly gone, the hills of Lanark gave back the afterglow of sunset, the whitewashed walls of cottages were pink and old dead grass was the colour of flowering heather. At half-past one next morning when the speedometer showed 500 miles, we pulled off the road on to the edge of a bleak, anonymous moor and slept in the front seats until grouse began to call and the light came again. We pushed on north and west all day, by Inverness, Invergordon and Lairg until the tar ended, the road became single track, and we entered the sodden grandeur of the west.

Fifty miles beyond Lairg the road reached the coast at a little township called Kinloch Bervie, though it had already met miles inland the head-waters of the great sea lochs. The ribbon that unwound from London in July sun petered out into rain-swept moorland two or three miles beyond Kinloch Bervie. Another fifteen or so miles of uninhabited, trackless moor and the cliffs turned the north-west corner of Scotland at Cape Wrath.

It had been raining for a week, said the old lady at the post office. We should find a hotel, a petrol pump and a shop farther on. Rain sluiced off the corrugated iron roofs of the houses. After day, night, and day again of motor-car buzz, it was good to soak in a hot bath in the small fishing hotel, which was full of anglers and fish.

A few weeks before, a timber loaded steamer had sprung a leak off Cape Wrath and had " by grace and favour," said the gentle proprietor of the hotel, managed to reach Loch Inchard

and take the beach. He had put up the crew in an empty
cottage against the loch while they had stopped the leak and
refloated their ship. They had left behind a large signboard
inscribed " Sailors' Home." We were welcome, me dear boys,
to the use of the cottage for ten shillings, said kind Mr. Macleod.
We moved in straight away, pulled some bracken from the
hillside for bedding and got a peat fire going. The watcher,
a young phlegmatic Highlander who was employed to keep
poachers off the hotel water, was already using the cottage.

The Sailors' Home would have made such a perfect base
for North Rona ! If only there had been a few fishing vessels
about. So there had been, once, but not now, nor likely to
be with the nearest railway fifty miles away at Lairg. The
wooden pier of Kinloch Bervie stood empty and open to the
west. The boatman of D. M. Reid whom we found at Rhiconich at the head of the loch, was kindly, but most of the
boat's engine was away being repaired. Stornoway was the
one and only place ; there were plenty of drifters there and a
big fishing industry. Of the islands with queer names there
was particularly Am Balg, Bulgie Island, on the way towards
Cape Wrath. It had a good landing place, the boatman said ;
he would have been pleased to have taken us out.

We looked out to green-topped Bulgie Island when we
walked over the moor to Sandwood Bay on the way towards
Cape Wrath. Its steep cliffs were skirted with white water,
to seaward and windward by a mile or more of grey, heaving
rollers ; it was not, after all, to be landed upon. Between
stinging flurries of rain, Cape Wrath lighthouse just showed
to the north. The solitary deserted cottage by Sandwood Loch
had a corrugated iron roof and under it, a bath. Five trackless
miles of stones and oozing peat separated the cottage from the
road-end. One day perhaps the bath would be retrieved across
the moor.

In the Sailors' Home the watcher sat large and slow before
the old iron kitchen range which, apart from his chair, was
the only furniture. His present job suited him fine, he said,
puffing at a pipe of the treacly black twist. It was easy living

about there, no unemployed. Glasgow-baked wrapped bread came once a week from Lairg. The mail van did the fifty miles to Lairg every evening and brought back the newspapers. The watcher complained that the pollis—there was a policeman at Rhiconich—now insisted that motor bikes be licensed.

The life of the district appeared to centre on the hotel. Its fishing made employment, and its newly built bar recreation. Contemporary manners were fast finding a way to these townships of Loch Inchard, though the nearest cinema was still in Lairg. There were half a dozen wireless sets in the district. The newer houses were identical, built of corrugated iron and match-boarding, their roofs secured against the wind by wires spanning the ridges and dangling at the eaves with boulders.

> Boswell : These stones hang round the bottom of the roof, and make it look like a lady's hair in papers ; but I should think that, when there is wind, they would come down and knock people on the head.

The sustenance of the scattered houses was not obvious. A few potato patches, some scraggy hens and cows seemed hardly adequate. One or two locked wooden huts turned out to be shops ; local knowledge was required to discover when they would open. But housekeeping in the Sailors' Home was easy enough : water from a burn a hundred yards along the road, milk and eggs from a nearby croft which also conducted a hut-shop, a sack or two of peat for the carrying. A pity it could not have been the Rona roadhead.

But if it was sea-birds we wanted, Mr. Reid's boatman had said, Handa Island was the place, down the coast off Scourie. All the sea-birds under the sun nested there. The watcher told us he had once spent nine weeks there himself, watching the sheep. At least it was an island.

Handa and its sea-fowl were evidently a show-piece for the fishing hotel at Scourie. And the hotel seemed also to have a monopoly of the place when we found, taking high tea among the stuffed eagles, wild cats and enormous fish, that the pro-

prietor owned the motor boat ; the price was high, and the
boatmen were engaged as gillies. Some fishermen at a little
place up the coast called Tarbet, directly opposite Handa,
might make an alternative. The switchback road over uninhabited country turned out to be nearly impassable, but it
ended at the door of a genial old crofter who knew all about
Handa ; his grandfather had been born there. A mile of foot
track led on and down to a strip of beach with two or three
heavy rowing boats drawn up, and two or three crofts standing
back from the sea ; this was the euphemistically named Port
of Tarbet. The island lay out in the evening sun, a long dark
hump across the sea. We arranged to be rowed there the
following day.

Next day we landed at the sheltered eastern corner of
Handa and stepped out across the width of the island ; the
boatmen would come and fetch us in the evening. The bird
cliffs were on the seaward side. There the flat top of the island
was cut off suddenly into cliff walls nearly 300 feet deep. Back
from the cliff edge the ground fell away gradually to the
southward by rough grass and heather to rabbity dunes and
a shore of reef and sand. The island was empty but for sheep.
The birds were sounding long before we reached the cliff edge ;
then, peering over, the void below was a snowstorm of flying
sea-fowl. The noise struck like a blast. It was new, all new,
a first introduction for both of us to the welter of a big scale
sea-cliff colony.

The Handa cliffs being of a rusty-looking sandstone, strati-
fied in nearly horizontal beds, had eroded into tier upon tier
of shelves and balconies, all now packed with vociferous fowl.
All the common cliff colonists were here, each making a noise
after its own kind—puffins, razorbills, guillemots, kittiwakes,
shags, fulmars, herring and black-backed gulls, in numbers
great or less. Straight below us was a small bay enclosed by
cliffs but accessible at the head by precipitous broken slopes
strewn with boulders and covered with a mat of bird-dunged
chickweed. We called it Puffin Bay.

Some of the birds were strangers ; we had never before

set eyes on the extraordinary puffin or the inscrutable fulmar. So brand new was this unique first sight of puffins at the edge of Handa, they might have been of fresh creation : bright fantastic dolls—but alive ! They sat about the broken slopes, seeming alone of all the hordes to have time to do nothing. Their earthbound breeding season was ending. They stood or sat, yawned or leapt overboard with whirring wings, top-heavy beaks hanging downwards, orange webbed feet spread fanwise behind. Surely familiarity could never stale the real oddness of a puffin. Most birds are not at all comic, but puffins from the beginning were funny of themselves, as domestic ducks are. When Doctor John Macculloch in his time—he for whom " years had passed in vain attempts " to reach North Rona—sailed past Handa he thought the puffins and auks " most ornamental " ; the long ranks of brilliant white breasts resembled edgings of daisies or rows of snowdrops. The mate fired a musket at them and the cloud of birds arising " looked as if a feather bed had been opened and shook in the breeze."

We clambered down a sheep track to the floor of Puffin Bay, where flat rock skirted the cliff base. Shags were nesting among piled-up boulders in a stench of decomposed fish and exclusive shag reek. The sites of their noisome dens were shown by the whitewash of young and old. The black adult birds flapped away making guttural noises, the young scrabbled into far recesses, defaecating over each other as they went, then facing about and trying to bring up. The stinking nests showed all stages from eggs and newly hatched, perfectly naked, coal-black nestlings to full-sized young.

Shags leaving their perches in a fright dived straight underwater ; the necks popped up well out to sea and twisted every way in curiosity. A shag coming in to land was good to watch. It would finish off with a few violent wing-beats, and as often as not, fall flat on its front as its own uncontrollable momentum carried it on ; pick itself up, shake the tail, waddle forward, surely trying to look as though nothing had happened. I peered into a small cavern and saw a shag before it saw me : fast asleep, head under wing, standing on its flat feet. A bird like a shag, fascinating but not inviting sympathy, could be seen for what it nearly is: a warmed-up reptile with feathers. Some hardy fishermen could still eat a cooked shag.

The cliff base was littered with eggshells of razorbills and guillemots and with young birds, alive, dead and half-eaten ; casualties from the roaring nurseries above. Yet the wastage was nothing to the careless seething overhead. The guillemot slums were crowded tier on tier, thus the pools of egg-yolk here below. No carefulness in the breeding of guillemots, none of the neat nests or quiet brooding of inland birds. They went headlong at the business, a-jabbering and a-rowing, knocking each other's eggs over the edge. They stuffed something down the offsprings' gullets, paddled about in the muck, whirred away to sea for more. They cared nothing for each other's excreta. On Handa only the puffins had time to stand and stare.

Kittiwakes' onomatopoeic cries increased the clamour. One huge piece of cliff, overhung like half the dome of a cathedral, was plastered with kittiwakes' seaweed nests, so that one could not go unsplashed below. The dank dripping place echoed with their screeches ; a kittiwake seen silent for a moment, standing neat and gentle beside its young, looked incapable of making such a row.

The fulmars' nesting was withdrawn and quieter and took place on exclusive, earthy ledges where the cliff was soft and green grown. The gulls hawked to and fro before the cliffs ; they had finished their breeding though they still kept one or two special promontories.

All day the tumult went on, the birds whizzed to and from their ledges, crannies and holes. We scrambled where we could and held in our hands young kittiwakes, guillemots and razorbills and drew out for a look a young puffin or two huddled at burrow's end. In the evening the boatmen came out again and we returned northwards to the Sailors' Home. There had been time to see only a little of the cliffs, nothing of the rest of the island. We should come back in a day or two and take up residence.

II

The First Island

THE large but minimum pile of bedding, food and etceteras lately heaped on the rotting wooden floor of the Sailors' Home, now lay dumped on the stone slabs of the shepherds' hut, Handa Island, transported thither by road, by our aching backs along the mile of track to Port of Tarbet, and by rowing boat. The hut stood inland and solitary, a low stone box with walls a couple of feet thick, a corrugated iron roof slung with boulders and a single door giving on to the mainland. This hut, the sheep, a dipping-trough and enclosure were the marks of contemporary human use of Handa. Two shepherds came and lived in the hut during the lambing season and again in late summer for the dipping, said the fishermen. Otherwise Handa had long been uninhabited. The father of one of the fishermen had been born in the island.

We mentioned some diffidence about moving in without even asking ; would it be all right ? The fishermen thought such doubts unreasonable and delighted in showing off the unexpected resources ; they were as pleased as children. Then their figures diminished down the slope to the Sound, leaving ourselves to five days of undisturbed possession (we hoped).

The hut stood on a slope with rising ground of bracken and rocks behind and the stone-walled sheep-pen to one side. A patch of bog delivered a tiny burn nearby whose trickle was diverted into an aqueduct of two boards nailed together and finished with a corned beef tin for a spout. It was dim inside after the outdoor seaside glare, though the hut was not at all the rude bothy we had expected. It was divided inside by a string hung with the stock of blackened bedding things : the near end by the door stacked to the roof with wooden sheep-

29

troughs, peat, peat digging tools, rabbit wires and indigenous junk—oddments found and kept in case they should come in useful, such as an old electric light bulb ; the far end beyond the blankets was furnished and had a fireplace in the end wall. We had intended to do without fire or cooking. The heads of the two beds were ranged on either side of the fireplace, one bedstead of old iron with a mesh mattress, the other of deal, without. This second bed (mine) was peculiar in having only three narrow boards to bridge the space it enclosed, one each for head, hips and feet. Above the beds were cuttings from *Punch* in driftwood frames. *Punch ?*—of course, old copies from the Scourie hotel. A sausage-maker's coloured calendar was for the current year but had not been torn off for four months. There had been a good deal of bad weather, judging by the amount of poker-work on the wooden bed. " A happy home " was carved on the door, and " Old Dan " had been here for five years running.

The rest of the furniture was a wooden table and an iron arm-chair with only the iron parts left. Mainland rubbish, rather than be thrown away, could usefully go to Handa.

Such light as there was indoors got in through two tiny windows and through a jagged hole in the roof made, so the fishermen had said, by the unexpected going off of a shepherd's muzzle loader. The chimney was topped with a bottomless bucket, wired on, upside down. The flue was simply a hole left in the middle of the wall ; later on the view down it to the glowing peat at the bottom was cosy enough.

We shut the door behind us and walked right round the four or five miles of coastline of our first uninhabited island. It fell far short of an ideal. A broadly oval island used by birds and sheep, limited by cliffs round the seaward side, sloping to a reefed shore facing the mainland ; nothing else. The interior was undifferentiated, a broad back of very rough grazing with boulders sticking out of it and two or three boggy little lochs. The old inhabitants had left only some inconspicuous nettle-grown walls and a few gravestones down by the shore. No

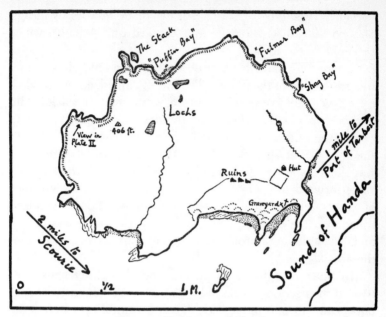

FIG. 1. *Sketch map of Handa*

sheltered indents of coastline into calm water, no detail of warm dell or little valley, no purling stream or plashing water-fall, no kind of tree or shrub, no flowers. The tallest vegetation was bracken. A little driftwood and a diminishing few leathery mushrooms were the resources. But we were the only inhabit-ants. A cold wind blowing in from the sea laid over the yellowed sedges and waved the tufts of cotton grass. The boggy little lochs were chill and grey. It was autumn already, in the first days of August. Barren wildness had to be the attraction of the Scottish islands, or there was nothing?

> *Where would the world be, once bereft*
> *Of wet and wildness . . . ?*

It put such value on one's shelter. We were soon enjoying sitting by the fire in the hut while rain rattled on the iron roof and hissed into the red peat, and the wind worried at the four stone corners. A chimneyless lamp was just made to work by means of a bottle with top and bottom knocked off. A haven when the light began to fail !

There must have been a full mile of bird-loud cliffs round the north coast of the island. The line of cliff edge was crinkled by a few small bays which gave a way down to sea level in one or two places. There was the original Puffin Bay, then nearer the hut came Fulmar Bay, a nasty place, and nearest, the low cliffs of Shag Bay. When the wind bore offshore there was silence a few paces back from the cliff edge ; then as one came forward the noise broke out suddenly like a blow—roar of waves, chatter and scream of sea-fowl. Loose boulders rolled over the edge exploded satisfactorily on the rocks below and left acrid sulphurous eddies ; the sea-fowl swarmed into the air.

In Shag Bay the shags sat close on their fishy nests and twisted their scraggy necks to look up at us. Their guttural dog barks came from dim crevices. Their beautiful eyes were jade green, in sunlight their fishy feathers were glossed and iridescent. The piled boulders at the bottom of Shag Bay were negotiable until we came to a gap of sea too wide to jump, where a seaweed forest heaved in the ground swell. One of those long wooden sheep-troughs would neatly bridge the gap. Back to the shepherds' hut and back again across the empty island, one of us at either end of an unwieldy trough. We manœuvred it down the cliff, manhandled it over the boulders. Too short. Ainslie wished to use it as a boat, but a demonstration run at the end of a piece of string was unsuccessful. Back over the boulders, up the cliff and again past the watching sheep to the hut.

Fulmar Bay, the nasty place, was a treacherous cliff of wet earth and lush greenstuff topped with a bastion of sheer rock. In one place an earthy cleft dribbling with water led down to discover three nestling fulmars squatting on a narrow shelf. The only site for an observation hide was between two of them. John set to, shoved tent poles horizontally into the soft soil of the cliff and draped them with rotting sacks from the sheep-pen. Everything had to be lowered on a rope or carried dog-like. The three young fulmars objected and sprayed us with their hot oil, their spluttered-out jets ranged up to two or three feet ; once a crab's leg came up. The nestlings sat surrounded by a circle of scurf from their own down, and looked like nothing so much as oversized grey powder-puffs—which was a cliché description for a nestling fulmar, but no other came so aptly.

Puffin Bay was the hub. On the evening of the 2nd of August the slopes and boulders were crowded with puffins ; on the morning of the 3rd not one was left. The sudden autumn exodus to the sea had happened. In a day or two a few birds reappeared, purposeful and busy, feeding late young ones. One evening after that the cliff-side air was again full of flying puffins going fast and in an urgent-seeming manner. They sat again on their slopes, but in silence ; they seemed unable to make a clean break with the land.

All the colonists' ledges were quickly thinning. Guillemots' activities in particular were easier to follow now that their ledges were less overcrowded. I saw the act of one late egg knocked overboard ; its owner waddled to the edge and peered after it.

> The idea that its shape allows it to twist round in the wind is exploded, as is the egg when a careless sitter sends it hurtling to the rocks beneath (T. A. Coward).

The full English name used to be, the foolish guillemot.

The Stack of Handa near Puffin Bay was a feature, probably the tourist feature. The crown of this great lump of separate rock was only a giant's jump out from the cliff edge. A leaning weathered stake stuck up from the grass on the top, the most startling of any human relic on the island.

A crossing to the Stack had been made in the eighteen-seventies and had been written about by John Harvie-Brown, famous naturalist of the time, who had twice visited Rona (his findings reported in *Ronay* and known nearly by heart). Two men and a boy from Uist in the Outer Hebrides had got across at the behest of the Scourie landlord, to destroy the nests of the great black-backed gulls which until then had bred there in safety and had increased to a nuisance.

> The invasion of the top of the Great Stack was accomplished by means of a rope, thrown over it from the nearest cliff-top of the main island, along which the boy scrambled. . . .

Somebody must have been over since the seventies to account for the inanimate, staring stake which we saw. It looked an impossible feat, but last across, according to Seton Gordon, were

> a fearless crew from Lewis—men who were doubtless skilled in fowling upon the cliffs of Sula-Sgeir and North Rona—and by means of a rope they traversed those giddy yards with the roaring surf five hundred feet beneath them.

From an empty piece of sea there appeared a large dog-like head, a Great Dane's head without ears : so startling was the first sight of an Atlantic grey seal. The head looked around, the nose slowly tilted upwards and slid back under water. Shag and Fulmar Bays had each a resident seal. They travelled at the surface, broad backs awash, so smooth, slippery and naked, they were different from any imaginable animal. The sea had taken a dog and had made of it, this. They submerged in a neat duck-dive, splashless and silent ; alarmed, and they were down in a flash, a resounding swirl of white water left behind.

The sea was always such a cold and unlikely waste, barren and heaving grey water ; I could never really credit that it should contain a teeming life and produce large warm-blooded animals. But from Handa the wonderful west coast fauna revealed itself creature by creature. Porpoises made their revolutions in the Sound, where cruised just below the surface the great bodies of basking sharks. Two black triangles cut the surface and moved along with a little bow wave. Basking sharks would bulk up to a length of thirty feet, said the fishermen of Tarbet.

The First Island

Black guillemots next showed themselves, called by the local men sea pigeons or tysties. They bred on islets in the Sound of Handa. On one crossing we were landed on an islet containing a foul-smelling crevice with a pile of dung outside. We withdrew the two nearly fledged black guillemots—weighty chickens in pepper and salt—then let them splash back through their ordure into the safe darkness. Adult tysties looked soft and plump and their dusky plumage, entire except for a white mirror on either wing, was set off by beautiful bright red feet. And when they opened their beaks the inside was vermilion. The white wing mirrors of birds whirring low over the sea looked like little patches of broken water. I saw one bird leave a rock and bounce on to the sea, like a painted boat shot from some lido water-chute. The tysties were as novel as all the rest.

One stretch of cliff belonged to a family of peregrines. A buzzard quartered the ground like an enormous moth. From the bracken beds of the interior flew a thrush, a blackbird ; there were wrens and starlings ; a young robin peeked in at the door of the hut. More remarkable were the ordinary house sparrows which inhabited the eaves of the hut, making their careless nests there. Sparrow chatter woke us in the early morning.

The iron roof groaned and the rain rattled upon it—cold, wind and wet. The mainland was easily lost in sea mist that swirled over the island ; a half-hearted sun appeared infrequently. All day long the sky emitted a uniform grey light and our days were timeless. We dragged up driftwood from the landward beach and searched for the last of the mushrooms. If it hadn't been for the birds there would have been nothing to do. One would soon have tired of walking round the island looking at the sheep. Ordinary seaside activities, such as bathing, appeared grotesque.

The mushrooms grew mostly at the back of the dunes where a close pasture reached inland to the ruins of the village. This had evidently been the cultivated land; the remains of drainage ditches still showed. Lying on the grass was a bamboo flagstaff which the shepherds used in their season for signalling to Scourie, two or three miles to the southward. (There continued to be no sign of them.) Only the walls of the crofts remained, standing up from a floor of turf and nettles. There had been nine.

The last generations of crofters had lived on potatoes and fish until in 1845, the year of potato famine, they had to choose between starvation and emigration. They chose America and the island was actually cleared in the spring of 1848. It so happened that none other than Charles St. John—of *Wild Sports in the Highlands*—very nearly saw them go. In the same summer, when he was engaged on his *Sportsman and Naturalist's Tour*, harrying the remaining ospreys up and down Sutherland, he made a day's visit to Handa. As his boat approached the shore he saw, sitting out on the point nearest the mainland, a large white cat.

> I could not help being struck with the attitude of the poor creature as she sat there looking at the sea, and having as disconsolate an air as any deserted damsel. " She is wanting the ferry," was the quaint and not incorrect suggestion of one of our boatmen. . . . I passed several huts, the former inhabitants of which had all left the place a few weeks before ; and, notwithstanding the shortness of the time, the turf walls were already tenanted and completely honeycombed by countless starlings. . . .

What had been the truth of this particular clearance ? There was the potato famine ; but also Handa was a good sheep-walk. Nowadays the local men said that the Duke of Sutherland had been most to blame ; it was a month's notice, the emigration ship called, then Canada for the rest of the crofters' natural lives. Charles St. John's evidence, though perhaps suspect, did not agree :

> Depending on the Duke of Sutherland's well-known kindness and liberality, the lower class of inhabitants take but little trouble towards earning their own livelihood. At whatever hour of the day you go into a cottage, you find the whole family idling at home over the peat-fire. The husband appears never

to employ himself in any way beyond smoking, taking snuff, or chewing tobacco ; the women doing the same, or at the utmost watching the boiling of a pot of potatoes ; while the children are nine times out of ten crawling listlessly about or playing with the ashes of the fire.

The Duke, having tried every plan that philanthropy and reason could suggest, has now succeeded in opening their eyes to the advantage of emigrating, and at a great expense sends numbers yearly to Canada. . . .

Charles St. John lay on the cliff brink of Handa and thought of a snowstorm as he looked down to the teeming birds. When he left the island the white cat still sat looking towards the mainland. When Seton Gordon visited Handa he was with a piper who marched up and down the turf by the village ruins, and played a lament.

*   *   *

The fishermen of Tarbet came and fetched us, we took two or three days at the Sailors' Home and then, washed and reprovisioned, came back for another spell. Three snipe got up in front of the hut door. Rain fairly hammered on the roof ; the inside was beaded with wet which was soon glistening in the light of a driftwood fire. The chimney smoked abominably. The burn became quite a little torrent. After forty-eight hours the wind blew itself out and the rain stopped, the mainland reappeared and the sun came out.

Of the thousands of birds still left we had chosen for a closer look the three young fulmars of Fulmar Bay and a downy razorbill chick, alone on a small ledge near the bottom of Puffin Bay and immediately beneath a big kittiwake colony. The rock below this colony was a morgue of young kittiwakes. Their parents bred on such narrow ledges and the nests were soon trodden down, so that falling off was too easy. One did so as we worked at hide-making below, and fell almost at our feet—plop—quite dead. Several of the nests above had dead young on them, adults only stood on others. The rock walls echoed with onomatopoeic screams, kittiwark, kittiwark, kittiwark.

The razorbills, for whom John thought boar and sow more suitable descriptives than male and female, were pleasing company. The razorbill stood there close in front of the hide, comfortably propped on feet and tail, twisting her razor-beak into every conceivable position. Or she paraded—hop, waddle and jump, up and down the ledge, with wing assistance for the difficult steps. Her disregarded chick followed her about and kept digging its head beneath her, trying to be brooded. Her white bib was so very clean, running up in a point to her neck ; her twinkling eye was nearly lost in the deep chocolate brown of her delicately modelled cheek. Her noise was of continuous hoarse grunts, sometimes repeated so fast that they ran into an astonishing trill. The bill of one parent, presumably the boar or male, was notably bigger and deeper than the other's. It was odd to see that the chick stood and ran on the webs of its feet while its parents followed the common auk fashion of shuffling along on the full length of the tarsi. It was like a nursery tale of evolution, demonstrating that razorbill ancestry had gone on its toes. Soon the chick would be paddling along with the rest of the tribe.

And what had environment done to the razorbill ?— peculiar, peculiar creature : boat-shaped body, stumpy wings whirring hard to get it up to the nesting ledge, cold webbed feet to drive it competently through the water and to mount it incompetently on dry land. But why should it so wreathe and writhe its neck, point up its axe of a bill and grunt until it was trilling ; why so jerking and awkward with its young ? Why indeed be what it was, instead of something else ?

At Fulmar Bay I spent an initial half-day cramped miserably into the little hide while the young fulmar in front did almost nothing. Notable activity when it pecked at a fly. Occasionally it preened a little, nibbling into its down. Once it presented its rear end to the edge and powerfully voided a white stream. Now and then it yawned or looked at the sky and settled more deeply into doing nothing.

Old birds circled the bay, flap and glide, round and round, each time nearly but not quite alighting by one or other of the powder-puff young. Their wing-beats looked inartistically mechanical because of the stiff style of wings worked from the shoulder without any flexing at the wrist. The young ones sat unattended, spread out as if they had been dropped from a height, looking as boneless as cowpats. When adult birds did alight they sat motionless and took no notice of the young, When they did move it was with an unbirdlike deliberation, no sharp birdlike turn of the head or quick glance, no bird nervousness. Their big black eyes looked quiet and gentle ; some naturalists had used the word " demure " for fulmars. It was misleading ; fulmars bite viciously ; " inscrutable " was the word. With most birds one could tell roughly what they were at ; one watched them and they did something recognisable. This was not the case with fulmars, we found ; their actions were baffling.

Below, past my feet, were rocks and breaking sea. Farther out I could see the seal which frequented the bay. In another view gulls and a hooded crow were feeding on offal, two rock pigeons preening. A misty rain began. A herring gull standing near its young one with a far-away look suddenly regurgitated a lump of fish. The sacking of the hide touched me all round and I was weary of examining its weave.

For a short time my young fulmar did exercises. It flopped over on one side and slowly stretched out a wing and a leg until they were quivering stiff, a deep luxurious stretch that I watched with envy. Then it stood up on the flat of its weak legs, held out its wings stiffly and worked and jerked them from the shoulder joint—practising for the grown-up, board-winged style of flying. A peculiar farmyard cackling began ; it was adult fulmars alighted on another ledge. Two birds sat opposite each other ; one opened wide its bill, craned up its head and deliberately cackled at the other. Nothing came of this.

The Scourie motor boat chugged past the bay with a load of sightseers. The seal submerged, the hoodie flew away.

An outcry arose from a razorbill's ledge farther on. I saw a great black-backed gull flying off with a young razorbill in its beak while a cloud of feathers drifted down from the ledge where the parent sat bewildered. The gull carried the chick down to a rock and hammered it. Four other black-backs flew round making, with the wretched chick's squeaks, a great noise. The parent razorbill stayed on its ledge for the rest of the day but had gone by next morning.

The hide soon weathered until one sat in mud and wore the sodden roof like a very heavy hat. In later watches fulmars did at least come to the ledge in front, where they bickered. To start it one bird had only to wave its head at another, opening its bill and loudly caa-caa-caa-ing ; the other would respond similarly. They sounded rather like ducks. It might get as far as one bird spitting into another's face but usually the outside bird gave ground until it overbalanced over the edge. Our young one would have nothing to do with any of them, its angry pumping kept them all at a distance. The one ordinary relationship between young and adult I saw only once and distantly. The parent opened its bill and worked its neck, the young one pushed its head inside ; a semi-solid mass passed between them.

The clue to fulmar behaviour was its primitiveness ? Recent watchers have thought that the way the limited caa-caa-ing performance—courtship, display, posture, whatever it may be called—has to express the gamut of the emotions, is a sign of primitiveness ; and the queer separate bones of the bird's bill is morphologically primitive. The birds we watched on the ledge were probably non-breeders. The phenomenon of " visiting " by non-breeding birds or by breeders from other ledges is now well known ; the flighting round and round, making passes at the ledges, is part of it. Probably the parent of our young one never appeared at all, which would not have been surprising if we had known then that fulmars are supposed to feed their young only once a day. And it seemed that after their first youth the young were no longer brooded. The early August young of Fulmar Bay sat habitually unattended.

The First Island

On our last evening on Hånda half a gale blew from the north. We dismantled the derelict fulmar hide, the breeze whisked the sacks up the cleft and deposited them on the cliff top. Fulmars' stiff winged soaring was magnificent, but now it was not all. They limbered up, became loose and supple, and forgot the board-winged style. They hung careless by a cliff corner, every feather quivering, tails fan-spread, wings flexed, legs hanging loose. In glass cases in museums flying birds dangle by a thread : the thread was to be imagined as suddenly snapped ; like that the fulmars slipped away across the wind, then banked and broadsided to fetch up into it again and ride the upward blast. They lowered themselves in jerks to the offing of a ledge, like a lift going down, then hung as puppets before raising their wings, breaking the spell, and landing. One almost felt relief when they did land—tightrope walkers safely across.

The fishermen of Tarbet came again the next morning. We wired the door shut and walked off through streaming rain. White water chased the stern across the Sound ; the heavy old boat sagged in the troughs or surged youthfully on the crests.

*　　*　　*

We last saw Handa from the summit of Foinaven, the commanding mountain of the district, rising some five miles inland of the head of Loch Inchard. The map was brought to life : north to Cape Wrath—a white strip for Sandwood Bay —the two great sea lochs of Inchard and Laxford—a winding line for the Rhiconich and Kinloch Bervie road. Handa lay out beyond the coast, fifteen miles away. The setting for the landmarks was the fantastic Sutherland beach of loch and stone, like a rocky shore at low tide. A big wave would have covered it all.

The next day and night we drove south along the route by which we had come ignorantly north a few weeks before.

An elementary exercise in island-going ! But we had had

the first wonder of meeting sea-fowl in bulk and the pleasure of a mild though uninhabited island. We had seen something of the north and west, cold seas and seals, we weren't quite so green as when we had started. Next year perhaps, as initiates, we should get a landing on North Rona.

Handa Island, July 31, August 2-6 and 9-12, 1935

FIG. 2. *Shepherds' hut, Handa Island*

SECOND YEAR

NORTH RONA
SHIANT ISLES
CANNA

*

1936

III

North !

THE old story looked like repeating itself. We plagued D. M. Reid again and Malcolm Stewart of *Ronay*. I met Tom Harrisson, who had written an exciting paper in the *Ibis* on the " Resident and Migratory Birds of North Rona, the remotest Scottish Island." The three successful visitors each wished us luck and Tom Harrisson lent us his unpublished notes on Leach's petrel. But when we got the name of an owner-skipper of a Stornoway steam drifter he wanted £50 for the job ; and D. M. Reid thought the North Atlantic too wild for any Stornoway motor boat.

All the same we did realise that Stornoway was the only hope, even if we had to turn up there on the chance. If only we knew the place or someone in it ! However, transport of ourselves and all our gear would require a car. As an act of faith I had already bought one. This was a curious vehicle in a breaker's yard.

Cars that came into breakers' yards—the well-established dumps of the contemporary scene—were classified into " stiffs " and " runners," the stiffs being too far gone for anything but breaking up. Unsold runners soon became stiffs. I found my car in mid-winter with half-thawed snow weighing down the hood and masking the rust-eaten mudguards. All four tyres had long since subsided; it sat in a final looking way on its wheel rims. A car could hardly have appeared so obviously past any further activity on the public highway, yet this was a classified runner. " Reliable ? " said the dealer, " Gawd yes, bloody fine engine, do fifty." And the extraordinary thing was that after some mere wiping off of moisture the engine started and ran quite smoothly and even registered oil pressure. " There you are," said the dealer, flourishing the receipt :

" To one Motor Car . . . £3." This might have seemed like deliberately adding to our difficulties, but finance called the tune. And if only this car would go it would be perfectly suited to the job, being of economically small horse power yet provided with a large bath-shaped body behind with room for any amount of luggage.

The car stood in the dump through the various snows and rains of winter and spring while rust went on eating at it, white mould crept over the woodwork and algae greened its ancient hood. The carriage of two people and several hundred-weight of gear for six or seven hundred miles was the task in front of it.

In the spring came a letter postmarked " Stornoway." In the course of trying everything I had written to a director of a company of Fish Curers, Coal Merchants, Shipbrokers, and Steam Drifter Owners. The reply was a shaft of wonderful light from, literally, a perfect stranger. He owned a 32-foot auxiliary cruiser himself, wrote Kenneth MacIver. He had never been to North Rona himself but understood that very good weather and a good-sized row boat were necessary for the actual landing. He would quite likely be able to arrange for a drifter skipper, probably one of the visiting drifters, to land us and bring us off for about a quarter of the price we'd been quoted so far. If we did get landed and drifters had to leave suddenly for other ports he would see that we weren't stranded. He explained how unpredictable were the fishing and movements of drifters. Think it over and phone if necessary, he said. I hurried to John in the next county and we rejoiced over the letter. The same spring evening, by faint Scots exchanges, I phoned Stornoway and tried by shouting to convey our delight.

Now real preparations could go forward : lists of things to take, to buy and to make. Being ignorant of the resources of the Outer Hebrides we got a month's provisions for two people " in cases not exceeding 50 lbs." from the Army and Navy Stores. Should we ever, in some rude shelter and by the light of a storm lantern, be seated on these packing cases ?

Night photography would require some sort of apparatus set off by a trip wire (to be tripped by Leach's petrel) which would work the camera shutter and fire a flash-bulb. I experimented unprofitably with an electric bell, without the bell. John came forward with a remarkable device : Leach's petrel would fall over a wire, which would set off a mouse-trap, which would slam down on both shutter and flash-bulb releases ; and which would remain experimental. Tarpaulin, meth, gumboots, sacks for building a hide, torches, fishing tackle, a thermometer for petrels' temperatures if not our own, consumption of the Primus meticulously worked out—there was plenty to think about. We got up the *Life Histories of North American Petrels and Pelicans and their Allies*—the coast of Maine knew Leach's petrel. I felt I could visualise North Rona—some slope of flattened sedges, gulls keeled over in the wind, a rocky coast with grey seas breaking white—yet knew that if ever we did see the island it would be altogether different from preconceptions.

At the end of the May Term I went down sadly for the last time, but all the summer stretched free ahead.

The car was insured with difficulty and licensed. It went well on a test run, though naturally fittings such as lights, battery, dynamo, self-starter, were either out of action or missing. During a speed trial downhill the whole hood took wing and collapsed behind in a tangle of metal and green-aged cloth. The speedometer surprisingly worked, and no shaken passenger doubted its truth. I thought it best not to tamper with the engine, though a drip-tray underneath contained many dropped-off nuts, and far worse was the discovery of coarse filings in the crankcase. A scrap of newspaper under the back seats, dated September 11th, 1925, put the car's age at an honourable minimum. The old Singer was no longer " it " but " she " and the jeers of the populace were hurtful.

I constructed from the remains of the original hood a small collapsible shelter to cover the front seat only, leaving the bath-shaped rear seatless and unencumbered to accommodate the great pile of luggage. Loose bits of mudguard were sawn off with a hacksaw, a leather dog-strap fitted to hold the bonnet together. She was ready to go.

Only July 11th, 1936, Mr. MacIver sent a famous telegram :

if unable get you rona myself think could get drifter do so for about five pounds stop impossible make bargain with any particular vessel beforehand as no guaranteeing will be at stornoway on your arrival stop come fishmarket on arrival mailboat

The next morning, fair and sunny, we started off.

*   *   *

When the seven Army and Navy packing-cases and John's gear had been added to mine, the rear tyres were nearly flat. We pumped them up again and tucked groundsheets over the load ; the collapsible shelter leant back against the pile. John pushed, the slope of the drive carried us away past the rhododendrons.

The first few miles were naturally apprehensive. Driving, one felt oneself to be in charge of more than a car, the gross overload produced a disturbing sway, and there did not seem to be anything holding the front wheels to the ground. Some people smiled to see us pass, others pointed rudely, even hooted or whistled. My preoccupation with the oil gauge diminished as it continued to keep steady faith with the busy old engine.

Towns were difficult but we were getting on famously— Aylesbury, Buckingham, Northampton, Leicester. Hay had been carried from the meadows ; farther north it still lay making ; still farther and the grass stood uncut under a grey sky. Rain started, setting to nought the collapsible shelter. On wet tar the load became nearly unmanageable. We rounded Scotch Corner with a noble slide.

Peculiar sounds were always growing or receding from the generality of noise. The fan gave a high-pitched squeak, the petrol can on the running-board drummed crescendo and diminuendo, the silencer was punctured ; we progressed in a hammering bruit. " Is that noise the fan ? "

" What ? "

" I said, Is that noise the fan ? "

" What van ? Oh, can. I thought we'd cured it."

" Oh, never mind. I said, It doesn't matter."

But we had crossed the border and done 330 miles when the light began to fail ; and having no lights ourselves, fell gratefully into bed at the small transport café of Kirkpatrick Fleming. We really thought we should reach Kyle of Lochalsh the next evening.

Six o'clock in the morning, and an uninviting prospect of rain-sluiced road. The sheep were sodden and the heaths were blasted. Manufacturing villages lasted for grey wet miles. At last the day began to brighten, the clouds about Glencoe looked as solid as the mountains. Fort William, Invergarry, rain again—the last frightful stretch to the coast was hard to bear. We had had a rule that the springs should not be allowed to bottom—the dead thud each time they did seemed likely to be the last—but we must get to Kyle before dark. The engine chugged yet more gamely as we bucketed across the moor and, juddering in every limb, charged into deep turbid potholes. The footbrake had grown gradually feebler until it was useless. The cornucopia horn, once a comic, a small boy's toy, now sounded a serious warning.

The last obstacle before Kyle was Dornie ferry, where the hazard offered was a steep slope of seaweed-covered boulders and a right-angle turn over two boards on to a barge. John, who had got out, so convinced himself that the car would either overturn or run straight over the barge and into the sea, that he offered a small bet. However, we left no more than a cloud of blue smoke at Dornie and soon after ten o'clock rolled triumphantly into Kyle. We ached and throbbed and buzzed.

Rain was streaming down again in the morning. We were relieved when the wonderful Singer, which caused some comment, had been safely hoisted on board the mailboat and her eccentricities covered by a tarpaulin. Sea, and the sea-fowl were showing up again sort by sort, each to be seen freshly after an inland year.

This mailboat service was Stornoway's daily link with the Mainland. Mail, passengers, cargo, sheep, the Glasgow morning papers, the morning milk, all crossed the Minch in MacBrayne's *Lochness*. She would turn round in Stornoway and sail the same evening, said a man. But she lay in Stornoway from Saturday to Sunday evening because of the Scottish Sabbath, though she sailed before midnight struck on Sunday. Oh yes ? If you wanted to freight a car on the Sunday evening sailing you must get it aboard on Saturday evening, no one would work on a Sunday. No ? Just now a steward from this ship made the newspaper headline : " Church Tries Man For Working on Sabbath." There were unusual compulsions up here ?

To the southward, six miles away, some dark cliffs stood out of the sea: the Shiant Islands. The Outer Hebrides came up ahead, the inhospitable coast of Lewis, first distant blue, then grey and barren rock. In the early evening a few fishing boats were coming out of the entrance into Stornoway. Some were steam drifters—the sort we should go to Rona in ?— going out for the night's fishing ? They fished at night, no doubt, but how ? We knew nothing about it. The steamer approached a stretch of grey houses at the end of the harbour.

There seemed to be a very large crowd to meet the steamer. Of course ; it was the event of the Hebridean day. The Singer was swung ashore right in front of the barrier, the crowd greeted her with laughter and hoots.

" Come fish-market on arrival mailboat." The fish-market on the quay was a circular one-storied building with a red iron roof splashed by gulls. The interior was an empty floor with a circumference of hutch-like offices. In one of these was to be found Mr. MacIver.

" Well," he said almost at once, " I've arranged for a drifter to take you to-morrow morning for five pounds." We should find the coal. She'd sail at ten o'clock in the morning. Well !

He explained that the drifter had sailed in the afternoon and that it depended on the fishing whether she would be back in the morning or not. If she got any fish she would be in and she would take us to Rona. If not, he'd have to try to find another skipper who would be willing. The old wells on Rona were a doubtful quantity, we thought it provident to take a supply of drinking water, in case ; this also would Mr. MacIver arrange. We didn't know how to say our happy surprise and thanks.

We set up in the waterfront hotel and hid the Singer round the back of the fish-market, hoping that lights were not required. Stornoway had rather the look of a Scandinavian fishing town, the smell and atmosphere fitted though the building was of stone and the iron railings in the more affluent parts were in the very spirit of all grim cement-washed Scottish apartment houses. What elsewhere might have been promenade was here stacked high with herring barrels. Sheep and hens roamed pleasingly in gritty back streets. In the shopping centre standardised shop fronts—Woolworth's, Montagu Burton, a twopenny library, the Playhouse café—went cheek by jowl with ship chandlers, tweed merchants and fleshers. There was a cinema.

In the morning the quays were crowded with drifters, slim steam drifters and hefty motor boats nearly as broad as long. All their galley funnels smoked quietly, the galleys of *Girl Ethel, Rising Sea* and *Seven Seas' Spray*, of *Speedwell* and *Express, Verbena, Dove, Ellen & Irene, Lews, Home Rule, Harvest, Comrade, Corona, Provider, Cailleach Oidhche* (Gaelic hieroglyphic). " You're out of luck, your boat's not back," said Mr. MacIver, but by the afternoon he had arranged the same terms with a visiting drifter from Buckie. There was leisure to gather up a last few stores—the paraffin, some emergency oatmeal, potatoes, a water bucket. In the ironmonger's a very large genial fisherman, buying a lavatory brush, told the story of the two shepherds of Ness who, back in the eighties, after a religious dispute, had retired to Rona to do penance. " And they found them lying there "—as it might be just there among the buckets and stoves—" dead." So that was still a live story in Lewis ; we knew about it from *Ronay*.

" You know, this is the usual Stornoway weather," said the hotel barman, propping up the entrance and looking out at the grey drizzle. Buses converged from townships all over Lewis and Harris to park their bruised metal along the waterfront and to await the mailboat. The *Lochness* came in again. The chemist-newsagents' of Mr. Roderick Smith, lately provost, opened for a hectic evening hour and thus distributed the morning papers on the same day. After one day one seemed to know Stornoway by heart ; it was an original, and already I felt fond of it.

Next morning we were woken to be told : " The drifter you're going in is waiting, you're to go down and see the skipper." Mr. Buchan was skipper, a small cheerful man with white hair, and his ship was the steam drifter *Rose*, aged and wooden. He thought he'd get us a landing the day. " This northerly wind'll die away as the sun goes round "—but the sun might not have existed. The Singer was backed up ; all our miscellanea were heaved on board. After careful instruction a fish-lorry driver, amused, drove the car away for a month's rest in a herring-curing shed. The fish-market was receding through a curtain of steam-coal smoke.

Mr. Buchan kept close inshore to show off the sea-bird cliffs ; a hard desolate coast. The old ship went with a good thrust and throb, but it was a long drag up the length of Lewis, about four hours before we passed the Butt and cleared for the open Atlantic. There was the swell then ; the *Rose* barged and rolled her way north-north-eastwards, chucking up spray which flung against the glass of the wheelhouse ; her course cut across the grain of the sea. The Butt lighthouse grew slowly smaller.

The nine or ten of a crew were east coast men, but they knew their Hebrides and the western summer season like natives. Stornoway was entirely a drifters' port. A drifter rode drifting to a long wall of nets through which herring sometimes tried to swim ; the mesh let only their heads through and they could not back out because their gill-cases acted like a barb. Herring were smoked or salted in Stornoway, mostly for export. It had been a bad fishing season so far.

The landward gulls were left astern ; there was no land left. The waste of waters was empty, no single other ship in sight all day. Had we heard the story of the two shepherds of Rona ? Or of the race between the men of Lewis and the men of Cape Wrath for the claim of Rona ? The stiff-winged silent fulmars were St. Kilda gulls—pronounced St. Kildy—named from the old days when fulmars in Britain swarmed to no other cliffs. The day was one of those timeless, endless days, with the displeasures of an unaccustomed sea voyage : queasy, unwarm, yawning, wedged in the wheelhouse ; nothing to do, only a passenger. Talk ran out after a few hours. One had already smoked too many cigarettes ; wanted, and didn't want, to eat. John, always a dreadfully bad sailor, was at last down below and exhausted into sleep. A freshening of wind came before each rain squall, a good sign, said the men. They also began to say : " I hae-me-doots on the landing." The wind streamed our trail of black smoke low over the sea.

At last, at last, was Rona sighted, a tiny blotch on the horizon that kept on disappearing. It slowly became a little hump, still elusive. That would have been Toa Rona as named on the map, the 355-foot hill at the eastern side of the island. Another lower hump rose beside the first, " the paps of Rona," said the skipper. The two humps joined up. Rona's companion rock Sula Sgeir began to show farther to the westward. The island imperceptibly grew—" she's lifting quicker now "—it was going to be much bigger than I'd thought. Under the excitement I had then just one moment's trepidation—what had we really let ourselves in for ? But now to get there, and land !

> *Then mark their little home exposed to view,*
> *Like some low cloud that stains th' äerial blue ;*
> *Bless'd, on the spot they gaze with fixed delight,*
> *And deem to reach it ere th' approach of night. . . .*

The land took colour, a green back which sloped into grey-brown cliffs and to a low peninsula of broken rock at the south-west corner. The cairn showed on top of Toa Rona ; we had risen the island fast. A squall blotted out everything. When it cleared we were quite close ; there were white spots of sheep and a dark heap on the hillside—the village.

The borrowed chart was brought out and we read over again the summarised excerpt from the *West Coast Pilot*, done in the fish-market office. "Towards the south-east end of the island a hill rises steeply with a vertical cliffy face to the southward." Yes, agreed, but where was the landing place " on the south side of this hill, in a small creek ? "

A patch of white water on the starboard bow. "Watch out for that rock."

" Och, it's only——"

" LOOK OUT ! " The wheel fairly spun, and the *Rose* sheered off. " Och, it's only the spit of a wave." We nosed in more carefully, with a look-out posted in the bows. John came up on deck, very green, longing for any shore.

The skipper rang down for " Stop " ; the *Rose* wallowed, her black smoke eddying about. There was a bit of a lee, a half-enclosing curve of rock and cliff before us, but all fringed white and flung with spray. All seemed cold, windy and bare ; no part looked like a landing place.

The business of getting the small boat over the side was apparently a not very common manœuvre among driftermen, even as Malcolm Stewart had here noted it among trawlermen. The junk was cleared out of the boat, it lurched uncertainly from its chocks, was manhandled over the gunwale and took the plunge. A crew bundled in ; they pulled away to see if they could pick out a sheltered place.

The island colour was degraded by the grey day, not a living green ; chill, not exhilaration, in the sea wind. The old *Rose* was in keeping, hulky old seafarer with her smoke and her soot-blackened mizzen and the herring scales everywhere. Watching the boat, Mr. Buchan said, " I fear we'll no' land ye," but the boat's crew brought back as it were an olive twig and shouted up that it was worth trying. All our gear was handed across as the two gunwales heaved within passing range, and was piled in the dirty water swilling about the bottom-boards. Mr. Buchan shook us by the hand and gave us his blessing. " Heave ho, me hearties," said the fireman at one oar.

The first inlet was hopeless with swell, the spray was thrown back over the boat. We were going to fail. A little more sheltered place farther along looked better, where the rock had a vertical wall. The boat edged in : we leapt lightfoot ashore. Not so easy to land the gear. Each piece came hand to hand as the swell allowed, or was flung upon the rock. The crew pulled away as quickly as they could—hadn't thought they would manage it.

We watched them bob back to the ship, saw the boat manhandled inboard and the *Rose* move and turn ; the men were waving. The hectic moments were over. We could appreciate that it really was the rock of North Rona under the soles of our cold wet feet ; no longer any hurry for anything at all. It was about eight o'clock in the evening, the 16th of July.

We had been landed on the southward face of the rocky peninsula called Sceapull, sticking out from the south-west corner of the island. We picked up the tent and our rucksacs and started walking on to the main body of the land. Everything was strange, each boulder and rock ; every blade of herbage was strange because it grew on Rona. An uproar of sea-birds arose as we walked along, they had all come down to Sceapull to look and protest—gulls, mostly the big raucous great black-backs—arctic terns going round with lazy dropping flight, screaming—yelping oystercatchers—silent fulmars keeling past. We clambered over some boulders full of shags. A boulder-strewn seaside sward began, of thrift, buckshorn plantain, the yellow flowers of some dandelion sort of weed. Young fulmars were sitting right out in the open where they had been hatched, perhaps against a boulder but on level, quite inland ground ; they streamed their oil as we passed.

Young gulls were running about. As the slope rose inland the ground was covered with long coarse grass and sedge. We came to some earthworks.

So this was the village. A jumble of grass-grown mounds and walls—impossible to tell where one building ended and another began or what was the proper ground level. Tortuous underground tunnels were roofed with slabs of rock and grown over with turf. There were several oblong holes in the ground, lined with stones : houses. Recesses were let into the sides—this was the prehistoric type of wall-bed ? Beehive-shaped stone huts roofed with living turf were more recognisable. The ground was covered with a thick mat of silverweed, in flower.

The *Rose*—we had forgotten her—was a speck with a trail of low blowing smoke.

At the top of the village was the obvious chapel. This famous survivor was an oblong enclosure of enormously thick drystone walls. Three of its walls were more or less fallen, but the western end still stood seven or eight feet high. At the eastern end of the chapel the unique and even more precious cell of St. Ronan was a mound of turfy earth and stones—but hollow. You looked down into a small rectangular dungeon, nine or ten feet deep and nearly all underground, lined with close-laid inward leaning stones : this extraordinary cell was one of the earliest untouched Christian churches in the British Isles. A powder-puff fulmar squatted in each corner.

Abutting on the chapel was a circular area inside a turf wall, and within it, stuck up in the silverweed, stood a Victorian gravestone : the graveyard and the memorial stone to the famous two shepherds of Ness. The so-called manse was below this, another oblong hole in the earth with a chickweed-covered floor, but the ground so lay that one end was open ; you could walk in. At the other end was a fireplace. A stone chimney stack, two or three feet high, rose from the turf. More young fulmars were tucked away in recesses of the houses and walls. Small holes in the grass walls were the burrow entrances of Leach's petrel ?

We chose a flat pitch of silverweed near the manse and in

the stiff breeze set up the tent. Down to the landing place again—the sea bobbing with glistening seals' heads—to bring back an Army and Navy case and a breaker of water for food and drink. The ten-gallon water breakers weighed about a hundredweight each and had nothing to catch hold of; getting one up to the village was a fearful labour.

The northern half of Rona was unknown from the village, dead ground shut off by the broad ridge at the top of the slope. Before we turned in we had to look down the precipitous hill on the other side, to where it narrowed at the bottom to a bottleneck of land and opened beyond into the sprawling rocky peninsula called Fianuis. The sheep had disappeared when we landed ; we saw them trailing their ragged dirty fleeces down on Fianuis.

We shouldn't do anything about Leach's fork-tailed petrel the first night but should save up, like a Christmas present, the first experience of a night out in the village ; have a good sleep first. All the birds had quietened.

> *Nought broke a silence gloomy as the grave,*
> *Nought, but the wind, and hoarse-resounding wave.*

At eighteen minutes past eleven, happening to look out of the tent, I saw a little dark bird flit quickly like a bat across the sky above the ruins. So that was it.

When it was darker the air became full of flitting shapes and our piece of night was alive with loud exclamations. The shapes dashed about so fast and close it seemed they must hit the guy-ropes of the tent. We lay in our sleeping-bags : I reflected on last year and this, on now and on the near future, and felt extraordinarily content.

IV

" *A World Alone* "

THE very first morning on Rona was brilliantly fine—
flawless. The sun shone hot, the sky was blue, fleecy
clouds floated, the breeze was kindly. The flowering silverweed
buzzed with insects ; a square yard of it might have been anywhere, until the pleasure of looking up to see all round the
empty ocean !

After breakfast I lifted a loose stone—beneath sat Leach's
petrel and young. In the hand, in the flesh, this remote bird
was attractively original, sized between thrush and sparrow
but slim and light, dusky feathered except for a white rump
above its notably forked tail. The neatly miniature black-
webbed feet were cold to the touch. It had a dark passive eye
and a petrel's queer hooked beak, black, with the soft-looking
tubular nostril along the top. A high forehead made its head
look an unusual shape. Leach's petrel was silent, turned its
head about and tried to bite. When we let it go it circled once
low over the grass—long sickle wings, jerky flight—then made
off south-eastwards and flickered out of sight over the sea.
We lowered the stone over its chick, a ball of grey fluff from
which stuck out a bill like its parent's ; its beady eye was
nearly hidden by fluff.

A peculiar smell hung about the village, musty, sweetish :
Leach's petrel's own odour. We soon realised that the turfy
walls were all riddled with petrels' burrows. A few puffins and
starlings shared the walls ; young fulmars were parked indifferently about. Most notable of the fulmars were the four in
St. Ronan's dim cell, where also lay nestlings' skulls of other
years ; probably chicks hatched in that little dungeon often
failed to get out. One young fulmar in a recess of the manse
had been hatched on a heap of rusting sardine and bully beef

Lisgear

Fianuis

Storm Beach

Tunnel Cave
(Sgeildige)

Fanko

Old
Wall

Geodha a Stoth
(standard landing place)

R I D G E

Village ⌂⌂ ⌂ Chapel

○ Best well

⌂ 355 ft.
Cairn

Toa
Rona

Hasrgeir

Seapull

Leac na Sgrob

Stoc a Phriosain
Poll Heallair

Poll Thothetom

Loba
Sgeir

Landing place
16·7·1936

Caolas Loba Sgeir

Gealldruig Mhoe

0   ¼   ½   1 Mile

Fig. 3. *Sketch map of North Rona*

59

tins, the only trace to be found of the last human residents.

We began a desultory carting of gear up to the village, but kept breaking off. There was everything to see. A scrabbling among the rocks revealed a young grey lag goose, already a first new record for the island. A stretch between Sceapull and the village was a black-backs' breeding ground, the old birds in uproar, their speckled young splashing through the slimy green puddles whenever we passed. We tried to avoid going too close to the young fulmars for it set them coughing and bringing up ; a pity to see their parents' providence so wasted. The mutes of flying gulls splashed on the rock with a smacking noise.

Down at the landing place the sea was calmed. A seal lay basking on its back, lazily gnawing at its flipper—saw us—twisted round its sleek head and stared, then bundled itself into the sea. The black guillemots of Sceapull sat engagingly about the rocks, planted on bright red webs, yawning and showing each other the vermilion insides of their mouths. We followed Sceapull to its land's end where it was separated from the ultimate, off-lying Loba Sgeir by a lane of deep water called Caolas Loba Sgeir. We stripped and plunged in. The Sgeir was a large, flat, entirely bare expanse of rock which winter seas would wash over. Arctic terns rose from it in a screaming cloud though it was not their nesting place. Loba Sgeir was pleasant to skip about on after the fearful chill of Caolas Loba Sgeir, but the sharp rock and the greeny swell were no place for white indoor human bodies, soft and vulnerable ; anything but natural for them to walk about in their state of birth. We plucked up courage and returned to the mainland. It was warm enough in the afternoon sun to idle naked indefinitely.

So many thousands of sea-fowl ! We looked over the west cliff—impossible to encompass the seething tumult of colonists. All the roaring party were there: kittiwakes, guillemots, puffins, razorbills, fulmars. The swell beat against the foot of the wall far below, bobbing with white dots. You could fix on one flying speck from the snowstorm and follow its way, to the cliff, bank and turn, out again and round. Along the south coast were innumerable shags with green eyes, kittiwakes again, puffins on station along the cliff top turf, feral sheep bolting away. I counted eighteen seals' heads within a few feet of each other. The patches of floating shags were thicker still.

A little bit of the cliffs, some stretches of the grassy southern acres of the slope—each new area was a precious exploration. Only once can one tread new ground for the first time. All this would soon be familiar ; now it was novel with a strangeness almost of unreality. The twist was in the coming from ordinary life, no doubt, from human affairs all-pervading to a wholly extra-human country—which teemed. Everything had more than ordinary significance ; it had nothing to do with us. The fulmars' breasts were snowy as they circled the ruins, gliding and beating mechanical wings, more than ever enigmatic. And all the others, thousands and thousands, each of its kind, each had its own egg or young, its own style of flying and chosen place. The seals basked unasking on their known rocks. Loose stationary stones lay about, unused, " secure in mystery." The village grass was Yorkshire fog a foot deep, a mauve sheen of bloom buzzing with bluebottles. Yorkshire fog ?—but it was on Rona, growing on its own, unnamed.

*   *   *

The weather was changing again. The breeze freshened and chilled, turning the village silverweed so that the leaves showed silvery. The far visibility of the evening must have been rare. A cloud of gannets stirred above Sula Sgeir, ten miles away. The sea was empty to the hard horizons.

> *Far on old Ocean's utmost region cast,*
> *One lonely Isle o'erlooks the boundless waste. . . .*
> *Dim from its cliff, but far-remote, is shown*
> *One distant coast ;—'tis else a world alone !*

And indeed, far, far away were the mountains of Mainland, the mountains south of Cape Wrath and inland of Kinloch Bervie or Scourie, a year and seventy miles away but sharp and clear from this Rona evening. Even the rather mean cliffs of the Butt of Lewis were showing, from forty-odd miles.

The sun passed low over Sula Sgeir and went down in a flaming sunset out of a mackerel sky. The strange great bird that happened to flap across it was a landward heron.

We collected up the litter already surrounding the tent and secured it under the old rickcloth which, in a projection from the Home Counties, I'd felt sure would come in useful. A sheltered place for the Primus was inside a stone-roofed tunnel leading into one of the houses. We had a first mug of something hot. Clearing up, we made a bitterly disheartening discovery —the case of flash-bulbs—it was missing. It must have got left in the drifter ; everything had been stowed down below and it must have been put out of sight. So much for the unique night photographs of Leach's petrel. The only hope now was that the sheep people might bring it ; presumably they would be coming sometime. Would the crew of the *Rose* have realised the value of that small box, would they have the savvy to hand it to whatever Stornoway drifter Mr. MacFarquhar might charter for the sheep ?

The breeze by dusk was strong and cold, north-easterly ; the grass lay over before it and the ruins were dark graves against the sky. Eleven-thirty—time for the first petrels, I thought, looking out from the cosy tent. We were missing another night because John had developed a shivery cold, probably not improved by Caolas Loba Sgeir. A good deal of weird noise sounded later on, but the wind blew much of it away and the tent was flapping and straining. John snored full blast ; I thought then, as often afterwards, that I would not care to be alone in Rona.

On our second and more to be expected morning, wind-driven rain pelted loud against the tent, the view through the chink where the door flaps joined was of wind-laid soaking grass and vibrating thrift heads. The guy-ropes were twanging taut. At the moment the little tent with sleeping room only for two was our total shelter. After indecision we dressed against the weather.

The conventional headquarters for residents on Rona was the manse, as called, a convenient place though not more than a pit walled with stones. Its only overground wall was built across the flat-floored gully at one end and contained two gaps, doorway and probable window. I remembered the photograph in Malcolm Stewart's book ; it had been one of the most emotive of illustrations, showing, as well as the heaped stone and recognisable thrift, Evidence of Man—a sack hung over the window hole and a spade leaning against the doorway.

You stooped under the lintel stone and were indoors, in a useful pit-house about sixteen feet by nine and six feet deep ; fireplace and chimney at the far end, and the relic of a dividing wall across the middle. This was where the two penitent shepherds of the eighties had lived and died ; the chimney and fireplace and end wall would be their work ?—modern island period ? The floor was a lush plot of chickweed which soon got trodden into mud. We roofed the fireplace end with the rickcloth, secured round the eaves with boulders and some discovered quern stones. (Corn grown on that hillside !) Inside we set up house and arranged a cooking corner. The rickcloth roof was far from waterproof but it did cover enough of the pit to shelter the boxes and bags, camera apparatus and clothes. Outside its cover were enamel plates for the rain to wash up, and the water breakers and the seven Army and Navy cases, all contents packed in airtight tins. The rickcloth delivered some of the rain it received into a breaker ; we needed only to have brought an empty instead of four times ten gallons of best Stornoway water.

Having now a house, we set out to explore again. Wild Fianuis opened in the eye of the wind, rimmed with seething white. The real thing :

> *The northern ocean in vast whirls*
> *Boils round the naked melancholy isles.* . . .

Puffins were nesting even under the stones of the summit cairn of Toa Rona. From here all the island lay plain :

> *From the centre all round to the sea*
> *I am lord of the fowl and the brute.*

The peninsulas of Sceapull and Fianuis sprawled on either side of the broad east-west ridge, the island's backbone and height of land. Toa Rona at the eastern end was a rounded down, 355 feet high, chief pap and first to be lifted from seaward. The summit fell away on three sides by slopes steeper and steeper until they were cliffs, grass to thrift to bare rock ; the fourth side stretched westward and inland into the grassy whaleback. Three-quarters of a mile away the far end of the ridge was chopped off sheer, the western cliff dropped like a wall. The north-looking face of the ridge was a steep slide down to Fianuis ; the southern, in which the village was dug, a more gradual slope, bigger and broader, tailing off into the south-western spur of Sceapull. The mantle of rough grazing seemed merely a skin laid over adamant rock ; it seemed that it might be peeled off in one piece and rolled up as a carpet of woven grass roots, leaving clean rock underneath. The edges of the land were cliff-bound except at the two peninsulas, and they were rock-bound. From the point of Sceapull, up past the village, over the ridge and down the other side, and along the length of Fianuis, was a mile and a half on the map. Rona was a large island thus cast away in the northern ocean.

Fianuis began at the foot of the ridge as a narrow neck undermined by Sgeildige, the tunnel cave, an island feature. In some geological future Fianuis must become another island. Meanwhile, in any Rona guide-book the tunnel cave would remain second only to the village ; the storm beach might be a poor third. A shaft led down to the sea floor of the cave ; we found it a dripping slimy place with seals and shags inside and a diminished swell swilling at the walls. On the neck of Fianuis were works of man, the drystone square of a sheep fank and a partly fallen wall from sea to sea.

The geologist's storm beach, inland a little along the west side of Fianuis, was a boulder bank set with wind-ruffled puffins and fulmars. Fianuis was obviously the seals' chief ground, being a great rocky plain easily accessible from the sea in many places and usefully provided with off-lying skerries.

64

The north-eastern rocks faced wind and sea directly—" thus far, incalculable main ! "—and made a boiling surf from which seals' heads looked up curiously. Eiders were the same, not concerned with the cauldron but looking at us ; and we from solid rock looked out to them. The swell ran down the east side of Fianuis to throw up against the cliff of Toa Rona and stream back in waterfalls.

Fianuis presented the isolation : a desert of cold rock, low-lying, with the sea near and strong all round. When you turned your back to the wind and looked south there was only the stark skyline of the ridge. The wind of the ocean searched it over ; no rest from it or shelter from stinging squalls. The black-backs were like hawks, swinging in the wind with their wings half furled and their legs hanging loose. This was high summer.

A black guillemot's home under a boulder was marked by a heap of dung—the young exchanged secrecy for cleanliness. We thought we should like an intimate view and so built up a hide of stones, after several avalanches, drystone walling being like that.

And so home over the ridge. We had now had a superficial look over most of our island.

*　　*　　*

We sat waiting for darkness to bring in Leach's petrel from the sea. This was the night for which we had come so far and, odd, here we really were, sitting on our luggage in the manse on North Rona in the stormy dusk of July 18th, 1936. Now let the petrels show their part. The storm lantern was hung and lit ; we sat in oilskins and gumboots and counted the drips through the rickcloth roof. Outside a rain mist swirled down from the ridge.

An astonishing noise began to issue from the end wall of the chapel, a long loud churring as of rolled rr's, a frog's noise, but periodically broken off by a sudden exclamation, as if the maker had been overtaken by a hiccup. This, as we afterwards realised, was a storm petrel's churring. It soon stopped and we stumbled our ways about the village.

John's torch beam was a golden rod in the running mist. Dark flitting shapes were beginning to materialise and disappear ; the first birds were in. They made no noise but the rustling of wings as they dashed close by. Occasionally there was a momentary brighter glimpse—the white rump of a recognisable bird.

I was standing alone in the chapel, savouring the experience. The weird things darted and fluttered round—close to the ground—sweeping up against the sky—turning and twisting and going at breakneck speed. They still flew in silence.

On lulls of the wind there came an unearthly ululation, the forsaken wailing of seals. The sound heard unexpectedly was something to make one's hair stand on end, despairing, moaning, unnatural. The village was enclosed whichever way you shone the light by the moving wall of mist.

The little birds began to call. The sharp cries, loud and uncouth, came faster, tumbling over each other, more and more. The activity of dashing and shouting worked up to a pitch and sustained it full tilt—eccentric, abandoned aviary in the night above the village.

The darkness was full of excitement and haste—but facts ? It seemed impossible to sort out anything from the headlong rush of wings and ejaculations. John, always the prime mover in petrel research, was already trying to write phonetic words from the pell-mell staccato voices. I saw two birds collide with a smart flop and fall to the ground, pick themselves up and dash on again. Noise came loud and hollow from underground as well as from the air, the walls were all alive inside. Birds were scuffling on the ground—we saw them momentarily as we stumbled to and fro—they were looking for their burrows ? An urgent cheeping of chicks sounded from behind the screen of turf and stone. We made a beginning of sticking in pegs to mark subterranean noises ; we had already cut a supply of pegs from the lid of a food-box.

Hopeless to try to follow the flights with a torch beam ; all you could do was to hold the light steady and see the birds illuminate themselves for a flash. I caught one on the ground in the beam—just time to register the instant vignette. That was how it went : from the anonymous rushings of the darkness a bird was suddenly discrete in torchlight—momentarily still, bright eye and sickle wing—and gone.

The headlong fair lasted perhaps two hours, ourselves bewildered and fascinated in the middle of it.

The excitement was beginning to wane ; gradually the air became less busy, the noises lessened. The first doubtful signs of another day were showing. The petrels were dispersing—going back to sea ?—going underground ? Their calls now only punctuated the breeze. They had finished another night. We didn't wait for the rest of the dawn.

V

A House and Grounds

THE fork-tails now set our routine ; we stayed out with them every night thereafter until about three o'clock in the morning, and attended a run of twenty-five performances without a break.

Once we had settled on a number of burrows for observation, each night's work became a series of routine rounds from our home in the manse. It looked misleadingly cosy from outside, the storm lantern glowing within, but sitting there like a couple of troglodytes we knew too well the habits of the rickcloth roof. In a wet wind the slack would suddenly billow upwards, then, subsiding, tautened with a vicious crack which showered everything with spray. Between rounds of the village we sat munching a ship biscuit and watched the raindrops run glistening along the seams. The two fastest deliveries dropped splosh into a barrel, and tinkle into a bucket ; up sailed the roof and we ducked with our mouths full while it fired its charge. In one bad night the barrel was filled to the brim. As the famous Mr. Martin Martin had noted of another of the Western Isles,

> The moisture of this Place is such that a Loaf of Sugar is in Danger to be dissolved.

It was convenient thus to have water without any carrying, though at first we conserved our Stornoway supply carefully and used for washing-up the gull-water from stagnant bird-polluted pools ; this before it was brought home to us in the manse, somewhat literally, that we could rely on rain water. Seepage water of a sort was always to be found ; there was an inch or two in a muddy well by the village. The map

68

marked five old wells dotted about, small drystone squares
a foot or two across and a foot deep, sometimes covered with
a flagstone. The best well in the island was about half-way
along the southern cliff edge, where almost a stream trickled
over after heavy rain.

The passing days sometimes brought sunshine as hot as on
the first day, when a body could go naked, but we did not
bathe again. At mid-July the summer season had already
passed its peak, the eider ducks swam offshore with well-
grown broods, the longest twilights and the fairest days of the
year had already gone. On one or two days the sea was nearly
silent and perfectly blue, only the low heave of swell. Then
the occasional crash when the march of swell matched with
the cliff, came unexpectedly, like a stray gunshot. The weather
was always of first moment, since we lived in it ; the island's
one-time natives had taken their names from " the colour of
the sky, rainbow and clouds." Driving mist had been considered the Rona norm, but that damp cold could clear
extraordinarily quickly, to cloud shadows racing over the
southern slope and to a sea at once blue and sparkling and
dotted with white horses. Sula Sgeir used to get the sun first ;
the sullen rock would wonderfully light up under a low sky
all aslant with sunbeams ; the sunshine would cross the sea
to Rona ; you felt the quick warmth.

Above the village were ancient grassed-over lazy-beds, the
old natives' arable ground, which a late low sun would make
to seem contemporary again, by so stereoscopically marking
light ridge and black hollow. It re-made the cliffs to new, so
that they had had no weathering ; they were knife-edged and
cast chasms of darkness. The matted grass of ridge and slope
was made smooth as green velvet. The sun going down threw
a shadow upon the end wall of the chapel, the one wall tall
and bare of thrift ; the shadow slowly pushed the yellow light
up the wall, as indeed it had done at intervals for something
like a thousand years. On each fine evening there was the
stage when the sun was behind Sula Sgeir and the black rock
stood at the head of the sun-road across the sea. In any

moderately fine weather Sula Sgeir was always bringing up one's sight, being the only mark in the ocean.

Sometimes we saw a stray fishing vessel. On rare days the mainland mountains showed again, and once or twice at night we could make out in the ultimate distance the faintest winking of the Cape Wrath and Butt of Lewis lighthouses. Cape Wrath alternated red and white ; the Butt blinked only white.

*　　　*　　　*

A common reaction of one set down in an island swarming with life is to try to make it manageable by counting—a naturalist's census. We took a bit at a time and counted steadily in various weathers for several days, until we had got all round the five miles of coastline and all over the 300 acres. The swarming auks of the boundary walls and the shags whose young had mostly taken to the sea were too difficult, but as we patiently went round we did begin to see some of the relationships of the different birds to each other and to their summer land.

Our reckoning at the beginning of August was : A minimum of about 380 pairs of Leach's petrels and numerous storm petrels, not estimated ; at least 250 pairs of great black-backed gulls ; about 1000 pairs of kittiwakes ; 7 pairs of starlings still nesting in the village and a flock of some 70 birds which fed among the sheep ; at least 50 pairs of rock pipits ; 3 or 4 pairs of wheatears ; 2 herons ; about 20 pairs of eiders (we found two or three just distinguishable nests up on the ridge, mats of wet down overgrown by the grass, with greeny eggshells left to tell of successful hatchings) ; 587 nestling fulmars ; 30 oystercatchers ; a small party of turnstones and another of redshanks ; about 60 pairs of arctic terns ; 20 pairs of herring gulls and 6 of lesser black-backed gulls ; 15 to 20 pairs of black guillemots ; very many shags and razorbills ; puffins and guillemots unnumbered.

On one day we counted 250 Atlantic grey seals round the coast, nearly all of them about Fianuis. The sheep numbered about 200 ; they and the seals were the only mammals. No rats, mice or rabbits, no reptile or amphibian, " no sort of trees here, no, not the least shrub " ; not even heather. There were less than fifty different species of plants, mostly drab. No one had yet attempted a collection of invertebrate life and nor did we, knowing nothing of that endless department. Our belongings became infested with earwigs and silverfish ; lifted stones revealed an invertebrate scuffling. Sometimes we turned up the large peculiar shore slaters ; their small familiar relations, woodlice, were common in the petrels' burrows, and so were beetles, centipedes and more earwigs.

The adult great black-backed gulls were masters of the island, eating but not eaten. That was first and obvious. The rest of the birds suffered under them and their corpses made in places almost a litter on the ground ; a puffin's corpse turned neatly inside out was one of the commonest of island sights. The black-backs cast up in large pellets the indigestible beaks and legs of unfortunate auks and kittiwakes. A sample dozen pellets, borne home to the manse and dissected, contained the remains of one small petrel (adult and whole—this made one complete casting), two young fulmars, one young great black-backed gull, two adult and two young kittiwakes, one puffin, the remains of five adult auks (razorbill or guillemot), two young and two eggs, some fish bones and fragments of a shag's egg. (Nothing to tell, of course, whether victims had been taken alive, ailing or dead.) An inexplicable red rubber balloon turned up in another dissection.

One puffin was nesting next door to the manse, a familiar neighbour called the house puffin. A sad day when a black-back came and killed it and started eating it on its own erstwhile doorstep.

In a few days at the beginning of August we collected 166 corpses left by the gulls. Eighty extroverted adult puffins and 36 adult kittiwakes made the bulk, but it was a pity to find 10 adult Leach's petrels, a storm petrel and a black guillemot. However could the clumsy diurnal black-backs have got hold of the nocturnal petrels, quick and slick as mice ?

The black-backs included cannibalism in their unpleasant habits—there were eight young of their own species in our collection of corpses.

The first young kittiwakes fresh on the wing appeared like a new species, soft and weightless, moth-like, and in their bold black and white plumage quite unlike their parents. We saw the first of them flying on the first of August and the first corpse on the second ; 26 a day or two later. Young puffins were safe in their burrows, so were young black guillemots under the boulders of Fianuis and Sceapull. Arctic terns nested among loose pebbles on Fianuis, ground which black-backs continually flew over. It seemed a confident example of protective coloration ; the eggs were extraordinarily difficult to find, but the scarcity of young terns and of such as oyster-catchers appeared striking. The population of black-backs seemed a disproportionate tax on the rest of the birds.

Young fulmars were practically immune from the black-backs and oil-squirting seemed to be their obvious protection, particularly for those which sat out in the open, single and unattended. In fact this is supposed not to be a defence weapon at all, but as fulmars young and old throw up oil as an emotional reaction and usually face the cause of disturbance, it came to much the same thing. Both young and adult shot at first clear oil, a first pressing as it were, but as they went on pumping the spoil thickened into vomit. Old birds sometimes turned sideways and sicked up gently, and this perhaps was a plain analogy to the alarmed vomiting of, for instance, herons. It was the first strong jets from chicks facing the alarm that looked so usefully defensive.

Fulmars were really the badge of Rona, for teeming Fianius of the seals and black-backs was a place apart, shut off by the ridge, and the kingdom of the auks was cliff-bound. But fulmars were always flying strange and silent over the body of the land, and the inland nesting of many of them was the remarkable feature of Rona. Squab young sat 300 yards from the sea, more were on the flat rocks of Fianuis and Sceapull, and 21 were scattered in the village. One could understand why the old naturalists had flocked to St. Kilda, drawn by the fulmars, arctic and inscrutable, but with yet that one southern outpost in Britain ; and so the excitement of the pioneers when they came to Rona in the eighties and first found fulmars spreading there. Now the sight was to see fulmars nesting on level inland ground, and the pleasure that this was the very mark of a place where human beings were rare foreigners. In the early mornings from the manse or from the sleeping-tent we used to hear the farmyard noises of courtship going on, as on Handa Island, on a wet ledge of indifferent memory. The feeding of the young, the retching transfer, we rarely saw, and the old birds seldom attended their young. After a rainy night many would be bedraggled for want of a parent's shelter. Sometimes a village fulmar would get bogged down in the long grass, unable to take off. As for the young fulmar in the manse, it was very unfair that we should have claimed the house. We couldn't leave it to starve, so, experimentally, we ate it, fried in its own grease. A chicken cooked in engine oil might have been similar.

Always something to find on the dawdling walks of census-taking or exploration ; always something to see on this wind-scalped foreign land in an empty sea ! A couple of seal's teeth to be knocked out of a discovered jawbone, a nestling fulmar hatched alongside a dead sheep, some new plant to be looked up, the horny, totem-coloured capping of a puffin's bill, sloughed from an old skeleton. We investigated the many underground noises of the island, lifted stones and felt gingerly down burrows—young puffin here, black guillemot there, a whiff of petrel from a heap of boulders. In a new country some things are novel in themselves but also the familiar becomes remarkable because of the new context. It was so on Rona : if one plant or bird were new, another surprised by familiarity.

The map was marked and ticked off bit by bit. A stretch of the west coast, southward to Sceapull : forty or fifty pairs of guillemots down there, some old birds still incubating their eggs, sitting half upright, egg between legs, continually poking at it and readjusting it with their bills—it was a wonder that any ever did hatch. Below them just two pairs of kittiwakes, right in the line of splashings from the ledge above. Farther on, under a dripping overhang, two razorbills' eggs—one warm, the other cold and wet, long abandoned. A pair of black guillemots next, a few toady young fulmars, three noisome shags' nests ; then a party of oystercatchers, a wheatear flickering among the rocks, two separate colonies of nesting gulls, more shags, malodorous and dismal. The most notable of all the cliff-dwellers was a solitary razorbill perched with its egg on a bracket of thrift which grew like a fungus from the 300-foot sheer west cliff. The bracket razorbill became an old friend ; the egg hatched safely, but later on the chick either fell off or was taken by a black-back.

The cliffs were varied in many places by caves or over-hangs and by geos,[1] some fit for exploration. On the south coast we got down the cliff and managed to work round into the narrow cleft called Stoc a Phriosain. The entrance was blocked by an enormous rock, past which there was squeezing room if you took your coat off. Inside was a dripping dark exciting place, scattered with rare driftwood and with dead birds and decomposing seaweed, and roofed with a slit of far sky. The noise of the sea was distant thunder. A tunnel led in and on ; we crawled through and emerged into the next geo, Poll Heallair, with rock walls rising sheer a hundred feet, kittiwakes crossing the strip of sky, and no way out but back. No doubt there were several such places still to be found and explored, probably only from the sea.

Nothing happened ; all was content (except for nagging regrets about flash-bulbs). What should one expect, cast on an island with everything found ? In only a few days anything outside our immediate doings seemed of no interest. We slept late after seeing the petrels finishing, then used to issue from the village in the afternoons. Island life seemed normal, not like a holiday or a journey but an everyday life, in which there

[1] Geo, a narrow cliff-walled inlet of sea.

was never enough time for all our affairs. One day was much like the last and the next would be much the same. The first experience of living apart from the body of mankind lasted only a few weeks, but trite formulæ about escape from the senseless rush of modern civilisation—commonly uttered by those immersed in it—didn't apply. The core of the matter was, being able to do something interesting entirely without interference. Selfish, self-centred? Of course. I believe our enjoyment was almost smug.

VI

Leach's Petrel

THE peculiarity which attaches to all the tribe of petrels and shearwaters is by no means lacking in the four kinds —fulmar, storm and Leach's petrels, and Manx shearwater— which brush a wing tip at British coasts. All are thoroughgoing pelagics, marathon fliers who, if they could, would no doubt even hatch upon the face of the waters (as indeed old salts traditionally held was the habit of the stormies, Mother Carey's Chickens, the bringers of evil weather). All are very oily and have the odd tubular nostril and hooked beak, all are hopelessly ungainly on land, have a musky smell, lay one white egg each year, and, except for the fulmar, venture ashore only at night and then go underground.

Leach's petrel, most inaccessible and least known of the four, began in Britain as " an undescribed petrel with a forked tail " in the collection of the ornithologist, Mr. Bullock, who obtained it at St. Kilda in the summer of 1818. It might have become Bullock's fork-tailed petrel if the specimen had not been bought for the British Museum by the curator, Dr. Leach. Little was known of the new species in life. Robert Mudie (*Feathered Tribes of the British Islands*, 1834) wrote that these birds were

> seldom seen at the places where they breed, as they nestle in holes of the rocks ; and, though they make a sort of croaking noise there, it is made only during the night. . . .

The distribution became better known but hardly any other information was added in the next century. Illustrations commonly showed the bird in a stance it could not support in life, and even contemporary books had no word for the nocturnal performance.

Personally we came to regard these small petrels, which had

begun for us as a name in an index, with a baffled affection—
what *were* they up to ?

The village, silent and deserted of petrels all day, showed
two signs of their habitation. One was the musty, musky, nearly
sweetish smell always hanging about, the other the burrow
entrances among the green walls, sometimes looking like
reduced rabbit burrows, with miniature heaps of excavated
earth. Any large stone lifted up was liable to reveal an egg
or a chick. We had so found the very first, and we found
several more like it by accident. John, for instance, going to
block up the manse chimney against some of the draught,
pulled up a cushion of thrift and laid open an incubating petrel.
The daytime investigation of burrows, how they could be short
cul-de-sacs or nesting chambers leading from a labyrinth, their
measurements, nesting material and so on, was straight-
forward ; it was different after dark.

For an observer the sensational part of the fork-tails' life is
naturally the nightly aerial ritual, and up to our time it could
only ever have been witnessed on Rona by about a dozen
visitors. Each evening in the manse we waited for it as the
village dimmed into dusk; each night the gentle thrills of " first
bird seen " and " first call heard."

At dusk, perhaps an hour and a half after sunset, a first
shadowy bird would appear circling over the ruins, seen intermittently because of its wide circuit in the thickening light.
The fast jerky flight seemed feather-light, to have a buoyant
butterfly aimlessness. Another appeared, and another.

The crowd gathered : no sound but the brushing of wings.

There was usually a company of birds before the first call
broke out. Noise was soon continuous, the air alive with
random headlong fliers. In daytime the village sounds were
of passing black-backs or terns, starlings' chatter and the intermittent cacophony of fulmars' courtship. At night, except that
seals' ululations sometimes came faintly on the breeze, the life
was all of loud petrels. The animation seemed heightened by
the place, where all else was inanimate.

In the village hive a human being seemed of no more

account to the birds than the stone wall of the chapel. They rustled past our faces or slipped aside just in time though they did occasionally crash into each other and tumble to the ground. Crashed petrels sometimes sat as if dazed ; once I found one with a blooded head. (These collisions have since been interpreted—by Kenneth Williamson, from Faroe observations—as possibly deliberate meetings, to lead to some underground ceremonial.)

Although the flighting was the overwhelming impression, it did not seem to be more than a decoration to the real work of the night. Petrels plumped down on the grass and quickly shuffled into their burrows. There they regurgitated to their chicks, whose desperate peeping added to the noise. Digging went on spasmodically at unfinished burrows even as late as August. The digger straddled down and scraped energetically backwards with a webbed foot ; little showers of earth were thrown out from the burrow mouth. Subterranean calls and invisible scrabblings sounded as if activity underground was as desperate as that above.

The cries soon sorted themselves into a flighting call and a remarkable burrow croon : churr-r-r-r-r—(it went)—an undulating crooning, suddenly tripping over into a high-pitched yet soft exclamation—ooee ; r-r-r-ooee-churr-r-r-r, for minutes together. Fascinating to put one's ear to a bank and hear the astonishing noise unwinding within. The flighting call, uttered indifferently in flight or underground, made the volume of noise. Our rendering looked somewhat ridiculous : her-kitti-werke—kek-ek-eroo ; loud, staccato, with many variations. A third call, a harsh skhee, skhee, expressed anger, we thought.

The flighting and calling, the peeping of chicks and underground regurgitations, the crooning, colliding, digging, scuffling and scrabbling went on into the small hours, until at the earliest trace of dawn activity began to wane, the gramophone gradually ran down. Departures were subdued and silent, a flitting away low over the grass. Birds remaining underground ceased their bickering. The first black-backs came planing over the village. The state of day was sour dawn half-light, enough light to show the white rumps of the last departing fork-tails. The indifferent ruins gave no sight or sound of the late teeming activities.

Three hundred and twenty-seven was the number of occupied burrows we counted in the village. On night walks we came into minor replicas of the village hive, perhaps another fifty pairs of fork-tails nested in other parts of the island. Fianuis, for instance, at three o'clock in the morning— there were petrels flighting about the storm beach. Puffins, bright vignettes, stared at the unaccountable torchlight before they whirred off. In the village again, at nearly four o'clock, the last two or three petrels still flitted. We decided to stay up, made some coffee, while the day life gradually awoke. Gull noises increased, fulmars renewed their interminable stiff-winged perambulations of the village. I called on the young fulmars of St. Ronan's cell and received their oily greeting. Sula Sgeir showed again. Some terns came loitering overhead. On a veer of breeze a faint chorus swelled from the colonists of the western cliffs. The few village starlings began to squawk and feed their young. Now it was broad daylight, another day, the 26th of July. The sun rose briefly and disappeared into dark cloud. Rain began.

At midnight in July there was still an afterglow of sunset in the north-western sky. Sometimes Sula Sgeir was still visible when the first fork-tails arrived. I went to the western cliff edge, wondering if one could sight them in silhouette coming in from the sea. One could not, but still the hubbub of the cliff colonists wafted up with the ocean's everlasting grind. The bracket razorbill was at home, its eye sparkling red in torchlight, shone down into the abyss.

*　　　*　　　*

Sitting of a night in the manse, we did not have to go outside to be among petrels ; they came in ; even the vertical walls lining the manse fairly crowed with them. A storm petrel would flutter in and lose itself in the lantern light. It had a burrow in the fireplace and would promptly go in when shown the way, so that we couldn't have had a fire even if there had been anything to burn. At first the mixture of species was confusing, but there were only about twenty pairs of stormies in the village, nearly all in a heap of dry stones beyond the chapel. The reeling noise they made in their crannies, which had so intrigued us from the chapel wall on our first night of petrels, was easily told from the fork-tails' analogous crooning. Stormies had all the attraction of the petite ; they made the larger, more grey-brown Leach's seem almost gross.

A thump against the rickcloth and a bird would fall among the cooking things and old tins—a fork-tail this time. This was a particular bird called the Primus Leach's because its burrow was in the bottom of the wall by the Primus, past which it would scuttle and disappear. Tampering with its affairs— natural behaviour elucidated by tampering?—we introduced a strange bird after it. At once there was a torrent of harsh screams, the foreigner came out forthwith. You could soon tell if a burrow were occupied by introducing a foreigner. The easiest way to catch petrels was to crawl into the entrance tunnel of a house, where they scuttled like rats. When handled they were apt to vomit.

The burrows we had chosen for detailed watching were provided with a lattice across the entrance made of matches or slivers of packing-case wood, easily brushed aside, and with an observation window cut over the nesting chamber and kept covered with a bung of thrift or a stone. That F's lattice was newly down, that H had already been and gone, that B was still incubating and no sign of its mate to relieve it, that J had failed to turn up at all—such was the night news as we stumbled on our routine rounds, repairing lattices and peeping through windows. We ringed birds as we caught them, and this, with information laid by lattice and window, began to yield some indication of what went on below ground. Sheer inconsistency soon appeared to be the only keynote to the life of Leach's petrel ; the further we looked into it, the deeper the puzzle. The birds' time of arrival varied, so did the amount of activity, but most striking was the apparently haphazard irregularity of attention to both chicks and eggs.

One night of easterly storm practically put a stop to petrels' activity. Hardly a bird turned up ; the few that did made the record latest arrival time. Torchlight showed only beaten swathes of soaked weeds and dripping vibrating thrift clumps ; the blast tore at our swaddles of woollies and weatherproofs. Odd birds flickered momentarily against the sky before the gale whisked them away. For the observers, between rounds, under the frenzied rickcloth, such a night called for hot rum punch brewed from the single precious bottle.

> The Natives qualify it sometimes [the weather] by drinking a Glass of *Usquebaugh*.

While outside,

> *Outflying the blast and the driving rain*
> *The petrel telleth her tale in vain.*

On more normal nights the irregularity of the petrels was such that one chick might be fed twice, another once, another not at all ; it wasn't all or none throughout the colony but some and some. A catch phrase soon developed between us : Dull Calm Night of Maximum Activity. Birds arrived early and stayed late in such conditions, the darkness was at its busiest, and most of the observation burrows would be visited (probably). However, a large number of birds flighting did not necessarily mean that a proportionate number of burrows would be visited. Even incubation was irregular though this matter, most of all, set the difficulty of deciding how much was natural behaviour and how much the result of unavoidable interference by ourselves. The normal course appeared to be share and share alike, each bird sitting for a day or two at a stretch, visited at night and presumably fed by the other ; but a bird neglected by its mate was quite capable of leaving the burrow at dawn and giving the egg a whole day in which to incubate itself. When the egg did hatch a parent commonly spent only the first few days with the chick, and thereafter attended it only at night.

Some eggs never hatched, some chicks died, perhaps of neglect. In the summer there was the black-backs' unexpected toll of adult birds, in the winter there would be the shore-driven casualties of gales, though this was apparently the petrels' only seaward hazard. (It looked like an opening missed that no ocean-going predator had evolved to hunt the pelagic, flitting lives.)

The American, William Gross, observing Leach's petrels on an island in the Bay of Fundy, considered black-backs to be their worst enemy :

> One can pick up the regurgitated remains of dozens of birds in the morning along the shore after a night of full moonlight. The awkward, erratic flight of the Petrels makes them easy prey for the Gulls who stand guard along the shore and exact a heavy toll upon the bewildered birds which come fluttering in from the sea at night time.

Moonlight on Rona made the fork-tails late to arrive and early to go.

Chancy and casual though the whole nesting economy did look, it worked. And after all, the ordinary foolish guillemot was in even worse case—single-brooded, laying but the one egg and that easily knocked from precarious ledge, its young watched over by black-backs, itself the prey of winter storms and ships' oil waste—yet no one had suggested that its hordes diminished. Such birds *must* have a long breeding life. Darwin said, " the Fulmar petrel lays but one egg, yet it is believed to be the most numerous bird in the world " . . . and he worked out that one pair of elephants, producing only six young in a lifetime of one century, would after less than eight centuries have left descendants numbering nearly nineteen millions.

*　　*　　*

Observation of the fork-tails could never keep up with

question and argument. How did they—or any petrel—find their way at sea, how did they find their own burrows in the thickest night ? Why the night flighting ? Had the odd smell any significance ? Were the birds properly diurnal, with nocturnal excursions, or were their eyes adapted for night vision ? What could account for the irregular feeding ? Would daily weight and temperature records of the chicks show any correlation with the apparent eccentricity of their parents' visits?

The scales were constructed with a penknife out of packing-case wood, with nail bearings and two empty butter tins. Weights were coins and matches, afterwards converted by immense arithmetic into grams. Thermometer and scales came out every evening before the adults arrived. . . . John sitting in the manse with a tiny fluff of petrel on his knee, with a thermometer tucked under its wing stump. . . . Both of us crouched over the scales, one coaxing the chick to stay in its butter tin, the other manipulating the coinage, the petrel slowly oscillating against 3d. plus 20 matches. The record increase in twenty-four hours was 12.8 grams, from 4d. plus 20 matches to 5½d. plus 6 matches ; the scales were sensitive to half a match.

We did not know of Mr. Gross's American observations until long after we had left Rona. His weighings had been properly done in a field laboratory. The resulting graph showed a remarkable zigzag climb, due, he admitted, to the adults' irregularities which in turn might " be caused to a certain extent upon the conditions of the food supply at sea." The question of the food supply of petrels foraging from Rona led far beyond the resources of a few weeks on the island. In one direction it led to an inquiry into the nature and habit of plankton.

In the sea as on earth, all flesh is grass. The grazing of the oceans, the basic greenstuff, is the thin soup called phyto-plankton—chiefly of diatoms in their bacterial numbers, unicellular, shelled, free-floating, but yet green plants building organic foods from the faint mineral solution of the sea. On the diatoms feed some of the vast body of minute floating organisms collectively called zooplankton—protozoa, all sorts of larvae, tiny fish, pelagic shrimps, copepods, molluscs—all the etceteras of marine biology.

Plankton in the North Atlantic ocean is most abundant within a broad band stretching right across from east to west. All the known Atlantic breeding stations of Leach's petrel lie within the band, from the outliers of the Outer Hebrides, to the Faroes, to Icelandic islands, South Greenland, Labrador, and southwards to Maine. Leach's petrel, it explains itself, is a plankton feeder.

Plankton is most abundant in surface waters by night and sinks to lower levels by day. This is the wrong way round for a diurnal petrel, though storms may stir up plankton into the surface waters in daytime. (It was immediately after a storm that one of our petrel chicks made its record weight increase.) And driftermen say that herring, plankton feeders of course, come to the surface in bad weather. The creature we found most commonly in the vomit of handled Leach's petrels was afterwards identified as *Meganictyphanes norvegica*, a small nearly transparent pelagic species of shrimp, described as a constant and important constituent of northern oceanic plankton. The next more pregnant fact was that when *norvegica* spawned it did so on the surface, in shoals. Its spawning season varied with location, but to the north of Rona and also off Mr. Gross's coast of Maine, it went on all the summer. Successive spawning shoals would (and evidently did) provide Leach's petrel with an easily accessible food supply over a long period. Things began to hang together.

Floating oily or greasy matter is another petrel food. Mr. Gross trolled up petrels to his boat by streaming a bait of " odorous cod livers." A shoal of herring leaves an oily scum which attracts petrels, and fishermen use the birds as a not very reliable sign of herring. The old writer, Robert Mudie, thought that petrels skimmed the oceanic oil film with their breast feathers as they flew, and picked it off afterwards with their bills.

A food supply was provided, why then the shoreward

irregularities? Yet food and weather combined seemed to be the chief factors involved. Probably most birds came to land irrespective of their fishing success, as long as the weather allowed it. The obstinate point was that the chicks fed on any one night were not all or none, but some and some. That required the assumption that the Rona petrels foraged in small parties or singly, else all or none would find food and, presumably, all or none would feed their chicks. Against this were ocean records of the speed with which petrels congregated at the presence of food, appearing as if from thin air, so there had to be a further assumption that the Rona fork-tails foraged over an extremely wide area.

The argument had a pretty sequel. A copy of the article in *British Birds* which ended our labours happened to reach Mr. Jack Beach, director of a Yarmouth firm owning herring drifters. There was the spawning of *M. norvegica* to the north of Rona and the *norvegica* in the fork-tails' vomit; and there was that latest of all arrival times of petrels at Rona when the gale was *easterly*. Next spring Mr. Beach, having steam drifters at Stornoway and at Wick, sent them to try the seas north and west of Rona. They made some useful catches. But one felt that, like the fork-tails, they might just as well have not.

* * *

Another puzzle was the extraordinarily long incubation and fledging periods, not only of Leach's but of petrels generally. A blackbird had its eggs hatched and its young flown within a month. The British petrels took six or seven weeks for hatching and another seven or eight for fledging. Why? The quickest possible breeding season would have seemed an advantage for birds so shy of the land. Shore-going was apparently their most dangerous expedition, else why come under cover of darkness?

Mr. Gross kept four Leach's eggs on his laboratory table in temperatures varying from 45° F. to 85° F., yet after eight days they still contained living embryos.

Under actual conditions the egg is often left unincubated by the adults for several days. . . . The long incubation period may be correlated with the low temperature and great humidity of the burrow, and to the low body temperature of the adults (106° F.). . . .

No doubt the hardihood of the egg lessened the damage of inefficient brooding, but would an egg in an incubator hatch any more promptly than in nature?—or was the slow pace of embryological development set wholly by hereditary constitution?

The fledging periods of petrels, not only of unconscionable length, were also apparently variable from chick to chick. In the case of Leach's petrel, the irregular feeding of the chick looked a likely starting place, though irregular or at least infrequent feeding is common to other petrels, possibly all. An ordinary chick treated like a fork-tail's would promptly die of starvation. How did the petrel chicks survive?

Petrel chicks evidently had the capacity of surviving at a low basal metabolic rate—that is, at a low rate of living. If their metabolism went on at the normal high rate for birds they would quickly burn up their available food and probably be dead of starvation before the next meal. A low metabolic rate implied the inactivity of the young, sitting toadishly in their burrows all day and conserving themselves inside their fluffy insulation. Or, contrariwise, their very inactivity depressed the metabolic rate and made a meal last longer? However, though the fork-tails' nocturnal habit condemned their chicks to infrequent feeds, this was not the case with the diurnal fulmar; yet the fulmar chick is said to be fed only once in twenty-four hours. Was then the quality of the food itself, so largely fatty, of overriding importance?

Petrels, of course, shared their oiliness with other sea feeders such as herring and the blubber-sheathed whales and seals. The oiliness originated in the diatoms which tend to manufacture oils and fats rather than carbohydrates. As food, fats are characterised by great energy value, ease of storage, high concentration, and by slowness of assimilation. Just the thing for a far-flying, oceanic bird ! In the case of a young petrel intermittently topped up with the oily brew from its parent's stomach, the slow assimilation of fats would in itself require a wide spacing between feeds ; so the fulmar, with unfettered access to its chick, yet fed it only once a day ? Irregular feeds and slow assimilation—thus slow and irregular growth, and long and variable fledging period ?

Young petrels soon overtake their parents in weight. Possibly, because of the unbalanced nature of the food, young petrels were unavoidably overfed with fats in order to get enough of the other food elements. By the time they are fledged they are grossly fat and unable to fly. At this stage they are deliberately deserted by their parents, so that they starve into flying condition.

Was then all the long drawn-out nesting and peculiar habit of petrels to be traced largely to an excessive imbibition of oil ?

There remained the distinctive petrel smell, varying in flavour from genus to genus, but musky of them all. Was it an irrelevance of oiliness or did it have some hidden significance ? William Gross wondered whether it might not be " a highly differentiated characteristic of the individual bird." If so, " we can explain the ability of the birds to single out their mates in the dead of night." No end to petrel conjecture. Robert Mudie even wondered whether petrels discharged oil in rough weather " to procure a calm for themselves, in order that they may repose " . . .

The thrust of evolution and the mould of environment had together shaped the petrels, fitted to exploit the oceans and able to assimilate the oily skimmings. However petrels' economy might work, theirs had been an extremely successful venture, branched into many species, supported by enormous strength of numbers, and cosmopolitan of the oceans. And the answers to nearly all the puzzles about them, from their smell to their sense of direction, remained with them.

So, petrel, spring
Once more o'er the waves on thy stormy wing.

VII

A Rona Annual

SOMETHING was at the tent doors, a voice saying, " Are you receiving visitors to-day ? " We struggled from sleep to account for this—of course, the sheep people. In fact it was Malcolm Stewart himself, revisiting Rona with the shepherds and with Mrs. Stewart. The first thing in our minds was, did he know anything about our box of flash-bulbs ? No. The island was strangely dotted with men beginning the round-up ; cold rain and mist were sweeping over it, at six o'clock this morning.

The tenant passed, a tall man with rain dripping from his somewhat straggly moustache. "It's Himself," John whispered. " Fine sport for a hazy day, boys," said Mr. MacFarquhar.

The first manœuvre was a wide sweep to clear the southern half ; small black figures in streaming oilskins worked round the rim of the island—faint shouts and barking of dogs. The shepherds had used the standard east-side landing at the neck of Fianuis, called Geodha Stoth. Our help was not yet wanted, so we sat out of the way under the lee of the ridge and looked down to their drifter heaving uncomfortably below, hardly within the bight which Fianuis and the cliffs of Toa Rona sheltered between them. She was one of the elderly paraffin-engined Stornoway boats, a heavy sluggish thing without the attraction of a steam drifter ; her wet-darkened deck no doubt slippery with fish scales and sheep dung, and swilling with dirty water as she rolled.

Scared sheep began to move down the north slope of the ridge to retreat into Fianuis. The sheep fank at the foot of the ridge was artfully placed. Its entrance gave northwards on to Fianuis and faced a gap in the old stone wall across the neck of land. All that the master of the round-up had to do was to push all the sheep north into Fianuis, make a fencing funnel from the gap to the fank entrance, and drive the sheep back at it. It was not as easy as it sounded.

Men and dogs appeared over the ridge. Now we could go down and find out about flash-bulbs without danger of heading the chase. The skipper was just ashore ; we asked him. " Ar," he said, " the *Rose* has gone down." What, gone down ? " Aye, she's away on the east coast now." But had he got a box ? The box. A square box. Well, he said, he knew Mr. Buchan and Mr. Buchan had come to his house and said the boys he'd landed on Rona had left behind this wooden box. He, the skipper, was going to bring it to Rona.

Somehow the transfer had failed, but as near as we could get to a straight answer was : " Well, the *Rose* is away now."

The sheep were out of sight somewhere at the far end of Fianuis. The wire-netting funnel was put up. We were directed to lie down in yonder drain, which we did ; the wall had shortcomings as a barricade and had to be manned at the breaches ; one was to rise out of the ground if they were threatened. At other thin places on either side of us were stationed morose driftermen in black cloth caps. Many men were shouting in Gaelic, some with their mouths crammed with hasty food. From our drain we watched the sheep slowly coaxed towards us. They broke back. They were gathered again and broke again. They broke a third time. The dogs were getting tired. Some of the men took off their boots and stockings and rushed barefoot over the rocks, screaming in Gaelic. The fourth time the block of sheep wavered in the very mouth of the funnel—behind them a close cordon of men beside themselves with shouting and flapping their oilskins, of dogs barking their heads off—in front the open passage to the fank. The suspense must break. It broke, a solid wave of sheep surged forward at the wire-netting fence, flattened it and scampered away up the north slope beyond. A few were left struggling in the wreckage.

The fence was put up again, the sheep fetched from the

hill once more. Most of them pelted through the gap where the wall stopped a yard short of the western cliff—the arch of the tunnel cave at this point—then an airy drop to the sea. This time the return drive went off without a hitch. Stragglers were run down individually and carried in. The men settled down to hours of shearing the trailing, dung-matted fleeces. A lamb was killed and put to cook in an iron cauldron over some lumps of coal against the fank wall. Forty of the sheep which had been counted on the island a year ago were now reckoned missing from unknown causes, and the spring crop of lambs had to survive the black-backs as well as all the other hazards. A sheep's life on Rona could be no picnic.

The wind had been freshening steadily all day and blowing an unrelieved screen of rain or mist. Mr. MacFarquhar said he doubted they'd get away the night ; they would be waiting until the sea eased down for fear of losing sheep overboard. At dusk an emissary came up to the manse to fetch Mr. and Mrs. Stewart, and they walked off in the streaming rain. The drifter continued at anchor until half-past four next morning and then suffered a dreadful nine-hour passage to Ness. The expedition was duly reported by the Ness correspondent of the *Stornoway Gazette* :

> VISIT TO RONA.—The drifter " Cailleach Oidhche " (the owl) left the Breakwater, Port-of-Ness, on Wednesday, 29th inst., at 10 p.m., with Mr. A. MacFarquhar (lessee of Rona), his men, lambs, dogs, and other requirements, for their annual visit to Rona for the purpose of shearing, counting and other-wise looking after the sheep which are wintering there. It was quite nice weather when they left the Breakwater, but they had not gone far when we heard the foghorn at the Butt blowing. We then felt sure the weather conditions were not favourable. However, the " Cailleach Oidhche " got back to the Breakwater about 1 p.m. on Friday, the 31st inst., having accomplished the work she set out to do. It was a relief to see the drifter and all safely back, for the " Rona annual " has always been considered locally a precarious trip.

We returned to our settled ways. One of the newly

imported, ignorant lambs walked across the already disintegrating rickcloth roof and left a track of large rents. These new young rams stayed about the village at first as if glad of company. The expedition had brought us newspapers which we could only find dull, though useful in other ways ; the saying that all news is local seemed particularly apt. We should have made headlines of Young Shag Disgorges 26 Fish, Is This A Record ? and of Quaint Clay Lamp Discovered In Deserted Ruin. It might have happened to any one, says Finder. This lamp was in fact a precious find by John, in one of the walls, a traditional cruse for burning seal, fish or seabird oil ; the maker's rough thumb-marks were impressed on the ancient clay. We did not know there was any clay in the island until, digging down through the debris to find the true floor of St. Ronan's cell, I struck a pure seam. There was no sign of clay anywhere in the thin island soil, so presumably clay for pottery and flooring had been imported from some pocket of glacial boulder-clay in Lewis. I had hoped to find a stone-paved floor to the cell, to which I could have excavated without risk, but the clay put me off.

We tried the desert island method of communication by letter-in-bottle. The old-time natives of St. Kilda had used to send off letters in toy mailboats, which were more often picked up and delivered than not. We heated a nail in the Primus and burnt " Please Open " on a piece of wood. The letters went into an empty tin with a shilling and a note To The Finder. Then we tied the piece of wood and the tin on to an old fisherman's mark-float, found washed up, and flung the contraption from the northern cliff edge of Toa Rona. The seals were particularly interested in it as it carried away rapidly towards the north-east.

Ocean Mail.—On August 10, Mr. George Spence—appropriately enough a minion of the Postmaster-General—found a tin can, supported by a wooden surround, floating and stranding on the shore at Birsay. Within the can he found a foolscap envelope and a message, neatly hand-printed on a sheet taken from a school essay book. Also enclosed was a shilling, and a

three-halfpenny stamp. . . . What " John," the writer of the
message, has been doing on North Rona, or how he got there,
is a puzzle. It is possible that the sender of the message may
have been ashore from a yachting cruise.

The cutting was from *The Orcadian*, Orkney weekly newspaper ;
Birsay was 90 miles from Rona and the mailboat had taken a
fortnight for its voyage.

*   *   *

Fianuis was always alien territory. Coming over the ridge
and opening the broad sprawling rock below, nearly a separate
island, we looked down to another country where human
entry caused surprise and alarm. And when I chanced on an
old sea-eaten mooring-ring let into the rock down there, I
stared at it and it stared unmoving back. The seals did not
expect to wake up to see a sudden Man standing and watching
them. Fright, and bundling flight—one stood harmless but
powerless to allay it. Once safe in the swirling surf the inquisi-
tive heads watched openly, bright with interest, and the so-
controllable nostrils opened and shut.

The warm sensuality of seals basking unaware surpassed
even the voluptuousness of a domestic cat. It was an extrava-
gant wallow, luxurious abandon to the summer sun. As
observers we were merely occasional passing foreigners, without
time enough to attach ourselves and get to know separate
individuals. We saw them only at their borderland, sleeping
and basking, labouring in and out of the sea, apparently
enjoying the fearsome surf and apparently unsexed. The rest
of their lives were hidden in the sea and they would not be
hauling up for their autumnal season of calving and mating
for another month or two.

Sometimes the seals' silky hides were smeared with fresh
blood, presumably the damages of getting in and out of the
sea. One I came upon without its knowledge lay flat on its
back and presented to the sun a belly patched with scars and
raw places. I sat down and waited, a warm sunny place on

the sheltered side of Fianuis. In its doze the seal stretched out
its flippers as they might have been hands released from torturing cramp ; it spread its hind flippers like a fan and the
stump of a tail stood up until it quivered. I thought of a
labouring man interrupting a purgatory of hoeing, slowly
straightening his spine and jerking it into the opposite curve.
The supporting rock was knobbly but the seal breathed blissful
sighs, cushioned in blubber ; it half rolled over to scratch
with one hand. The feverish season of sea-fowl was the seals'
time of detachment from sex ; they had all the summer long
for peaceable idling and basking rest and more rest : very
Hebridean.

Seals' wails and groans—best heard after dark and alone
—wafted over the water ; the mammalian slugs lay parked
about the off-lying rocks. One day we counted up to eighty
on a skerry where they lay so thickly that there seemed to be
more seal than rock.

Glistening seaweed followed the measured sea-swirl round
slippery boulders. The white patches to seaward were parties
of auks, and gannets from Sula Sgeir were fishing the heaving
swell farther out. The seal woke and saw me, rolled over
and urged itself to the sea, fell in. I waited the long pause.
There broke the doggy whiskered head, looking back with
the usual bright-seeming interest. A person tied hand and
foot for some dreadful party game, laid on his stomach and
told to hurry, might look much like a seal making for the sea.

Another day I was sitting in the hide overlooking a boulder
that hid a young black guillemot. This was a day when one's
eye at the peep-hole shed tears from the wind. A clamour of
gulls and waders retreated with John as he went away, the black-
backs resumed their eminences, life returned to the non-human
norm. Ridiculous fuss and self-assertion the black-backs continually made, standing and aark-aarking stupidly with their
beaks pointed to the sky, or sticking their necks out as they
flew ! In every view they stood staring about with a detestable
supercilious-seeming gull stare ; no, not altogether unlike the
conventional glaze of English upper class. The large un-

beautiful young of the black-backs pestered after their parents, making querulous piping noises. Both young and adults picked at a seal's carcase, overlooked by another hide. There, for instance, an old bird came sidling up, pit-a-pat on large webbed feet, and began to nibble tentatively, blubber oil glistening on its beak. Soon it was jabbing its beak down like a pickaxe and pulling and tugging with its feet braced. It lost hold and fell over backwards—ha ha—readjusted itself and stood staring all round : who dared laugh ? I never felt any difficulty of anthropomorphism in recognising dignity, or rather loss of dignity, in birds such as black-backs.

My black guillemot, coming to its home boulder, waddled in quick bursts over the sea pink and swung a little red fish from its bill. Each time it was the same sort of fish, long and thin and nearly as red as the guillemot's own feet. It was stuffed in under the boulder without delay, in a crescendo of noise from the chick which subsided as the old bird whirred away—a brief view of whirring mirrored wings and retreating red webs splayed out astern. All that was to be heard of the chick was a laryngytic peeping and all to be seen an occasional rear view which presented itself at the entrance, muted vigorously, and withdrew into the darkness again.

Each pair of black guillemots nested discretely but they were not solitaries ; in twos and threes they shuffled on the rocks, dipping their heads and opening their beaks to each other, uttering a worried-sounding and doggy whine. When two faced up to each other, whining, the ceremony was like a marionettes' act. The stiffness of courtship looked as if of outside control, analogous to circus animals going through a set piece, without understanding, like the trained elephant which holds up a hand mirror in his trunk but looks at the back of it. The family resemblance between black and foolish guillemots was strikingly close ; it was odd to think of heredity bringing different habit and plumage to each, yet a set of mannerisms and movements peculiarly the same.

On the 3rd of August, a Monday, which elsewhere would have been Bank Holiday, a whole gale blew from the west.

" War, 'mid the ocean and the land ! " The west cliff of Rona presented an astonishing display, sea-fowl flying in what might have been a new medium for all the resemblance left to their normal whirring excursions. The gale struck full on the cliff and rushed up the rock wall in a vertical stream, buoyant like water. A clump of thrift thrown over the edge came soaring back. On the cliff top the wind beat at the grass with inorganic fury and the grass seemed that it must tear its roots out to escape, it was so flailed and so scurried with rapids.

The puffins were best; the air supported them as a fountain of water supports a ping-pong ball. They moved slowly past, correcting slips and wobbles, much in the way of a nearly overbalancing and very unconfident skater. When they came unchoosingly close, they were helpless ; one moved to within a literal foot of John's face but was powerless to get to a more comfortable distance until the wind should take it. The skater again was heading for a hole in the ice but for the life of him could not turn. The puffins themselves looked anyhow, breast feathers all over the place, spread tails cocked up ridiculously, feet no longer neatly tucked in but carried as if they were paddling in water. If they lifted their wings they dropped suddenly ; spread them and they rose vertically, whoosh, like a lift. Two capsized when they found themselves out of control and about to collide.

The razorbills, no longer chubby bodies with high revving stumpy wings, were now fierce predators poised on arched wings far above the sea (though a little uncertainly). Fulmars hung stationary or hurtled across the wind with an express-train rush of air past wings bent but held rigidly stiff. Even young kittiwakes fresh on the wing looked confident. The under-powered auks, for whom air was usually too thin, were the ones to profit from the new buoyancy.

*   *   *

The view from Toa Rona did not change, but our seeing eyes became residents', not strangers'. Now the whole bare sweep was dotted with significances, the places of birds and seals, plants and human relics ; the large scale of rock and sea's edge was familiarly detailed into all the little asides of topography. We had been long enough in the island to appreciate a move of season, and a shift of whole populations. Summer was on the wane. By the 8th of August many of the sea-birds had finished their landward days and had gone out into the ocean again, with their increase of offspring. By the 12th the black-backs' numbers were down to 70 adults. Only the whitewashed cliff shelves were left to show where guillemots had been, as carved and ink-splashed desks are left in a silent schoolroom.

Another use of Rona began to be revealed : a stepping-off place for south-bound birds migrating from Iceland and from lands within the Arctic Circle. A turtle dove of all creation— this was familiarity made strange enough—flew over the village. A rarity, a barred warbler, came flitting about the old walls. Parties of whimbrel and curlew landed and took off again. A teal, a sandpiper, were new records. A bunch of golden plover got up from the ridge, a Greenland wheatear arrived, peewits' cries came from the night sky. The first half of August showed only the pioneers of what would become a rush, though already on Fianuis flocks of white wagtails were 150 strong, southing from Iceland or Faeroe or Greenland. . . .

> *The tribes repair*
> *From every isle along the fields of air ;*
> *Of every varying wing, and every name,*
> *The wild, the fierce, the gentle, and the tame.*
> *All peaceful met on RONA'S lonely shore. . . .*

On Fianuis an inexplicable crossbill pecked at the seeding chickweed. Whatever was it doing out here in the Atlantic, tame enough to let us stand watching in the sea wind a couple of yards away ? It knew no incongruity, was perfectly orientated. The odd quality that birds conveyed when seen apparently out of context was altogether subjective. Crossbills carried with them a history of waves and seashores as well as of inland pine trees ; and what about the turtle dove, last heard crooning from umbrageous copsewood ?

So we continued, happy as the days were long, until one day, just on a month after landing, a ship was to be seen steaming towards the island.

VIII

The Visitors' Years

Our happy residence came near the end of Rona's first century of visitors' years. The surviving native, an old man called Donald M'Leod, had left the village in or about the year 1844, an indefinite far away date which yet set an end to one lingering history of Rona and began another. Since then, once in ten or twenty summers of the new history, some ship or other, a stranger, had nosed in towards the cliffs of Rona and had sent off a boat's crew to find a quiet place among the rocks. The curious gentlemen had come ashore.

Who were they all, what had brought them to Rona, how had they come and where landed, what had they seen and thought, coming over the ridge and opening the village ? Leach's petrel had drawn ourselves to Rona, but once there, and of affection, I wanted to learn everything else to do with the island. One could not live regardless in the manse, and we came at the tail of a splendid inquiring procession of Victorian, Edwardian, Georgian irregulars . . . ornithologists, archæologists, geologists, yachtsmen, a botanist, an ecclesiologist, officers of His Majesty's Commission on Ancient and Historical Monuments, officers of Her Majesty's Ordnance Survey, a duchess, even medical men and police for an island exhumation and post-mortem. I felt proud that we should be adding our own news to the island chronicle, something of Leach's petrel, of bird notes for the *Scottish Naturalist*, of new plants found since the day botanist Barrington was ashore in '86. We had come as young amateurs, nineteen and twenty-one (owing all to others' help), yet our term of residence was by far the longest since 1844, only excepting that of the two shepherds of Ness, both of whom had died in the island.

I must see what all the visitors had written, not only those of latter days but the others of the old history before them : Doctor Macculloch and the Minister of Barvas, Martin Martin, Sir Donald Monro and the rest, who had called to see the natives or had written down the curious reports they had heard of this oceanic extremity of the parish of Barvas, Lewis. Afterwards, it was fascinating to come to know the different personalities of different interests who were separated by years and had never met each other, who were yet all joined by the thread of Rona. Most of them had acquainted themselves with the findings of their own predecessors ; it was long after leaving Rona before I was content that I had.

(1) An Ecclesiological Note

About the year 1847 it seems that one Captain Burnaby, R.E., was conducting the original Ordnance Survey of Lewis. Before he finished he took his party to Rona and Sula Sgeir, perhaps in 1850 or 1851, and made the six-inch maps so invaluable to every visitor after him. " Benign Reader, hast thou seen, studied, and digested, this exquisitely-laboured and faithful performance of high Art—this Ordnance Survey ? " asked, for instance, the rhetorical Mr. T. S. Muir, ecclesiologist, who was soon to be Captain Burnaby's first successor at Rona.

The activities of Captain Burnaby's party must have caused a good deal of curiosity throughout Lewis. A piece of gossip was recorded by Mr. Muir in his favourite device of reconstructed conversation, in this case an interminable chat with his pilot, Iain Mackay, which took place in Stornoway in July, 1857, when they were just back from their own visit to Rona. Muir had noticed a hole in the roof of St. Ronan's cell. Mackay (born in Rona about 1800, left in 1810), now taking a glass with his gentleman, alleged that the sappers had made it :

" Maybe you don't believe it ; but some of the Ness men, who were over to clip the sheep, told me they saw them do it, because they wanted to know what sort of a place it was inside, but couldn't make up their minds to the trouble of going in by the door."

" That was a shameful thing for men of their sort to do," said Muir ; had Sir James heard of it ? (Sir James Matheson of Stornoway Castle had not ; he was the contemporary landlord of Rona and in about 1850 he had offered his island as a free gift to the Government for use as a penal colony ; the Government had declined.) If Sir James were told, said Muir, perhaps he would ask Mr. Murray the tenant " when next over, to build up the hole again : it's not very big.". . . In 1936 one entered St. Ronan's cell through the hole in the roof.

Captain Burnaby's own account of Rona was severely geographical, and all that he had to say of " five or six rude, flat-roofed, ruinous huts " was that one was said to have been a church. The six-inch map marked forty-five place names on Rona. The sappers must have taken someone with local knowledge on their surveying expedition, possibly even Donald M'Leod himself, lately King of Rona, of whom Captain Burnaby said :

> He resided there about six years ago, for about twelve months : he appears to have been weary of his solitude, and expresses a horror at the idea of being left there again. His residence on Rona, together with his rude, yet muscular figure, has procured him the above-mentioned title.

*   *   *

The small trading sloop *Ada* was in July 1857 discharging a cargo of fish-curing salt at Port of Ness. Mr. T. S. Muir was not far off, perhaps saying over to himself his apostrophe to Rona :

> O these endless little isles ! and of all these little isles, this Ronay ! Yet, much as hath been seen, not to see *thee*, lying clad with soft verdure, and in thine awful solitude, afar off in the lap of wild ocean,—not to see thee with the carnal eye, will be to have seen nothing !

Yet, three score miles—rocks—surge—uninhabited—uncouth landing-places : how to get to it, and upon it,—that is a question !

The answer was that he simply chartered the sloop *Ada*, landed easily at Rona and measured up chapel and cell during a quick run ashore to the village—

There, then !—the spot where Iain first drew breath,—his father's *troglodyte* habitation, which, forty-and-seven years ago, and whilst yet a child, he left to join the " world's unquiet waies,"—'tis desolation now !

He returned to Stornoway to hold for the benefit of his readers a protracted conversazione about it and about, with Iain Mackay, whose memory went back to childhood years in the village at the beginning of the century.

" You saw the houses we lived in ? " [asked Mackay].
" Yes [said Muir] ; and some with low stone-covered passages, partly sunk into the ground, leading crookedly into them : these passages were not in the least broken down—having been very strongly built,—but the houses themselves were roofless, and empty of everything ; only there was a quern, or the like, still lying about here and there."
" And the cross ? " inquired Iain.
" I saw three or four crosses, though only one that was whole—a rough weather-worn stumpy thing, standing some two or three feet high, in the middle of the burying-ground."
" With three holes bored through,—you saw it ? "

The three-holed cross had gone by 1936[1] and the others lay fallen in the graveyard, rough weather-worn stumpy things in their bed of silverweed. But the three-holed cross had been particular, a focus of old folklore. Iain Mackay tried to remember,

[1] It is now to be found in the church of Teampull Mholuidh, Ness, a restored Christian-archæological monument, the key of which used to be kept in the shop of the local General Merchant but somebody did a mischief in the church (*mercator qui dicit*) and the canon of the Episcopal Church in Stornoway now has it.

" There was something—if I could mind it—that the big folks used to talk of,—something about the holes. The night before the New-Year, they came to look through them, after they had put the candles on the altar."

They put a candle at either end of the teampull (St. Ronan's cell), Mackay explained,

" and then went outside to see the light coming through the door and the window over it : and after that we went to the cross ;—but I cannot well remember ;—it is a long time ago and I was taken away out of Rona before I could know or think very much more about it."

He did not know the wherefore : " it was the custom." Muir asked, Was there anything else about the teampull ? Mackay said that nothing was missing there except a wooden pin,

" a wooden pin, turned up like a hook, that Saint Ronan hung his hat upon, when he went in. Before I left the island, you could see it sticking out of the wall at the side of the door, after you were through it and on your legs again. I remember it quite well : we used to hang things upon it—we children, I mean, for the older folks did not go in so often, the door was such a hinder—any little thing we had with us—a wool-waif, or the like—we hung it upon the pin, to see if it would be still there when we came back next time. I looked for the stick, the other day, the very first thing I did after I crawled through, but could not see it—it was away."

Muir said he fancied that the teampull must be more tumble-down that it used to be. " Yes, on the outside it is," said Mackay, but inside—" just the same as ever it was." And there had been no particular change in the eighty-odd years since they saw it : the same unique little dungeon leading out from the remains of the larger later chapel ; the same inward leaning walls, dark and buried, and the hefty crossways roofing slabs on top. Only the fulmars were new. The tiny doorway from the chapel was no longer negotiable though it can have been little less silted up in Muir's time or even in Mackay's childhood when "the door was such a hinder." "To get through it," said Muir, "I had to draggle myself forward, lying full-length on the ground." . . . In our time there were still bits of lime mortar clinging to the beautifully bonded inside walls.

> "We laid turf also on the top of the chapel, [said Mackay], and put lime made from shells in among the stones, to keep them together ; for we thought a great deal of the teampull, and would not have liked it to fall down. . . . I mind we were often on the top of it putting on turfs ; for the wind was always blowing them off in the winter time, so that we had every now and then to be putting them on again."

Muir said he fancied Iain did not know of any other building like St. Ronan's?

> "I am sure, I don't ! [said Mackay]—nowhere !—the least like it, or so small : it is only three or four steps, when you are in it, from one end to the other ; and so narrow, you might, by standing in the middle, and holding out your arms, touch both walls at the same time with your fists, or the ends of your fingers—have you all that down ?"

Muir had ; and Scottish Ecclesiology, said his publishers, had been created and sustained by his researches. Certainly neither archæology nor ecclesiology can ever since have been adorned by such a one or the *Characteristics of Old Church Architecture, &c., in tne Mainland and Western Islands of Scotland* (1861) been so ambushed in prolixity and allusion. *Characteristics* was followed by "a series of booklets thrown off from time to time as occasion or inclination prompted," and finally by reprints and second thoughts collected in the much more sober *Ecclesiological Notes on Some of The Islands of Scotland* (1885).

A couple of hours on a July evening of 1857 did not exhaust Muir's interest in Rona. "I should like to try it anew," he told Mackay, "there is a craving to return" . . . and the piquancy of his second visit was that he attached himself to the Rona Annual, 1860.

Muir did not realise that he was watching a play ; he never thought to wonder whether the island festival would outlive, how many generations of shepherds and sheep ? Continuity through the perspective of time was the attraction, now, of that far away trip. Then as now went the same outing from Ness, July then and now for the island round-up and the shearing in the self-same sheep fank on the neck of Fianuis ! The " annual wool-gathering trip," as Muir called it, was more of an expedition then, under sail only ; the men hauled up the boats and had a night ashore. They—Muir and the faithful Iain Mackay, the tenant Murray and a Stornoway schoolmaster—landed from the yacht *Hawk* on Tuesday evening, July 10th, 1860, at the tunnel cave—a " very avernian-looking gap." The boats went round to Sceapull and were hauled up for the night by Caolas Loba Sgeir (where latterly Ainslie and Atkinson rashly swam).

> There was something wildly-picturesque and almost spectral in the aspect of this desert spot, after it had been lighted up with the glare of our midnight fire. But our stay in it was only of short duration ; and what we did the whiles may be guessed —a bit of farraginous supper—a hot drink—a pipe and talk— a swatch of sleep (bless the mark !)—and, now, for the sheep-shearing !

This seems to have been somewhat inefficient, as the sheep, " which had to be collected without the assistance of dogs, were every now and then breaking over the *crò,* so that the men were compelled to be constantly going off in pursuit of them all over the island." Muir spent his day in careless wanderings :

> Throughout its durance, the day was delightfully sunny and calm, and our strollings, now along the edges of the beetling precipices of the higher parts of the island, and anon down among the low bristling rocks forming its northern extremity, were about the most pleasurable I have ever experienced.

Unlikeliest of visitors !—who could have forecast so unexpected or admirable an eccentric to walk the island in a mid-Victorian summer day as this Mr. Muir, resurrected from his own well-bound, expansive volumes? There could never be another like him in all the rest of the visitors' years.

Muir's hot July day was ending; he went over to fetch his things from the Sceapull bivouac:

> This took us a little time to do, for the carrying of a load through the Sceapull rocks is a feat not to be so quickly performed; but finding Murray quite ready for the start on our arrival back, we all at once, and without more delay, went down to the *Geodha'a Stoth*, where Iain was encaved with his boat to lift us out to the *Hawk*, and there, with almost a tear in my eye, I bid a final adieu to Rona—Beloved!

(2) MELANCHOLY EVENTS

In the spacious days of the nineteenth century, naturalists' yachts began to turn to the north and west. The pioneering voyages ticked off the islands one by one; St. Kilda soon became practically a compulsory pilgrimage for an ornithologist while Rona survived yet undiscovered. Rona Annuals went on, and men of Ness made their intermittent sealing expeditions. Sailors from passing ships sometimes stole a few sheep. From five hundred to a thousand puffins were caught on the annual visits and salted down, like the gannets of Sula Sgeir. An island tradition ran out when Daniel Murray, the tenant of Muir's day, gave up twenty-three years later; the tenancy had been in his family for well over two centuries. Old ways continued with the new tenant, but in this same year came Rona's turn to fall at last to the first of the yachting naturalists: June 20th, 1883—Mr. John Swinburne, sailing yacht *Medina*.

Swinburne got ashore somewhere along the south coast soon after three in the morning, having visited Sula Sgeir the evening before. He had with him as pilot one Norman Macleod of Ness who, being pumped about the birds of Rona, had included one which " answered to the description of a petrel of some sort." So after landing they made straight for the village and began to heave out boulders and to scrape with their bare hands.

> Five minutes' steady digging, and the first petrel with its egg was brought to light. I examined it eagerly, and was delighted to find it was a specimen of Leach's, or the fork-tailed petrel. . . . Subsequently we dug out twenty-two more, with their eggs, all within an hour and a half, and could easily have obtained a great many others had we wished.
>
> This colony is, I therefore imagine, one of the principal breeding stations of this species in the Eastern Hemisphere, and certainly the largest in Great Britain, the only other one yet known being on one of the St. Kilda group. . . .

At midday, with the twenty-three fork-tails and a List of Birds Seen, Swinburne went back on board and " having seen all sail made, turned in, with the gratification of imagining that I had contributed my small mite in the way of ornithological discovery." And indeed he had ; his visit started a train of naturalists' voyages of which our own in 1936 was but a latest instalment.

> " As an Appendix to the valuable account given to this Society in December, 1883, by my friend Mr. John Swinburne,"

said Mr. J. A. Harvie-Brown to the Royal Physical Society of Edinburgh some two years later,

> " I beg to offer, *first*, a drawing of the islands of North Rona and Soulisgeir (or Sula Sgeir) as seen by myself and a friend —Mr. Hugh G. Barclay of Norwich—when approaching the former island from the S.E. by S. ; and I offer, in the second place, some slight account of our visit to Rona in June of the present year—1885. . . . I will at the same time give a short account of the melancholy event which occurred there last spring. . . ."

Here was the famous story of the two shepherds ; the civilised world afterwards reaching out even to North Rona, with a question in the House, an Inspector of Police, a suspicion of foul play and an island exhumation. Mr. Harvie-Brown told his learned audience that he was quoting his friend Mr. Carmichael, who had collected the facts.

" The names of the two men who went from Lewis to Roney[1] were Murdoch Mackay and Malcolm MacDonald, two good representatives of the Danish and Celtic types. Having objections to the appointment of a layman as preacher to the church at Ness, and being grieved at some feeling shown them in consequence of the action which they took along with a few others of the congregation, they were desirous of making some atonement for their opposition, and resolved to leave the place.

" Accordingly, on the morning of Monday, 20th May, 1884, they sailed for the island of North Roney, where they landed that night. Ostensibly their reason for going there was to take care of the sheep on the island, but in reality it was to atone for their action against the minister that they went into exile. Twice did boats go out to North Roney—in the following August and September—and the friends endeavoured to get the two men to return to their families and friends, but in vain. The men were then in good health, and apparently enjoyed their island home, and employed themselves in building sheep fanks, fishing, and killing seals." Mr. Carmichael here relates a curious instance of a sort of second sight or presentiment of evil regarding the men, which occurred in the person of an old woman called Flora MacDonald residing near Ness, but we need not relate that here, and only mention it in order to point out that, in consequence of her repeated urging upon the people of Ness, strong efforts were made by the relatives to reach Roney. " It was only, however, on the 22nd April, 1885, after two previous unsuccessful attempts, that they effected a landing. No one met them. At the door of the little half-underground house occupied by the two men the boatmen found the body of Malcolm MacDonald in a sitting position beside an improvised fireplace, as if he had fallen asleep. On the floor of the house, beside the fireplace, lay the body of Murdoch Mackay. His tartan plaid was placed neatly and carefully over and under him, showing that the deft hands and warm heart of Malcolm

[1] " Mr. A. Carmichael, than whom there are few more capable judges, holds that Roney is the correct way of spelling the word. . . ."

MacDonald had performed the last sad office to the body of his dead friend. The bodies were wrapped in canvas wrappings, and buried side by side in the primitive and beautifully situated burial-place adjoining.

" It was feared that the poor men might have met with foul play, and the matter having been brought up in Parliament, the Crown authorities ordered an investigation. Accordingly, the procurator-fiscal, Stornoway, and two medical men, proceeded to Roney in the fishing cutter ' Vigilant.' The bodies of the two men were exhumed, and a *post-mortem* examination made. There was no appearance of foul play ; it was ascertained that Murdoch Mackay died of acute inflammation of the right lung and left kidney, and that Malcolm MacDonald died from cold, exposure, and exhaustion. The opinion among the friends is that Malcolm MacDonald assiduously attended his friend day and night till he died, by which time he himself became so weak that he could not bury the body, and being unable to remain in the hut had sat down by the improvised fire and died. There was a small pot on the little fireplace at the door, indicating that Malcolm MacDonald meant to prepare for himself some food, which, however, he was never destined to eat. The medical examiners found nothing in his stomach but a few grains of meal and a little brown liquid—probably tea. An abundance of unconsumed food was found in the hut. On this occasion the son of Malcolm MacDonald took two coffins with him to Roney, and the two friends were re-interred again side by side as before. Mr. John Ross, jun., joint-fiscal, Stornoway, Dr. Roderick Ross, Barvas, and Dr. Finlay Mackenzie, Stornoway, Mr. Gordon, inspector of police, Captain Macdonald of the ' Vigilant,' together with some of the officers and several of the crew ; MacDonald, son of Malcolm MacDonald, and one or two other relatives of the deceased men, attended the re-interment, which all present felt to have been of a most touching nature.

" The men would seem to have spent their time in prayer and meditation, and in reading the Gaelic Scriptures, in which they were well versed. Neither of them could write, but they kept a record of their time—of the days, weeks, and the months —in a very ingenious manner. This was accomplished by means of a bar of red pine wood, evenly and accurately dressed, 2 feet long and $1\frac{1}{8}$ inch in the side. A notch is neatly cut in the corner of the bar for each day of the week, and then a deeper notch for Sunday, while for the end of the month a cut is made from side to side of the bar. The plan is simple, clever, and intelligible. The markings begin on Friday, the 21st June, 1884, and cease on Tuesday, the 17th February, 1885. Towards the end the notches are less neatly and accurately made, indicating very clearly that the deft fingers which fashioned the rest were becoming weak and powerless to cut into the hard pine wood. These notches are no less touching than instructive, and speak to the eye and to the heart and the imagination with a pathos all their own. Through a hole in the end of the calendar is a looped cord by which to suspend the stick. It is singular," concludes Mr. Carmichael, " if nothing more, that it was about the very time that Flora MacDonald began to see her " warnings " that the last notch of the stick records the cessation of the last life. These " warnings " became so all-absorbing to her that she walked fifteen miles to the friends of the exiled men about them ; " and Mr. Carmichael further relates that he himself interviewed a young man in Edinburgh —Donald Morrison—who was on his way home from Canada to see his people at Ness, and who related that : A fortnight before he had received a letter from Ness saying that the friends of the men in Rona were in a state of extreme anxiety concerning them in consequence of Flora MacDonald's statements ; and when the said Donald Morrison landed at Liverpool, he was greatly astonished at the corroboration of Flora MacDonald's fears, or the coincidence, if you will, between her statement and the friends of the men. . . .

The habit of sheep-stealing is still carried on by passing ships or fishermen. In the summer of this year—1885—both sheep and the oil barrels and the plenishings of the house belonging to the dead men, consisting of tea, sugar, butter, soap, a grinding-stone, etc., were stolen by some Grimsby fishermen, who have since been apprehended. These articles were all upon the island at the time of our visit in June, and there seemed to be considerable honourable feeling even amongst the proprietors against touching the dead men's effects. . . .

The episode of the two shepherds being closed, the island returned to normal. The black-backs no doubt had been harried and no doubt they soon regained their numbers and their position as predators in chief. The seals could safely leave their skerries and come ashore on to the main body of the land ; the manse was available again to fork-tails and stormies.

Later on the shepherds' friends came back and planted among the older, ruder slabs a memorial stone inscribed, in the unaccustomed English of the men of Ness :

SACRED TO THE MEMORY OF MALCOLM MᶜC DONALD NESS WHO DIED AT RONA FEB 18 1885 AGED 67 ALSO M Mᶜᶜ KAY WHO DIED AT RONA SAME TIME Blessed are the dead who die in the Lord

Men of the sheep-shearing party used to whitewash the stone at their annual visits thereafter.

There is no sanction for calling one particular pit " the manse," but it has come to be so known, and suitably, considering the motives which had caused the shepherds to colonise it : a faint suggestion of the *Mayflower*, and St. Ronan for precedent.

Harvie-Brown was twice at Rona. The first time was worrying and rushed, the two hours ashore spent in hasty digging for petrels. The chartered steam yacht *Eunice* was not up to the North Atlantic, " in fact, a river boat." In the two years before he could get back for a longer look a landing was made by the botanist, Mr. R. M. Barrington, a shadowy and unforthcoming visitor, who was yet the first camper in the village, from June 29 to July 1, 1886.

I was too early [he reported] ; but the flora is remarkable for its poverty : *Plantago maritima* absent, and *Ophioglossum vulgatum*, var. *ambiguum*, abundant. These are the two salient points. I noticed 35 species, to which a few might be added later on.

His list, " Plants observed on North Rona, July 1, 1886," remained first and last until we in our year started gathering the island vegetation into the manse and I sat long and often, laboriously identifying the pieces by means of Messrs. Bentham and Hooker. The *Ophioglossum*, adder's-tongue fern, remained abundant : little green tongues scattered deep in the mat of long wet grass, each inch-or-two plant a spike paired with a spearhead blade. Barrington's *Plantago maritima*, sea plantain, remained absent ; buckshorn plantain instead made patches of squishy gull-littered turf. The flora was a botanist's ; there

was no spectacle of wild flowers. Certainly thrift was sometimes a rosy drift, sea milkwort's tiny flowers had a faint shell-
like quality, some yellow-headed composites were bright, but
the most of it was a sour northern mat. I could not see the
soft sweet verdure with which some of these writers had clothed
the island.

When Harvie-Brown came back again it was in the pride
of his own ship, his sailing yacht *Shiantelle*. Fianuis was in the
peak of the season when he landed at Geodha Stoth, June '87.
Thrift " filled the air with delicious fragrance, faint but sweet,"
oystercatchers yelped and gulls cried, eider ducks squattered
off their nests.

> Huge caverns, göes, gloups, and rock-arches, stacks, and
> detached masses of rock, abound, and at once attract attention ;
> and the booming of unbroken Atlantic waves, and giant rollers
> lashing deep into their recesses, and filling often to the roof
> some of the great arches, proved a very fascinating scene to
> me. . . .

With Harvie-Brown were his friends Professor Heddle, geologist, and Mr. Norrie, an early cameraman. Next day they
landed again and Mr. Norrie was " successful in obtaining
several fine views." He set up his brass and mahogany at the
edge of the graveyard looking towards the chapel. . . . " Old
Chapel, N. Ronay : Breeding Haunt of the Fork-tailed Petrel."
The corpulent man in the photograph, dressed in some sort
of marine rig and lying on the graveyard grass, must be Harvie-
Brown himself—" already very much overgrown," as a friend
recollected him about that time. Another man stands beside
him with a satchel over his shoulder; the professor no doubt.
The old chapel has changed in the winding back of time, the
south wall is clearly standing and the doorway is intact. The
special cross with the three holes in it is just below the chapel.
It is a sunless day, close and still probably, the thrift heads
have shown no sign of movement during the exposure. Mr.
Norrie's lens does not cover quite sharply to the corners of his
plate though at the right-hand edge the hump of Toa Rona

and its cairn show clearly. The lazy-beds above the chapel are sharper now, nearer their days of cropping, and the graveyard herbage looks less rank. Mr. Norrie has stopped it growing for an instant ; the latent image is carried away from Rona in the yacht ; and fifty years later the old collotype plate in Harvie-Brown's *Vertebrate Fauna of the Outer Hebrides* (1889) preserves the same power of silent frozen time as a stereoscope. I could stare and stare at the print, looking back into the silent summer day long gone. . . ."Summer—summer ! The soundless footsteps on the grass ! "

Harvie-Brown tried to find a first fulmar's nest on Rona, a few birds were flying past one cliff face only :

> I crept on hands and knees to the edge, and craned over to get a better view of the face ; and my delight was great when I saw one Fulmar sitting, apparently on its nest. . . . Wishing to see if she were breeding, I threw down several small stones, and, not without some trouble, managed at last to dislodge her. My disappointment was as great as my previous delight, when I saw an empty nest. . . .

August, 1936 : 587 nestling fulmars counted on Rona. Rarity —how artificial ! Yet Harvie-Brown's excitement as he peered could only have been for a rarity, a fulmar petrel could only be seen as it really was when not yet dulled by familiarity or numbers, as literally outlandish as any mollymauk or mutton bird found by old seamen in another hemisphere.

This visit exhausted the nineteenth century naturalists' discovery and exploitation of Rona which, begun in '83, missed out the shepherds' year of '84, waxed in '85 and '86, and now ended as *Shiantelle* stood away on June the 19th, 1887.

(3) Steam Yachts Downwards

The thrift which had scented the air for Harvie-Brown was in bloom again for the twenty-third season since his day, this time for Her Grace the Duchess of Bedford,

but by no stretch of the imagination could I have detected its
fragrance amidst the all-pervading stench of the nesting-places
of hundreds of Fulmars, Great and Lesser Black-backed Gulls
and Herring Gulls, [said she].

Latterly the newspapers called her, unavoidably, " The
Flying Duchess." She held an " A " licence and still flew her
own light aircraft when over seventy years of age, until on a
spring day in 1937 she took off for a flight over the North Sea
and did not return. In the years before the Great War
she had been a steam-yachting naturalist, four times at Rona.
But the pioneering was over and done ; now it was only nature
notes in the *Annals of Scottish Natural History*, to report fulmars
established in the village and the (" horrible modern ") tombstone in the graveyard. In August 1910, on her third visit, she
landed at the Tunnel Cave :

> An easier landing was effected by rowing to the extreme end
> of the cave. From here there is a curious gap [an *avernian-
> looking* gap ?] sloping up from the sea to the grass-covered
> surface above. The opening being very narrow, daylight cannot
> be seen from below, and, bending almost double, one has to
> feel one's way in comparative darkness for the first few yards.
> It is moreover extremely slippery, but the actual landing is less
> risky in a swell than jumping on to wet sea-weed at the mouth
> of the cave.

When she was back again in 1914 there were fewer fulmars in
the village :

> I attribute this to the fact that two gentlemen had put up a
> shelter in one of the houses and spent a few days there about
> three weeks before my visit. Tame as the Fulmars are, as a rule,
> they probably resented this interference and the fumes of
> tobacco, which must have been very necessary to any one
> sharing a house with them. (I found the remains of a cigar !)

She saw a pair of whimbrel on the ridge " but had not time to
search for a nest " . . . and there was never another opportunity.

—1914, August 23rd—. . . destroyers *Rifleman* and *Comet*
collided in a fog, the latter being considerably damaged.

The *Sappho* was sent to search North Rona Island, a statement having been received indicating that it might possibly have been used by the enemy as a base for aircraft. She reported, after examination, that the island was, as expected, unsuitable for such a purpose.

The *Ajax* reported having burnt out a boiler and the Admiralty[1] . . .

Rona Annuals were interrupted. A shepherd who had lost a dog in the island found it still alive after the war and the sheep unharmed. It was running wild and was finally shot. This was just the sort of incident to make a local legend. In 1936 it was still well remembered ; in one telling the dog was stone blind and running with the sheep, " he wass dodging the men and in the end he wass clubbed to death."

One day in 1924 a different order of visitors came to look at the ruins, the first strangers since the war, the representatives of the Royal Commission on Ancient and Historical Monuments and Constructions of Scotland. The three-holed cross still stood in the graveyard, though, said the Commissioners, at large and mentioning no names,

> There is evidence that private parties landing from yachts have not scrupled to interfere with ancient monuments and even to remove such as were portable.

(The fork-tails would have agreed.) St. Ronan's cell, " conjectured to be an early, possibly Celtic, chapel," was put on the short list of " Ancient and Historical Monuments and Constructions which the Commissioners deem most worthy of preservation and in need of protection," but nothing happened. One day perhaps an embossed iron notice-board about H. M. Ministry of Works, for the sheep to read ?

Cheviots replaced Blackfaced sheep as the island breed, the tenancy changed again and went to Mr. Alec MacFarquhar, upstanding in a snapshot of the sunny Rona Annual of 1927, master of the party brought then by steam drifter *Pisces*, even as of the rain-soaked party from *Cailleach Oidhche* in 1936. The

---

[1] Admiral Viscount Jellicoe of Scapa, in *The Grand Fleet, 1914-1916*.

photographer of 1927 was John Wilson Dougal, Glasgow manufacturing chemist, amateur geologist and well-loved summer migrant to Lewis. The custom of whitewashing the shepherds' tombstone had been given up ; only the birds did that now. Of the graveyard Wilson Dougal wrote :

> For a little time we rested, with tender thoughts of those who lay at our feet. We were in the grace of a living glorious day, heard the swirling waters at the foot of the cliffs, and saw the circling birds overhead.

In 1930 Malcolm Stewart made his first visit to Rona, with D. M. Reid; he was back again next year with T. H. Harrisson ; his *Ronay* was published in 1933. We ourselves entered, seeking ways and means of reaching the island. So to Harrow and D. M. Reid, he of " Our Loneliest Isle " in the *Cornhill* ; to T. H. Harrisson and the " Resident and Migratory Birds of North Rona, the remotest Scottish island " in the *Ibis* ; to their rusting sardine tins found by ourselves in the manse.

IX

A Dull Calm Night

ON the fair morning of August the 11th John went off to Fianuis to occupy a hide by an arctic tern's two eggs, and I stayed behind to borrow a young petrel from its burrow to photograph it. A small ship three or four miles away might be a passing trawler, it might even be a drifter coming to fetch us. Provisions were getting short but the thought of going was dreadful, to have to uproot ourselves from habitual residence in the manse.

I finished with the young petrel and set up the camera in one of the house tunnels to take an interior photograph by flash powder ; lay half inside the entrance thus blocking it, lit the touch paper, seized the powder tray and held it at arm's length, shut my eyes. The faltering fizz-z-z-z went on and on—touch paper must be damp—dare I look—PFOUF !—the explosion left a choking cloud of smoke which poured out through the chinks of the walls. This process, in default of flash-bulbs, was naturally no use on petrels though indeed we had spent one entire night at it ; a night punctuated by these fearful explosions, so that at dawn the environs of the manse stank like the aftermath of a fireworks display and we were singed and limp. We had sat all night behind two cameras and a torch, all pointed at a petrel's burrow in the manse, with a lighted candle stump at hand for ready fire. When a petrel appeared, one prodded—in an extremity of aversion—a flaming paper spill into the heap of flash powder. After each explosion and with the gradual return of eyesight, we tried to reconstruct what had happened. None of the photographs was any use.

I withdrew backwards from the tunnel and retired to the manse for a rest. The ship had come nearer.

Suddenly her siren blared loud and long. She had turned

northwards, quite close now, and was steaming round the eastern hill. By the time I had breasted the ridge she lay stopped in the east bay, cautiously far offshore. I could read the fishing number on her funnel, BF 70, Banffshire, an east coast Scotsman again. I was in time to see John issue from the hide on the neck of Fianuis and wave his arms ; surprised, no doubt. When I joined him at Geodha Stoth we could see through glasses that we were being looked at through glasses. Puffins were like dust across the field of the lenses ; most had gone away to sea, but to-day there were hundreds flocking out from the huge flank of Toa Rona, raised by the alien echoes of the siren. There was an unhurried movement to the stern of the drifter, the small boat was prised from its resting place abaft the mizzen and urged to the gunwale ; it wavered in the balance, then flopped into the sea.

The boat rose and fell on the slight swell in the bay, approaching imperceptibly with insect-like oars. It got well within hailing distance but still nothing was said ; one even felt slightly shy. Then, " Wheer's yer landin' ? " The boat creaked her side against the rock of Geodha Stoth.

Had we enjoyed ourselves, the fishermen said, ashore in their rubber thigh-boots. Yes ; and I foolishly asked if they had come to take us off. Aye. They mentioned casually that there were a couple of letters on board, and a case. Too late ! Some of them went off to search Fianuis for any green glass net floats which might have washed up, while we were rowed out to the ship ; strange to look up to the bulk of Toa Rona from a floor of sea. The small boat came to the drifter's steel flank, *Alert*, her painted name. We scrambled on board, entering again a steamboat's own warm aura ; under the cliff she hissed quietly and lifted gently to the swell. Mr. Sutherland the skipper came down from the wheelhouse and handed us the two letters (always to be preserved for the precious address —" Isle of North Rona ").

Long-suffering Mr. MacIver in Stornoway ! " After a deal of persuasion I have prevailed upon the skipper of the steam drifter *Alert* to take you off Rona.". . . He knew all about the wretched box of bulbs, had arranged for it to come with the shepherds' chartered steam drifter, then this ship burst her boiler and a motor boat had been substituted without his knowledge. He now sent the flash-bulbs because we should almost certainly have to spend a night on board and might like to photograph the shooting and hauling of the nets. This seemed like a hint, but the position was delicate : the skipper was already doing a large favour (saving, it turned out, a trip by the Stornoway lifeboat) and had steamed far out of his way. Could we decently ask for more ? The skipper said he wanted to get back to the fishing grounds in the Minch by nine in the evening. I related to him the whole unhappy story of the flash-bulbs and ended by boldly asking, could we have just one night with the bulbs, while he should lie off ? He was very doubtful, anyway he would have to ask the boys first, and it depended on the fishing reports. A long, long wait while the sky clouded, and it began to rain. Below in the little cabin we hogged fresh bread and butter. The wireless gave out genteel music until, at last, the fishing reports : the voice saith that Stornoway's fishing had been poorly. Oh, what bad luck ! What might a night's fishing be worth to the crew ? Well, it might be nothing, a waste of coal, or it might be £500. Oh. Most of the boys were still dispersed, whistling at the seals or looking yet for glass floats. In the end procrastination won the night, for by the time a quorum of the boys had been gathered to discuss our offer it was too late to get back to the fishing grounds. I sat in the stern of the small boat with the box of flash-bulbs in my lap. Some of the boys would come off in the morning to give us a hand with the gear, half-past seven sharp.

The prospects for this unique night of flash-bulbs could hardly have been worse. It was still raining hard when we got back to the village. Under the rickcloth we put the apparatus ready, and began the hopeless job of packing in the mud and wet. Then the rain stopped, the sky lifted, and there fell a benign and perfect calm.

Whichever way one looked there seemed to be one of our

gaunt tripod derricks stark against the sky, each commanding a chosen burrow entrance. The fork-tails came in early.

In the circumstances there was only one way of operating : to catch a petrel, pop it into a burrow, and let off the flash as it came out. We plunged somewhat literally into the hectic business of catching petrels, crawling in and out of the tunnels, grabbing wildly, sweating, losing skin, soon covered with wet black earth and drenched from the sopping grass. A Dull Calm Night of Maximum Activity !

The trouble was that a petrel having been popped into a burrow was often quite content to stay there ; and if it did come out was far away by time one could see again after the blinding flash—off again to catch another. Another difficulty was that the lenses kept steaming over. The fumbling haste of working cameras in the dark, changing plates, losing petrels and catching petrels—not a moment's rest, everything earthy and wet, oneself practically panting—made the most remarkable night either of us had yet passed.

The calm held throughout and the sound was all of petrels, but for the faint intruding wakes of the seals. The most useful burrow was one with an extremely small entrance drilled through thrift turf ; on other nights we had sometimes noticed a bird stuck in this entrance, so that now a bird wriggling its way out gave more time, or even sat wedged and momentarily still while our lightning laid bare the night. One automatic gadget was set up by a burrow whose history was of nearly consistent visits, but the bird chose this particular night not to come at all.

At last the calling and flying began to die away. John unprofitably waved his landing net in the fading night, pouncing and grabbing could yield me no more catches in the tunnels. Dishevelled, wet, dirty, and quite exhausted, we stood out in the graveyard to see the last birds flitting over the chapel or making out to sea. When the last bird had gone it was half-past four : played out.

We made some hot drink and packed the Primus and ate recklessly of the short provisions. The wet rickcloth still glistened palely in the light of the storm lantern. We sat and looked at the litter of gear and rubbish scattered on the mud floor of the manse. We threw spent flash-bulbs at the walls, where they exploded with a final plop. Whatever images they might or might not have illuminated, both flash-bulbs and petrels were now a closed episode. In fact, most of the negatives turned out to have been spoilt by misted lenses, and when those had been thrown out, and those others showing a streak of petrel across the plate, or no petrel at all, there remained three or four indifferent records of the extraordinary night, genuine enough, but as we well knew, not sufficiently spontaneous for any sense of trophy.

The new day opened slowly under a high pale sky, cool in the dew-drench, a heavenly August morning ; it would be a scorcher later on ! I stood out to see and feel it when I should have had my nose to the packing. The air touched fresh but there was no movement of breeze. There was a glow where the sun was coming up and a grey sheen glittering on the horizon ; hazy out to sea and flatly calm. Time must stand still, just for a minute or two ! The sea, the village, the deep wet grass—I knew it for a morning to be looked back on.

In three hours we had everything stuffed into boxes and bags, roped up and stacked. The manse looked impersonal and inhospitable without the rickcloth ; so that was how it had strangely looked a month ago ? On the first journey to the ridge we thankfully met three of the drifter's crew. The drifter lay below, perfectly still and black against the early light, with her reflection black beneath her. With the sun came torturing hordes of midges which rose from the sparkling acres of wet grass. Gradually we removed the pile of gear from village to ridge, sweating and cursing at the midges.

One of the men said he'd rather be in jail than live in that place, and they all remarked on the petrel smell. They had seen a lot of flashes in the sky during the night.

Now we had to take a last look at the village, the un-changing ruins and the fulmars circling stiff-winged on their early morning flights ; our own marks were only the churned mud of the manse, the tent's scar, and the trodden path between them. We trudged away with the last load and left the village lying quiet and deserted, redolent of petrel, thin singing with midges.

Residents in the village should not use the east bay landing ! No. It was a sweltering grind down and up the north face of the ridge, bad enough with the month-reduced loads travelling downwards. At last we brought up the rear of the caravan on its final dripping journey and sat down puffing by the pile of goods at Geodha Stoth. The small boat was having a nice row round the cliffs. The drifter's siren blared out for it, the ever-curious seals dived in a swirl, the cliffs sent forth clouds of puffins. The boat came, was loaded and pushed off ; unloaded and by brute force manhandled inboard.

This time it was a steel deck that pulsed to the propeller's slow thrust. The land soon lost all colour to a hazy grey, lost height and became a low mound. Then it was a single little hump that grew blurred and elusive in the heat haze.

The drifter stopped, clumsily backed and started to get alongside a single glass float. Bad engine usage, said the engineman, full-ahead, stop, full-astern. She steamed at half-ahead on the telegraph, meaning three-quarters to the engineman. At full speed she burns half as much again, he said. Quite so ; we were paying for the coal. The steam drifters would soon be making their ways down to Yarmouth and Lowestoft for the East Anglian season. After that some of the fishermen would finish the winter in deep-sea trawlers. One man said he always chose the labour exchange first. Some others would fish the sea lochs until the spring when the Scottish herring season came in again. If the Rona grounds were ever fished it was in the month of May, but it was too far away for anything but a big steam drifter. Like most of the Scottish boats, *Alert*—or in common usage *Alairt*—was share-owned, except that engineman, cook and fireman were on a weekly wage. The ship's owners took a third of the profits, the owners of the nets and the share-fishermen themselves each got another third.

Half a day's steaming to reach the Butt, steady throb, deep oily swell lifting and falling, August haze. Then down the starboard side drew the slow procession : the Butt, on the bow, abeam, on the quarter ; Cellar Head, on the bow, abeam, on the quarter ; Tolsta Head, Tiumpan Head. The view about Tiumpan, " Chump'n," gave deep into Lewis, piece-patched with crofters' modest claims. The sun was late and yellow by the time we rounded Chicken Rock and Holm Island and drove in down the length of the quiet harbour.

There were green trees, proper trees, above the water at the end of the harbour. There was the waterfront hotel, the fish-market ! We might never have been away.

North Rona Island, July 16–August 12, 1936

X

The Shiant Isles

THE *Alert* had shot her nets in the Minch and had got nothing ; had come on northwards to ourselves in Rona, and missed that night's fishing. As soon as she had put us down in Stornoway she turned round, and next morning came back with one half basket of herring. Meanwhile the two boys, having scrubbed and soaked in hot water, slept for fourteen hours in soft clean sheets.

In the hotel bar Mr. Sutherland the skipper told us more of a dark bird he'd already mentioned, which flew like one o' they St. Kildy gulls. Never saw them anywhere but offshore between Castlebay and Barra Head, he said, and he had been up and down the coasts of Scotland time and again, man and boy, etc. Now these birds were evidently shearwaters, the fourth and last of British petrel-kind, and Castlebay was down at the other end of the Hebrides, Barra Head was the opposite pole to Butt of Lewis, 130-odd miles between them. A shear-water hunt might make a good finale to our Hebridean season, we thought, but not just yet, because the same evening more islands cropped up, the Shiant Isles.

The Shiants were the dark cliffs as seen from the *Lochness* a few weeks before, of no significance to ourselves then, coming first and innocently across the Minch. Now Kennie MacIver was going off with his brother Duncan in their *Sulaire* for a week-end. They would put us down on the Shiants if we liked and pick us off after a few days. There was an old house there, the islands were uninhabited and full of birds. Yes indeed.

(1) EILEANAN SEUNTA, THE ENCHANTED ISLES

The Minch was having a rare mood of fog ; the sea dark

and glassy ; steamers' sirens sounding somewhere beyond the blank wall. *Sulaire* kept close in down the Lewis coast, patchily seen ; found the light Gob na Milaid and the headland Srianach beyond, northern horn of Loch Shell. Thence by dead reckoning, thicker than ever, across the Sound of Shiant, answering steamers with her own lugubrious hand-pumped noise machine. The sea looked darker ahead, lighter astern ; there was a dark loom in the fog : dead slow : stop. We were up against some cliff or other. Sea-birds were bustling all round, looking double-sized in the fog. We started again, cruised to and fro, then lost the land altogether. The engine was stilled . . . unaccustomed quiet . . . we listened for the land. A faint sound came, sea breaking against a shore, and there—a faint baa-ing of sheep, muffled clamour of sea-fowl. The engine coughed out its watery exhaust again. Nearer to and the sea-birds were louder. Kittiwakes' cries meant sheer bare cliff—one listened upwards towards them—an imagined wall rising from the stilly pond. And caves probably, those dim characteristic kittiwake clefts, dripping wet, overhung, and footed in dark water where the swell would pulse in like a tidal bore. Puffins flew in loaded with fish. A dark outline of cliff loomed up again ; *Sulaire* was anchored there and then.

The Shiant Isles, not counting various outliers, are three, two of them joined together by a narrow strip of shingle. These two, Garbh Eilean and Eilean an Tigh, lie roughly north and south as a two-mile-long barrier. The third, Eilean Mhuire, stands off to the east of them so that the distance between makes a broad open bay.

At dusk the fog lifted enough to show the way into the Bay of Shiant. As we steamed in, the oily dark sea was lit with the watery sparks of phosphorescence, the foam so bright that it threw a glow on to the ship's side. Ahead, the shingle strip showed as a black line whose either end went up into black cliffs, on the one hand Garbh Eilean, on the other Eilean an Tigh. " Temporary anchorage can be obtained during summer, if necessary only," said the *West Coast Pilot*.

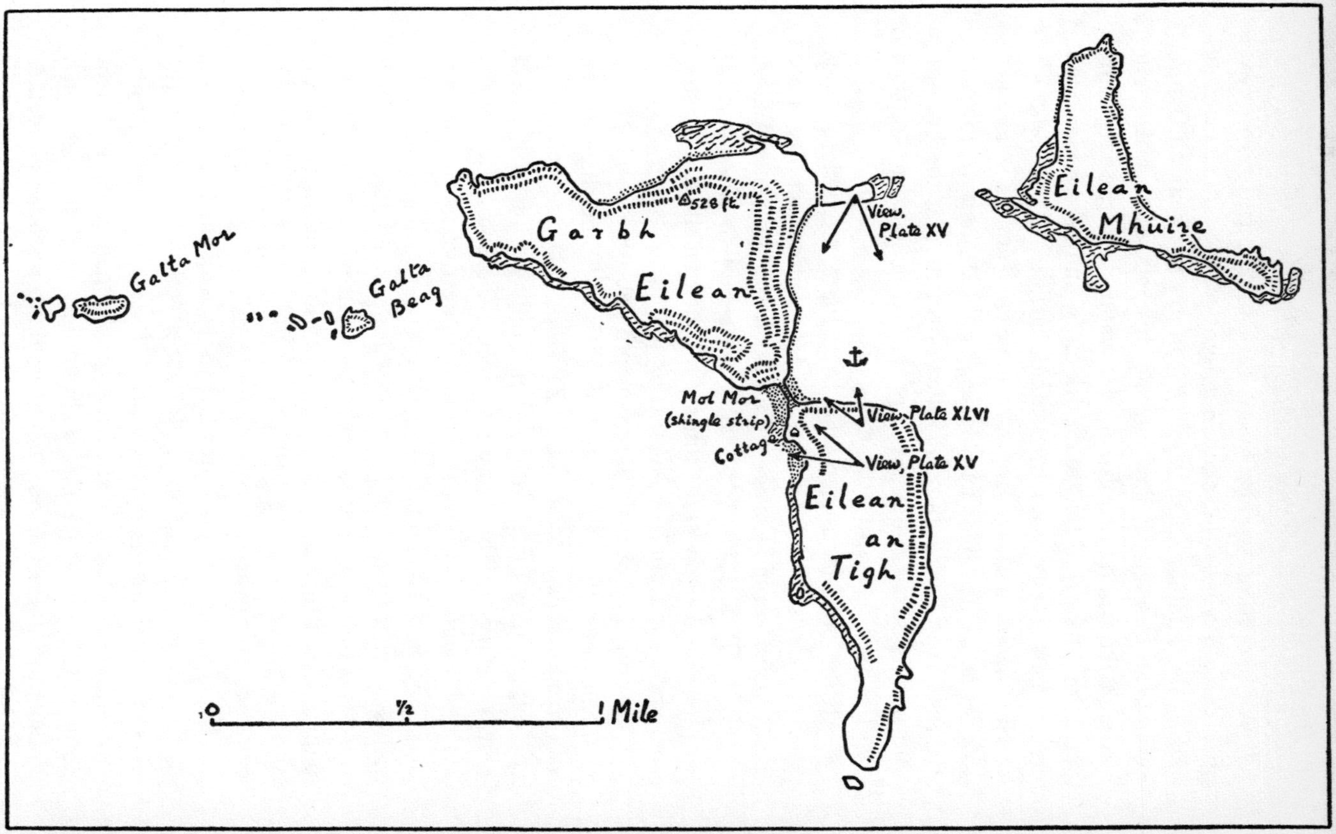

Eilean Mhuire

View, Plate XV

Garbh Eilean

528 ft.

Mol Mor
(shingle strip)

Cottage

View, Plate XLVI

View, Plate XV

Eilean
an
Tigh

Galta Mor

Galta Beag

0   ½   1 Mile

Fig. 4. *Sketch map of Shiant Isles.*

We had come to the Shiants as if blindfolded, so in next morning's daylight the first clear sight was an impact : new lands all round, a high strange country ! Great cliffs rose pillared to tops lost in slow-moving mist, sun-glare was bright through the ceiling of mist. Quiet waters below, a large surround of lofty green hills and dark cliffs, and here under one's feet, *Sulaire* still lying off the shingle strip ! All this east side of Garbh Eilean was a length of majestic columns, whose feet rose from a scree of fallen blocks, tumbled anyhow down to the sea. A gentle lapping of water down here at the bottom, late puffins buzzing in and out of the old lichened stone, then five hundred feet up to the misty edge.

All the old island-goers had been there, from the famous Martin Martin to indefatigable Dr. Macculloch, to Lord Teignmouth on his Voyage round Scotland and James Wilson on his, to T. S. Muir and J. A. Harvie-Brown. For ourselves with our bits of goods, the dinghy touched on the shingle strip on Sunday the 16th of August, 1936.

We crunched over the large smooth pebbles and stepped up into Eilean an Tigh, the Island of the House, and there, round a corner of rocks, stood the House—an old stone box with a corrugated iron roof. This was not only the one-time shepherd's cottage but also a past residence of Compton Mackenzie. He had bought the islands, had had a new roof put on the cottage, and had lived there for a summer. We shoved open the rain-swollen door upon a thick reek of damp and disuse. There were two rooms, one empty, the other strewn with old newspapers and furnished with a very old table, one or two chairs and an infested-looking bed. Wet ashes in the fireplace, rat evidence everywhere.

Except that the house was not yet ruined, the Shiants were in the common condition of almost any of the smallest of the Western Isles. The *Ruins*, the *Landing Place, Well, Pile, Graveyard* and the rest dotted over the six-inch map were sufficient pointers to a long-gone island community of crofter-fishermen sufficient unto themselves. Yet the Shiants were not altogether abandoned ; they were still a reservoir of grazing and fishing ;

Shiant mutton was a local speciality and lobstermen still came over from Skye. Besides, there were even the odd visitors.

To us just back from the dourness of Rona, the Shiants seemed the kindliest of kingdoms. Eilean an Tigh had all the amenities. However you looked down on to the house, the little green coastal flat seemed made for it. Beyond the house a tiny stream delivered on to a shore well provided with driftwood. A seashore was novel after Rona. The stream issued from a small snipe bog where willow saplings grew—proper ligneous tissue, unheard-of on Rona. Reeds from the bog had been used to thatch two satellite bothies squatted beside the house. Here for a first time was an island, remote but convenient, which had all the desirable features to be imagined for a small island—house and stream, driftwood, inland detail, a sheltered bay (more or less), beach as well as cliffs. Eilean an Tigh sloped up from a low rocky shore along the western side to the crest of a range of the characteristic columnar cliffs along the east ; in between was a knobbly acreage of rough grazing, a strong-coloured country of heather and ruddy sedge. The cliffs were inaccessible, the departments of kittiwake and fulmar often only to be heard and not seen from above. Garbh Eilean was the naturalist's island. Eilean Mhuire, across the bay, remained unattainable.

After scoured and salt-bitten Rona, perhaps we could not help finding a hothouse quality about anything growing over a foot high. We felt ourselves set down in the midst of a natural sanctuary, blossoming with flora and busy with small perching birds as well as flat-footed sea-fowl. There was no clue to the fiendish gales which must howl about the isles every wintertime, but then it never has seemed reasonable to me that the west coast of Scotland, so rugged and peat-ridden, should also be in character with a dripping proliferation of vegetation as rank and strong as on a sewage farm. The ideals of the vegetable kingdom must be far from those of warm-blooded creation ; what passes for mildness to a herb is to sentient beings raw and searching seaside chill. What a climatic ideal to put before any furred or feathered or clothed creature, loving hot sun overhead and dry ground underfoot, and only to be braced by a day of sunny frost !

Even at the edge of Scottish autumn the Shiant soil burgeoned with flowers. Earlier in the summer when day was hardly divided from day the place must surely have been Eileanan Seunta, The Enchanted Isles. There were roots of primroses and violets and kingcups, bushes of wild roses, the willow withies. Meadow sweet grew in the bog and forget-me-not by the stream ; there was water-mint enough to make the lovely river reek. The highlands of Garbh were deep in heather and one or two sheltered hollows up there were a yellow blaze of gorse from ancient twisted stems, very ligneous. Weedy composites spread their sunny discs, pink and white campion trailed down the cliffs, where perched creaky great clumps of roseroot. Starry stonecrop and rockrose and milkwort blue or pink, were summer bright ; yarrow and sneezewort, mauve-blue scabious with its wine-coloured stamens, pink lousewort with its blown-up calyx, calamint and yellow rattle, buttercups and daisies. The wiry knapweeds topped with dark knobs—hardheads—had yet to break out into bright purple autumnal tufts. The clovers red and white grew best on the faint square which must once have been potato patch. Little field gentians grew among the west-facing crags above the house, where the soil was warm in afternoon sun.

The Sunday morning mist vanished in a day of sunny breeze, and laid open a fill of ocean and land. At sunset we sat with a map and tried to name the great hills of the horizon, of Lewis and Harris, Skye and Mainland. In the north-east was our own outriding Eilean Mhuire, and beyond, the ocean-seeming Minch, unencumbered by any more land.

You could live a summer here ! Cut peat and stack it to dry, dig up the potato patch again and grow some lettuces. The boat would be light enough to pull up on the shingle strip, and on all the little cliff-foot bits of beach where her keel would grate. You would fish, and go over to Eilean Mhuire and find the popish chapel, and on a glassy day, nose under the vasty cliffs and rub against their feet. You would lie timelessly in the heather and watch the basking seals and the peregrines bickering with the hoodie crows. When it rained you would sit indoors and wait timelessly for it to clear up.

There would be, however—there was—one unpleasantness. The rats of Eilean an Tigh were large, bold and wily, and in possession of the house.

We set up in the house, using its two chairs, table and fireplace, but the infested-looking bed was not inviting, so we pitched the tent down on the fresh seaside sward. John snored away ; I lay awake to the sound of the sea, and to him ; bright moonlight outside. Something was tickling at the back of my head ; what else but an oversized rat. The beastly thing went tittupping over the turf back to the house, trailing its obscene tail.

After that we took war into the enemy's camp. We set about decontaminating the wooden bed, carefully removed the heap of ancient clothing, and one by one the old sacks. This started no rats, only their hard little leavings, which tinkled like hail on to the floor. We left some dry rushes on the boards of the bed for body insulation, pulled the bed well away from the wall and next night went to bed with torch, sticks and a loaded .410 shotgun. The rats began to move as soon as the fire flickered down, while outside highland-and-island type rain beat against the window. The rats were scuffling behind the matchboarding and in the other room, then, tittup-a-tittup-a-tittup one would go scampering across the top side of the matchboard ceiling. This went on all night and every night. Once I woke up and saw by torchlight a large rat sitting on our clothes on the back of a chair at the foot of the bed. I had just drawn a bead on him, holding the torch along the gun barrel and aiming above my feet, and was just about to rouse John with a considerable explosion against his ear, when the rat disappeared. It was the only chance offered. Again and again in the evenings we crept ineffectually round the house and bothies ; we never even got a shot. I stood at sunset in the doorway—a rat somehow scampered up the vertical jamb beside me. We found a rusty old break-back trap and

set it ; the bait disappeared. The rats no doubt had experience
of similar encounters with shepherds and lobstermen, with
Compton Mackenzie himself perhaps.

These Shiant rats then, they were free of enemies ?—for the
human challenge was unfortunately a flop. One afternoon I
was mushrooming on the green peninsula sticking out from
the north-east corner of Garbh. This hump of ground had
been one of the cultivated areas and was still strongly marked
by furrows and ridges, the turf very rich and green. As I
started home carrying the crop of horse mushrooms (the large,
the medium, and the button) I saw lying in the sun on its
back, a kitten. The offspring of a cat. I gaped at it, and it fled
beneath a pile of stones, the fallen walls of some sort of bothy.
The place was perfectly littered with the remains of young
puffins. There were anyway two kittens in among the stones.
I said " puss puss " to them but they were wild as hawks, and
spat and crackled, so I gave up the immediate idea of taking
one home. They looked in perfect condition, with bright blue
eyes and piebald coats.

I remembered now : we'd been told that Compton
Mackenzie had put down a pack of seven cats some years
before, in hopes of clearing the rats. One of these cats was
remembered—for its size perhaps or ratting prowess, I don't
know—anyway it had had some publicity at the time. This
animal had been a great piebald tom. His line was carried on !
The beast himself might even still be extant. No reason now
why Shiant cats should not flourish indefinitely ; and the
rats too.

A plague of rats in a Harris township was reported by
Martin Martin. The natives could not extirpate them.

A considerable number of *Cats* was employed for this end, but
were still worsted, and became perfectly faint, because over-
power'd by the *Rats*, who were twenty to one ; at length one
of the Natives of more sagacity than his Neighbours, found an
expedient to renew his *Cats* Strength and Courage, which was
by giving it warm Milk after every Encounter with the *Rats*,
and the like being given to all the other *Cats* after every Battle,

succeeded so well, that they left not one *Rat* alive, notwith-standing the great number of them in the Place.

The Shiant cats, like ourselves, had been worsted ; or perhaps, failing warm milk, they had not even tried. Summers were soft living for them, as the puffin remains showed, but the long winters must have been lean. The living then would be beachcombing—dead fish, oiled sea-fowl, any sort of fleshy debris, braxy mutton, shellfish even ? And rats ?

The rats will also be beachcombing. How are they to live, vis-à-vis the cats ? Is there some uneasy understanding of neutrality, always smouldering ? Or will the stress of winter sometimes stage dreadful pitched Battles ? A nightmare bluff of Unnatural Selection. . . . ?

Soon the rats never go abroad but in packs : their members, continually weeded by cannibalism, grow horribly fitter and fitter—their rodent tusks ever longer and yellower, their tails more obscenely squamous, their hides scarred, their size horrifying. The cats meanwhile, the greater cats, " They prowl the aromatic hill, And mate as fiercely as they kill," they too get fitter and fitter. They are few and solitary, gaunt and shaggy, with blazing eyes ; nearly always now their lips are curled in a soundless snarl. Sometimes one of them snatches a rat which wasn't fit enough, sometimes one finds itself cornered by the rodent pack, swarmed over, torn alive. They have become the last British wild beast, *Felis catus mackenzii*. They have long since pulled down the last sheep. A man dare not land at the Shiant Islands.

(2) Garbh Eilean and Eilean an Tigh

In the Shiants, both beetling cliff and abounding flora had their source in basalt. The islands, " an eruptive cluster," said Professor Heddle, ended a " line of orifices of volcanic outflow ", of which Giant's Causeway and Staffa were other examples. Few things were rougher than an Elisabethan collar, he said, and that was what the circumference of Garbh Eilean (The Rough Island) most resembled. The northern cliff face, for instance, was not broken, nor flat, nor stepped into ledges ; it was, in dark magnificent simplicity, a row of basaltic columns. At best the columns protruded in half-diameter and sheered up to heights far beyond the scale of a humanly made pillar ; fluted columns rearing up to the blue sky ; " Nature herself, it seem'd, would raise A minster to her Maker's praise ! "—as Sir Walter Scott noted of the similar columnar show at Staffa.

Many visitors had been to appraise the spectacle, and it was surprising that the Shiants remained so little known. If the columns lacked the regularity of Staffa, said Dr. Macculloch,

> they exceed them in simplicity, in grandeur, in depth of shadow, and in that repose which is essential to the great style in land-scape.

The pillars of Fingal's Cave were eighteen feet high, the cliff face of Garbh, five hundred.

The two-mile cliff circuit was negotiable in only two places, one of them leading straight up from the shingle strip ; an ascent, said Martin,

> somewhat resembling a Stair, but a great deal more high and steep, notwithstanding which the Cows pass and repass by it safely, tho' one would think it unsafe for a Man to climb.

Once up there, one was in the elevated plain where the gorse bushes grew and where small inland birds, skylarks and pipits, twites and stonechats, flitted and sang. Where, said Muir,

> you ramble and skip about like an antic, full of your deliverance from the qualms of the late seafaring and tricksy cliff-work.

On Muir's day in 1859 the islands had been empty. Lord Teignmouth in the eighteen-twenties had watched, of all improbabilities, haymaking, but the crop was taken away by wherry and the summering shepherds too ; " no consideration could induce them to remain longer." In 1815 the shepherd's family had been fully residential, but Dr. Macculloch had been disgusted by their apathy and filth ; a century and more since the self-sufficient crofters of Martin's time, when Eilean Mhuire " hath a Chappel in it dedicated to the Virgin *Mary*," the islands were " fruitful in Corn and Grass," and the cows were " much fatter than any I saw in the Island of *Lewis*."

But habitation of the Shiants had had a temporary renaissance since Muir's 1859 report of : " uninhabited." The present cottage had been built, or rebuilt from ruins, and in '79 Harvie-Brown and party were entertained by the shepherd's family of mother, two daughters, deaf and dumb son, and a little girl. This unnamed family dwindled to an old man and his daughter, perhaps the little girl of 1879 grown up. Their end was a typical island story, which we heard afterwards in Lewis, and which dated back to about the turn of the century. They lived in the house, "just the two of them"; the daughter used to row herself seven or eight miles across the overfalls of the Sound, to visit her betrothed ; when the old man died it had been ten days before she had been able to get in touch with Lewis. These two had been the last inhabitants.

The waning of human habitation had kept pace with the waning of the islands' grandest and immemorial ornament : a pair of sea eagles. As the mark of the Shiants for passers-by was always the cliff spectacle, so for visiting ornithologists it was the sea eagles. Generation after generation of eagles occupied the same eyrie in the north face of Garbh ; generations of men had recorded them from a first account in 1703 to a last in 1903.

Before my own eyes, as I walked over Garbh, there rose a very large brown bird which flapped slowly up and away with heavy, full wing-beats, and diminished to a speck in the direction of Harris. Excitement, of course, was colossal. John was pecking about on some boulder beach far below and never saw the bird. It was probably an immature golden eagle.

Eagle has always had in traditional antithesis, wren ; so

the wrens of Shiant, having been spared description as a unique island sub-species, span freely about the boulders at the feet of these huge cliffs where eagles once flew. One half-expected the great overshadowing scale of their surround to silence them, as a cathedral is silencing, but their briskness and the absurd cock of their tail stumps seemed to out-perk even the homely wrens of the south. The first time of hearing their song took me unawares—spontaneous burst of spring song— as I tried to place it I found a sudden out-of-season feeling of April sunshine and green-sprayed hedges—then to Hebridean boulders and a tiny vibrating wren.

Wrens and puffins shared the half-mile of boulder scree, footing the east cliffs of Garbh. There was the sense of sea-fowl coming in from limitless ocean, little wrens pioneering sea-wards from the hinterland, and meeting here at the edge in a sea-washed tumble of basalt. Even now in the third week of August, puffins still buzzed to and fro, loudly, because the cliff face behind conserved and threw back the whirring noise of wings ; and wrens' spring song was the odd punctuation.

*　　　*　　　*

We had our four days, Sunday morning to Wednesday evening. That was well enough : we scrambled up and down the islands, and in the evenings sat very cosily before the drift-wood fire and listened to wind and rain beating on the window, retired to the rat-proofed bed and listened to the rats. But unfortunately we ran out of food. Of course it had been too easy, we had thrown together a few provisions saying airily, and most inaccurately, Oh, that'll last a week. On Wednesday evening, having eaten the last of the food, we packed up and carried our goods down to the shingle strip, and waited to be fetched. No ship came in sight, so at dusk we rejoined the rats. No ship came in sight on Thursday either. Hungry Thursday evening we employed in poker-work ; John engraved on an old ram's horn, " Shiants, 1936," and filled the room with a stench of burning horn. We thought probably we were being

given an extra day to make up for one bad one which we'd
spent indoors, fitting together the rat-bitten pages of some
ancient magazines, while outside half a gale slashed rain
against the window ; at high water, seas had been washing
right over the shingle strip and streaming down into the bay.

The food resources of the islands were scanty indeed : no
rabbits ; sheep reserved for a state of desperation ; no noticeably edible vegetation. Man, as Edmund Sandars has noted,
" cannot digest grass, even cooked." The first meal under the
new régime was boiled nettle tops, elderly and rather blighted,
and leathery horse mushrooms, found previously and then
passed over. And the first supper we'd had in the house had
been young mushrooms done in butter and milk, a fragment
of snipe from the bog, scrambled eggs, coffee, and bread and
cheese.

We found an ancient fish-hook and gut, and rigged a line
from bits of string with a bolt for sinker ; the gut broke at the
first cast. We found a discarded lobster pot, mended it, baited
it with an old piece of seagull found lying about, and placed
it in the sea at low water ; it drew no lobsters. We explored
the shore, rejecting little green crabs and limpets but collecting
a saucepanful of small black shellfish, which we called winkles.
These, boiled and cooled, one ate with a safety-pin until one
began to feel sick. The muscular part was gristly, the guts
green, soft, and revoltingly sweet. They were a kind of small
whelk, we found out afterwards, not poisonous. After two
days of this somewhat palæolithic diet, a step outside the door,
and there, all smiles, Kennie MacIver.

What he did not reveal for a long time, and which really
was rather funny when it did come out, was the real reason
why we hadn't been fetched before : he'd clean forgotten.

Shiant Islands, August 16–21, 1936

XI

A Shearwater Hunt

WE roused the motor car from its long rest in a fish-curing
shed and made tourism of Lewis. We rode it up to the
northern district of Ness, where the worldly connections of
Rona had always been centred. Houses stood scattered alongside the gritty potholed road without enclosure or path or
visible means of support, a populous string of townships—
South Dell and North Dell, Cross, Swanibost, Habost, Lionel,
a turning down to Port of Ness. Knockaird, Five Penny Ness
and Europie led on to the Butt. We called on old Mrs.
Macleod, Ness correspondent of the *Stornoway Gazette*, whose
column had recently reported the Rona Annual, and on Mr.
MacFarquhar the tenant, whom we had suitably first met on
the island. We made a round of tourists' features, black house
and tweed loom, summer shieling and experimental peat farm,
the standing stones of Callanish ("the Stonehenge of Scotland").
The artefact stones of Rona were warm with human solidarity,
compared with that grove of dolmen at Callanish, stamped
and staring with a sinister, alien intelligence.

Time and season were running out. If we still expected to
find shearwaters we had better get on with it. We removed
to Castlebay at the other end of the Hebrides.

The tail-end islands beyond Castlebay had not harboured
shearwaters for years, we were told ; Canna was the place,
and a fisherman there called Mr. MacIsaac would be our man.
We removed to Canna, Inner Hebrides.

As the steamer crossed the Sea of the Hebrides towards the
Parish of the Small Isles—Canna, Rum, Eigg and Muck—
indisputable shearwaters crossed her bows : fined-down,
piebald fulmars, flying and gliding, as seen by the skipper of
the steam drifter *Alert*. In darkness and rain the steamer

approached a small wooden pier lit by two or three storm lanterns. We got off—no one else—and a flock of sheep was urged to get in. The mailboat slid away; various men went off swinging their lanterns. We remained with our heap of luggage in the wet darkness. The road or track from the pier was a pale strip of rutted mud leading faintly into the unknown. We pitched the tent on a sodden patch of long grass.

The dawn which eventually came was of Saturday the 5th of September, a somewhat unlikely season in which to go birds-nesting, though still within the shoreward season of petrels. We dressed in wet clothes and went in search of the fisherman, Mr. MacIsaac.

A minister of the Small Isles had once remarked that their roads were

almoſt in a ſtate of nature

and nowadays the one and only road of Canna—which no car had yet traversed—was three miles long and led from the pier, along the south coast, to an outlying farm called Tarbert. We walked past the nuclei of Canna life, a church, a hut-shop, one or two cottages, the shack-type post office, the laird's house. Canna had such a prosperous air ! The houses were neat and freshly whitewashed, the inhabitants—some fifty souls—looked so healthy and well turned out.

Cheerful, rubicund Mr. MacIsaac knew all about shearwaters. Once when he had been ferreting, he related, and listening at a rabbit hole, a shearwater had come up and nipped his ear. On Sunday afternoon he walked us along the road to show us the best place. We passed the terminal farm called Tarbert, where a boy said that the birds—" sheerwaters "—were still as noisy as ever, and went on until we came to a tumbledown stone and turf bank on the cliff edge.

This bank was the very place where Mr. MacIsaac had had his ear tweaked nine years before.

The bank was riddled with burrows which did not look quite like rabbits' works. We began to dig with a penknife but got nowhere. Rain began again, in a freshening wind ;

137

we went home, deciding to come back after dark, with a spade.

When we started out again a full gale was blowing at our backs and the sky was pelting with rain. The farm was showing a beacon of one lighted window which led us so far, but after that we stumbled about almost anywhere. It was pitch-black and sheeting, the turf stood in wind-whipped pools of black water. We fell over, stepped into bogs and streams, found ourselves suddenly at a cliff edge—but it was a short inland drop. By pure luck we walked into the shearwater bank. Obviously there was no sign of shearwaters, no bird could have landed. You could not look out to sea, the rain hurt too much. The place screamed with wind. Struggling back we found a pale streak across the hill, a landmark wall. It turned out to be a waterfall over the cliff edge, only the gale was blowing the whole lot back again. The pale volume of water went twenty feet up into the dark, and fifty yards inland you could feel above the rain the heavier lumps of stream water coming down. We stumbled inland among crags which did not seem to have been there before and suddenly found ourselves right on top of the farm, whose light was out. We walked into a flock of geese and then into—" oh, its only a horse." We found the gate to the road and were congratulating ourselves until it turned into a completely other, strange gate. When we did find the right one it was in the wrong place, but after that it was a straight trudge up and downhill along the road, straight into the gale. I remember trying all ways to carry the useless spade, its blade so caught the wind. At midnight, exhausted and as wet as if we had been swimming, we found haven in a wooden annexe to the house of Mr. MacIsaac.

Beginning again next morning in dried clothes but still carrying the spade, we returned to the bank. We dug and dug, and burrows branched deeper and deeper into labyrinths. The inside of the bank was dry as dust and the tail end of the gale blew earth into our eyes and ears and mouths. The nearest we got to shearwaters were some dead remains and a dirty old egg.

A Shearwater Hunt

We left Canna in a flood of yellow evening sunshine ; it had been a fine day ! Long drag across to the Outer Isles, long drag up the length of them, another return to Stornoway. Now our season was over and it was sad to have to take our turn on the plump shuttle 'twixt Islands and Mainland, to leave the Hebrides where you could go how, when and where you pleased, lie in bed all day if you wanted to or walk about all night. Visitors' freedom was perhaps only the freedom of any non-breadwinning stranger in any slightly foreign and unenclosed country, but it didn't seem so. The inhabitants evidently lived notably circumscribed lives within the narrow permissions of Calvinism, though an exception was always to be made for the careless freedoms of Stornoway. By now the nightly event of the town, departure of mailboat, was altogether familiar, the singing and waving and bagpipes and evidence of whisky, the good-sized steamer sliding out astern and taking away the lights, the crowd on the dark quay straggling home to bed.

As a very large shiny American car was swung on board one heard a chance remark . . ." belongs to the two boys who were on Rona." Indeed ! An unsteady man addressed a wailing Gaelic dirge at two girls who looked embarrassed. Cheerio Chrissy, ta-ta girls, all the best, Murdo !

The novel woods beside the Mallaig road were already autumnal, fungal and damp. The car suffered without disaster the fifty-mile switchback of potholed scree between Mallaig and Fort William, but it was progressively falling into the genre of the comic crock. It shed nuts and bolts freely on its way ; a larger piece called tie-bar fell off at the back and trailed in the road ; I accidentally trod on a floor-board and went through.

Again the crawl across the floor of Glencoe and again all the difficult towns of the north. By time the car was home and put to rest in a field it had done nearly two thousand miles, which wasn't bad for a three pounds' worth.

Canna Island, September 5–7, 1936

XII

Rough Island-story

ON North Rona—to hark back to the island and ourselves
standing in the silverweed of the village—it was just
incredible to look about and to know that the place had once
had its own natives. Not some unwilling shepherd over for a
few months, but a happy permanent colony of not-so-remote
men, women and children, who were born and lived their whole
lives there. Almost as incredible to know that farm crops,
soft-haulmed potatoes and thin-stemmed barley, had grown
instead of this mat of wind-and-salt-scrubbed foggage. We
ourselves nonchalantly made free of some old tunnels and pits
in the ground. One of these pits had been a most holy place,
and the rest of them houses for living in, for meals, for childbirth and death, and days and nights of winter storms. Under
the wet rank grass, under our own gumboots, the remains of
these natives still lay. It was a feat of imagination to try to
resurrect them and set them digging, harvesting, cooking and
worshipping. What even should they be, under-sized Erse-
chattering troglodytes, or slow big-boned seaside yokels of the
Norse blood, blue-staring beneath an unkempt thatch of straw-
coloured hair? Or ordinary people from Lewis?

Some of the lives had been documented. As I traced it
back, two texts seemed apt to the story of the bare back of
rock sticking up from the northern ocean. The traveller in
Scotland, said Dr. Johnson in 1785,

> now and then finds heaps of loose stones and turf in a cavity
> between the rocks, where a being, born with all those powers
> which education expands, and all those sensations which culture
> refines, is condemned to shelter itself from the wind and the
> rain. . . .

And in the Hebrides, Benjamin Crémieux added in 1934,

> all that man, isolated by mist, wind and cold at the edge of
> the ocean, has been able to invent to reassure himself and to
> calm his fears—magic, legends, superstitions—all are to be
> found here.

For a textbook the only possibility seemed to be the Old
Testament. Despite dissimilar climate there was the same
overwhelming surround of inanimate nature, fearfully seen, the
same precarious livelihood and the same recurring sheep—
shepherd motif.

(1) A Hundred Years of Decline

By 1815 the population of Rona as visited by Dr. John
Macculloch had dwindled to a single family of six, whose
matriarch had been forty years in the island. As for the
visitor himself, the forthright and fluent geologist, " the Stone
Doctor," enough to say that he was the chief island investigator
of his time and that he voyaged persistently among the Western
Isles between 1811 and 1821, " forming a universal guide to
that country." It was he for whom " years had passed in
vain attempts " to reach Rona, and when he did succeed his
revenue cutter had some trouble even to find the islands ;
" the map-makers had forgotten them, and the manufacturers
of longitudes and latitudes had tabulated them, each according
to his own fancy or belief."

> The first objects we saw as we reached the surface of the
> cliff, were a man and a boy, who, with a dog, were busily
> employed in collecting and driving away a small flock of sheep.
> No houses were visible ; but, a little farther off, we perceived
> two women, each loaded with a large bundle, who seemed to
> have arisen out of the ground, and were running with all speed
> towards the northern side of the island. It was plain that they
> had taken us for pirates or Americans. . . .

A hail in Gaelic made the shepherd and boy bring to, " but it was some time before the females came from their retreat, very unlike in look to the inhabitants of a civilised world."

The barley, oats and potatoes of the six or seven acres under cultivation had already been harvested, the winter's fuel store of turf was cut and stacked. The shepherd, Kenneth MacCagie, was a servant or cottar employed by a tacksman in Ness who in turn held the island (and did very well out of it) from the Lewis landlord. MacCagie was allowed as much as he wanted of island-grown food ; the surplus and the wool of the flock of fifty sheep were taken away by the tacksman's boat twice a year. MacCagie had also to find eight stone of sea-fowl's feathers annually ; his wage was two pounds a year, paid in clothes, and " as there were six individuals to clothe, it is easy to apprehend that they did not abound in covering." There was not much danger of his trading on his own account as,

> excepting one or two visits from the boats of the *Fortunée*, while employed in cruising after the *President* in 1812,[1] we understood that he had, for seven years, seen no human beings but ourselves and the people of his employer. . . .
>
> We might have expected that the use of money would almost have been forgotten here . . . but Kenneth MacCagie was fully as aware of the value of his commodities as if he had been an inhabitant of Stornoway itself. . . .
>
> We were amused with one trait of improvidence, quite characteristic of a Highlander. The oil of the coal fish [2] served for light, and a " kindling turf " preserved the fire during the night ; but had that fire been extinguished, " but once put out that light," no provision was at hand for rekindling it, nor could it be restored till the Lewis boat should return. . . . MacCagie only shrugged his shoulders at the suggestion of a flint and steel ; he had lived seven years without one.

The MacCagie household consisted of wife, infant, two boys

---

[1] Hove to off Rona and sounded in 60 fathoms. Sent a boat ashore for information. (Summary from the log of the *Fortunée*, in Public Record Office, London.)

[2] . . . " cuddy-oil candles they were—just what we had in the island. . . ." (Iain Mackay to T. S. Muir, in 1857.)

and an aged and deaf mother. The women's clothing was

something in the shape of a blanket . . . but scarcely sufficient
for the most indispensable purposes. . . . The wife and mother
looked as wretched and melancholy as Highland wives and
mothers generally do ; but MacCagie himself seemed a good
humoured careless fellow, little concerned about to-morrow,
and fully occupied in hunting his sheep about the island. . . .

During the long discussions whence all this knowledge was
procured, I had not observed that our conference was held on
the top of the house ; roof it could not be called. The whole
spot seemed to consist of an accumulation of turf stacks ; and,
on the lowest of these, we thought ourselves stationed. It was
the house itself. . . . We could not perceive the entrance till
it was pointed out. This was an irregular hole, about four feet
high, surrounded by turf ; and, on entering it, with some
precaution, we found a long tortuous passage, somewhat
resembling the gallery of a mine, but without a door, which
conducted us into the penetralia of this cavern.

Inside sat the ancient grandmother, nursing the infant by the
embers of a turf fire.

From the rafters hung festoons of dried fish ; but scarcely an
article of furniture was to be seen, and there was no light but
that which came through the smoke-hole. There was a sort
of platform, or dais, on which the fire was raised, where the old
woman and her charge sat ; and one or two niches, excavated
laterally in the ground, and laid with ashes, seemed to be the
only bed places. Why these were not furnished with straw, I
know not ; and, of blankets, the provision was as scanty as that
of the clothes. Possibly, ashes may make a better and softer bed
than straw ; but it is far more likely that Kenneth MacCagie
and his family could not be fashed to make themselves more
comfortable. . . . Every thing appeared wretched enough ; a
climate where winter never dies ; a smoky subterranean cavern ;
rain and storm ; a deaf octagenarian grandmother ; the wife
and children half naked ; and, to add to all this, solitude, and
a prison from which there was no escape. Yet they were well
fed, seemed contented, and little concerned what the rest of
the world was doing. . . . The women and children, indeed,
had probably never extended their notions of a world much

beyond the precincts of North Rona, and the chief seemed to have few cares or wishes that did not centre in it.

" This was a variety of human life worth studying," said Macculloch, " but the difficulty of carrying on complicated investigations through the means of interpreters, is sufficient at all times to excuse greater omissions than you will find in the history of this State." MacCagie did not seem to have made up his mind whether or no he would renew his engagement, of which seven years out of eight had passed.

All that we could discover, was a desire to go to Lewis to christen his infant. In another year, his wish will have been gratified. I shall never know the event ; for assuredly, in leaving North Rona, I have left it for ever ; but I shall be much surprised if some future visitor does not find Kenneth, twenty years hence, wearing out his old age in the subterranean retreat of his better days.

Final decline on Rona had started long before 1800 ; " once five families residing upon it," said the *Statistical Account* of 1797, " but now only one." Although Macculloch saw social life in Rona at its lowest ebb, he had to admit that the MacCagies seemed contented and well fed. And of a time only ten or fifteen years before this, the boyhood memories of Muir's Iain Mackay were all of island-pride and content :

Muir : " You Eilean Rona folks, Iain, must have had a heap of odd old stories to tell one another, as you gathered round the fire in the long winter nights ; for then, I fancy, you had little else to do."

Mackay : " Nor in the days, neither, often ; for sometimes the days and the nights were so alike, you could scarce tell which was which. But in the summer-time it was a bonny place—so green ; and you would not see such barley and potatoes as we had, anywhere. There was only a few of us altogether, big and little, and it would be lonely, often : but we were content, and had no strife—if we had, things didn't go right, and if bad words were spoken when we sowed, the seed never came to anything, or it grew black and withered.

I could tell you a great deal about that and other things, if
I could but now think of them." . . .

Habitation of a sort had hung on until 1844, yet all these
years later we ourselves—back from the Shiants and inquiring
into the Lewis connections of Rona—heard of a very old man
of Ness, a Mr. Macdonald, who was said to be son of a shepherd
of Rona and to have been born in the island. The name was
wrong, but if the King of Rona, Donald M'Leod, had had his
woman with him in 1844 she could have borne him a child
who would now be 92 years of age. Alive in Ness? In 1936
the person to ask about such things was Mrs. Macleod, Ness
correspondent of the *Stornoway Gazette*.

Mrs. Macleod was full of local gossip and memories, as
befitted a journalist ; she seemed quite pleased that the two
boys who had been on Rona should have come to see her in
search of news. She had written a little birthday verse of
thankfulness in her column in last week's *Gazette*. But
wouldn't she recite it? said John politely. *Eighty-eight To-day*
it was titled. . . .

> *I am aged but not old, for His promises unfold*
> *The joys that await me, more precious than gold,*
> *And though griefs and perplexities have furrowed my brow,*
> *If ever I loved Thee—my Jesus—'tis now.*

"Oh, how charming," said John. We were soon deeply
bogged in the histories of innumerable, indistinguishable
Macdonalds and Macleods and others of old time, but the
Mr. Norman Macdonald, the allegedly Rona-born, turned
out to be a fraud.

An aged Mr. Murdo Macleod was fetched from a croft
nearby and came forward to testify. He spoke (in translation)
of the eviction from their crofts at Gress near Stornoway of his
own grandfather and of a Macdonald. This Macdonald and
the grandfather Macleod had both gone to Rona : evicted,
looking for unoccupied land, where else to go? Grandfather
Macleod was said to have done a stretch of thirty years in the

island and then to have left ; Macdonald had stayed on, either importing a wife or having had one with him from the start. She had borne him three sons and a daughter. " And never a cup of tea," said Mrs. Macleod. They brewed ale from island-grown barley and made ewes' milk cheese ; they had no means of relighting the fire if it should ever have gone out. Cod smacks used to fish about there and the sailors would come off and buy cheeses. Once a crew landed and poured a bucket of water on the fire and then showed the bewildered Macdonald how to relight it with flint and steel. This was all quite nicely in keeping with Dr. Macculloch, but neither his MacCagies nor the earlier Mackays, who had an assistant called Angus Gunn, were recalled. The youngest of the Macdonalds' sons was the Mr. Norman Macdonald still alive in the Ness township of Cross.

We found the house. A very old man opened the door. He had little English and none at all as soon as he realised that we wished to photograph him ; such an idea was remotely out of the question and he gave off such a string of " Och-no-och-no-och-no " that it almost ran to a trill, like the voice of the razorbill on Handa. We came back with the enlisted help of old Mrs. Macleod's daughter, Miss Daisy, who dealt volubly in Gaelic with Mrs. Macdonald, but Mr. Macdonald had retreated to a safe back room and would not appear. His fraudulence now came out : his two brothers and his sister had indeed been born in Rona but not himself. And they, Miss Daisy Macleod whispered, had all passed over (but surely it would have been more surprising, even unnatural, if they had not ?). The reason why Mr. Macdonald would not be photographed was that his " people " would never forgive him if he were to be pictured in old clothes. Very well, would he make an appointment and dress up ? Two o'clock the next afternoon was fixed by Miss Daisy Macleod.

We came chugging out the thirty-odd miles from Stornoway again. After an interval and some curtain-rustling, the door was opened a couple of inches and a quantity of white beard was visible. The naughty old man had not dressed. More och-no, the beard withdrew and the door shut; Mr. Macdonald jnr. remained unphotographed.

This time we found old Mrs. Macleod sitting quietly by the peat fire with another Mr. Macleod, whose great-grandfather had unavoidably lived in Rona. He had no connection with that other Macleod whose grandfather had been evicted from Gress. (Always in the Hebrides one had to be saying over to oneself, No Connection with any other Firm of the Same Name.) Had either of these Macleods anything to do with the 1844 one, Donald the King? Who knows? Never mind, the great-grandfather of the present Macleod had been a Bard. His first composition had been oddly inspired by an accusation against himself of sheep-stealing. Mrs. Macleod spoke out clearly, reciting one of the incomprehensible verses. We had heard her mention what sounded like " cayley "; in sudden alarm we identified this with the " ceilidh " of the *Official Guide to Stornoway* :

> At the ceilidh the old superstitions are recalled by the stories that are told of the " daoine-sith " (peace-folk, or fairies), the " gruagach " (the long-haired one) [etc., etc.] . . . The evil eye figures prominently . . . unlucky to meet a woman when on their way to their fishing boats—a red-haired spinster especially so . . . to hear a cock crowing before four in the morning . . . gloomy forebodings. . . .

We found ourselves in the midst of a ceilidh? It wasn't so alarming; indeed, a cup of tea, a peat fire, some Gaelic gossip, and there you were. Mrs. Macleod translated her verse into these unremarkable words :

> " Is it not a shame that a man who speaks both English and Gaelic be accused of stealing the sheep that were drowned in the cave ? "

It was odd that gossip of Rona seemed to have ends but no middle. It dealt in family memories or in the most distant and misty mythology; the generations of proper inhabitants through several centuries seemed to have left little news. Thus

Mrs. Macleod was full of St. Ronan and his doings at one end of history—traditional stuff continually kept up to date and retold with topical allusions, like a pantomime—and at the near end of time she chatted about Rona Annuals, the death of the famous two shepherds, and so on. And Alec Mac-Farquhar the tenant jumped equally freely from St. Ronan to, for instance, a puppy found in a black-backed gull's crop, to the increase of seals since the men of Ness had given up sealing expeditions to Rona, and to his perennial complaint about the damage that he claimed the seals' oily bodies did to his island pasture. Trying to trace records of Rona was certainly easier in the visitors' books than in the field of Ness.·

An undated incident belonging to the years of declining habitation was told to naturalist John Swinburne by his pilot. A crew from Ness lost their boat when landing at Sula Sgeir. They lived on sea-fowl for several weeks until a passing vessel transferred them to Rona. Months afterwards a revenue cutter found them eating the last of the shepherd's potatoes. Swinburne's pilot had himself once been a shepherd in Rona ; his name was Norman Macleod. It seemed that at times in the early nineteenth century there could barely have been standing room upon the island, so great a congestion of grandfathers and great-grandfathers ; and the sheep must have been hopelessly outnumbered by all the Macleods and Macdonalds, Mackays, MacCagies and Gunns who vied to be shepherds.

(2) THE ANCIENT RACE

Martin Martin's *Description of the Western Islands of Scotland* made something of a stir when first published in 1703—our own Hebrides, yet remote as the South Sea Islands. An odd result the book had was to inspire one John Ogilvie, D.D., to write a long moral fable : " *Rona A Poem, in seven books.* . . . London : 1777." " The Author was amused with the account which Mr. MARTIN gives of the simple inhabitants of this little isle," he explained ; but a stuffed owl often perched upon the resulting verses.

Martin himself never visited Rona. He got the news chiefly from Mr. Daniel Morison, the minister of Barvas, who did.

Upon my Landing (says he) the Natives receiv'd me very affectionately ; and address'd me with their usual Salutation to a Stranger, *God save you, Pilgrim, you are heartily welcome here ; for we have had repeated Apparitions of your Person among us,* after the manner of the second Sight, *And we heartily congratulate your Arrival in this our remote Country.* One of the Natives would needs express his high esteem for my Person, by making a turn round about me Sun-ways, and at the same time Blessing me, and wishing me all happiness ; but I bid him let alone that piece of Homage, telling him I was sensible of his good meaning towards me : but this poor Man was not a little disappointed, as were also his Neighbours ; for they doubted not but this ancient Ceremony would have been very acceptable to me ; and one of them told me, That this was a thing due to my Character from them, as to their Chief and Patron, and they could not, nor would not fail to perform it. They conducted me to the Little Village, where they dwell, and in the way thither there were three Inclosures ; and as I entered each of these, the Inhabitants severally saluted me, taking me by the Hand, and saying, *Traveller, you are welcome here.* They went along with me to the House that they had assign'd for my Lodging ; where there was a bundle of Straw laid on the Floor, for a Seat to sit upon ; After a little time was spent in general Discourse, the Inhabitants retir'd to their respective dwelling Houses ; and in this interval, they kill'd each Man a Sheep, being in all Five, answerable to the number of their Families. The Skins of the Sheep were entire, and fleas'd off so, from the Neck to the Tail, that they were in form like a Sack : These Skins being fleas'd off after this manner, were by the Inhabitants instantly fill'd with Barley-meal ; and this they gave me by way of a Present, one of their number acted as Speaker for the rest, saying, *Traveller we are very sensible of the Favour you have done us in coming so far with a Design to instruct us in our way to Happiness, and at the same time to venture your self on the great Ocean : Pray, be pleas'd to accept of this small Present, which we humbly offer as an expression of our sincere Love to you.* This I accepted tho' in a very coarse dress, but it was given with such an Air of Hospitality and Good-will, as deserv'd Thanks : they presented my Man also with some pecks of Meal, as being likewise a Traveller ; the Boats-Crew having been in *Rona* before, were not reckon'd Strangers, and therefore there was no Present given them, but their daily Maintenance.

THERE is a Chappel here dedicated to St. Ronan, fenc'd with a Stone Wall round it ; and they take care to keep it neat and clean, and sweep it every day. There is an Altar in it on which there lies a big Plank of Wood about ten foot in length, every foot has a hole in it, and in every hole a Stone, to which the Natives ascribe several Virtues ; one of them is singular, as they say, for promoting speedy delivery to a Woman in Travel.

THEY repeat the Lord's Prayer, Creed and Ten Commandments in the Chappel every Sunday Morning. They have Cows, Sheep, Barley and Oats, and live a harmless Life, being perfectly ignorant of most of those Vices that abound in the World : They know nothing of Money or Gold, having no occasion for either : They neither sell nor buy, but only barter for such little things as they want : they covet no Wealth, being fully content and satisfy'd with Food and Raiment ; tho' at the same time they are very precise in the matter of Property among themselves ; for none of them will by any means allow his Neighbour to fish within his Property ; and every one must exactly observe not to make any incroachment on his Neighbour. They have an agreeable and hospitable Temper for all Strangers : they concern not themselves about the rest of Mankind, except the inhabitants in the North part of *Lewis*. They take their Sirname from the colour of the Sky, Rain-bow, and Clouds. There are only five Families in this small Island, and every Tennant hath his Dwelling-house, a Barn, a House where their best Effects are preserv'd, a House for their Cattle, and a Porch on each side of the Door to keep off the Rain or Snow. Their Houses are built with Stone, and thatched with Straw, which is kept down with Ropes of the same, pois'd with Stones. They wear the same Habit with those in *Lewis*, and speak only Irish. When any of them comes to the *Lewis*, which is seldom, they are astonished to see so many People. They much admire Grey-hounds, and love to have them in their company. They are mightily pleas'd at the sight of Horses, and one of them observing a Horse to neigh, ask'd if that Horse laugh'd at him : a Boy from *Rona* perceiving a Colt run towards him, was so much frighted at it that he jump'd into a Bush of Nettles, where his whole Skin became full of Blisters.

ANOTHER of the Natives of *Rona*, having had the opportunity of travelling as far as *Coul*, in the Shire of *Ross*, which is the Seat of Sr. *Alexander Mac-kenzie*, every thing he saw there was surprizing to him, and when he heard the noise of those who walk'd in the Rooms above him, he presently fell to the Ground, thinking thereby to save his Life, for he suppos'd that the House was coming down over his head. When Mr. *Morison* the Minister was in *Rona*, two of the Natives Courted a Maid with intention to marry her, and being married to one of them afterwards, the other was not a little disappointed because there was no other match for him in this Island. The Wind blowing fair, Mr. *Morison* sailed directly for *Lewis*, but after 3 hours sailing was forced back to *Rona* by a contrary Wind, and at his Landing the poor Man that had lost his Sweet-heart was over-joy'd, and expressed himselfe in these words : I bless God and *Ronan* that you are return'd again, for I hope you will now make me happy, and give me a right to enjoy the Woman every other Year by turns, that so we both may have Issue by her ; Mr. *Morison* could not refrain from smiling at this unexpected request, chid the poor Man for his unreasonable demand, and desir'd him to have patience for a Year longer, and he would send him a Wife from *Lewis* ; but this did not ease the poor Man who was tormented with the thoughts of dying without Issue.

ANOTHER who wanted a Wife, and having got a Shilling from a Seaman that happen'd to land there, went and gave this Shilling to Mr. *Morison* to purchase him a Wife in the *Lewis*, and send her to him, for he was told that this piece of Money was a thing of extraordinary Value, and his desire was gratified the ensuing Year.

ABOUT 14 Years ago a swarm of Rats, but none knows how, came into *Rona*, and in a short time eat up all the Corn in the Island. In a few Months after some Seamen Landed there, who Robbed the poor People of their Bull. These misfortunes and the want of supply from *Lewis* for the space of a Year, occasion'd the death of all that Ancient Race of People. The Steward of St. *Kilda* being by a Storm driven in there, told me that he found a Woman with her Child on her Breast, both lying dead at the side of a Rock : Some Years after, the Minister (to whom the Island belongeth) sent a new Colony to this Island, with suitable Supplies. The following Year a Boat was sent to them with some more supplies and Orders to receive the Rents, but the Boat being lost as it is supposed, I can give no further account of this late Plantation. . . .

This account was all of the Ancient Race, the immemorial endemic community of—as Macculloch called them—the North Ronenses, whose extinction made a dividing line in the island story more decisive than the lingering end of 1844. Thereafter was only the system of absentee tacksman employing resident servants, a family or two of shepherds at the best. Money came to be used, potatoes were introduced, sheep replaced cattle, the shepherds finally abandoned the sheep. There was no real break between the disasters of the late seventeenth century and present times.

A tradition of further disaster when all the men were drowned in a boating accident was recorded by both Dr. Macculloch and Captain Burnaby the sapper. This must have happened either to the new colonists, Martin's " late Plantation," or to the boat's crew sent by the minister to collect their rents ; or to both. In any case, once the thread was broken, new colonists had no better fortune.[1]

The Ancient Race consisted immemorially of five or six families : " ordinarlie . . . five small tennents," said a seventeenth century fragment, and " five families, which seldom exceed thirty souls in all," said another—a report by Sir George M'Kenzie of Tarbat. He went on :

> They have a kind of commonwealth among them, in so far if any of them have more children than another, he that hath fewer taketh from the other what makes his number equal, and the excrescence of above thirty souls is sent with the summer boat to the Lewes to the Earl of Seafort their master. . . .

" Their sheep there have wool," explained Sir George, " but of a blewish colour." The inhabitants were so well satisfied with their lot that " they exceedingly bewail the condition of those, as supernumerary, they must send out of this island."

A thought of this island thrown out by Dr. Macculloch was even more apt as a text to earlier centuries than to his own :

[1] The legendary next inhabitant, so Captain Burnaby was told, was a female who tested the tradition that " the fire never quenched in Rona " and found it a fallacy ; she prayed fervently and her fire was miraculously re-lit. Had grand-mamma MacCagie become a legend ?

To find inhabitants on such an island is a strong proof, among many others, of the value of land in this country compared to that of labour. There are few parts of Britain where Rona would not be abandoned to the sea fowls that seem its proper tenants.

But in these times there was nothing for comment in the fact that so small and remote an island as Rona should be inhabited; all the little iles were inhabit and manurit, semi-underground housing was quite the norm. Dr. Johnson's being, sheltered by loose stones and turf, came home to roost with Benjamin Crémieux's magic and legends at the edge of the ocean.

By the twentieth century the Rona village had long become unique in that it had hung on unchanged but by weathering, while in other islands there had been replacement and progress. What Macculloch saw was to all intents a Stone Age village inhabited in the year 1815. In 1936 it had just the look of archæologists' photographs of some excavated Pictish village, only the manse chimney and the overground stone huts built by the shepherds of 1884-5 had to be discounted. (And the shepherds' residence had hardly been of a piece with previous natives', what with the chimney and the window-hole and imported foodstuffs : comparable to the standard of our own domesticity.)

A hundred and fifty years before Martin, the first known account of Rona was written by Sir Donald Monro, "Heigh Dean of the Iles," who travelled through the Hebrides in the year 1549 on some sort of pastoral inspection. The archaic uncouthness of his report seemed of itself to reduce the islanders to a more primitive state, though probably there was no change at all in the interval : the island set the standard, not the centuries outside. " A harmless race on this sequestered shore Pass'd the long round of lingering ages o'er," as Dr. Ogilvie wrote. And Sir Donald Monro . . .

Towards the north northeist from Lewis, three score myles of sea, lyes ane little ile callit Ronay, laiche maine lande, inhabit and manurit be simple people, scant of ony religione. This ile is

153

uther haffe myle lange, and haffe myle braide ; aboundance
of corne growes on it by delving onlie, aboundance of clover
gerse for sheipe. Ther is an certain number of ky and sheipe
ordainit for this ile be ther awin ald right, extending to sa
maney as may be sustainit upon the said gerssing, and the
countrey is so fertill of gerssing, that the superexcrescens of the
said ky and scheipe baith feidis them in flesche, and als payes
ther dewties with the samen for the maist pairt. Within this ile
there is sic faire whyte beir [barley] meal made like flour, and
quhen they slay their sheipe, they slay them belly flaught, and
stuffes ther skins fresche of the bear meil, and send their dewties
be a servant of M'Cloyd of Lewis, with certain reistit muttan,
and mony reistit foulis. Within this ile there is ane chapell,
callit St. Ronay's chapell, unto quhilk chapell, as the ancients
of the country alledges, they leave an spaid and ane shuil,
quhen any man dies, and upon the morrow findes the place of
the grave markit with an spaid, as they alledge. In this ile
they use to take maney quhaills and uther grate fisches.

For the rest, for St. Ronan and the Dark Ages, there was
no choice but to attend a ceilidh.

(3) The Legend

Someone must have built St. Ronan's cell. *Ron*, in Gaelic,
a seal : Rona, Ronay, Ronin, isle of seals ; St. Ronan was
their patron saint. The historicity of St. Ronan ?

The chapel, said Muir—and one clung to his single sentence
if only because it was written down in English and not Gaelic
spoken—was

> dedicated to St. Ronan, son of Berach, a Scot mentioned by
> Bede as having had disputations with Finan, bishop of Lindis-
> farne, regarding the true time of keeping Easter ; and who,
> near to the close of his life, is said to have retired to the island
> of Rona, and there died about the end of the seventh century.

Muir himself dated St. Ronan's cell from the eighth or ninth
century. Saints of early Christian times were well known to
have been in the habit of retiring as hermits to remote isles.

There were innumerable little dedicated chapels. What was remarkable about St. Ronan's was that it should have remained holy and the place of worship for all the inhabitants ever after. And since St. Ronan himself could hardly have existed alone upon Rona—" Upon this isle whereas he had abode, Nature, God knows, had little cost bestowed "—the inference was that habitation, in the fixed conservative mode imposed by the island, might well have stretched unbroken from even before the eighth or ninth century right down to the modern disasters of the late seventeenth century. The Ancient Race !

" A deal of legendary story is still afloat among the ' idle-headed eld ' at the north end of Lewis," said Muir, and we ourselves heard some of it from Mrs. Macleod, the Ness correspondent, and from others. Muir had a version of the traditional story of St. Ronan from the contemporary tenant of Rona, who had it from an old man called Angus Gunn, who had it on the spot when he was a young shepherd in Rona in about 1800. What the story amounted to was that a God-fearing man named Ronan, who lived near the Butt of Lewis, was grieved by the scolding and quarrelling of women and prayed to be taken away. His prayer was answered and a large whale appeared at Port of Ness (" a great black whale," said Mrs. Macleod, " but not quite so big as the Loch Ness Monster "). The man Ronan embarked on its back and was carried to Rona. He found the island inhabited by monstrous hairy animals with long claws and round red eyes glowing like hot coals. He contended with them until they backed out of the island and were drowned. As they slid down the sloping rock face on the south coast called Leac na Sgrob, their claws left some (unimpressive) wavy scratches in the rock. " We used to go there to look at them often," said Iain Mackay ; " nothing more than slickensides caused by differential land movement," said Malcolm Stewart. Ronan then built his cell and the devil raised a tempest to blow him and his teampull clean out of the island, and St. Ronan leant against the (west) wall of his cell to prevent it blowing in and when the devil had done his worst, there was a bend in the wall, and there it remained to this day . . ." as you have it drawn in the book," said Iain Mackay to Mr. Muir.

In some cases St. Ronan had a sister, the beautiful and virtuous Brenhilda, who accompanied her brother to Rona but who then " for reasons variously explained " removed to Sula Sgeir and sat pining on a stone called *Suidhe Brianuille*, the Seat of Brenhilda ; and when wandering seamen found her skeleton, a shag was nesting in her bosom. John Wilson Dougal had recorded this story ex-ceilidh.

Like other outlying isles, Rona had to have a boat-race legend. Traditionally crews competed for first possession of an island, invariably ran neck and neck, issue in doubt to the last, and the winner won by some unexpected dramatic turn. The race for Rona was between the men of the Mainland and the men of Lewis, " and if you had seen them coming," said Mrs. Macleod, " you would have been frightened." The Lewismen's ruse was to throw ashore a lump of burning (Lewis) peat, and so to this day. Certainly, as Wilson Dougal remarked, there was " a treasure house of folklore amongst the Ness people." Personally I could never find such stuff anything but tedious, although, as James Boswell said patronisingly of Martin's book, " one cannot but have kindness for it." There was something pathetic in the contrast between the fanciful, immemorial legends, told and retold by indoor firelight, and their subject, the far-off, obdurate island that had worn out life after life and smashed boats since ever boats had sailed there. In spite of all its history Rona in a view from seaward was the same this day as a hundred or a thousand years ago. A little shifting of earth and stones counted for nothing ; no change ; all that had happened was the passage of time.

THIRD YEAR

FLANNAN ISLES
NORTH RONA
EIGG

*

1937

XIII

Rock Station

THERE were the Flannan Isles or Seven Hunters or Seven Haley Isles, twenty miles westward from Lewis in the Western Ocean,

> seven little islands, named Flananae, some holy place (in old times), of girth or refuge, rising up in hilles full of herbes. . . .

They had sheep in them, and Leach's petrels, and a lighthouse. No question of anything but a return to the Outer Isles, though this year no fair stretch of summer lay ahead, only three weeks to be squeezed from so-called gainful employment. We might be lucky and fall in with the chosen day of the Rona Annual. The Monach Isles off the Atlantic coast of North Uist might be a place to look at. Or Eigg—last year on Canna we had been told that Eigg was the place for shearwaters by the thousand.

The borrowed Morris was fitted with lights, so we drove day and night and at dawn retraced the remembered hazards of the Mallaig road, where the Singer had bucketed gamefully on its last homeward grind. The car embarked for the Outer Isles. Sea-fowl again bobbed upon the waves, puffins beat away furiously without rising ; other, later, puffins whirred towards the dark cliffs of the Shiant Isles. The car disembarked and took up the old stand behind the fish-market, where the Singer had used to drip its pool of oil. Herring barrels were piled high along the waterfront, gulls splashed the corrugated iron of the fish-market, a chill wind rattled the windows of Stornoway. A homecoming !

Up at Ness, Alec MacFarquhar was dusted with white meal, grinding barley at the mill. He would be away to Rona before long ; the skipper of the *Provider*, a paraffin-engined Stornoway drifter, had said he might do the job. Calling sociably at Butt of Lewis lighthouse we were told that the best chance of getting out to the Flannans would be with the sheep-boat that sailed from Bernera in Loch Roag, on the west side of Lewis. The Flannans did not seem impossibly far ; even without plans aforethought we might reach them. Last year they had seemed quite near when we had heard Light speak to Light—the Butt winding up the radio telephone and calling forth from the ocean, a voice of the Flannan Isles. " Hallo hallo the Flannans, Butt of Lewis calling the Flannans. . . . Good morning, Mr. Black." " Your generator's louder than your voice, but I can hear all right," had said disembodied Mr. Black, himself faint and tinny.

The moors had never been so wet !—and only last year we had seen them for the first time. This time we were no casual visitors happening to be back again ; no ; returning islanders, greeting old friends and familiar places. Back to Stornoway by Europie, Five Penny Ness, Knockaird, Lionel, Habost, Swanibost, Cross, the Dells, the Galsons, Mid and Five Penny Borves, the Shaders, and Barvas crossroads.

(1) Eilean Mor

The grazing tenants of the Flannans and old Mr. Malcolm Macleod, whose boat *Rhoda* annually took them there, all lived in the island of Great Bernera in Loch Roag. Great Bernera had a post office in it, so after some complicated telegraphing Mr. Macleod received an unknown voice, mine, asking whether two of us might please come with him to the Flannans, if and when he was going. He would have gone yesterday, he said, but the weather was not chust favourable. Now he was going in an hour or two and could pick us up at Breasclete pier. We threw some provisions together, made a headlong rush across Lewis, and found the pier, deserted and grass-grown, a concrete wall against the empty waters of Loch Roag. We put the car against a peat stack and waited. A crofter girl said her mother

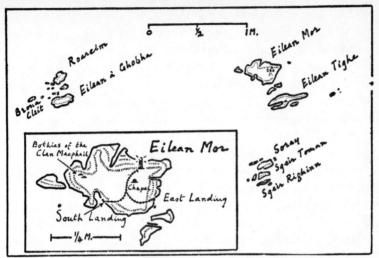

FIG. 5. *Sketch map of Flannan Isles or Seven Hunters*

would never forgive her if she let two strangers away without
a cup of tea. At last a motor boat approached the pier. Since
Malcolm Stewart had been out in her to the Flannans, the
Rhoda had acquired a second-hand Kelvin. His own passage
under sail had taken thirteen and a half hours.

We chugged away from Breasclete pier, the patriarch at
the wheel. Mr. Macleod's white beard stirred in the breeze;
he had a happy smile and he was in his seventy-eighth year.
The chosen of sheep, about to begin their thalassic year, had
to be picked up from the islet where they had been collected.
The boat nudged in among the rocks and a quick round-up
ended against her side. Then out round Gallan Head and into
the Western Ocean.

Eilean Mor, chief of the Flannans, soon began to show as
an ultimate speck under the westering sun. Heavy old *Rhoda*
chugged up and down the swell, the wisps of paraffin fumes
blew away to leeward and vanished. The twenty-five sheep
supported life as one block in the fish-hold. Long, cold, clouded,
oceanic afternoon while Eilean Mor grew slowly out of the
sea. It wasn't worth all the fork-tailed petrels in the world,
said one of the shepherds sympathetically to naturalist Ainslie

in his customary prostration of seasickness. On this sort of occasion, to have lived in Rona was the best possible credential, valid throughout the Western Isles.

A haze closed off the island for a time. It came out again with a pin-point of lighthouse added, a new low whaleback alongside, and a couple of outliers to the southward, all standing clear-cut and dark with the light behind them. The swell still kept hiding the islands. The engine's racket never faltered. Daylight faded. The lighthouse began to twinkle at the bottom of an enormous red and yellow sunset. At last we were close up to steep cliffs.

The *Rhoda* presented her stern to some steps in the cliff face and rolled sluggishly, bubbling her exhaust under water, while the sheep were thrown and caught hand to hand like so many sacks. And now,

Know first, on FLANNAN'S desert isles you stand,
Far-famed ;—a lone, but consecrated land !

Two of the men and ourselves followed the sheep up the steps, which were accompanied up and across the cliff by a railway track. The crown of the island was a good height up from the sea ; short stony turf showed a glimmer of mayweed flowers where it fell away into cliff slopes. The sheep dispersed into their new land. We followed the railway towards the large block of lighthouse buildings and the silent revolving light. The shepherds knocked at a door, and waited, and knocked again—very queer. Someone called " Come in," and there was revealed the Principal Lightkeeper putting on his trousers.

The shepherds, of course, already knew the three keepers : Mr. Black . . . Ainslie, Atkinson . . . Charlie . . . and Johnnie. They made coffee and something to eat for all of us in the big lamp-lit living-room. We spoke of our tent and were offered spare bunks. John retired to one of them to sleep off his ocean misery ; Mr. Black retired ; the shepherds went back to the boat, saying that they would lie overnight in a quiet place against the rocks, which seemed confident. It was about midnight. Charlie took me up to the balcony of the tower. The island lay spread in pale moonlight. I leant over the railings and listened once more to the night-time voice of Leach's petrel. Later on I walked out into the middle of a usual performance . . . sea noise away and below . . . and above, commanding the night, the slow unvarying revolution of the light-beams. I chose an underground churring and dug down with my hands through thrift cushions and slabs of peaty turf : the old familiar smell, the bright black eye, forked tail and tidy webbed feet of Leach's petrel—a year and how many miles over the sea from here to Rona !

In the morning the shepherds rounded up and loaded the island-fattened sheep. The sheep were lashed by the horns, thrown into the sea, towed out to the boat and hauled aboard, fat, dripping and helpless. The Flannans were purely a fattening pasture, there was no lambing and the stock was completely exchanged every year. The sheep of the other islands of the group would make another load. Mr. Macleod said he would be back for them in two or three days ; the lightkeepers had hospitably taken us in ; we said we'd stay until he returned.

The shepherds had been catching puffins, pulling them out of their burrows during the night. They took away a sackful for home consumption. We used two dead puffins they had left lying to bait a couple of lobster pots, cast into the sea from the east landing. Lobster tea in the lighthouse, served with the lighthouse hammer.

*   *   *

The framed card hung in the tower read :

The Commissioners of Northern Lighthouses hereby give Notice, that on the night of Thursday the 7th day of December next, and every evening thereafter from the going away of daylight in the evening till the return of daylight in the morning, a Light will be exhibited from a Lighthouse which has been erected on Eilean Mor, one of the Flannan Islands. The Light will be a Group Flashing White Light showing 2 flashes in quick succession every half minute. The power of the Light will be equal to about 140,000 standard candles. The Light will be visible all round and will be elevated 330 feet above high water spring tides, and allowing fifteen feet for the height of the eye will be seen at about 24 nautical miles in clear weather, and at lesser distances according to the state of the atmosphere. When close to, the stacks lying to the westward of Eilean Mor will obscure the Light over two small angles. The top of the Lantern is about 75 feet above the island.

By order of the Board

Edinburgh, 30 Oct. 1899   *James Murdoch Secretary*

To which should have been added : God Save the Queen !

The Flannans, one of the remotest of Lights, was served by four men of whom three were always on the island, while the fourth was over in Lewis at the barrack-like shore station. Each man did two months on rock station, as they called it, and then a month ashore. This was the place of one of the most publicised of lighthouse mysteries : a passing ship reported that the light was extinguished ; no trace was ever found of the three keepers. This was soon after the Light was established and since then men had been lost in landing and one had been killed by falling off the tower. The Flannans, naturally enough, had an evil reputation.

Lighthouse life hinged entirely on lighting-up and putting-out times. " About dusk " was " about lighting-up time " ; rain came on not at dawn but at about putting-out time. Twice a day Flannans listened for Butt of Lewis and then called Monach Isles. " Hallo hallo Butt of Lewis calling the Flannans, hallo the Flannans good morning good morning Mr. Black over." It was either a fine day here or not a fine day here and that was about all. Like paired commentators, when one couldn't think of anything else to say he said " over," switched off the screaming generator and transferred the onus to the other, who would probably say, " Well I'll be getting along now cheerio over and down." We told Monach we might be calling on them.

The focus of lighthouse life was the big living-room-kitchen with its polished coal range, varnished deal-boarded walls and old-fashioned trumpet loud-speaker, which could produce tinny dance music if required. From the living-room led off the tiny bedrooms, two bunks in each, the wireless-room, store-rooms, workshop, engine-house and a passage to the bottom of the tower. The living-room at least had windows but once inside the tower one might have been anywhere ; wind and rain and Atlantic surge were remote. The lantern house in brilliant hurtful glare and the echoing stone stairs had an empty laboratory-hospital cleanliness. Silence was broken by mathe-matically regular clangs from a bell as the driving weights slowly unwound their way down the tower and revolved the great cage of prisms up above ; then, every half-hour of the night, a ratcheting noise as the weights were wound up again. The paraffin lamp burnt with a steady purr. It had a burner much like that of a Primus stove, surmounted by a single incandescent mantle hardly bigger than those of the mantle lamps common in the crofts of Lewis. It seemed a poor sort of centre-piece for the wonderful cage which a push set moving, and for the undefeated skill and determination which had reared the tower of great stone blocks, and laid railways, and made concrete jetties, on a rock in the Atlantic Ocean. At lighting-up time the cage had to be revolving at its settled speed before the lamp was lit, or a false signal would go out. But the lightkeepers hardly ever sighted a ship.

On a clear day St. Kilda showed in the south-west, and the mountains of Harris and of Uig in Lewis were lowly in the south-east and east. From the balcony the rest of the Seven Hunters lay spread near and altogether inaccessible, nearly twenty various foam-fringed islets, sgeirs and stacks. Eilean Tighe, Isle of the House, was only two hundred yards beyond the east landing. It had some sort of ruined stone and turf bothan in it, and a dozen sheep, and the keepers said they would see hundreds of geese on it in the wintertime. On beyond to the south were Soray and Sgeir Toman with attendant reefs, eight-and five-acre green-crowned humps ; even these had a few sheep perched on them. In the west across nearly two miles of unencumbered Sound stood seven-acre Roareim with three sheep, and twelve-acre Eilean à Ghoba with eight sheep. These with Eilean Mor made Six Hunters, a better title, for to make seven you had to choose between the westward needle stack, Brona Cleit, and the southward three-acre Sgeir Righinn, both sheepless. The six-inch map from surveys of 1851-2 had not yet been corrected to mark the lighthouse works.

Mr. Black, the Principal Lightkeeper, was a small quiet man who had been a keeper for thirty years. He sat much in his chair, saying reflectively to no one : " aye, aye." Often he went outside to pace up and down and up and down the concrete path. Sometimes he played his concertina. He was a wild man in Stornoway, what with the concertina, we heard afterwards.

Charlie was First Assistant and had been a sometime painter and decorator in Glasgow. He liked the job. He was a kindly man who went with a fixed and inward smile and something of a glare to his eye. He was noted for reading Dickens and for carpentry, but it was hard to stick to anything on rock station, he said ; start something, keen as you like, but then it sort of faded out. Johnnie from Shetland, stout and placid, was still in his early twenties. The job suited him too and, like Charlie, he took to seriousness and reasons for the Universe. They made little demands of each other, the routine was so well settled. Once an argument about duty watch became suddenly heated, John and I sat back glancing at each other, but a flare-up scene was avoided. Each man had his own private store of sweeties and cake ; some cake produced by one of them had gone bad in secretive hoard. No one could have been more unreservedly hospitable than they, taking us into their way of life for three or four days.

Apart from the lighthouse compound, the features of Eilean Mor were the unnumbered ranks of puffins, the railway and the sporting five-hole golf course, all of which were inseparable. Even this chief of the Flannans was not much more than a sea rock, only 39 acres elevated nearly 300 feet above the sea and entirely enclosed by cliffs. (" On all sides it rises in mural

precipices and very steep turfy slopes, at once from the sea "
—of course T. S. Muir had been here.)

The single track railway emerged from the engine-room
of the lighthouse, where a great drum was coiled with steel
wire rope, one end of which was hooked on to a four-wheel
bogie. At Charing Cross the railway forked, with proper
points ; one line curved down to the east landing, the other
to the south. Innumerable puffins sat about the railway. They
were everywhere, puffins yawning, billing, fighting and
tumbling like sparrows, standing about with beakfuls of fish
or of grass. They were whirring up to the cliff edge, braking,
dithering, dropping away to get momentum for another try,
finally managing it and plopping down on to solid ground.
Hundreds stood still doing nothing, the green turf was " like
a meadow thickly enamelled with daisies "—to-day as on Dr.
Macculloch's day of 1815. As you walked the island groups of
puffins buzzed away as thick as dungflies from a cowpat.
The underground snored and grunted with them, they dashed
out from underfoot and bundled themselves away, often hitting
the ground and overturning all of a tumble in their haste.

Puffins and the lighthouse hens fraternised at the cliff edge,
above the teeming strata of kittiwakes and razorbills, guillemots and shags. Fulmars were surprisingly scarce considering
the nearness of the St. Kildan metropolis. There were a good
many skinny rabbits, descendants of thoughtless introduction
experiments by early lightkeepers. It was odd to see the
smallest of baby rabbits sitting twitching its nose in the middle
of a group of solemn puffinry. The lightkeepers had a story
of a rabbit picked up by a black-backed gull and dropped on
one of the smallest stacks, where it escaped ; they had seen it
there alive—there was a little grass on the extreme top of the
stack—but being neither gravid nor capable of partheno-
genesis, even if of the right sex, the emigrant had not reproduced
its kind.

The sporting five-hole golf course with bogey 17 took in
some of the more level earthworks of rabbit and puffin. Puffins
looked on at the inconclusive match of residents *v.* visitors.

Charlie and Johnnie exchanged uniforms for modern shorts and gym shoes. Surprisingly no balls were lost. After one bonny swipe, which was thought to have carried over the edge, the ball was found safely, and expensively, bunkered in the mouth of a puffin burrow. Two pairs of oystercatchers flew anxiously round as we played off to the second, the long hole west of Charing Cross. All this tilted crown of the island was barefoot ground, a close turf with thrift and seaside plantains. The lightkeepers afterwards wished to bathe. We joined them momentarily in the appalling chill of heaving green water off the east landing.

With all the thousands of puffins there was hardly a black-backed gull, and perhaps that was why. We saw not more than six pairs of great black-backs, and Eilean Mor was free of the carcases and extroverted puffins that had so littered Rona. Did the two pairs of Flannans ravens discourage them ? We applauded one as it stooped at a black-back ; we saw a black-back take a puffin only once, snatching it up from the golf course.

(2) Flannans Night and Relief Day

In the night a sea mist solidified the lighthouse beams. The loom of beams swept deliberately over the petrel ground, where lush chickweed glistened with mist moisture. The clanging of the bell sounded faintly as the weights unwound within the tower. The three rays struck out from the lantern house like those from the Dong, the Dong with the Luminous Nose. A little breeze brought drifts of faint clamour from the cliff colonists. Puffins were sonorous underfoot ; the lively petrels fluttered in a warm dark air and sometimes flopped into each other. They appeared to be indifferent to the Light.

We spent two nights out with the fork-tails and guessed that a good 200 pairs were nesting in Eilean Mor, scattered into five discrete colonies round the edges of the island. Below ground, puffins and rabbits were hopelessly mixed up, and fork-tails sometimes had their own private nesting chambers in the general labyrinth ; a specimen excavation yielded first a young puffin near the entrance and then much deeper in a small fluffy fork-tail's chick. Probably most of the fork-tails dug their own small, exclusive burrows, and these, unlike the often obvious and worn entrances in the village walls of Rona, were exceedingly inconspicuous and overgrown and showed no sign of use. This had been particularly noted by W. Eagle Clarke when in 1904 he had made the first record of Leach's petrels nesting in the Flannans, and had thus added a third to the two already known stations of St. Kilda and Rona.

The underground reel of storm petrels was even more fetching than fork-tails' churring. The stormies themselves, such little featherweights, so neat and smoothly glossy, with black bills tiny and hooked, little spindle legs and diminutive cold webs, made fork-tails seem almost clumsy. Stormies always liked to nest under a pile of dry stones ; they had an exclusive colony in one of the two local Ancient Monuments and Constructions : it was from beneath the stones of Bothien Clann Igphail, The Bothies of the Clan Macphail, that their reeling was to be heard.

Adult puffins were either at sea at night or underground. From beneath humped thrift cushions or mounds of mayweed there came more noises, long-drawn, meditative-sounding groans, something like a distantly heard foghorn but much personalised and conveying half resentment, half solicitude. One smiled with delight at the swelling and falling voices of this sonorous underworld, could have sat and listened to them indefinitely.

> *The isle is full of noises,*
> *Sounds and sweet airs, that give delight, and hurt not. . . .*

The underground of petrel and puffin recalled nothing so much as the effect of a pondful of frogs in full spring song.

Young puffins ready to fly evidently went down to the sea under the safe cover of darkness. We came across one or two, unaccompanied, steadily waddling and tumbling downhill, their backs dewed with drops of misty rain. We floated one off from the east landing ; its first action was to drink. Afterwards one read how R. M. Lockley on Skokholm had elucidated the young puffin's journey to the sea, how the full-grown young, too fat to fly, were deserted by their parents, just as young petrels were ; how they fasted for as long as a week and then emerged alone and made their own way down to the sea, at night and only at night. In daylight only a tithe could survive such a passage. An eighteenth-century minister of the Small Isles wrote :

> It is believed, that the young puffin becomes so weighty with fat, as to be unable to take the wing and leave its nest : To remedy this inconvenience, the old puffin is said to administer sorrel, to extenuate, and render it fit for flying. It is, at any rate, a known fact, that sorrel is commonly found to grow near the puffin's nest.

Strange : the same association with sorrel as corrective of fat (" for digestion's sake, as is conjectur'd ") was persistent in old accounts of petrels' ways. Sorrel has indeed been taken from the proventriculi of fulmar petrels, and old-time islanders themselves used sorrel to qualify their diet of oily sea-fowl. But sorrel did not grow in the Flannan Isles.

*   *   *

The red flag meaning " East Landing " was flying from the flagstaff, beside the Northern Lights ensign with the figure of a white lighthouse on it ; the *Pole Star* lay off to the east : Relief Day. The engine-room had steam up : the drum unwound, the bogie went clattering away downhill, forked left at Charing Cross, and disappeared round the cliff slope.

This was oil-landing day and a whole year's supply for the lantern—twenty barrels—was coming ashore. *Pole Star's* motor-boat came off and lay plumbed below the derrick ; a lot of men wound the handles ; the weighty pendulum of a pair of barrels swung and descended into the bogie. There

was much shouting up and down the uni-directional telephone
between lighthouse and landing. The drum up at the lighthouse began to turn, the cable tautened, the bogie moved up
the cliff across the mayweed-covered wall, set above and below
with watching puffins ; rounded the cliff shoulder, passed
Charing Cross, drew over the golf course, and disappeared
within the lighthouse. The barrels were pumped out into
storage tanks and the bogie came clanking back on slack cable
at alarming speed.

At each Relief the *Pole Star* brought a single live sheep,
which grazed tamely about the lighthouse until it was wanted
for butchering. We understood that the Commissioners had
not been able to come to an agreement with the tenant about
a suitable price for his own local sheep.

Charlie was pathetically excited for his month ashore, his
own end-of-term feeling infected the place. Relief Day was
unsettling to the placid round, all the bustle and appearance
of strange men going in and out. Mr. Black said he was
always glad when it was over. By midday it was over : the
new man had come off and Charlie went away with the
boatload ; *Pole Star* diminished trailing thick black smoke.
She would be back again before the next Relief to land coal
and water.

The new man settled in very briskly. He was friendly and
cheerful and we wondered why he had not long since been
murdered by his mates. He bragged and was loud and know-
ledgeable of all things, could not converse without clutching
one's arm and pinching and prodding. Johnnie needed all
his placidity, but even he could no longer smile at jokes about
his young self and the girls ashore.

Sea mist swirled about the islands all the afternoon. It
cleared in the early evening for a round of golf, interrupted
by Mr. Black shouting from his caged constitutional on the
lighthouse concrete, and pointing to the eastward. A small
dark blob approaching the islands. This time the *Rhoda* went
straight on to the two western outliers, where, in spite of the
swell, old Malcolm Macleod took her up against the rocks until

the wild men could jump ashore. They had lost seven sheep during the year from a total of fifty, they told us afterwards. One of the small stacks had had only two sheep put down on it the year before ; one had died during the winter ; the survivor was taken off and two more landed in its place. In the round-up another sheep fell over a low cliff, first thirty feet to strike its skull against a rock edge, and then on into the Atlantic, where it swam round to the other side of the rock and landed itself ; it was safely retrieved. Such an anachronism of shepherding was yet worth doing.

Again *Rhoda* lay overnight against one of the islands. This time the men shot a sackful of guillemots and shags. The young men laughed (behind his back) at old Macleod's fancy for a bit of fishy sea-fowl ; they belonged more to the toothless age of food in tins. For the rest the five of them slept in *Rhoda's* tiny forward quarters, a noisome black den. All this seemed pretty hardy, particularly for a man of seventy-seven, but it was summer luxury compared to the legendary hardihood of earlier sailors from Lewis and Harris. Then, in midwinter and long before engines, men in little half-decked boats had used to go out line fishing, it might be for seven days at a time and twenty miles beyond the Flannans. " And when you would see them step ashore you would think they were drunken men."

The sackful of birds was a last token of centuries of fowling expeditions to the Flannans. The rent for the islands was now £5 ; in Macculloch's time it had been £10,

> a price paid rather for the birds by which they are inhabited than for the grass they produce.

The High Dean in 1549 thought more of the sheep :

> Infinit wyld scheipe therein, quhilk na man knawes to quhom the said sheipe apperteines. . . . M'Cloyd of the Lewis, at certaine tymes in the zeir, sendis men in, and huntis and slayis maney of thir sheipe.

Some change in dress and manner, no doubt, a different breed of sheep now firmly owned, but otherwise the same hazards and hallooing round-up of . . . " wyld sheipe in the seven iles forsaid, quhilk may not be outrune." The sea-fowl remained as heretofore, their football-crowd noise swelled from the cliffs. Shags continued to paddle in their own ordure, guillemots jostled on slimy ledges, razorbills in crevices, kittiwakes clamoured in dark gloomy clefts above the slapping swell, puffins darkened the air. But casual latter-day shooting of a few birds was a very different matter from the formalities of one-time subsistence fowling. Martin described an extraordinary rigmarole of punctilios and taboos with which contemporary fowlers surrounded themselves, how novices had each to be accompanied by an old hand, how the first injunction given after landing was, "not to ease Nature in that place where the Boat lyes," how exactly the various rituals of prayer-making at the Chappel were observed, and so on. Martin interviewed one of the fowlers, who explained that the Flannans were a place of "inherent Sanctity"; no one had ever landed there "but found himself more dispos'd to Devotion there, than any where else."

The chapel of St. Flann, Teampull Beannachadh or Blessing House, which, as Malcolm Stewart said, resembled a large dog kennel, stood obviously in the middle of the island. Being dry stone built and enduring quite stark and free from lichen or turf, it must have looked the same when brand new, perhaps a thousand years before, though the slab roof had sometime been roughly remade. A flock of starlings perched on it and flew down to feed among the sheep ; enterprising colonists, one pair had nested within the teampull. Rabbits hopped in and out of the single low entrance, sheep sheltered inside, rock pipits crept between its stones. It was enclosed by a broken-down fence, presumably to keep out the sheep.

It seemed, just to look at them, sufficiently unlikely that the Flannans should ever have had inhabitants, ecclesiastic or lay, before the Lighthouse first spread its beams, at the going away of daylight on the 7th of December, 1899. Inherent sanctity would not have built the Blessing House, ancient in

Martin's time. Muir, who might have been expected to help, merely said of it : " a very primitive-looking thing, composed of rough stones joggled compactly together," and went on to describe the sheep as the tenant's " four-footed pets." Macculloch had chosen to come on a Sunday, " and the sound of the mineralogical hammer, as not in the authorised list of necessary works, was not heard." He was more forthcoming :

> Two saints seem to contest for the honour of giving their name to the Flannan islands. Flannan was Bishop of Killaloe in 639, and he is canonized in the Irish Calendar. But St. Flann was the son of Maol-duine, Abbot of Iona, who died in 890 ; and who is to decide ?

Had the early fowlers who presumably ran up the Bothies of the Clan Macphail built also Teampull Beannachadh ? Would they have done this *de novo* and thus inaugurated a tradition of sanctity, or would they not have built unless the sanctity were already inherent ; and who is to decide ? The remoter islands were anciently holy of themselves, with or without Christian remains, not only Flannans, but St. Kilda, Rona of course, Shiants and others less withdrawn ; early Christian missionaries were known often to have adapted existing pagan sacredness of place and usage. The Christians themselves were apparently pleased to exist in a hut and a sheepskin, with a bag of meal and an occasional sea-fowl.

> Not a few of the *English* and *Scottish* monks, were superstitiously fond of solitary and remote places, fond of little isles, fond of keeping their bodies under a cruel mortification. . . .

But if a lone residence by St. Ronan upon Rona was too much of a stretch for modern imagination, so much more was anything of St. Flann's upon the Flannans.

> . . . feem to have been the refidence of ecclefiastics in time of the druids,

said the old *Statistical Account*.

In spite of its suggestive name the next door island, Eilean
Tighe, Island of the House, caused no comment among the
earlier writers. Harvie-Brown landed upon it briefly in 1881
and Malcolm Stewart in 1932 ; the house was " a collection
of stones arranged in an oval to round formation " (Stewart).
The Royal Commissioners on Ancient and Historical Monuments had neither seen nor mentioned it, though they had not
thought much of either the Bothies of the Clan Macphail or
of the dog kennel Teampull Beannachadh ; they had scheduled
neither for protection nor offered any word of their possible
origin. Probably fork-tails were nesting in the house nowadays.

Harvie-Brown at the Flannans had not done so well as
usual ; he was out twice in bad weather in June, '81, but
managed to land only upon Eilean Tighe, once, at hazard, and
for only a few minutes to look round and to pick up some birds'
eggs. When he was back in the boat Professor Heddle got
ashore, but fell and hurt his knee. " Query," put H.-B. in a
footnote, " as the ' Punctilios ' of Martin were not adhered to
on our first landing, was this not just retribution upon our
heads ? "

Had John A. Harvie-Brown, F.Z.S., M.B.O.U., F.L.S.,
F.R.S.E., etc., indeed eased nature in that place where the
boat lay ?

*   *   *

Mr. Black and his assistants came down to the south landing
to see us off. They would soon be really lonely, he said, when
the sea-birds were gone ; and I realised with a sort of shock
just how lonely it would be : everywhere the silent abandoned
riddles of puffin burrows, all the deserted whitewashed cliff
ledges. Again and again the refrain . . .

> *The Northern Ocean in vast whirls,*
> *Boils round the naked melancholy isles. . . .*

For a final signal there would be all the migrants to pass,
going south—and to be harbingers again after the elemental

season, coming north. The joy of the sea-fowl's vociferous bright-coloured return in spring !

The loggish *Rhoda* was livened by the northerly swell. There were twenty-two sheep below and two more lashed on to the hatch above the engine, enormous creatures like yaks, with thick matted fleeces. John settled up against one—there was nowhere else ; " as warm as a girrl," said one of the shepherds. The dwindling islands moved in and out of mist patches, and sank, until only Eilean Mor with a speck of lighthouse remained. The Flannans, yes, they were well enough ; not much to them perhaps, so bare and elevated ; necessary ever to return to them ? Probably no, never.

" Far off the petrel in the troubled way " ; fulmars were with us, and shearwaters as smaller black and white versions thereof, both board-winged, banking and cutting out their set figures.

> *She rises often, often drops again,*
> *And sports at ease on the tempestuous main.*

Little black birds came singly skimming the swell. " Here ran the stormy petrels on the wave " . . . or Leach's ? A near one paused momentarily to pick up some food scrap ; in the instant of its uplifted wings the white rump showed and a short, square-cut black tail : stormy. These were the birds to be called sea-swallows, not gross and squawking terns.

After four or five hours the *Rhoda* rounded Gallan Head into the calm of Loch Roag.

—Last week the motor boat " Rhoda " as is the annual custom, made two trips to the Flannan Islands. On both outward journeys " Rhoda " had a good number of sheep on board for wintering in the Flannans, and those which were on the Island since last July were brought home. These were landed at Callanish, and from there they are sent to Stornoway, where they get a ready sale. This year the weather was more favourable for both trips as there was only a slight breeze of wind and the sea was not rough. (The Bernera correspondent, *Stornoway Gazette*, 30.7.37.)

Eilean Mor, Flannan Islands, July 21–24, 1937

XIV

Another Rona Annual

CELTIC SUNDAY : puddles stood in the half-dry empty streets ; all life was withdrawn indoors ; cigarette packets and beer bottles from Saturday night lay about the pavements ; deserted piles of herring barrels—drifters' decks empty—quiet drifts of galley smoke—gulls' cries and a grey breeze : all Stornoway Sundays were rolled into one.

There had been no danger of missing the Rona Annual, it turned out. I went Sabbath breaking and called with misgiving on *Provider's* local skipper. Still a bit too much north in the breeze, said he, red-eyed in his doorway, too much for working up to the rocks in the small boat and the like o' that. There remained too much north in the breeze for a day or two. At intervals of keeping an eye on the *Provider* we looked into the interior moorland of Lewis.

> The island is compared to a gold laced hat ; the internal part of which consists of this soft and useless moor, and the circumference of which is in part more or less cultivated at the sea-side.

Eight ravens got up in a body from the moor ; an occasional blue mountain hare sprinted away ; we walked through the territories of golden plovers, handsome goldies, jet black and golden, querulously piping. Coming over a rise in the tundra, we opened a small loch upon which floated a pair of red-throated divers and a single black chick. The nest would, of course, be on the small grassy islet in the middle. In such cases the best writers found an addled egg sunk to the bottom ; we found the second chick hiding under the bank and giving itself away by small clucking noises. Floated off, it was buoyant as a cork, but had no idea of directional swimming. The dreadfully cold water lapped about a naturalist's fork.

177

The old birds could submerge imperceptibly until only periscope head and neck were showing. As one of them flew he uttered the queer hollow cry of his kind, the loon's traditional prognostic of rain :

> The rain goose, bigger than a duck, makes a doleful noise before a great rain. . . .

but as rain was generally falling or about to fall, the loon's call hardly signified.

One noted again the Ainslie method of fly-fishing, first seen on the burns of Sutherland and since unimproved, whereby some wretched little trout, in doubt whether or no it was hooked, found itself whipped from the burn and cast high over the fisherman's head upon the moorland far behind. Or we went past summer shielings into a higher country of tussocky sphagnum and sedge cut up with black bare peat drains. The shielings were turf-and-stone bothies roofed with tarpaulins— the country people's quarters during the annual migration of themselves and their cattle to the summer pasture of the moors. The all-black women went in and out, fetching and carrying.

*   *   *

In Stornoway, *Provider* lay at Number Two taking in paraffin for the Rona trip. They would be at Port o' Ness at seven in the evening, said the skipper, with a steadying hand against the bar ; " pick up Alec MacFarquhar and his boys." John was firmly not going to come. Some time after the drifter had sailed I drove up to Ness, giving a lift to a noted Scottish author who was joining the trip. " And did you rehabilitate the ancient ruins ? " he asked. A long wait at Ness ; Mr. MacFarquhar and his boys arrived and waited. The party was about a dozen men and boys and four dogs. This time the tenant had to supply the necessary small boat ; it was a leaky flat-bottomed wooden box pointed at one end. *Provider* at length turned up ; the fence posts and wire and dogs and ourselves all got out to her in the wooden box.

Butt of Lewis lit up as we left it on the quarter. The glass cage would already have been revolving, the weights sinking down the inside abyss of the tower, while meth still cooked up the burner.

> *The lights began to twinkle from the rocks:*
> *The long day wanes: the slow moon climbs: the deep*
> *Moans round with many voices.*

Provider rolled lifelessly in the swell, driving slowly N.N.E., steadily relinquishing the land. Looking after my own interests, I crept beneath a piece of sailcloth on deck. " Towards the north-northeist from Lewis, three score myles of sea. . . ."

At about four o'clock I woke and saw that we had found land, saw at once that we were steaming past the eastern cliff of Rona. The new day was half light with a chill sourness over the cold swell. *Provider* turned into the bay and anchored, still feeling the swell. All the flying clamour of sea-fowl ! The sea bobbed with seals' inquiring heads, young shags in a flock made the water boil where they dived. This was it—as at each island—but most of all at this farthest one : to come into the teeming, self-propelled, extra-human world. They all came out, flying in the steely dawn light to see what was up, the black-backs slowest and loudest, whirring auks, silent fulmars, oystercatchers yelping and terns screaming, kittiwark-kittiwark-kittiwark iterated and reiterated. Well, they would soon know. Once men, not black-backs, had ruled here and they still came back each year for one swift raid.

There was no difficulty over the landing at Geodha Stoth, once the wooden box had been thrown overboard, and baled, and more or less rowed in. The usual schedule, to land at break of day.

Part of the stone wall across the neck of Fianuis was down, and at first from the fallen stones came the beckoning purrs of a nursery of storm petrels. I listened in the ill-tasting dawn with much delight. The season's gulls' nests were already weathering ; a sheep lay dead and pulled about in the fank. The salt-bitten orache and the chickweed were the same, and the bird litter of feathers and corpses and white-splashed mutes and brought-up pellets—the heedless sea-bird slum of Rona !

I went with the shepherds up the old killing slope to the ridge. They followed the cliff edge round and came back up the southern slope in a mile-long front. Battered-looking sheep and scurrying grown lambs jostling with them began to move before the line. The necessary panic caught on and a body of sheep streamed in one pelting scare down the north hill and away into the rocky fastness of Fianuis. And there they stayed for five full hours while the men repaired the wall and erected the funnel fence leading into the fank. Poor stormies, that was the end of their new colony under the so suitable heap of dry stones.

I was free to go to the village. From the ridge again Sula Sgeir was rain-clear and even the mainland mountains just showed. The dawn had come out to a bright glare under a dirty white sky and to an air not rough enough to be cold.

The earthworks ! As John Wilson Dougal remarked of the Hebrides, " the first requisite when visiting these islands is to have been there before." So : the old cultivation ridges sweet with clover, the graveyard, the shepherds' stone set deep in silverweed, the musky smell of petrel, the chapel, the manse. I walked into the manse. The floor we had trodden into mud was again a virgin bed of chickweed, from which stuck out bits of bird-whitened packing cases. Starlings had been nesting in the chimney above the old tins we had left in a heap in the fireplace. There was a young fulmar in the usual cranny in the manse, two young fulmars and a failed egg in the gloom of St. Ronan's cell ; the old birds continued their inscrutable circlings of the village.

The scar where our tent had stood was now only a closer patch in the silverweed. The well below the chapel was quite dry. Another house puffin was back in the village.

Everywhere in the green walls were signs of new petrel diggings, trickles and piles of dry earth outside the miniature rabbit burrows. Some of last year's burrows were still complete with bung and marking peg, and it might have been the identical toady balls of down, " D " and " O " and " H " and the rest, which now sat inside. I lifted the flat stone under which we had found the first petrel chick on our very first morning in Rona : now, another generation of fat and fluff.

A walk on Rona attended by protesting sea-birds was timelessly as before : the view from the elevated hump, down and round to the inescapable sea, the same ground detail of puffin corpses scattered on the grass, young fulmars urgently pumping as one passed, occasional dead sheep or their skeletons. (Dead animals lying about, not cleared up : the mark of nature without man.)

Down at the fank the customary wild Gaelic shouting went on, the barking of dogs and the surge of terrified sheep. Hebrideans were about the only countrymen left who could still throw off their boots and run barefoot without a thought ? The mass of rams, ewes and fat bewildered lambs wavered in the mouth of the funnel. The decoy sheep, an earlier capture, baa-ed furiously at its tether. The fencing held, sheep gushed into the fank and stood in a panting baa-ing mass ; the dogs trotted over its continuous back. Shearing began, a merciful stripping of tattered fleeces. The fat lamb was killed and put to boil in the old iron pot over a fire of coals against the fank wall.

Now the sea-birds could be attended to by those not busy at the shearing. The one day raid of men was a sorry sight but its damage would not have equalled even a day's taking by the black-backs—and the black-backs caught it too. The rusted guns went off at the ranks of interested puffins, and of guillemots, and of shags ; a bloody sackful was collected for return to Lewis. Young fulmars could not help pumping and squirting when a man passed, so they got kicked out of their places or killed with a stone. One young fulmar kicked dead into a stagnant pool had filmed the water with its oil, as if it were a pad of oily cotton waste thrown out of an engine-room.

Seeing again all the young fulmars sitting so openly and

undefended, I felt sure that their oil-throwing was now defensive, whatever its origin. They survived—until to-day—under conditions where other nestlings would not have lasted five minutes, and to-day's sudden decimation emphasised their previous immunity. Neither John nor I had yet seen any black-back—fulmar encounter, of young or old, and last year when we had found the remains of two young fulmars in our collections of black-backs' castings, that had been after the shepherds' visit.

I had hoped, though without confidence, to get taken across to Sula Sgeir while the shepherds were busy in Rona ; the skipper had indeed said " aye." By now the driftermen were asleep or had dispersed to look for glass floats or to whistle to the seals. I knew it was no good when I saw the skipper come ashore with an ancient fowling-piece in one hand and a box Brownie in the other. But he did lend me the gun after he had killed four or five seals, " or anyway wounded the devils." John had asked me to try to get him a fulmar for dissection. Fulmars had wisely all cleared off to sea, and I could not find one until I had trudged to the other end of the island, to the rocks of Sceapull, where a few were still flying about. The skipper's gun was a very old double-barrelled 12-bore, red with rust and literally tied up with string and an elastic garter ; with it he had given me five cartridges, each loaded with a few pellets of AAA shot, a suitable size for despatching bullocks perhaps, or for dispersing mobs. I clicked back the hammers very gingerly indeed.

A fulmar came flying towards me. At about ten yards' range I let off both barrels. There was a deafening report and a far whistling of lead, but the fulmar remained inscrutable. I tried again carefully with one barrel and again clean missed. Two cartridges left; must get a sitting shot. I crept up to a fulmar, drew a bead on it and pulled the trigger as it took off. Nothing happened, but as I took the gun down it went off into the air with a vicious kick. No more fulmars until as I walked back just one came flying towards me. I knew it would come to no harm, nor did it.

182

One by one the sheep were shouldered and carried down to Geodha Stoth. A line had been rigged from drifter to shore and the sheep-box was ferried along it hand over hand, to and fro on the many journeys until some forty sheep had been loaded ; then the bags of wool and the fencing. Many sheep dripped from involuntary bathes as they stood jammed in the box with dirty water swilling about their legs. They were fenced in along the port side of the drifter's deck; the mess they made of a ship was the unpopular part of the charter for a Rona Annual.

Provider rolled to the swell, the engine putt-putted again from the exhaust port, paraffin vapours eddied round the sheep-boat. Microcosm of the sea, the dirty putt-putt-putting exhaust of a paraffin engine, dipping and choking under water ! The drifter stopped on her way out of the bay to pick up a dead sheep.

Sula Sgeir was tantalisingly clear, standing well below the horizon. No time for a try now, and anyway it was discovered that the ship had run out of fresh water, with six hours' steaming for Port of Ness. We all got very thirsty.

Provider reached Port of Ness by dusk. The sheep-box lost another large piece of gunwale going over the side and took another fill of water.

Only two or three weeks before the *Stornoway Gazette* had said :

—It is not Ness readers only, nor those resident in Lewis, but many people in distant parts of the Globe who will learn with regret that our Ness news no longer will come from the pen of Mrs. Macleod, Ocean Villa, Port-of-Ness. On grounds of health, Mrs. Macleod has been obliged to give up writing. For the past few years she has fought bravely against her failing eyesight, writing her notes on specially ruled paper, to guide her hand ; but now, on doctor's orders, she has been compelled to discontinue.

The Rona Annual was no longer reported.

*   *   *

I was back in Stornoway by midnight. We were now working to a very close schedule, to catch a steamer from the far end of Harris to go to North Uist and thence, hopefully, to find a way out to the Monach Isles. We packed up and set off on the 60-mile drive to Rodel, Harris, got there about five in the morning, slept a couple of hours in the car, and woke to bright sunshine. An early maid came out from the Rodel hotel and said that it was no use waiting for the steamer to come at seven-thirty a.m. because it came at seven-thirty p.m. A pity, that slight error in time-table reading, because now the Monach Isles could not be fitted in. Sixty miles back to Stornoway, to the *Lochness*, to the mainland. In twenty-four hours' time, early next morning, we were waiting in Mallaig for another steamer to take us to the Island of Eigg, for another try at shearwaters. Eigg stood a dozen miles away in the south-west, a raised plateau land with its Sgurr sticking up at the far end.

We breakfasted in Mallaig. Harvie-Brown would have done that, going off somewhere, or Charles St. John : Victorian breakfasters, breakfasting at the Inn in Mallaig.

North Rona Island, July 28, 1937

XV

The Voice of Eigg

THE steamer ploughed flocks of shearwaters. The birds
flew so low they nearly met their images in the oily calm ;
the set performance of flap and glide was as much a rhythm of
rise and fall as telegraph wires seen from a train. The mountains of the Small Isles stood mirrored in the sea.

We had hardly asked the captain about Eigg, her resources
and shearwaters, before his ship started cutting through the
flocks. Three friends of his were aboard, he said ; schoolmistresses, they knew all about Eigg. The captain was a large,
ruddy, hearty man with liquid eyes. He breezed up to his
three schoolmistresses in their deck-chairs and pulling up
above them, shouted : " There's a pretty girl for you now,
isn't she, eh ? "

It was a stroke of luck to meet Miss Macmillan, schoolmistress of Eigg, then on holiday. Soon she had given us two
strangers the run of the schoolhouse. We should find a garden
and were to eat anything we found growing in it or else it
would be wasted. We never got over the pace of Scottish
hospitality. The tent voyaged to the Flannans and back, and
to Eigg and back, and never came out of its bag.

A motor boat came out to meet the steamer. A lorry—or
the lorry—waiting on the jetty had the laird's title emblazoned
upon it : Sir Walter Runciman of Eigg. We put our goods
in the mail-cart and followed it up the hill, into the interior,
along the only road.

Eigg, obviously, was a nice island. Inner Hebrides of
course, and therefore after the Outer Isles seeming to burgeon
with well-being. The day before yesterday I had been a
hundred and fifty miles northward, in the far harsh desolation
of Rona, milling with sea-fowl under a dirty white sky.

185

To-day Eigg lay in southern summer hat and the white road was dusty.

The cultivated parts looked like a model farm, with the neat richness of whitewashed and freshly painted cottages, fuchsia bushes, small gardens and stone paving. We passed a real wood, and hanging thickets of hazel. Well-grown sycamores sheltered the steading of schoolhouse and schoolroom. The garden had a potato patch and rows of cos lettuces and carrots. We set up in the kitchen.

A little way on were the post-office, a shop and a cottage, three houses sharing a common iron roof. Beyond them the road curved downhill and opened the western seaboard of Eigg, the broad coastal plain of Cleadale, piece-patched with crofts and edged by the silvery sands of the Bay of Laig. Inland, the plain rose to a two-mile rampart of cliffs, which fenced off the plateau moorland. The works of man fitted nicely into island topography. Thus the road crossed the saddleback between the huge southern block of the Sgurr and the northern moorland plateau, and thus the unit of shop—post-office—school stood on the saddleback, at the divide, equidistant between the north-west community of Cleadale crofts and the south-east township of jetty and boat anchorage (" haven for heighland bottis ").

We took several opinions about shearwaters from Cleadale crofters. They agreed that the inaccessible " up there "—the rampart of inland cliffs—was shearwaters' nesting ground. We climbed up to the foot of the cliffs in sunshine at the end of the day. The cliffs went on up another four or five hundred feet to reach the thousand-foot level. Down below was the crofters' patchwork of potatoes and oats and hay, long shadows to the dotted haycocks. Beyond them lay the deserted sands and the silvery sea, the black shadow side of the peaks of Rum and, soon to sink behind them, the eye of the westering sun.

We had not had a night in bed lately so for a start we went back to the schoolhouse and had a good sleep. During the rest of our four days in Eigg the remarkable thing that hap-

pened was a heat wave. We splashed in and out of the not
unwarm sea which tide by tide advanced and retreated across
the sands of the Bay of Laig, slept in the sun or shuffled bare
feet into the hot sand, the Singing Sand, and made it produce
its unnatural squeaks and grunts. Blue sea, hazy sky pale and
hot, not a soul about.

At night, after the evening rise of midges had subsided, we
stood in the doorway of the schoolhouse and heard the distant
eerie cackling of shearwaters. The road was a pale gleam, the
still air heavy with the scent of meadow sweet. When we
came down into the plain the warm darkness was a living body
of noise, the whole cliff front above threw down a steady roar
like distant cheering. The cries of individual birds nearer to
but high out of torch range were sharp punctuations to the
background mêlée. We sat down at the roadside in the stilly
dark : one way the sound of the sea, the other, shearwaters ;
nothing else. Whatever number of such sharp discontinuous
exclamations must have been required to blend into one steady
roar ? It was not, for instance, like motor-car noise that easily
merged to make a roar of traffic. Rather, how many cuckoos
to make an unvarying surge of sound with no element of
" cuckoo " recognisable. The near, individual, shouted-out
calls were something like kok-kok-kar-ooo (sort of), with many
variations ; the last syllable sounding like a gasping intake of
breath. It was the same loud abandon as of fork-tails' nights
but on an altogether different scale, over a couple of miles
of ground instead of an acre.

We scrambled up again to the base of the cliff breastwork.
Even up here the sound of breakers nearly a mile away was
so clear it seemed that a jump would reach the sea. The birds
were still above us, streaking in wide circles and all the time
yelling out their calls. Patches of mist made torches little use.
An invisible bird would go tearing across the sky, shrieking as
if pursued of fiends, then abruptly in mid-sentence the noise
would cut out ; most eerie ; as if a knife had suddenly sliced
off the bird's head. The noise of loud beating wings sometimes
came so near that one felt like ducking. Black blurrs loomed

187

instantly from the darkness. Bats outa hell, the circus of the cocklolly birds.

Several times we heard the plop of a bird landing, and finally had one in the torch beam, particularised from the darkness, pinned and seen. It shuffled down a burrow. We pulled away turf and soft earth and laid open a nesting chamber, completely filled by a large lump of grey down. This young one was both heavier and bulkier than its parent. It was calling disproportionate baby-bird squeaks, trying to make its parent feed it, indifferent to both torchlight and excavation. An adult shearwater's beak was very damaging, we soon found. We patched up the burrow and left them.

With more practice we caught torchlit glimpses of shearwaters shuffling down or leaving burrows. They seemed to need some little eminence to achieve a clear take-off; otherwise they issued from their burrows at speed, wings half open, and as often as not got bunkered in the fern lower down. I heard a bird crash with a loud cry and spotted it awkwardly placed in a honeysuckle bush. It half opened its wings and used them like arms to clamber towards a burrow entrance higher up. When we came back in daylight and took out the heavy obstreperous young one from the first burrow, it worked its wings in just the same way, and used its beak like a grappling hook to hoist itself uphill.

Dawn began to spread, gradually to silence the birds and to drive them back to sea. The sun came up, travelled round, and sank, shining full on to the silent empty face of the cliffs.

Next night was clear to the stars. The starry host was so thickly sown it seemed that one must be able to trace the path of a calling shearwater across the sky by the stars it would eclipse on its way. But no, though in the clear air torchlight could find the flying birds. One felt about with the beam for the travelling noise above . . . suddenly caught the white cigar-shape and followed as it went on quick, shallow-beating wings. The long narrow wing area of course made shearwaters magnificent high-speed fliers, but carried also the penalties of both a high landing speed, and thus many crashes,

1. NORTH RONA, *from the wheelhouse of stem drifter "Rose" July 16' 1936*

2. THE MANSE inhabited

FIANUIS on a wild day   *John Ainslie*

3. LEACH'S PETREL OBSERVED: *petrel-weighing scales constructed and in use; lattice at mouth of burrow, disarranged by petrel's entry; petrel chick and adult*

4. RAZORBILLS, *west cliff of Rona. "Bracket" razorbills (see p. 74);*
razorbills and puffin airborne in a gale. (Composite Photograph.)

5. CHAPEL, *North Rona. The left-hand end is St. Ronan's cell. Below: Looking down into the cell; plan of chapel and cell; the three-holed cross from the graveyard, photographed in Teampull Mholuidh, Lewis, with T.S. Muir's drawing of 1857 copied over it*

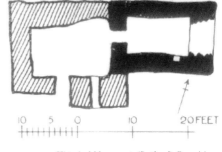

10   5   0   10   20 FEET

Historical Monuments (Scotland) Commision
Malcolm Stewart

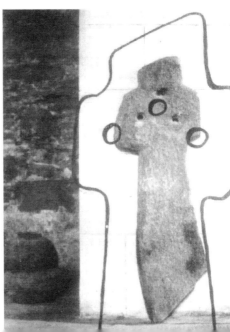

6. VILLAGE, *North Rona*. Above: *View from the chapel, looking south-westwards over the earthworks (manse at centre) towards Sceapull.* Below: *Old lazy-beds above the village (chapel at centre)*

7. Loading Sheep at the East Landing, *Rona Annual, July 28, 1937*

8. RED-NECKED PHALAROPES,
*chick and male parent, photographed
on a North Uist loch*

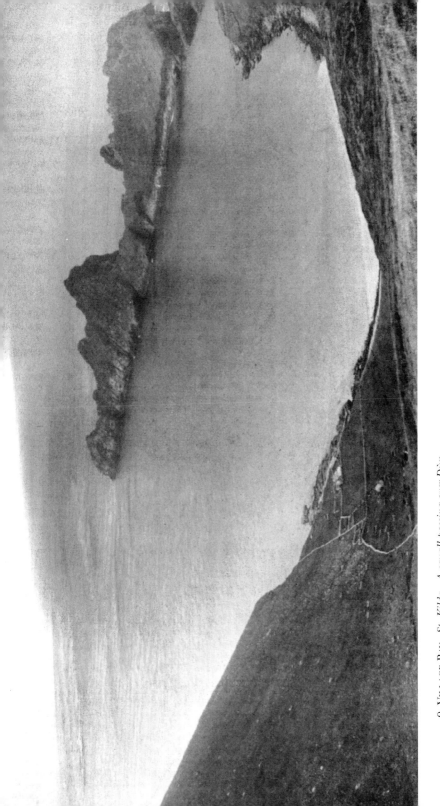

9. VILLAGE BAY, St. Kilda. *A squall passing over Dùn*

10. St. Kilda Village, July 1938

11. St. Kildans: *Finlay MacQueen bottom left); Mrs. Gillies spinning outside Number 11 and Neil Gillies sitting within; Neil Gillies at the post office*

12. Soay Sheep and St. Kilda Field Mouse: *A young ram in the Great Glen; a mouse in captivity; home-made mouse-traps baited and set*

13. FOWLING, *St. Kilda. Finlay MacQueen catching puffins in 1938 and in 1896; -and a visitor's drawing of 1876*

J. Sands

Cherry Kearton

Northern block (Lunndastoth) from the southern

½ mile

Lunndastoth

View

¼

Landing place

Geodha Blatha Mor

View

Bothies

"Teampull" (Tigh Mhaoldonuich)

Sgeir an Teampuill

Creag Trithaiga

Cairn 229 ft.

Bealach an t-Suidhe

O

Southern block (Sgeir an Teampuill (L) and Creag Trithaiga) from Lunndastoth. Teampuill shows against sea in centre

14. SULA SGEIR,
August 3 1939.
(Area of gannetry dotted in)

15. BOTHIES, *Sula Sgeir, by day and by night, August 3-4, 1939; the night flighting of Leach's petrels*

16. THE "HEATHER" AT THE SHIANT ISLES, *lying under the cliffs of Garbh Eilean,
July 22, 1946*

and of difficulties in taking off, thus the required eminence. Shearwaters had a hardly perceptible petrel-type smell and they did not vomit or throw oil. Being largely or entirely fish feeders—their tongues and palates serrated—they went different ways at sea from petrels proper ; it was unpetrel-like to flock close in to the shores of Eigg, in daylight. However, their night life remained of a kind with stormies' and fork-tails', though on a mob-like scale. For them, too, even with their vicious bills, the land was dangerous. (Again it was only the fulmar that was able to leave its oil-spitting chick out in the open.) We saw three or four shearwaters' carcases, one of them turned inside out—the black-backs' trade mark. Camp followers, we thought, clearing up the injured or dead.

Another dawn began to show. There were loud rustlings of wings as birds came out of their burrows and took off for the sea. We heard particular noises from a deep crevice under a boulder. The bird had been on its way out but torchlight turned it back. We sat down and waited, hoping that the out-to-sea impulse would be strong enough to dare the bird to emerge before daylight should put a final stopper on the hole. I had one flash-bulb left. The dawn grew while we waited and waited. Deadlock : we couldn't see without torchlight, and that immediately turned the bird back.

At last came a louder, faster scuffle. Torchlight caught the bird half-way out. The blinding instant of the flash showed it crouching under the rock, looking fierce and reptilian as it stretched out its head. In the reaction of complete darkness we heard it launch out and go whirring away.

The flash—the stab of brilliance that broke instantaneously as one jabbed a thumb on to the contact button—lasted about a fiftieth of a second. In that time the eye recorded a tableau of extraordinary detail, brighter and sharper than photograph ever was, a fixed unchosen mind picture. My tableau arrested the beady-eyed shearwater, crouching black and white, momentarily hesitating before it took off—more lifelike than life. The photograph recorded by the same flash was by comparison lifeless and posed ; and out of focus.

Next morning the schoolhouse alarm clock got us up in the darkness of four o'clock : perfectly still and warm. The mail cart came rumbling along the gritty road and halted to load our goods. We locked the schoolhouse door and hid the key in the place in the garden wall, as we had been told ; and in the half-light and still half-asleep, trudged off behind the mail cart to catch the bi-weekly steamer.

Eigg Island, July 30–August 3, 1937

FOURTH YEAR

NORTH UIST
MONACH ISLES
ST KILDA

*

1938

XVI

Sea-board, North Uist

"ST. KILDA enjoys the distinction of being the remotest of
all the Isles of the British Seas," wrote Dr. William Eagle
Clarke, who ought to have known better than to deal in
journalists' superlatives. (North Rona for one was handsomely
remoter, farther and lonelier.) "Surrounded by a halo of
romantic interest," he went on, and this sort of thing was
liable to prejudice a later island-goer. However, "much
bewritten St. Kilda . . . far-out group of islands," was the
best mark it got from Harvie-Brown. In his time fulmars were
a chief draw, still almost confined there, and were "invariably
seen and noted by all naturalists who have *done* the St. Kilda
trip." So, back in 1935, John Ainslie and I had opted for
Rona, rejecting Flannans with a lighthouse, and overdone St.
Kilda with a tourists' steamship service and who knew what
else ? Picture postcards for sure, some sort of home-made
trinket or memento, even orange peel ?

Second thoughts went to the other extreme. In 1930 the
remnant population of St. Kilda had on their own petition been
evacuated and resettled in mainland crofts. A few of these
natives still went back to the island for a month or two in the
summer, for the sake of old times. For three weeks in the
summer of 1931 a joint Oxford and Cambridge University
Expedition had been there to record the whole state of fauna
and flora, to make a control at the end of centuries of habitation, for change and comparisons to come. By now the village
must be falling into decay, early stages of ruin long passed by
other island villages. The pleasurable melancholy of far,
abandoned places would no doubt be there already. Change in
some sort must be showing in the face of the land, to any

193

one—to myself if possible—coming this eighth year after the evacuation and primed with the findings of the 1931 expedition. The place in desertion must be more than ever a naturalists' mecca. Leach's petrels of course, but also St. Kilda wrens, St. Kilda mice in two sorts, the wild race of Soay sheep. These were known, but what natural encroachments might there not be for the finding out ?

No doubt the romantic interest was well founded. It would be new to see the tourist trade so far-flung, documentary to note picture postcards of the desert island and orange peel in the crumbling village ? Besides, the only way of getting there would be by cruise steamer, go out with one cruise and come back with the next, so rationalising was essential. Having got amongst the Western Isles, absurd not to have St. Kilda in one's repertoire !

It came to this, that I abandoned my employment in order to go to an island. Not without misgiving, I hoped to pick it up again in the autumn. The proprietor of St. Kilda, Lord Dumfries,[1] generously gave permission for a stay on the island. I was to live in the one-time factor's house, and I nursed a letter to the watcher, Neil Gillies, who would be on the island during the summer. I had Martin's *Late Voyage to St. Kilda* of 1698 and John Mathieson's six-inch map of 1928, another box of flash-bulbs and a stock of mouse-traps.

John Ainslie was a doubtful starter, but would anyway come up to the Hebrides for a week or two. To begin with, we thought we would try again for the Monach Isles. This time he came forward with his own car, a silvery-bodied beetle of a thing with no ground clearance, which scraped its tin bottom even on the provocation of our respective byroads. Off we went on the sunny Monday morning of July 4th, 1938.

Lights on at ten-thirty p.m. and off again at four-thirty a.m. The car's bottom clanged and grated along the Mallaig road. The early morning hung overcast for an hour or two before opening to broiling sun. The islands had never looked so well ! Eigg lay like a grey man-o'-war in a deep blue sea

[1] Now Marquess of Bute

flecked with white, Rum's screes and lifting slopes were velvety
under the sun and patched with shadows. The high tops rose
into cumulus, seeming to support the snowy pile. A pall came
over and brought a shower of large hail, whereby lumps of
ice bounced on the hot deck. Gradually the increasing chilling
breeze killed the sunshine ; this was more Hebridean ; the
annual relinquishing of precious summer. Our different car
was parked in the usual niche at the back of the fish-market.

They had had no kind of summer at all, people said. The
peats had not dried at all, they were still using last year's. Old
Mr. Macleod over at Bernera had had his lobster pots aboard
the *Rhoda* since early in the month of June, and never a chance
yet to put them down, with the big northerly swell.

(The oldeſt people affirm, that ſince their youth, the climate
and feaſons are greatly changed for worſe.)

The Shiant Isles had been sold, and Canna too ; MacBrayne's
steamer had just landed the first car on Canna for the new
proprietor (one imagined it tearing from one end of the road
to the other, captive). Up at Ness, Alec MacFarquhar said that
the mutton prices were not worth a trip to Rona, but he would
have to go next year. If you left a wether there for three years
it would run to fat and be useless. It was the oil on the grass,
the film from the sea-birds' droppings. The sheep couldn't
take the grass and leave the oil. At Port of Ness, Miss Daisy
Macleod had opened a lonely tea-room, while yet in black for
old Mrs. Macleod.

After a day or two of old acquaintance we spread out maps,
West Coast Pilot and MacBrayne's time-table, and planned the
car and steamer route to North Uist ; and thence to the
Monach Isles ?

*   *   *

Table decoration in the Lochmaddy hotel was cut glass
bowls of wax water-lilies—but they were real ones ! Cosmopolitan potted palms and brassy jugs accompanied the necessary

195

stuffed wild cat and glazed 32-lb. salmon. The nearest we were to see to a tree in North Uist was a ten-inch fir, dead, in a pot outside the hotel.

We drove on westwards across the island, scraping and clanging, going anti-clockwise round the circular road. North Uist was moor, stones and lochs, at once more desolate and derelict than Lewis and Harris to northward, or Barra to southward. The dusk wind was chill. We came to the shore and there, far and faint in the Western Ocean, stood the pin heads of St. Kilda.

The road went on southwards and started to recurve south-eastwards before we had a good view of the Monach Isles. They made a low-lying green strip with a gleam of white beaches, five or six miles offshore ; at the northern end the tiny stem of the lighthouse was just discernible, regularly locating itself by the white flashes. We had spoken it a year ago. At that, night falling and since we couldn't get any nearer by land, we turned off into the moor along a cart-track. This led to a large sunken sheep fank with a concrete dipping-trough. The fank gave some shelter from the wind so we pitched the tent in it. The patter of rain on tent-cloth soon began. Next morning in the rain, I sat on a stone outside the tent, dressed in two extra sweaters and an oilskin, and my hands were blue with cold.

We went down to the shore over the machair. Proper, large-scale machair was new to us and surprising, after the accustomed waste of Hebridean bog and stone, yet in the same climate. It was the belt of close, flowery, sweet turf, stretched acre on acre immediately inland of the marram grass and dunes of a sandy shore. The turf was but a web of roots filled with sand ; the machair did not look green, it was either yellow or clover-white. There were very fields of yellow, low-growing buttercups with double-sized flowers. Heartsease and the yellow balls of bird's-foot trefoil were like the oversize blooms of alpine flowers. The cupped flowers blew with their backs to the wind ; the cover of plants was only two or three inches deep ; the machair was a counterpane of flowers laid over the sand. The cold wet wind came straight off the sea and at once picked up the smell of clover. In any less wet climate the machair sands would have been desert; the calcareous shell-sand offered nothing that a plant could use for coarse growth, so it was scented flowers all the way, kept going by daily rains.

Inland of the machair the sand progressively darkened with peat humus. This made the crofters' arable ground, little strips and squares of potatoes, corn and hay, so wind-blown and full of weeds that only near-to were they perceptible as under cultivation, except where corn marigolds marked them from afar. Intermittent fences of drooping wire were gated with bits of iron bedsteads. Crofters' sheep, cattle and horses were tethered each in its circle of grazed and trodden ground. Crofters' Uist was a hotbed of corncrakes; they were grating away day and night, even all night until the first larks went up with the dawn, and then on again through the full round of daylight.

Inland of the sown, solid rock began to stick out and so led away into the universal wilderness: rock bare or rock hidden below the ever-building peat, and every hollow full of water.

Wind-streamed marram grass bound the dunes. Where marram gave way to machair it was as if it were gracefully retiring, handing over the captive sand to sweeter flowers, but if bare sand showed in some loosening bunker the marram was on to it again like a knife. Between dunes and sea were fifty yards of flat hard beach where the wind blew sand clouds, so that the whole plain looked to be moving and the billions of running grains made a loud rustling noise. The Sound of Monach was green, not bottomless Atlantic grey, a short, steep, green-and-white sea, too tumbled for a small boat. It continued so for a few days.

All the time in wind and rain dunlins were trilling, and larks singing in the wet sky, and peewits calling everywhere. They and other things soon made an impression of something other than Hebrides, some other time and place. As soon as it was conscious, it clicked. Of course, this was early spring again. The cold, but all the flowers, the wet unsheltered feeling, the singing birds, the open unleafed space, everything so fresh. The feel of it had built up unconsciously, then, suddenly, was conscious and recognised. How dunlins' fresh trilling by a bleak northern seaside should so force the impression of southern, inland, early spring, I don't know, but it was so.

At Locheport, A. Ferguson, General Merchant, was magnate and monopolist. His was the petrol pump (embossed with a Scotch thistle), his bus ran to and from Lochmaddy, and the post-office was incorporated in his store, where he sold provisions, ironmongery, Harris tweed, clothes, and the miscellanea called fancy goods. No single food in A. Ferguson's shop was endemic to the Isles or even to Scotland, unless canned Scotch broth by Heinz should be counted. The slightly unusual black or green treacle was an imported sweetie common to all Hebridean shops. Tea, margarine and Glasgow wrapped bread were staple here as elsewhere.

In the Lochmaddy hotel Highland cattle were glazed in mist, but round about our fank a herd of the shaggy creatures grazed animate. The herdsman in oilskins turned his back on the weather and leant on his stick. We had a flat tyre, he said. He had used to drive a car in the island himself; he used to break a spring every week, he said, not without pride. Now this was the job, taking the cattle out to graze at six in the morning, standing by them all day keeping them off the crops, taking them home at seven in the evening. But the money was good and he would qualify for the relief. That was the only idea the young men had—to qualify; they would be away in Glasgow in a job, and then come back for six months on the relief. If you asked a man to do a day's work at the peats he would want his card stamped first. They were nearly all unemployed in Uist. And at the hotel, the moneyed fishers : Why did the islanders want a daily mailboat ? So they could stand and watch it every day instead of only four times a week—ha ha ha.

Each morning the herdsman left an old whisky bottle of new milk beside our tent. His own croft was half a mile away, a done-up black house with a chimney and the neatest fringe of boulders round the eaves. The tiny living-room with a sanded floor and a large stove contained hens and friendly collies ; there were also two enormous counterfeit dogs, in china, on the mantelpiece. The windows were hardly more than loopholes in the three-foot-thick walls ; wire netting and geraniums at the outside entrances to the tunnels blocked what little light they might have given. The address of the croft, planted alone beside the pot-holed track across the moor, was 2, Main Road.

*   *   *

While the weather continued too bad to go to the Monach Isles, we inquired after the great rarity, red-necked phalarope, said by bird books to survive in Uist.

Our first visitor at the sheep fank was the postman, who jumped down from his cart of post-office red. We stood and talked of this and that while the rain pattered on the backs of our oilskins. Now, had the postman possibly ever seen, or heard of, a small bird called a phalarope ? (to rhyme with see). He had not. This was a small bird something like a snipe, which lived in marshes. Ah, just over on yon loch he had sometimes seen a rare bird. It was very neat—he cupped his hands—it had a thin neck. "You know, it's an awfu', bonny wee bird." Had it any red on it ? Aye, pinkish it was, on its neck. Phalarope then ? (to rhyme with hope). Aye, that was it, that was the name. John Macdonald now, he had been a gillie in the island of Skye and had known Mr. Seton Gordon ; he might be able to tell us a definite place to look. We wondered if we had fluked the right place, first time and without even trying.

The home loch pointed out by the postman was a stretch of rain-swollen water overflowing banks of close-cropped grass or quaking bog ; there was no cover at all. The wind whipped up waves into a line of foam-suds along the lee shore. There was no sign of any small bird with a red, or pinkish, neck.

John Macdonald when found was an old man and lame. He said there used to be plenty of phalaropes in a loch along the road. It was the first loch after the old church grave. We should ask for Angus Macdonald at the first house that met you after the new church.

We failed to be met by Angus Macdonald's house. We tried a tin-roofed cottage which indeed contained two Angus Macdonalds, but they were both the wrong ones. It seemed that one of them was the old man with a snowy beard who came up to us and shook hands, saying, " I'm eighty-one years old." " You're doing fine," I replied and he was delighted. Did we think he would last another twenty ? But he might die to-morrow . . . aged chortle.

At another house two more Angus Macdonalds were living, but they were both out. One of them might have been the right one, particularly as the cottage was " Church View 1933." All the bleak landscape hereabouts was an undulating area of crofts, unfenced crops, moor, and seas of bankless loch and bog. The tethered beasts stood miserably tails to rain. The one describable landmark was a raised stony track leading past a green islet in the bog-and-water featurelessness. On the islet were the ruins of a possible church ; this was perhaps the church grave. We splashed and gurgled in the vicinity but saw nothing.

Angus Macdonalds were again away from Church View next morning and all day. At intervals of splashing about on our own we returned to the tent, laced ourselves inside, and tried to keep warm. Every now and then we ate more bully beef and Glasgow wrapped bread, and drank cold slimy water from the sheep-trough. I happened to ask a spectacled crofter, pushing his bicycle, if he had ever heard of a rare bird called a phalarope (see) or phalarope (hope). Aye, it was the red-necked phalarope he called it. (Englishman in stumbling French met with perfect English.) He had seen a pair of the birds on the shore of the loch against his own croft. " I would think they must be breeding,"

He laid down his bicycle and led us along the same track past the church grave islet. We got to the corner of the loch and there promptly enough was the neat little dark bird, swimming about among the water growth a few yards out. It was going in fits and starts, pecking at something it saw on the surface ; it answered to the life any photographs, drawings or descriptions we had ever seen, here on this chance-found loch of all the innumerable lochs of Uist. John stayed by it, to see what it was up to, while I went right round the shore in the hope of flushing its mate.

Red cones of polygonum rose in a little forest from the water ; the wind made flags of their leaves, which slapped and crackled with a noise like burning wood. I saw no phalarope but kept flushing dunlins and incidentally captured a baby coot. This little morsel, a warm ball of fluff with cold wet feet, was covered with long sooty down streaked with tawny hairs ; its head was surprisingly totem-coloured, both fluff and skin beneath it were blue, orange and red, and most of its bill was scarlet. When I had completed the circuit an old man came up and asked, Was I looking for birds' nests ? Yes, phalaropes' nests. Well, then, he would show me one against his croft. A small wader sprang up from the grass some way ahead : the nest was a deep cup quite overarched and it contained four pointed eggs, a dunlin's nest.

All that Angus Macdonald could say when next day we did meet him face to face, was that the birds were very scarce and nested in April and took their young to the sea. He had little English. In the summer he would see them but not now. The Uist summer was evidently evasive.

For a long time we worked a nearby marsh. The wind drove curtains of rain and mist across it ; we only persevered because two or three phalaropes accompanied us, calling their pleasant chippy calls—pleasant at first but soon irritating. Part of the marsh was quagmire divided by bottomless black leads of open water. The crust heaved and swelled like thin ice before a skater. It gurgled up thick black bubbles and gave off a very ancient and fish-like smell. The rest was grass, flooded by six inches of water. Uist was sinking fast.

I sat down on a single rock sticking out of the flood. The stage of a July birds'-nesting expedition : rain down your neck, flapping oilskins, numbed fingers, leaky gumboots. John splashed to and fro with a couple of phalaropes chirruping round his head. The only dry land was on two or three rabbity mounds and they were smooth as a lawn. We went back to the car for more bully beef and Glasgow bread, and a good sit-down.

" I believe you would also see the birds on a big loch over there," the spectacled crofter had said, so for a next cast we followed his direction, and came to a bay in the shore of a wide loch. It was obvious from first sight that this corner was a perfect hive of wild birds ; at once a phalarope was floating on the water.

Here a corncrake got up, spilling a brood of coal-black chicks. A coot had laid six spotted eggs in a clump of butter-cups on an islet in the bay. A baby dabchick, so young that it could not swim but could not help floating, lay on the water with its legs straddled behind and its wing-stumps spread, looking helpless. When it tried to dive it got its head under, but its fluffy other end remained proud ; the frog-kicks of its legs threw up a miniature spray. Along the shore was a colony of arctic terns at every stage from egg to grown young. A pretty sight to see was an old bird quivering on the wing above its swimming nestling, and passing over a silvery fish. Here also were a wild duck's nest, a pair or two of ringed plovers, a summer party of turnstones. Dunlins, here as everywhere else, kept trilling their April-fresh calls in the rain, and running about with their black tummies of summer plumage looking as if they'd been wading in black sewage.

For a few minutes sunshine burst upon the boglands. Terns' squawking, blood-red bills and chalky wings were backed by a momentarily blue sky. You had only to stand still for a tern to swoop and deliver a hearty buffet. On the grass was the shadow of your own head, and near it the shadow of a hovering tern ; the tern released its spring, the shadows approached ; you saw the impact impersonally at second hand, but felt it at first hand.

But phalaropes were the thing. When we first walked round the islet in the bay two minute chicks went running and stumbling through the grass forest to the water. We caught both, phalarope chicks perhaps two days hatched, fluffy mites as lively as kittens. They swam wonderfully well and fast, buoyant as ping-pong balls, with so little displacement that it looked as if they must overbalance ; away they drove, leaving a tiny wash. Phalarope breeding economy being practically a reversal of the sexes, it was the male who fluttered down at the water's edge and stood clucking like a diminutive hen. The chicks hurried cheeping towards him, holding out their wing-stumps in their haste. We stood four feet away. He turned to meet his chicks and when they arrived, fluffed out his breast feathers and took them in, all motherly and inefficient, in an inch of cold water.

If red-necked phalaropes were as common as moorhens probably their cuckoo-extraordinary breeding habits and their irresistible trait of tameness would give them a popular status equal to that of nightingale or of cuckoo itself. The female was the handsome one, brightly coloured and disinterested ; the drab aberrant male was discovered doing the work. Evidently the female laid the eggs only because the male could not. He, dowdy and flustered, bustled round our legs when we were near his chicks, while she sat away on the water and looked distant.

Their indifference to oneself made phalaropes happy creatures to watch, so driven by their own high-pitched rest-lessness. The way they bathed, ducking and shuffling, was as if the energy of a dozen farmyard ducks was being released by one little bird like a snipe. Water must have been as sub-stantial to them as dry land, the way they jumped on and off it, or scooted feather-light across it. (I paddled in a foot of water over an uncertain bottom, trying to point, focus and

expose a camera on mercurial adult or fast-swimming chick,
while terns banged me on the head.) They flitted constantly
from one thing to another ; even the solicitous male of the
islet would flit off to bathe, his chicks apparently immediately
forgotten and, half a minute later, as suddenly remembered.
We spent two days with them, and left phalarope *père* gathering
his young along the green shore.

XVII

The Monach Isles

THE beams of the Monach Light came nightly through the sea mist to us in the sheep fank ; they swelled and faded on their unchanging travel, coming up and passing like a car's headlights across a bedroom wall. As soon as the weather should improve the fank was going to be occupied by sheep and we should remove to the Monach Isles. Meanwhile the source of light remained distant.

A head pushed into the tent one morning, said, " Och, but you're having a fine sleep ! "—which had been true a moment before. This was Norman Macdonald, jovial boatman, about to cross to the Monach Isles. We could share the trip with two botanist gentlemen who had also been waiting for weather. I went on ahead to see whether the car would be likely to manage the mile of cart-track to the shore. At first the arable soil was a little darkened by peat—hereabouts plough farming was on quite a large scale—but potato fields near the shore were so drifted with white sand that the crop seemed to be growing in a sea beach. Looking back, the car was a silver dot in acres of waving barley ; it lurched slowly along like a beetle in rough grass. It achieved the end of the track, where we left it more or less bogged in loose sand to look after itself. Norman Macdonald's motor-boat, a small double-ender with Kelvin housed in a matchboarding box, had already been brought round to the beach and now rode anchored as near in as she could float. The two botanists were very well equipped with enormous new rucksacs, drying presses and vascula, and large hobnailed boots. Norman Macdonald had thigh-boots so we all went aboard by his broad shoulders.

The Kelvin would not start until its plug—the engine had

but the one lung—had been taken out, blown on, and replaced. Then we thrust ahead like a speed-boat. The little Monach jetty was dried out, so Norman Macdonald, as he remarked, had to be a wee horse again. We pitched the tent in a perfect dell close at hand. The botanical dell was inferior and farther off.

The island we were on, Ceann Ear or Ceaner, still inhabited, was the biggest of the group. Locally, it was called Heisker, and written Heiskir by Martin. Counting from west to east it came number four of the five Monach Islands : Shillay with the lighthouse was westernmost, then came Ceann Iar or Ceaniar, Shivinish and Ceann Ear—all three interconnected by reefs and sands dry at low water ; " of the same mould with the big island," as Martin said. He mentioned neither Shillay nor the fifth island, Stockay, offlying to the east—two terminal islets not of the common mould.

After the rock-bound outermost isles this Monach group was different not in degree but in kind, being nothing but five miles of sand-dunes and machair. Certainly the islands had a backbone of rock, even breaking out into reefs and twenty-foot cliffs, but it was sand which met the assault of ocean. We were used to the stern resistance of great rock cliffs. Here the seas were subtly shallowed and spent themselves on flat sand. " They come—they mount—they charge in vain " . . . the marram-bound dunes remained dry.

On Ceann Ear the dunes made a wall round an inland amphitheatre of machair, a mile across, flat as a plate, hundreds of acres of smooth, sheep-dotted, sweet machair. From one end to the other the Monach Isles were barefoot ground. Buttercups and daisies and white clover made up most of the machair, then there were drifts of bedstraw, plantains with their heads a halo of stamens, eyebright bright open to the sky, dwarfed mauve crane's-bill, stonecrop, kidney vetch tough-rooted deep in the sand, bird's-foot trefoil, thyme, heartsease. Here as in Uist, sand always showed through, the plants' roots went down too deep to make the fibrous mat of an ordinary turf. Heartsease with double-sized flowers was

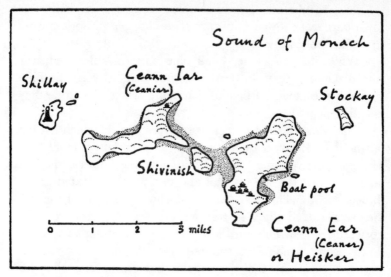

Fig. 6. *Sketch map of Monach Isles*

the beauty of the machair. Late low sunlight shone through the pretty pansy faces in a glow of orange and yellow.

Late sunlight threw into relief the webbed footmarks of terns, so slight in the loose sand that they were invisible when the sun was high. Terns' eggs were laid in scoops in the sand ; even as one looked the wind began to drift sand round them. After rain, the nests which had been sat on could be told by the circle of dry sand round the eggs. There was a big colony of arctic terns just along the beach from our dell. Nearly all the usual sea-birds were missing, for the want of cliffs.

Marram grass streamed as water before the wind, the sunshine marked each shaft not silvery nor yet white, but with the colour of light. The shadows of marram were like pencil lines drawn on the sand, like shadows of dead grass stems sticking up from snow ; the grainy texture of the white sand was like snow. The wind had carved the dunes into curves and crests as if the sand were driven snow. Sometimes the wind had undone the marram grass binding ; one ten-foot sand cliff was entirely screened by a network of bared marram

207

rootlets, as fine and closely detailed as a skeleton leaf. Our own bare feet showed hundreds of minute red pin-pricks from the marram points.

While the sun shone, small blue butterflies fluttered over the machair ; they fluttered over our dell between the blue sky and the moving fringe of marram ; when rain came they all disappeared.

The worst of the weather was fierce showers which fell for an hour or two and then passed away over Uist ; more blue sky spread from the sea and the blue butterflies came out again. When the sun was hot and fleecy clouds floated in the blue, the Monach Isles seemed the chosen place of the earth. Seaweed trailed slimy in tiny inshore waves, backwards and forwards in slow ebb and flow. The tide lines across acres of hard white sand were littered with worn, china-smooth shells. Near in, the sea would be green, stained with purple by seaweed forests—ah, the wine-dark sea ! Off-lying rocks were collared with surf. Farther out, the sea colour darkened, bluer and deeper blue, thicker and thicker with colour. The tide crept over the sands of the fords ; at high water a line of breakers showed the shallowest way from Ceann Ear to Shivinish and from Shivinish to Ceann Iar, whose single deserted cottage had once been the home of a Monach boatman. From there to Shillay with the lighthouse it was deep water.

On a winter afternoon two years before, two of the light-keepers, returning in their small boat from Ceann Ear to Shillay with mails, had been overtaken by the seas and drowned; now no boat was allowed.

These islands had not yet gone all the way common to outlying islands—dwindling population ending in desertion. Two families still lived on Ceann Ear, where ten years before there had been eight. Half a dozen houses stood roughly grouped on the bare turf—the village ; two were still inhabited. There were five children to attend the schoolhouse. Nowadays the living was mostly sheep ranching on the miles of machair. A little arable ground remained under cultivation in the south-west corner of the island, where the sand was slightly darker ; " a sandy soil, and very fruitful in Corn and Grass, [and] Black Cattle," said Martin. Time past, men working in island fields ! Even a personality had come down, a Macdonald naturally :

> *Neil Mackdonald* in the Island Heiskir is subject to the falling of the Tonsels at every change of the *Moon*, and they continue only for the first Quarter, this infirmity hath continued with him all his days, yet he is now 72 Years of Age.

Martin went on about the lack of fuel, how the inhabitants had to burn cow-dung, straw and seaweed. Nowadays they were burning coal in the two houses, " sea-coales," which gave an indoor atmosphere different from the usual Hebridean flavour of peat, though the varnished matchboarding and the wooden benches were correct. The crofters said it was less trouble to buy coal than to try to get men to cut peat in Uist.

There was no depressed area degeneration about the last two crofters ; they were the finest specimens of bullock physique I ever saw. In the sun, the giants worked at a pit-prop sheep fence to shut off Ceann Iar, or one of them mounted a sagging pony to move a parcel of sheep. But on a rainy day they sat immobile indoors, sometimes spitting into the fire, nothing to do. The hulking great crofter with his baby on his knee demonstrated the surprising animal gentleness of size ; in his enormous hand, like a ham, the baby's hand seemed too disproportionate—a mite for the mountain to have sired. The baby repeated his lesson in Gaelic : *a plut*—it rains. So it did.

Rabbits swarmed in the sand dunes and rabbit skins were profitable in a good year. The bright idea of introducing rabbits to compete for the grazing must have come since Martin's time, or surely he would have had a word to say about the island producing a prodigious number of coneys, purchased by the natives. In the evenings we went after the wary rabbits with .22 pistol. The stalk had to be done in style ; a beast picked at a hundred yards and approached upwind among the corries and bluffs of the dunes until, sighting through a screen of marram, one might get a shot at thirty or forty yards. The ones we shot were very tough, perhaps because we simply boiled them in water, without finesse.

The islands' other natural resource, available for export, was lobsters, and a party of young men came every year from Benbecula for a summer fortnight's lobstering. They lived in two rude bothies near the boat pool and kept their lobsters in moored crates. In the evenings they walked the island in pairs, threw stones, and smashed the terns' eggs with a boot heel. They were at a stage to havè boils on their necks, in a town would have been corner boys. One carried a tern's chick in his hand : " it's nearly dead I would think " ; he scooped a hollow in the sand and put it down ; we carried it back to the ternery where no doubt it became fully dead. Each morning the lobstermen sailed out into white water, to be lost in sea mist or to be seen far out in the sunny wind, working against the rocks, pulling up their pots at the lobster holes. They were fine daring seamen, and born to it.

When it rained, we retreated to the tent and read nine-pennies borrowed from one of the houses, imported thither by a lady home on holiday from Glasgow. Period 1923, the Misses Ayres and Bloom. When the rain stopped and the sun came out, millions of water-drops sparkled on the flowers and blades of the machair.

The machair invited beach cricket. Feeling half-witted, we asked at the house if we might borrow a soft ball. This was worse than the botanists, of whom the woman had said : " I don't know what they were at, they were looking for something under the stones." She thought at first that we wanted a bowl, and then said that they didn't play tennis on the island. We could look about, the children might have left a ball lying. So they had, what luck, a tennis ball, aged but entire. The necessary sticks came from an abandoned house in use as a cattle-shed and still containing box-beds with wallpaper peeling from the matchboarding.

The lobstermen who came to watch the so-English scene,

the sound of bat against ball on the village sward, would not join in, saying that they knew nothing of " all those games." (But Martin had written of the St. Kildans :

> They use for their Diversion short Clubs and Balls of Wood ; the Sand is a fair Field for this Sport and Exercise, in which they take great Pleasure and are very nimble at it.)

After watching for some time one of them said, " Does he try to hit the sticks ? " so he had grasped the fundamental idea. They appreciated only demon fast bowling or the lucky chance of the broomstick bat connecting squarely with the ball, to soar it away over the machair and beyond the pebble line of boundary six.

The botanists had no time for frivolities. They were " doing " a list of islands and were living and travelling on university grants. We turned over this information rather jealously ; one had heard that such grants were comparatively easy to get, but of course we had never actually got round to trying for one ; perhaps making a list of birds on each island would not qualify ; perhaps it was better to be free. The botanists scoured Monach with butterfly nets, pill-boxes and vascula, and after two days said they had " done " the group. Harvie-Brown and his kind, Martin's nature notes—and he had a nice account of the habits of Monach ravens—were long gone. Now it was a matter of collecting the sub-subspecies of beetle, the regional variety of a scruffy piece of grass, and sending them to specialists to be named. The islanders had no customary English ridicule for the minutiæ of science ; if poking under stones were scientific, then it would meet with interested and respectful agreement. It tied up with the general Scottish reverence for any sort of learning.

And the botanists were so efficient. Their enormous rucksacs had produced two featherweight tents. Passing, we noted that they were having eggs, corned beef and pineapple chunks to a meal—full-scale boarding-house luncheon ; we only had corned beef, and that two days opened. Well, each to his taste; we preferred to throw a few things into an old grocery box, not mess about with folding aluminium frying-pans; but then we never attempted anything without a car. A dog ate most of our provisions; our common inefficiency left us on the last morning with only a lobster and some green treacle to eat.

We rode back to Uist on a green swell with a deep view downwards, and landed at the white sand.

Sand had drifted and half-buried the car wheels; abandoned piece of machinery—leave it a few months and bits of it would have been patching fences. We reclaimed it and made it go and went lurching off inland through the barley fields. As we followed the track alongside our original local loch, the postman's loch, a phalarope flew up from the close turf just ahead. Not worth looking, but John got out, looked, and said, " Three eggs." I believed him when I saw them, three precious pointed eggs in a deep cup, like a lark's nest. This was a freak situation of course, and abnormally late in the season. Perhaps a first clutch had been flooded out and this raised track chosen as a drier place for a second laying.

In Lochmaddy a thrush sang out the evening from a tin roof, going on and on until eleven at night in the perfectly stilled and silent air. Twenty-six cars attended the call of the mailboat, possibly the full muster of runners in the island. The moon came up and put a road across the sea. At two-thirty in the morning the steamer's deck was deserted, the sea was flat and rippled like the sand on Monach beaches. Cold light already showed in the north-east; the ship's stem pushed out the bow wave—down there unseen sea-fowl splashed out of the way—surf creamed along her side; whoever looked after the black self-propelling bulk was withdrawn and unseen.

At Tarbert, Harris, at three-thirty in the half-light, chill shivers of sleeplessness were passing down the spines of many third class passengers. We continued by road. Headlights picked out whitely the march of telegraph poles. Dawn was perfectly still, mountains stood inverted in the lochs, the water-lilies were still closed. Only gulls were awake in Stornoway at half-past five, but already the earliest drifters were chugging home across the flat harbour water.

Monach Islands, July 12–15, 1938

XVIII

Going to St. Kilda

LANDING at St. Kilda was at the mercy of weather; if a
swell was running in Village Bay or if the wind had anything easterly in it you could not land and that was the end
of it. M'Callum, Orme's steamers, *Dunara Castle* and *Hebrides*,
made cargo-carrying round trips to the Western Isles, taking
about a week out from and back to Glasgow. St. Kilda
was added as a detour from Tarbert, Harris. Tourist
passengers booked for the round trip, and thus it became
a cruise. I planned to pick up *Dunara Castle* at Tarbert—
John was still hovering—and to come back in the *Hebrides*
on her cruise three weeks later. But so far this summer the
Dunara had only been able to land her passengers at St. Kilda
once in three trips. I tried hard for reassuring opinions, but
the landing must remain a matter of luck, " weather and
circumstances permitting."

As I provisioned in Stornoway, I included sweeties and
black twist for the natives who would presumably be there,
taking the hint from the Kearton brothers' shopping on their
own way to the island in 1896.

Stornoway was in a ferment, decorated for the act of con-
ferring her freedom on three of her sons who had made good
elsewhere. During the reception ceremony the leading citizen
unfortunately had his fingers shut in a car door. At the same
time the newspapers were making a great to-do over Rona and
Dr. Fraser Darling. A fishery cruiser had just landed him
there with his wife and school-age son. They were going to
stay right on through the seals' breeding season until Christmas.
His wireless transmitter was not working; no doubt nothing
but a relief to himself though of concern to the worried pressman in Stornoway who asked : " Could you land a plane on

Rona ? " Our own small proprietary feelings (Longest Term Residents Since 1885) were somewhat damped by the fishery cruiser, the wireless, the sectional huts, the newspaper headlines.

The pressman seemed to be a bosom friend of the grocer's. The grocer had delivered to the foot of the hotel stairs, where it remained, a huge box of provisions for St. Kilda ; now he fell over it. Stornoway was gay.

*   *   *

Dunara Castle, well-known figure in the Isles, was unloading second-hand furniture and sectional buildings at Tarbert, on the afternoon of July the 21st, 1938. She had just come in and her cruise passengers were streaming ashore, " free for one glorious week from cares, creditors and carping critics," as the cruise literature had it. Lashed on deck were a motor lorry and a dogcart ; the only visible concession to cruising was the marking for shuffle-board on the tiny afterdeck.

A few further passengers embark [only Ainslie and Atkinson] ; don't criticise them, you will know and number them as friends ere the week is out, for such is the fellowship of the sea.

Personally we could think of no more hellish way of spending a week's holiday than as cruise passengers, cold, queasy, and with nothing whatever to do, lurching from one rain-slashed Hebridean pier to the next.

The steerage quarters in the forepart of the ship measured two and a half paces by two and a half. We were the only occupants. The box was lined with shelves for sleeping on ; ventilation was by the companion-way or hole leading up to the deck. There was a stove which we got going with cotton waste and soon regretted, as it filled the place with choking smoke and the portholes were bolted and painted shut.

When the ship sailed at three o'clock next morning the air was so still that a match flame burnt without a flicker.

The sea got up with the light. Soon the whole ship was juddering. At first I enjoyed the sledge-hammer bangs as she punched into the seas, and daylight in the steerage flickered dim and bright as the two portholes buried and rose again. Then I suddenly realised what was happening : the ship should have turned westwards at Rodel and shaped a course through the Sound of Harris, but she had not altered, she held on southwards past the opening to the Sound and on along the line of the Isles. Disaster ! The captain shouted down from the bridge, St. Kilda was out of the question in this weather, he was making for Lochmaddy. He was hunched inside his oilskins, and glared over the spray-streaming canvas dodger. The sea had an inhuman powerful grey look ; the ship swilled with dirty water ; it was raining ; any land over a hundred feet high was hidden in a pall of running mist.

John was past caring ; I was in despair. And we had been so uniformly lucky so far, never turned back without a landing. And I had so set my heart on St. Kilda, even thrown up my job to get there.

The dogcart and the lorry went ashore at Lochmaddy. The business of loading and discharging cargo all down the line of the Outer Isles should have come after St. Kilda, the slow work at the piers of Lochmaddy in North Uist, Lochboisdale in South Uist, Castlebay in Barra, the intermediate meetings with motor-boats where there were no piers. But at Lochmaddy the captain casually said that he might try for St. Kilda from Barra, if the weather improved. This was a wonderful new hope. If she went at all, the ship always worked St. Kilda from the Sound of Harris ; the crew had never known her go straight to the island from Barra—clear Atlantic steaming for nearly seventy miles. There was no second chance of another cruise as far as we were concerned.

The ship lay for hours in Lochmaddy. We lay on our shelves.

At Lochboisdale we broke out for a couple of hours and walked a little way into the hinterland, the usual flat waste of stones and sodden peat.

The miserable day dragged out its heaving length. I found a little door to the boiler-room which opened to reveal an iron razor-edge. I sat backwards across this, overhanging the black inner chasm, which sent up a hot draught and partly dried my clothes. The state of the steerage lavatories, " Men " or " Crew," forbade even the most urgent ; I strode down the length of the ship, far out of bounds, clattered down the cabin class companion-way, through the brick-faced Glasgow tourists, and slammed the door of " Ladies Only."

Such unwanted life which remained to John, prostrate upon his shelf, was expended in seasickness.

> *Many a green isle needs must be*
> *In the deep wide sea of misery*
> *Or the mariner, worn and wan,*
> *Never thus could voyage on.*

I wanted to kneel before the captain and implore him : Did he realise that I had come seven hundred miles to him ? Did he realise that the St. Kilda wren had never been photographed at the nest, that it nested in dark places in the stone walls, that I had a case of flash-bulbs in yon heap of gear ? That the 1931 people had found only twelve St. Kilda house mice left —would they be extinct by now ? That the St. Kilda field mice should probably be all right and independent of human habitation, didn't he think ? That the cliffs were the biggest sea cliffs in the British Isles, that I carried a letter to Neil Gillies, the watcher, that I was to live in the old factor's house, that these last few years were the only uninhabited ones in all the known history of the island ? Then I could have thought to myself, there is nothing more that can be done. But the captain was dour and thick-necked ; he, also, was unshaven and unslept. He was a determined man, I had been told, who would make St. Kilda if anybody could. I wanted to ask him, Was he determined enough ?

At last the ship steamed in to the pier at Castlebay, Barra. I heard that a cargo of several hundred barrels of herring had to come aboard. There was no sign of them. This evening

John decided he should come no farther, for various reasons and uncertainties ; he should go back by air and leave the car for me to bring home the gear. I slept on deck on a pile of canvas.

Next morning was Saturday, *Dunara Castle* still lay in Castlebay, and there was no sign of a herring barrel. Then, trouble over Saturday afternoon labour. The weather was better, I felt more confident and less preoccupied with my own worries. I had with me the Kearton brothers' book of their own trip to St. Kilda, and knew it pretty well by heart. My copy of *With Nature and a Camera* was the one I'd first read at eleven years of age. The Keartons had been out in an earlier *Dunara Castle*.

> We arrived in Glasgow early on the morning of June 11th, 1896, and after getting our luggage on board the *Dunara Castle*, we went in search of a supply of tinned provisions for ourselves and a quantity of sweets and tobacco for the natives.

It suddenly came upon me that this ship was no new generation, she was the self-same, identical *Dunara Castle*, here and now. I could not get over it. She was herself an Ancient Monument. The date on her bell was nearly polished away : 1875.

And she was a lucky ship, one of the crew told me ; in all her long life she had only been twice ashore. She was deep in the water, built like a yacht, and though the modern diesel-electric mail steamers would carry more cargo in their round bottoms, the old *Dunara* was steadier and a better sea boat than they ; and she could still show them a clean pair of heels. This link by living ship was an abiding wonder and romance.

At two o'clock in the afternoon a lighter came alongside, laden down with herring barrels. At four o'clock *Dunara Castle* steamed out of Castlebay, turned south for a little while—then west—through the Sound of Mingulay—out into the Atlantic. She really was pointed towards St. Kilda and every minute she was another two or three hundred yards nearer. The long line of the Outer Isles was strung out to the northward, ending down here in the south with the cliffs of Barra Head. The Atlantic swell was mighty but it was blue. The captain was determined. Everything was going to be all right.

At ten o'clock in the evening St. Kilda was quite near. St. Kilda (Hirta) was centre ; to the left the sun was just going down into the sea ; outlying to the right were Levenish and Stac Lee, two black buttons, and Boreray, looking like a ruined castle. The sky above was streaked with miles of red. This landfall was sensational. How thankfully had it appeared to Martin Martin on May the 30th, 1697, after sixteen hours without a sight of land, in an open boat !

The islands had no depth or range of colour ; they were razor-sharp monotone silhouettes ; they looked like exaggerated cardboard cut-outs for a stage, stuck up on edge and lit from behind. Fulmars, as greeted by " all naturalists who have *done* the St. Kilda trip," flew round the ship, the St. Kilda gulls of the crew of the steam drifter *Rose* ! When the sun had gone, the opposite sky—astern, eastward, behind and done with— was a rosy light with a black trail across it of steam-coal smoke from *Dunara Castle*.

Where I now stood in the falling and soaring bows had stood the Kearton brothers in their little cloth caps with a button on top—their drooping moustaches—their precious specially made camera stowed below—the afternoon of June the 13th, 1896. And that was latter-day to the old ship. The Keartons had had a telegram of good wishes from Harvie-Brown himself, the G.O.M. of Scottish naturalists by then. He had been out in her seventeen years before, and before that, in the year 1877, she had herself originated the summer service to the island. And this evening, sixty-one years afterwards, the old *Dunara* was still steaming across the Western Ocean, to St. Kilda !

Boreray climbed out of the sea to yet more remarkable pinnacles. No wonder the silhouette was sensational, for Boreray by the six-inch map had a ground area of only 190 acres for a rise of 1245 feet—less than two-thirds the size of Rona and nearly four times the height. And the great mound of Conachair in St. Kilda fell from 1396 feet to the sea in a horizontal distance of a quarter mile; the best sheer drop was 300 yards of thin air. As the ship came nearer and the night darkened, a rocky ridge stood out against a soft bowl of land behind. The ridge was Dùn, guarding the south side of the bay. *Dunara Castle* drove wide round its point, and, listing on the turn, steamed into Village Bay. Her siren blared and echoed round the enclosing dark hills. An answering light soon flickered from the amorphous hillside. A narrow gap of sea showed between Dùn and mainland. *Dunara's* anchor rattled down, steam hissed from the winch, a touch astern, then, tinkle tinkle tinkle went the telegraph: Finished with Engines. A trip which should have taken seven or eight hours had come roundabout in nearly forty-eight, but the ship lay heaving gently in Village Bay.

I put my gear in a heap. This time the familiar well-worn pieces were numbered and chalked " St. Kilda." It was midnight. I made a mug of tea in the galley (steerage did its own catering) and prepared to sleep on deck. Then the captain sent word that I was to be landed now, " in case a wind gets up and we can't put you ashore to-morrow," he said. For one steerage derelict a lifeboat was swung out, lowered and manned; packages 1-11 inclusive carefully passed down, counted and checked. I often hoped that the captain realised something of my gratefulness for his determination. Blessed, ever to be blessed captain.

There was no light on the unseen jetty. The wash sounded on the shore. Somebody in the boat's crew shouted: " Are you there, Neil? " and " Show us a light." Two unintelligible voices came in reply, one an old man's. They must belong to Neil Gillies and to the famous Finlay MacQueen, who had been on show at the Glasgow Exhibition. We came in to a concrete jetty by means of a great deal of English and Gaelic argument in the darkness: "Come on in, there's plenty of water," " Chuck us a line then," " Come on in and I'll chuck you a line," etc., etc. I was ashore, and stood aside while the Gaelic worked itself out. Neil Gillies said, What was the good of coming on a Sunday when they couldn't sell post-cards? (Postcards—ah!) But he did sell both postcards and knitted socks and thereby got into trouble with the cast-iron Sunday observance of Finlay MacQueen.

Neil Gillies said I'd better go in the manse, the laird's house, for the rest of the night. We stumbled to and fro in the dark as he helped me to get my goods up there and under cover. A low wall surrounded the manse, as if to enclose a garden; a pebble path led up to the door. Mayweed loomed pale, overgrowing the threshold. In one room there was a proper bed with three sacks of straw on it. Neil Gillies found a candle somewhere. I thanked him and said " Good night." He said " You're very welcome " and " Good night " and went away. The stone-floored silent kitchen had taps marked H and C above the sink. I had heard of this H and C and had hardly believed it, though there turned out to be bath and water-closet as well. I unrolled my sleeping-bag on the bed.

Outside, in the small hours of Sunday, July the 24th, I leant over the garden wall and looked out to old *Dunara's* lights in the bay and to the dim crags of Dun beyond. Oh, this was going to be good!

*   *   *

It was the Shiants effect over again—island approached at night, then in the new day a strange surround high and close, all at once on the eyes. The first daylight look had this same suddenness and excitement but there was something half familiar in the newness. So much of St. Kildan literature read and photographs seen, it was as if a blindfolded man were to be uncovered in some known country: now where are you? And he would struggle to right himself with landmarks foreign until he could fix his place, find north and south, and rebuild the whole lie of the land.

From the manse a great encurving sweep of brown turf rose on three sides to a skyline nearly a thousand feet up, an enormous bowl to surround and beetle over Village Bay. The steamship floated tiny in the bay. Tide was low. A crescent of fine bright sand had uncovered below the stones at the head of the bay. The hills were dotted with cleits, and they made black knobs along the skyline. Cleits—one knew about them, a feature of St. Kilda, small drystone huts roofed with living turf, with a doorway at one end ; once used for storing crops, hay and fuel.

The line of about a dozen low houses was drawn across the bowl, a quarter mile back from the curving head of the bay. The manse stood apart—semi-detached with schoolroom and church—down here by the jetty, at the end of the grassed path from the village. Next up the path was the factor's house, my house to be, also apart. Beyond it the line of houses and byres fronted Main Street, with a full fair view over the bay, past the rock Levenish, to the south-eastward ocean. The other half of the island was dead ground from the village, shut in by the encircling skyline.

St. Kilda villagers in order of their appearance were : Neil Gillies, watcher, a middle-aged man with a game leg ; Finlay MacQueen, oldest inhabitant ; Mrs. John Gillies, senr., Neil's mother. All were St. Kildans born and bred and, as in every year now, they were back from mainland exile for a few summer weeks in the island. To-day all three were in Sunday best. Neil and Mrs. Gillies lived in Number 11 up towards the far end of the street. Finlay MacQueen lived in Number 2, next but one to the factor's house.

Boatloads of the *Dunara's* passengers came ashore during the morning and straggled up and down the street. I was carting my goods from manse to factor's house. A snipe flew up from outside the front door. A wren, a precious St. Kilda wren, whirred like a bumble-bee about a ruined cleit behind the house. The passengers looked in and out of the houses in the manner of people looking at ruins. When they found me and my housekeeping effects they were quite embarrassed and made to back out, apologising. No, no, do come in.

The rise of land behind the house was such that the two

upstairs rooms were reached by a door half-way up the back wall. The two ground-floor rooms were separated by a porch or hall whose width made a third tiny room at the back, possibly larder. Each of the two rooms had a window with glazing entire, giving on to the bay. The living-room had a wooden floor, walls lined with matchboarding, and a fireplace ; it contained two tables, two chairs, two canvas beds, a bench and a cupboard. I set up the Primus on top of the ornamented iron range in the kitchen, and fetched a bucket of gin-clear water from *Tobar a Mhinisteir*, the Minister's Well.

> . . . After sweeping out the plaster that had fallen off the walls . . . and lighting a fire on a grateless hearth, we began to set things to rights. . . .

It was in this same house that the Keartons had lived for their famous period piece of ten days ; and now an old copy of their book lay on the table forty-two years afterwards.

The kitchen was stone-floored with plastered walls, not so cosy as the living-room. Two packing-cases and an old door soon made a capital kitchen table—as the Keartons would undoubtedly have described it. The cubby-hole or larder opening from the kitchen was perhaps where Cherry Kearton had fallen through the rotten floor-boards when he had " commenced to prowl round in search of a ' dark ' room." I cleared out the fireplace and collected firewood, there was plenty of half-rotten deal lying about outside. Settling in was pleasurable, furnishing a base here at the hill foot from which to set out and explore. I pinned up the six-inch map on the living-room wall.

The passengers went back aboard the ship in the early afternoon but she lay on in the bay until the evening. I felt that nothing began until she had gone. Everything was waiting, and already there were one or two things. Snipe were obviously very common in the deep moist pasture, which was probably old arable ground ? This was something quite new since the 1931 survey. There was a corncrake in the grass too. Stout trunks of angelica rose from the soft swathes of Yorkshire fog ;

they grew almost over-lush, like umbellifers in the shade of some black-bottomed marshy copse far away in mainland. A dwarfed St. John's wort made yellow patches on the steep flank of the hill called Oiseval, into whose foot the factor's house was set.

When I walked up the path to the village Finlay Mac-Queen called me in. I entered to the old man sitting in his Sunday black on a stool before the fire. He had his spectacles on for reading the close print of the Gaelic Bible, which he held up slantwise to the window. He was excited in Gaelic and gave me to understand that he had been presented to the King and Queen at the Glasgow Exhibition. We went on along to Number 11 for a cup of tea and some of Mrs. Gillies' oatcakes; she had run out of tinned milk, so mine was handy. Neil said that Finlay had got very excited at the exhibition and had kissed the Queen's hand; I had gathered as much from the old boy's gesturing. While we were there *Dunara Castle* weighed anchor and steamed out of the bay, blaring her echoing siren. We villagers stood outside the door to wave.

Finlay MacQueen was going to conduct the Sunday evening service in the church. (And the Keartons' first morning on St. Kilda had been a Sunday. They had slept upstairs in the factor's house and had brought hammocks. They were up early and prepared for service :

Eleven o'clock came round, but there was not a sign of anybody astir on devotions bent. We waited with patient curiosity until half-past twelve, when an old ship's bell, erected on the top of a wall near the church, began to summon worshippers to the House of Prayer by a weird out-of-place kind of tinkle, tinkle, tinkle.

The indulgent minister (as they said) had given his little flock an hour and a half's grace, because of the labour of landing provisions from the *Dunara Castle* the afternoon before.)

Later on I met the St. Kildans returning up the path from church. There were two birds in the schoolroom, Neil said. I went and let them out : rock pipits.

Going to St. Kilda

The sky was overcast or raining ; the mountain Conachair remained under cloud nearly all day. Dusk enlivened the numerous snipe and the single corncrake. I set some mouse-traps round about. My lantern-lit window looked very cosy from outside. Again I flushed a snipe before the front door.

XIX

St. Kilda Now

ON A dull day (resident's experience) St. Kilda had the
drab ancient look of the other Atlantic isles ; the rock was
timeless grey, the grass brown, the sea-birds added to inhuman
desolation. The island then seemed a larger Rona, a barren
weather-beaten mountain top removed to the ocean.

The sun came out, there were cotton-wool clouds in blue
sky, and it was a different island. Village Bay gleamed with
pin-points of light, the water was fathoms deep of green and
purple. Cloud shadows moved across the flanks of Oiseval and
Conachair, where the old matted grass was burnished by sunlight. Lower down a small breeze set stirring the purplish
coloured swathes of flowering Yorkshire fog. Down in the
village, family parties of twites, " yellow-neb linties," used
to sit along the roof ridges ; in sunlight their bills were
sharp and brightly yellow against blue sky. The stone walls
were warm to touch. The surf was white as a seagull's
breast.

The evening sun went early off the village because of the
high rim of land against the west, but yellow sunlight slanted
late across Dùn and picked out the slopes and rocks in wonderful stereoscopic detail. I told the time, roughly, by the
shadow of the western rim moving up the flank of Oiseval
behind the factor's house. In the mornings I told the time
by the travel of shadows across the house wall.

A look across to Dùn through field-glasses showed precipitous green slopes dotted white ; the little white dots
were sitting fulmars, the bigger dots and splashes were
flowering clumps of mayweed. The white specks buzzing
in the air were puffins. I walked a first time across the sand of
the bay to puffin-dotted grassy slopes at the far side. The

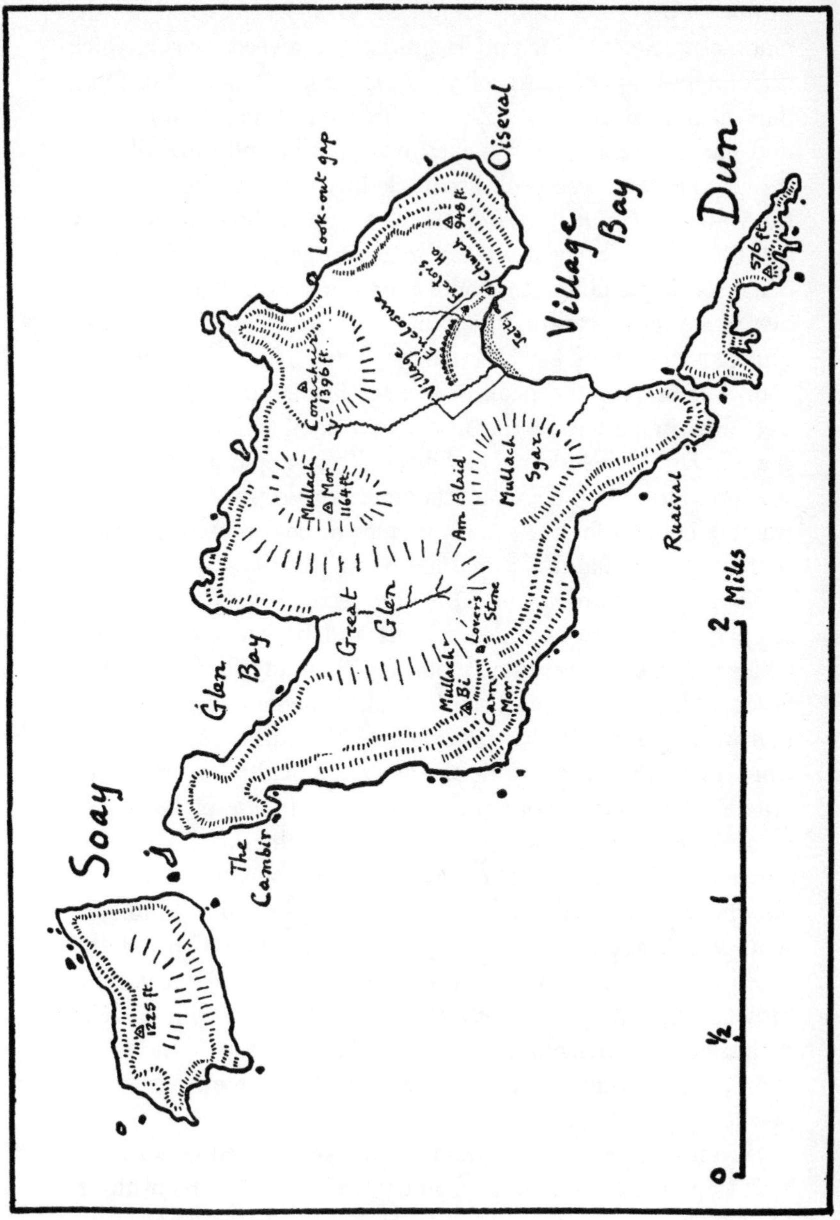

Fig. 7. *Sketch map of St. Kilda*

puffin slopes rose to be chopped off short to drop to the channel between Dùn and mainland. Seaweed swirled thick and sluggish in the channel ; no swimming that way to Dùn. The near face of Dùn opposite this narrow depth was sheer and dark. A black-back picked up a puffin and flew off with it over the bay ; the puffin struggled free or was dropped into the water, where it fluttered disabled ; the black-back quickly spiralled down after it. I sat in a sunny place and a wren came seeking among the stones four feet away. Gannets were over from Boreray and the Stacs to fish Village Bay ; they plunged and raised white shell-spouts. Late July was of course long past the peak of the sea-fowl's landward season, but even in mid-June the first two things which had struck the Keartons on landing had been " the apparent dearth of sea-bird life and the joyous songs of the Wrens." St. Kilda was big enough for the sea sometimes to be forgotten ; it was more than an island : a sea continent.

North-westward from Dùn the coast of Hirta was of steep grass slopes cut off into cliffs and broken by rock buttresses. The cliffs were mostly on the thousand-foot scale. Far down, at low tide, the surf swirled below the scummy line of the high-water mark all along the foot of the cliff wall. The cliff rim was marked with game-tracks which had worn away the grass. There were more traces, dung and tufts of brown or white wool, before I spotted a flock of wild sheep far away down the cliff slope. They were remarkably athletic, more like goats than sheep, with big curved horns and white tail scuts which showed when they turned to run. Some of the sheep were nearly white but the common colour was a various brown, anything from chestnut red to dark chocolate. The plant, Scotch lovage, grew along the cliff tops just as on Rona, an unremarkable umbellifer looking somewhat out of place.

From these western boundary cliffs you looked onwards to The Cambir, the northern promontory, with the green hump of Soay Island rising beyond it. Soay was the original home and place-name of the wild Soay sheep, some of which were introduced into Hirta only after the evacuation of 1930. Inland, the line of ridge and peak carried round three-quarters of a circle, Mullach Sgar, Mullach Geal, Mullach Mor, up to the crown of Conachair, dip to Look-out Gap, rise again to Oiseval, drop to Village Bay ; bay and Dùn completed the circle. From the rim of the bowl the stone-walled rectangle enclosing the village below looked as if it had been drawn to make a home acre, a little piece tamed from the soaring slopes of grass. The beach at the head of the bay was a fine shingle by the look of it ; when you got down there it was big boulders. A stream rose in the saddle between Conachair and Mullach Mor, a place of wet patches, with humps of sphagnum and stiff bog asphodel and spotted orchids nearly white. The stream fell seven hundred feet to trickle across the end of the street, it slowed down across the coastal meadow in front of the village for a fall of another hundred feet, and came out under the beach boulders for a final zigzag across the sand. Many primrose plants grew along the banks.

I climbed out of the village bowl and crossed the divide to open for a first time northern Gleann Mor, the Great Glen. Strange, far country ! Another stream wandered down the middle of a wide basin to the northern sea. The horizon was a bowstring strung across the open end of the glen. Wild sheep dotted this curving prairie, cloud shadows went slowly over the grass.

> There is no sort of Trees, no, not the least Shrub grows here, nor ever a Bee seen at any time.

Often and often in the south I was quickened to think of the Rona sort of desolation, but when I got into it the feeling was gone ; it would come again with recollection from a distance. All large-sounding melancholic verse of far-off place and lonely ocean-side was for recollection, not for the ground beneath one's feet and the sea in front ?

At first from the slope of Conachair I could see no sign of life in the village : the dark curve of houses and byres, lines of stone walls, cleits dotted innumerably, empty bay. Near at hand flies buzzed in some scanty heather. The surf noise which came up from the bay was unsynchronised, the small waves had sluiced up the sand before the sound of the break reached the flank of Conachair. Now there was some tiny sign of human life—the flickering white dots were Mrs. Gillies' washing. The queerness of no life was sometimes pressing when I looked about and listened from the door of the factor's house : the grass-grown street ; the line of silent mouldering houses ; the unseen sawing of the corncrake. Once yelping dogs had been the universal irritation of visitors. The manse chimneys looked so established, all the trappings of a human colony were there, but no humans. The evacuation was still near enough for this feeling ; for the first year or two it must have been overpowering to natives returning as summer migrants. There were still a few sticks of rhubarb growing in the long grass of the manse garden. A battered rose bush was in full flower against the wall of the house ; Neil had propped two old windows to protect it.

The village was alive with wrens ; their bold creepings in and out of windows and decaying roofs only underlined what was missing. In a calm a small smacking noise sometimes carried to the silent village, the noise of a sea-bird slapping the water on its take-off across the bay.

*   *   *

There were some cleits and broken walls up the hill, otherwise the works of man on St. Kilda were circumscribed by the village enclosure.

The first house, the manse with its H and C, I left alone as none of my business, but I took documentary inventories of church and schoolroom. The schoolroom contained two school-type pews, seating for fifteen scholars. The pews were fitted with mountings for ink-pots but only one of them held an ink-pot, which was of the common porcelain sort with black dried dregs in it. A square of linoleum on one wall had

served as blackboard. The walls were unvarnished matchboarding. A collecting box on a pedestal—" For the Maintenance of the Church "—stood by the door which opened
directly into the church. Bookshelves contained twenty-five
books, some of which had gummed labels bordered with fancy
scrollwork and inscribed " St. Kilda Free Library." The
books included a good many bound volumes of magazines,
such as *The Leisure Hour* for 1878, *The Family Treasury of Sunday
Reading* for 1863, *The Christian Guardian* for 1824 and '26, *The
Boy's Own Volume* for 1864 and '65, *Sunday Reading* for 1869,
'77, '78. Of the educational reading, *MacDougall's Suggestive
Arithmetics* was recent ; the rest was not. *Mechanical Philosophy,
Horology and Astronomy*, 1877, for instance ; *Class Book of
Geography*, new edition, revised 1881 ; *Clyde's School Geography*,
1873. MacDougall's teaching cards were spread about the
room, *MacDougall's Free-Arm and Blackboard Drawing Cards,
MacDougall's Speed and Accuracy Arithmetical Tests, Answers to
MacDougall's Speed and Accuracy Arithmetical Tests*. " If I sell
240 gals. of milk in 5 dys., in how many dys. will £12 worth at
5d. a qt. be sold ? " asked MacDougall. The poor bairns of
St. Kilda were to be civilised, when outside the surf was
washing on the sand and the seagulls were calling in the wind !

There were novels for non-educational, other than Sunday
reading. Some pleasant browsing here : *Lord Oakborn's
Daughters*, 1897, for instance. *Edgar Nelthorpe ; or, The Fair
Maids of Taunton*.

> A small country town in the heart of England was the scene
> some few years ago of a sad tragedy. I must ask my readers to
> bear with me while I relate it. These crimes, having their rise
> in the evil passions of our nature, are not of the most pleasant
> for the pen to record ; but it cannot be denied that they do
> undoubtedly bear for many of us an interest amounting almost
> to fascination.

Shades of detective-reading dons ! However, nothing had
happened by page 20, or seemed likely to, so I gave up.

A map of Britain on the wall included England but left

out Scotland. An empty gin bottle stood on one desk. A notice
said :

> All scholars between the ages of three to fifteen will be exempted
> from payment of school fees. Harris. 14 October, 1904.

The calendar on the wall (MacDougall's Educational Co.,
Ltd.) was dated 1930 and torn off to Sept.

There was a queer stationary quality about schoolroom and
church : silence ; still air and deep dust ; time arrested.
Archæologists uncovering a lava-buried city skip thousands of
years and find a household stopped short at the day of the
avalanche ; here was merely an eight years' silence.

The church was a large high-ceilinged room with windows
distinguished from the schoolroom's by being pointed at the
top in an ecclesiastic manner. The room was filled with two
close beds of varnished deal benches with a channel or aisle
down the middle ; the place had a lofty church-like emptiness.
I found myself walking quietly. The lectern of the pulpit was
a sloping shelf with a large English and a large Gaelic Bible
side by side. Dust was thick everywhere and the benches were
littered with dismembered psalm-books and Bibles in both
English and Gaelic tongues. Two of the windows were boarded
up, and for this reason : the jetty had been built in the early
nineteen hundreds and a box of gelignite left over then from
the blasting had been stowed away in a hut by the church.
Four or five years ago Neil had been clearing up, pulling down
the hut and having a bonfire ; on went the thirty-year-old
box of gelignite. But no one was hurt.

On May 15th, 1918, a U-boat shelled St. Kilda and knocked
down the house which up till then had stood beside the manse.
On first seeing it Finlay had wanted to go out and ask for
tobacco, Neil said ; then the firing started and the natives
promptly took to the hills. A trawler caught up with the
U-boat and hit it in the conning tower, so Neil said ; they'd
heard the pair of them banging away all day. He said that a
destroyer had finally captured the U-boat off the Flannans.

After that the authorities made concrete works in the hillside behind the manse and installed a large piece of naval ordnance, just in time for the Armistice. The gun was still there, though by now somewhat rusty and immovably pointed inland ; the date of manufacture was plainly legible : 1896.

Factor's house, being two-storied, and manse steading were the superior buildings of St. Kilda. All the other houses were alike : a row of sixteen low three-roomed cottages each with a chimney at either end. Their roofs were of zinc sheets, laid over planking and tarred. The tarring must have been regularly done, for the increment hung in sticky festoons round the eaves, like black icicles. The rise of land caused the eaves at the back to be at ground level ; a stone wall built against the earth two or three feet away from the back and end walls of each house made a surrounding trench ; these were now moats of standing water. Back and end walls were dead walls ; windows and doors all gave on to the street where the village life had gone on.

About half the houses were now roofless and five were complete ruins, abandoned even before the evacuation. Number 1 house had a hole in the roof, Number 2 was Finlay MacQueen's, Number 3 was a fair specimen.

—— Number 3, Main Street, July, 1938. The door is double, of two vertical leaves flaked with traces of red paint, kept shut by an oar roped crosswise. The two windows are one on either side of the door. You enter to a porch, a small space with a bench facing you and doors opening to right and left. This particular porch contains a trawl bobbin, a kettle and a cauldron both of bright red iron, the remains of an enamelled basin, a lot of loose plaster, straw and bits of match-boarding.

The door on the right opens into the bedroom-living-room. Here on the wooden floor are an iron bedstead, several trunks, tins, baskets and old bottles. The wallpaper is pink-patterned and ends in a loose mouse-eaten fringe an inch or two above the floor. On the window-sill are two small wooden tubs and a glass-bowled lamp with a broken chimney. The window

233

still has traces of a roller blind. A circular gridiron hangs on a coat peg. On the walls are a text, motif of wallflowers (?) embroidered round the legend, " The Lord is my shepherd I shall not want " ; a calendar for 1924 and a large, framed, nineteenth-century photograph of a son of St. Kilda dressed in some sort of mariner's costume, possibly a steward's. The mantelpiece is covered with two sheets of old newspaper, one of which is from an anonymous American weekly of 1925 and the other from a Scottish farming paper of 1924. On top of these stand a teapot, a school slate and some empty bottles. The ceiling of bare matchboarding is still fairly sound. One cupboard recessed into the wall is full of rubbish.

The kitchen is less well preserved, the stone floor is moist and dark brown and littered with such wreckage as wet turves, plaster, coal and old boxes. The air reeks of musty damp. Part of the wall is papered with the *Saturday Evening Post* of July 3, 1926. The rubbish to be found in the kitchen includes baskets, wood, an old lamp, a mirror, mouldered Gaelic Bibles[1], bottles and rope. The fireplaces of both kitchen and living-room are grateless and heaped with fallen soot. Iron chains for cooking-pots hang down from both chimneys.

The third room at the back, the width of the porch, is partitioned off with matchboarding. It has only half a ceiling, which leaves a hole for access to the loft above, which runs the full length of the house. This third room is a bedroom and contains an iron bedstead and some fallen beams and other debris.

*   *   *

The houses, except Numbers 2, 5 (Neil Ferguson's ; he had been in residence earlier in the summer) and 11, were deteriorating fast. Once the roofs were fallen, weeds quickly battened on to the wood pulp which had been floor. Unpainted window frames and doors soon softened and rotted away. Bits of china

---

[1] A Gaelic Bible is traditionally left behind in an abandoned croft.

which had been left eight years before on a wooden floor were now to be discovered buried in a dark weed-covered debris. Some roofless ruins had iron bedsteads still in place and overgrown with weeds.

I found a copy of *The Swiss Family Robinson* in one house. The large picture over the mantelpiece in the kitchen of Number 11 was of an Edwardian young lady, undoubtedly a gentlewoman, surrounded with ornament and suffixed with a verse. From most of the remains one might have thought the evacuation pre-1914. Evidently anything which came into the island was carefully preserved, and only at the evacuation did the natives take away a skimming of the most modern imports and abandon all the rest. No doubt even more Gaelic Bibles were taken away than were left.

The well-known post office fronted the street next door to Number 5. It had been quite genuine, though owing to the limited amount of business the office of postmaster had been held by one of the natives (Neil Ferguson). Inside I found a printed card headed " Inland Postal Rates " which started off : " Letter Post. Not exceeding 4 oz. . . . 1d." A paper pinned up on the wall was headed, " What the disabled soldier wants to know " and dated " War Office, August, 1915." The post office was a corrugated iron shack with a door and a window ; it bore a large crudely lettered notice-board : " St. Kilda Post Office."

Each house had its byre beside it, end-on to the street. The byre roofs were usually thatched and most of them had fallen in by now. The interior was often filled up with a heap of manure-like thatch, black, sodden, and nourishing weeds grown rank from the richness at their roots. Fallen rafters were tumbled anyhow, though the byres roofed with planking and felt had lasted better. The floors were beaten earth which remained hard though wet and slimy. The walls were dry-stone, sometimes plastered in the common mud-pie style of peasantry ; in this case cow manure slapped into the chinks and still showing the plasterers' fingerprints. The walls were three or four feet thick, and the eaves springing from the inside edge made the roofs look disproportionately small and perched, like the caps of elderly rowing men. The byres with roofs still sound were perfectly dark inside, and such as had a window were no lighter, because the moist tunnel through the wall to the window-frame made a congenial place for a thicket of fern. The interior of a byre was a pool of dark silence ; it was like being in a deep cave. To photograph one byre I cleared the window growth, propped open the door and gave an hour and a half's exposure (which was about right) while I went away to bathe and have a meal.

The sixteen houses were modern, only about seventy-five years old, an enlightened proprietor's building scheme. The present byres had been dwelling-houses before them, though for only a short turn. When they were built in the eighteen-thirties they had replaced a village of immemorial houses occupied continuously and unchanged, so it is supposed, since Martin's day ; and they must have been immemorial even then. The original houses seem to have been much on the Rona model, though unburied. A sort of tunnel led into a first compartment where the livestock lived and then into the natives' cavern : fire in the middle of the floor—smoke-hole in the roof, no other light—one or two wall-beds (boot-shaped vaults recessed into the thickness of the wall). And where Rona had St. Ronan's cell, St. Kilda had used to have three chapels, Christ's, St. Columba's and St. Brianan's, but all were long since erased ; even Muir could find no stone of them. Probably the ways of life in both villages were similar, except that St. Kilda would have been a good deal more sheltered and comfortable. When the byres were built as houses no trace was left of the original dwellings ; the site and crescent of street were as before, but nothing else ; and so the village lost its uninterrupted stretch into antiquity which it might otherwise have continued to share with the unique village of Rona.

Neil told me conversationally that the byres had been one-time houses—it was well remembered in island annals—but I heard nothing of the ancient dwellings before them.

Inside the byres nowadays there was the usual discarded

rubbish of old ropes, packing-cases, wood, sacks, boots and bottles. There were many cauldrons, tubs and barrels filled with an unknown liquid, thick, dark brown and stinking. The iron cauldrons had been for boiling up crotal, the lichen used by Hebrideans for dyeing wool, and for other, nameless brews. There were interesting miscellanea : a complete cradle, wooden hay rakes, flails (a wooden staff attached by a leather thong to a foot-length of very stout rope), spades and forks, scythes and sickles, the balloon-like sheepskin floats of authentic St. Kilda mail-boats.

There were piles of fulmars' feathers in many of the byres, which even after eight years kept their fulmar smell. Fulmars were a sort of *multum in parvo*, Swiss Family Robinson article to the St. Kildans, as if designed by a pre-Darwinian god with their requirements particularly in mind.

> " Can the world," faid one of the most fenfible men at *Hirta* to me, " exhibit a more valuable commodity ? The Tulmer furnifhes oil for the lamp, down for the bed, the moft falubrious food, and the most efficacious ointments for healing wounds, befides a thousand other virtues of which he is poffeffed, which I have not time to enumerate. But, to fay all in one word, deprive us of the Tulmer, and *St. Kilda* is no more." (The Rev. Kenneth Macaulay, visiting in 1758.)

The first pressing of a fulmar, so to speak, yielded its pure transparent stomach oil. Sometimes this seems to have been tapped from the living bird by means of some vessel on the end of a pole, otherwise the birds were smartly noosed from behind before they could throw away the oil, their necks were wrung and their beaks tied up to prevent it dribbling out. This was the oil burnt in cruses and it gave not a bad light ; it was also medicinal. Boiled fulmars yielded body oil, sold and exported by the barrel as train oil. Fulmar feathers used to be exported to London and used for soldiers' mattresses, Neil told me.

And though the rocky-crested summits frown,
These rocks, by custom, turn to beds of down.

237

The Keartons said that the feathers were first fumigated and then used for stuffing soldiers' pillows, and that after about three years the smell returned to them so strongly that

> Tommy Atkins refuses to rest his sleeping head on them until they have been again roasted.

Fulmar carcases by the thousand were plucked, split and salted down for winter use ; even in 1938 Finlay MacQueen took away to his winter exile a good stock of salted fulmars. Food, bedding, light, medicine, export trade—fulmars were staple in St. Kilda ; no wonder St. Kildans talked of the fulmar harvest.

The duster used by Mrs. Gillies was an old fulmar's wing ; she kept another by the fire for hearth brush.

*   *   *

No trace of cultivation remained ; the whole of the village enclosure was a meadow of deep wet weedy grass. The greenest grass was within some small stone-walled enclosures in which lambs had used to be shut up overnight, because the ewes were milked.

The cleits were thickest at the back of the village but they were also scattered far up the enclosing slopes. Their combination of drystone walls and weatherproof roofs were nicely adapted to a climate of wind and rain : the piercing draught between the stones dried anything inside and the thick crown of living turf, only possible in such an oceanic climate, kept it dry. Cleits were used both for storage and as drying chambers, for fish and sea-fowl, hay, the arable crops, and turves for fuel. The walls were sloped inwards and bridged by a ceiling of transverse stone slabs ; on top of the slabs was the mound of earth and turf. Nowadays the cleits had only heaps of old hay in them, or stacks of rotten wood useful for summer residents.

The graveyard was behind the village street. This was a piece of ground enclosed by a stone wall (" a small oval-

shaped space full of nettles," said Muir) where the gravestones
rose from a thick bed of grass, docks and yellow flags. Some
were rough blocks of island rock and some orthodox mason's
work, imported from the mainland and appropriate to their
period. Close by the graveyard was the prehistoric underground dwelling or earth-house, a trench partly roofed with
slabs and overgrown with fern, alleged to have been used by
Norsemen.

The grass was so lush in front of the village that I felt I
ought not to be walking in it; it had the sanctity of a meadow
closed for hay. Here lived the single corncrake of St. Kilda,
who rasped away day and night and who I never even glimpsed
in spite of much stalking and many wild dashes ; he must
have been unusually ventriloquial. On a still night the rocky
face of Dùn a mile away sometimes echoed his call. On still,
misty mornings, after a night's rain, every blade of grass was
weighed with drops, and cloud spread into mist down the
flanks of Conachair, where invisible ravens croaked. The wet
brought out big very Hebridean black slugs in the grass, and
if a pale sun warmed the moist air midges became unendurable.

Snipe were always jumping up from the village grass. This
was a good ecological change, obvious after the event, but
whoever would have guessed that of all birds snipe would invade
and take over the deserted village ? The flush of grass from
soft ground and the weed-blocked watercourses suited them,
and they had increased out of all bounds since the evacuation.
The ornithologists of 1931 had found a breeding population
of just three pairs in the whole of St. Kilda : " they were
restricted to the bogs, and hence to the high ground." The
village birds, scavengers of the middens, had used to be gulls
and hoodie crows, a parasitic flock of up to fifty crows much
disliked by the natives. Gulls did not come to the village now
and I don't remember seeing a hoodie anywhere.

On the last day of July I put up a snipe which flew as if
wounded ; it had sprung from a newly-hatched chick. The
old bird struggled in the grass close to, pretending a broken
wing. Two days later I flushed another snipe from four eggs.

These four eggs and the chick were presumably second broods, unusual in snipe. Possibly the rich food supply, still not fully exploited, had led to double broods?—even as the Scottish field vole swarms of the nineties had gathered all the hawks and owls and set them laying and hatching clutch after clutch.

The reason why I flushed snipe by the factor's house was because the drain round the back of the house had become a moat and had made the path in front into a slight marsh. I pulled off a continuous network of stolons of some water grass and uncovered a concrete gutter crossing the path and delivering into the meadow below. I thereby drained both moat and marsh ; in spite of the snipe one could not have a bog outside one's front door.

The factor's house had probably once had some sort of garden border, because I found a line of stones in the turf a foot out from the wall. I decided to reclaim this, borrowed a spade, stripped off the turf, reset the edging stones, and managed to preserve a few inches of soil above the rock bottom. I transplanted primrose roots from the Conachair stream. One plant still had two flowers, so far from the southern season, yet still of the authentic pale sweetness. I transferred a clump of thyme from a byre wall to the herbaceous border and added a clump of thrift, some mayweed and heavily fragrant white bladder campion. Corn marigolds had used to colour the crops, and I should have liked some, but the only plant I saw, growing in the decayed thatch of a byre, was already my indoor decoration. The vase was an *objet trouvé* : a cracked china toothbrush holder which had lost its washstand.

*   *   *

From high up on the slopes of Conachair or Oiseval the village works diminished to small proportion, the marks of a thousand years' habitation were a few heaps and lines of stone. A little higher up Oiseval and the village was dead ground, shut off by the line of turf which rose behind you as you climbed. Then all the view was a monotony of hundreds of

acres of brown grass and grey stones. Sunshine kindled it a
little, for the steep slopes took the light obliquely, as if midday
were evening. Usually by looking carefully through glasses
you could find a few wild sheep. They were to be treated as
game and at first their marks had a certain excitement, their
cliff-edge paths and a patch of flattened grass where an animal
had lately lain down, their dung—how recent ?

At a little distance even the dotted cleits merged into the
general grey-brown country, unless they stood on the skyline.
I was on the crown of Oiseval in the middle of a circle of brown
turf : all to see was the tremendous semi-circle of hills. This
was at the eastern extreme. From here Conachair led away in
the north-west, the slope fell westwards to the saddle which
begot the village stream, rose to the lesser hill of Mullach Mor,
fell again to the next divide, Am Blaid, the high watershed
between village bowl and the Great Glen. The skyline reared
up again to the eleven-hundred-foot crest of Mullach Bi on the
western cliffs, a couple of miles away. The curve turned back
towards the south-east and fell to Ruaival, a little rocky corner
in that view but steep and high to climb when you got there,
higher than the summit of Rona. Ruaival dropped to Dùn
channel, a tiny V. The five-hundred-foot crags of Dùn were
dwarfed.

At Look-out Gap, between Oiseval and Conachair, the
turf swept up strongly to the cliff edge, stopped suddenly, and
the cliff face was a wall five hundred feet deep. I lay flat and
peered over the edge. The wall was covered with grey lichen.
Fulmars swung past and the air wafted up fulmar smell. The
only near sound was of fulmars' wings, a windy noise as the air
rushed past the feathers. The white necks of some birds were
splashed with orange-coloured patches of oil and sick ; most
of them had bellies discoloured by the wet earth of their
breeding ledges.

The cliffs by which Oiseval and Conachair fell to the sea
were of the sort which start as extremely steep grass slopes and
grow ever steeper and more broken until the last few hundred
feet are sheer rock walls. Puffins and fulmars dotted the green

slopes, but the cliff colonists proper were so far down that their clamour was only to be heard in the murmur of beating swell. The ultimate walls were invisible from directly above; you had to look back from a projecting curve of coast to see the whitened ledges and to hear a faint waft of " kittiwark kittiwark kittiwark." The height was too great to see individual birds unless they were flying and showed white against the sea. On the ledges they were lost in the whitewash of their own mutes.

I looked across to Boreray four miles away, and its attendant stacs, Stac Lee, a haystack in that view, and Stac an Armin, a lop-sided pyramid. The top third of Lee was chalked white with gannets and their dung. A cloud of evanescent white motes buzzed above the rock—goose-sized gannets—like the protozoan stir on a microscope slide. Away in the north-east the Flannan Isles were just visible as two minute humps.

Fulmars were thick as puffins round the north slope of Conachair. Farther on the north slope of Mullach Mor was the most dolorous ground of all the island's sixteen hundred acres. It was a scarred area, rough turf zigzagged with black ditches and spotted with excrescences of sphagnum moss, a malignant yellow which looked as if a fungal disease had broken out over the ground.

From the summit of Conachair, where a bleached pole stuck up from a cairn, I saw rain coming. A black pall drew up from the west, covered and hid Dùn and spread across Village Bay before the rain broke on Conachair. These hills made their own quick changes in the weather ; by the time I was home again in the factor's house, thirteen hundred feet below, the sun was shining, though Conachair remained up in the mist.

In August the weather settled for a full week. After the first day of it, Neil said it had been the calmest day in St. Kilda since he'd landed at the end of May. We were to enjoy the island at its rare, far-from-typical best. Each morning came up dew-drenched and cool, and expanded in calmness and sunshine. Sometimes the hot stillness was diffused in glare. Then the ocean was glassy calm, a vasty pavement marked with streaks and bands. Sea and sky were fused in heat haze. The waves had hardly the power to curl and topple on the sand of Village Bay, though at the western cliffs you could still hear the slow grind of the swell and see surf swirling against the rock. It seemed impossible, looking out from the cliff top to the mazy level of ocean, that such a swell could still be moving it.

St. Kilda's heat had never the English desiccation. After showers of rain the humid glare buzzed with bluebottles ; the English context was turf scorched on cement-hard ground, ragwort, thistles, swarming rabbits, baked cowpats as thick as the thistles.

On one of these days of mazy sea and hot glare I found a place on The Cambir from which all the sea continent of St. Kilda was visible : Soay behind me, Levenish at the other extreme beyond Village Bay—a tip of Dùn showing—Boreray and the stacs in the north. The Cambir turf was almost entirely a wet squishy sward of tiny plantain plants broken up by small black tarns. A carrier pigeon resting by one of the tarns allowed me near enough to see the band on its leg. The neck of The Cambir peninsula and the lower reaches of the Great Glen stream were both gull areas, arrogant gulls overhead, the turf dirtied and trodden, littered with feathers and some extroverted puffins. The stream trickled down the middle of the glen, dropping by waterfalls from pool to pool. Some pools were waist-deep and a couple of yards across. The sky was a well of heat, the gulls planed round, disturbed, while I lay and splashed in the gasping cold water, all alone in Gleann Mor.

XX

Sheep, Mice and Wrens

LEACH's petrels were known to burrow on Dùn ; but the summering natives of Hirta had no boat. A hardy naturalist should swim over, carrying on his head his clothes, camera, torch, box of flash-bulbs and a sandwich ? I water-proofed a grocery box with putty—no end to island resources —to make a boat for my goods, to be towed behind me when I swam—if I did. Sunshine at once curled up the boards and opened all the seams. In the end I gave up the idea, being put off by the slimy forest of seaweed, the swell and the great chill of momentary immersions from the beach. All the same I felt a little guilty about it : here was the very source of Leach's petrels—where first found in 1818—where for nearly seventy-five years was its only known British station—where any nineteenth-century collector worthy of the name had helped himself—and all the time I was in St. Kilda I never saw or heard a fork-tail. The birds were likely to be breeding in Hirta itself, but where to begin in a coastline of nine or ten miles, and who was going scrambling alone on thousand-foot cliffs in the middle of the night ?

Instead I concerned myself with sheep, mice and wrens.

(1) SHEEP

Sheep in the other Atlantic isles were just sheep, Blackface or Cheviot as it happened, but these little brown animals from Soay were sheep for naturalists and for historians, even archæol-ogists ; and for sportsmen they were as *mouflon*—a couple of good heads decorated the manse.

Old writers apparently did not distinguish between the

aboriginal wild sheep of Soay and the then unimproved Hebridean breed. In his *General View of the Agriculture of the Hebrides* (1811), James Macdonald wrote :

> The native breed, or more properly, the Norwegian breed, (for it is the very same kind of sheep which we find all over the Norwegian coasts and isles that occurs in our Hebrides where modern improvements have not penetrated), has been the only kind known in these isles since the times of the Danish and Scandinavian invasions in the 8th or 9th century, till the present age. . . .

Traditionally Soay sheep were relict of the Vikings, whose aboriginal breed of sheep long survived in Iceland, the Faroes, Shetland, Outer Hebrides and Isle of Man. Only in the island of Soay have they continued true and unimproved. Authorities now distinguish between " Hebridean " sheep, now only in parks, and " Soay " sheep, only in or from Soay, and it seems that though they—and the little brown Shetland sheep—may have had common or similar origins, only the Soay race has remained pure.

The factor of St. Kilda, whose annual visit was accompanied in '96 by the Keartons, told them that the natives had wanted to cross Soay sheep with their own domesticated sheep—by then Blackface—but that Macleod of Macleod had objected, had taken over Soay himself and thereafter had charged the natives half a crown for each sheep they caught there. So the breed remained untouched, and only after the evacuation of 1930 were some Soay sheep introduced into the empty grazing of Hirta. Not, however, quite empty ; the islanders had failed to catch the last three or four sheep, so that the Soay breed in Hirta was probably now touched with Blackface.

Forty or fifty yards was as near as I was usually able to get to the wild sheep, and there was no hope of cornering one because they would go at full speed down places which I negotiated gingerly on my backside. In the old days when a boat's crew had used to go round to Soay to hunt the sheep, the Gaelic excitement of the occasion would drive some terrified

animals over the cliff. Even now Finlay MacQueen used to
shriek and wave his arms at them ; he liked to see them run.
When the Keartons went with a Soay expedition the dogs used
had their fangs broken, and they, helped by

> their barefooted masters, who sprang from rock to rock with
> great nimbleness and not a little excitement, literally ran down
> one of the timid creatures.

And Martin said :

> There are none to catch them but the Inhabitants, whom I
> have seen pursue the Sheep nimbly down the steep descent, with
> as great freedom as if it had been a plain Field.

Once I had a stroke of luck. It was on a hot day on The
Cambir and I was keeping along the cliff edge when I saw a
sheep's horns showing above a rock ten feet in front of me. I
immediately sat down and was fumbling with my camera
when the sheep came out from behind the rock and stood and
stared at me. " As near as I am to you," so I afterwards told
Neil, who translated to Finlay, who said : " Well, well, vary
khood, vary khood." I kept stock-still. The sheep did not
move, so I gradually lifted the camera and sighted it and let
it off. The sheep moved to and fro a few paces in an undecided
manner while I went on taking photographs. It made peculiar
grating and sneezing noises, shook its head and pawed the
ground ; a handsome beast to see so near to, with its close
dark chestnut fleece and its fine recurved horns : a young
ram. He was trying to work himself up to charge, I thought,
and didn't recognise me as quite human because I was sitting
down and wearing nothing but a pair of dirty white shorts.
Several times he started to go away, then stopped and was
puzzled and came back again to stare. In the end he made
off at a run to a distance of twenty yards, waited again, then
sighted and joined a party of his fellows, and they all went
away together across the floor of the Great Glen.

(2) MICE

Mice—I remembered Kennie MacIver saying that when he had made a yachting trip to St. Kilda in 1931 he had found the expedition of scientists in residence ; they had two or three St. Kilda house mice alive in cages, so precious he'd hardly been allowed to look at them.

The trapping of these and other mice was duly reported in the *Journal of Animal Ecology*, " The Mice of St. Kilda, with especial reference to their prospects of extinction, and present status," by T. H. Harrisson and J. A. Moy-Thomas. When the expedition left the island the mice were turned loose—twelve different house mice had been trapped altogether—but the species was thought unlikely to survive. House mice in St. Kilda were dependent on the food scraps of man and were not found apart from him. However, the independent long-tailed field mice should continue to prosper.

At first I could not catch a mouse. I had the usual penny break-back (" The Sentry ") and twopenny catch-alive traps. Neil then brought out an extremely patent mouse-trap, Made in Germany, and looking like a model of an industrial plant. The principle was that the mouse, perceiving the bait displayed behind bars, entered. In doing so he trod on a platform which tilted and released the catch of the entrance door, which dropped like a guillotine behind him. A wire tunnel now led him upwards past another trap-door which also shut behind him, to the top, where a hole opened to a second tilting board. This also tilted, deposited the mouse in a tin container, and reset the trap. I put some oatmeal in the tin as consolation prize and set the trap in the byre of Number 11. The next morning Neil came into the factor's house saying, " You've got a catch this time," and outside Finlay screeched, " Sleep, sleep, oh dear me, oh dear me." The mouse filled the entry to the trap and hadn't known how to proceed. I tipped him into an old schoolboy's caterpillar cage with a glass front and a back of perforated zinc, brought all the way to St. Kilda for just this occasion. The mouse seemed, first impression, the largest I had ever seen though otherwise much like any ordinary long-tailed field or wood mouse. He was at once provided with a matchboxful of oatmeal and raisins which he promptly settled down to eat. He sat bunched up, his large pink back feet comfortably splayed out while he held a raisin in his front feet. He had large bright black eyes and large paper-thin ears ; his fur was woolly and thick, not sleek. All the same it did seem a pity that this most special mouse should be so like any wood mouse to be caught on any row of garden peas. To zoologists *Apodemus sylvaticus hirtensis* differed in size and in fur ; it was the largest of all native mice.

Hirtensis twitched his whiskers round the cage, sat down in a corner and set to washing his face.

I visited the rest of the traps and missed a break-back in the cleit in front of the factor's house. I found it half hidden and attached to a live mouse, caught by the offside front and back toes. I felt uncomfortably cruel, but the mouse did not appear to mind, and in the cage at once picked up a raisin with the damaged foot and afterwards washed. The first mouse was George, the second Bessie, distinguished by size, and the extraordinary thing was that Bessie did turn out to be female and George male. They got on well enough together ; I remember seeing Bessie seated on top of George and briskly chewing a raisin.

Neil was amused at my delight with the mice ; Finlay, whose nights were disturbed by the scrabblings of mice in his loft, would have liked to have drowned them. I had as much pleasure from them as from any white mice of earlier years. In the evenings they ventured out with squeaks and scuffles and inquiring noses, upset their water trough (the tray of a matchbox waterproofed with candle grease) and took food into their sleeping quarters. Their most engaging habit was the way they washed their faces ; they used both feet together, busy combing movements starting well behind the ears and ending at the nose, just in the manner of a cat. I fed them on raisins, apple cores, biscuit, raw potato and oatmeal, and they did very well.

The house mice, it seemed, really were gone. At first I thought that the nibbled cheese of traps set in the inhabited houses meant house mice, but going on and catching only field mice I lost hope for *Mus musculus muralis* ; Finlay's active loft, the Gillies's bedroom—still only field mice. It seemed a sad little story, tacked on to the human saga of St. Kilda : common house mice had come in with men so long ago that their generations had gradually formed a new race ; now the men had gone and their small camp followers were to be written off as extinct.

In 1931 the scientists had caught no field mice inside the houses. Seven years later they were everywhere. I trapped them in the byres and houses, in the cleits, the old walls and in the long grass. At some time past, somehow, they had colonised Dùn ; Finlay told in translation and by gesture of a field mouse which had run up his sleeve there, when he was feeling down a petrel's burrow. (Oh dear me, etc.)

I did not like to set break-backs in the inhabited houses for fear of killing a surviving house mouse, but the catch-alive traps which I concentrated indoors were very inefficient. The 1931 people had been in the same difficulty. The weakness of conventional mouse-trap design was obviously that the trigger was loaded with the door-shutting spring. If the spring were strong enough to hold the door against the mouse's escape, the mouse wasn't man enough to touch off the trigger ; and if the spring were weak enough to be touched off easily, the mouse could easily force the door. A new design was called for.

I based my first model on the German trap. Materials available were old matchboarding, rusty nails, cardboard and tin lids. I borrowed Neil's saw, chisel and hammer, and an ancient rusty pair of tailor's scissors which could just be made to cut tin. The first trap was an open-topped wooden box with a trap-door at one end working like a guillotine. On the floor was a tilting platform of tin with either side bent down vertically and punched with a hole ; a nail driven through each side of the box engaged the holes and the platform was counterweighted until it tipped quite freely on its nail bearings. The guillotine trap-door was propped open by an arm of tin bent up from the platform. All that a mouse had to do was to walk along the platform until it tilted, which released the trap-door, which fell by its own weight ; no springs at all.

The second trap was an incredible mechanism. I puzzled over the problem of converting a downward into a horizontal pull. A mouse's weight exerted, one might say, a vertical force. You had your mouse on a tilting platform and it was exerting a vertical force ; how to redirect this force to pull away the trap-door trigger, which must be horizontal ? Of course, what else but a wheel ?—a wheel turning in a vertical plane—wires attached to the circumference at ninety degrees to each other and leading away to trigger and to platform. The downward pull from the platform would revolve the wheel which would pull with it the trigger release ; the guillotine would drop and there'd be your mouse—catched—perhaps. When I had finished this trap it worked about five times out of ten, but it had a lighter release than the first. Both the New Models were definitely indoor traps and could only be set by the inventor. The lids for them were two bits of glass weighed down with stones. The traps had such a rugged simple look that I felt sure the mice would be deceived. Neil and Finlay were scornful.

At its first setting the Second Model caught a mouse but let it escape. The mouse ate some cheese, churned up the complicated machinery, left its little black rice and gnawed its way out through the cardboard door. The same thing happened the next night to the First Model. But after repair and overhaul they had their triumph : on the night of August 1st the New Models, the German, and three ordinary catch-alives stood set in Number 5. Next morning the Models had a mouse apiece and the others were empty, though all showed traces of mice and two were sprung. There was no stopping them after that ; morning after morning they delivered their quota of St. Kilda field mice.

The mice George and Bessie were pets, while a selection of

later catches, the mice W, X, Y, Z and MacW., were merely specimens. When George and Bessie had been in captivity for nearly a week I noticed blood and something looking like intestines—Bessie had given birth. And now George sat holding one of the litter in his front paws, as if it were a raisin, eating it. It wasn't a litter of his siring, six days was too soon even for a mouse. I took out one of the dead young, a pink naked morsel, tightly curled up, hardly recognisable as an animal organism. George and Bessie were best left to themselves ; I covered them up with half an old wren's nest which lay handy. I hoped they would breed again, this time between themselves, but they never did.

(3) WRENS

Wrens—cheerful small troglodytes, needle-billed, bright-eyed, slipped in and out of the crannied walls of cleits and byres : busy—they halted momentarily for a song : flying—the little brown lumps whirred low and straight over the village grass.

Wrens, like mice, had been in St. Kilda so long that harsh isolation had moulded them into a distinct species—or sub-species—or island race. Late in their history Martin included them in his list of Land-Fowls, and so did the Rev. Kenneth Macaulay, after his visit of 1758, who added :

> How these little birds, I mean the wrens particularly, could have flown thither, or whether they went accidentally in boats, I leave undetermined.

And so it seems do modern biologists, unable to agree whether the wrens and field mice are pre-glacial relics or post-glacial immigrants.

Troglodytes hirtensis was launched in 1884, after the ornithologist Charles Dixon had shot a wren in St. Kilda and Henry Seebohm had pronounced it to be of a new species. From that day until the evacuation was the most dangerous period of all the wrens' long history. In 1904 St. Kilda wren and Leach's petrel shared an Act of Parliament to protect them, but collecting continued, the natives knew their value, and a clutch of wren's eggs would fetch £5 even within a few years of the evacuation. The 1931 party estimated the total population of living wrens as about sixty-eight pairs, forty-five of them in Hirta and the rest in Dùn, Boreray and Soay ; the village population was about a dozen pairs ; all the rest belonged to cliff slopes.

A family of five wrens lived about the factor's house, and sometimes slipped into my kitchen or living-room. The young were already nearly indistinguishable from their parents, whom they still pursued with fledglings' greedy hoarseness. It was soon obvious that now, late July, the wrens' breeding season in the village was over ; the village was busy with family parties of young birds all some weeks out of the nest. I was greatly disappointed. I had come with my familiars—the box of flash-bulbs, the ancient reflex camera which had to be draped in cloth to keep out the light, the black bloomers or plate-changing bag—and the bird had flown. This was puzzling and unexpected, because of the nests found by the 1931 people in late July, one had still contained eggs and the rest young at various stages. I should have been just at the right season.

Without any hope I set out to search the village for the chance of a stray late nest still occupied. I searched closely, inside and out, every one of the 130-odd cleits, byres and houses within the village enclosure. This took two days.

On the afternoon of July 29th I had nearly finished and had found thirteen nests, all done with. Those of the current year were easily told by their fresh look and green moss. If they had been intended for use, or used, they were lined with either fulmars' feathers (which yet kept their reek and were still available from old heaps in the byres or fresh from the small Tulmer factory which Finlay kept going) or with the pretty feathers of snipe (and this was the nicest little ecological link I came across). Nests from which young had flown were marked obviously with droppings, and inside by the thick dust

of scurf shed from nestlings' quills. Cocks' nests were unlined
—cock birds' careless running-up of nests was evidently
habitual in island as in mainland wrens.

Seeing me creep out of a cleit, Neil called me into Number
11 for a cup of tea. Afterwards I worked the scattered cleits
at the far end of the village. One of these, a small, rather
shabby cleit, had the doorway half blocked with stones. I
was going at the job thoroughly, no stone unturned, so I pulled
them away. There was a wren's nest two feet inside, tucked
into the angle between lintel and entrance wall. This one was
rather slightly built, certainly this year's, probably a cock's
nest. I felt inside to see if it was lined and my finger touched
a warm heap, soft, downy and fleshy—a nestful of young
wrens ! As the Keartons said,

> a situation over the door-lintel of one of these dark structures
> did not lend itself readily to picture-making.

They had managed with the help of two mirrors to make a
daylight time exposure of a wren's nest. This similarly placed
nest meant flashlight and a camera would only be able to see
it from one spot on the ground outside.

One of the last cleits was almost big enough to qualify as a
byre. As I came out of it a wren flew away from over the
doorway with something white in its beak. Ha ha, I thought :
fæces. Sure enough, there was the nest, and full of well-grown
young ones. This one was outdoor, high up and tucked deeply
under the turf eave, out of hand's reach. An eighteenth and
last village nest turned out to be a third occupied one, inside a
cleit right down by the shore at the head of the bay. This one
was fully indoor and so deeply tucked between the ceiling
slabs that only a straw or two of it was visible ; I could just
feel in, taking the skin off my wrist, to touch a nestful of warm
eggs deep in their feather bed. These three nests seemed like
second broods, but second broods had never been recorded of
St. Kilda wrens. The breeding season was puzzling. When
nests had been robbed for sale, the eggs had been taken in

late May or early June. This year the only nest Neil Gillies
had noticed, in the manse byre, had had five eggs at the end
of May. Yet in 1931 the very first young had flown on the
30th of July and there had been no sign of earlier broods.
There was more in it than met the eye, but for 1938 I plumped
for double broods.

The hide Neil and I built at the outdoor wren's nest was a
fine work in local materials. What was called for was a something to raise the camera eight feet above the ground and to
provide accommodation for the operator behind it. We found
two old tables, laid one upside down and anchored it with a
couple of hundredweight of boulders, and lashed the other
one on top, right way up. Two of the tripod's legs were
mounted on the table and the third was wedged into the cleit
wall in front. A home-made driftwood chair from one of the
houses stood on the table top and the whole was draped with
sacks ; most comfortable.

The hide at the indoor nest was easier and was simply a
low lean-to, leant against the outside wall of the cleit. One
lay full length inside. A bottle wrapped in silver paper from
a cigarette tin served as dummy, to accustom the birds to the
glitter of flash-bulb and reflector to come. When the hides
were finished I stood back and saw that both wrens accepted
them and returned to feeding their young.

Next day I mounted the dais, pinned myself inside the
sacking and sat back in the driftwood chair ; smoke was soon
swirling out of the peephole as from a chimney, while the
wrens were busy about their comings and goings. Both of the
pair came to the nest pretty well alternately ; they were easily
told apart as one of them was notably shabby. I supposed the
shabby one female until it flew from the nest to the graveyard
wall and there delivered, tail at full cock, a fine period of
spring song, as sweet and incongruous as the unseasonable
primroses by the Conachair stream. The wrens brought
insects and green caterpillars and fat white maggots to the
nest ; they flew away to forage particularly in thick beds of
docks. (St. Kildans had used to pluck dock leaves for their

cows ; a cow would hardly stand to be milked without a
bundle of them. Now you could walk the dock patches and
flush wrens, like partridges from a field of roots.) The young
wrens were big enough to lean out of the nest to gape yellow
maws at the parent, which, having unloaded its beakful of
food, remained clinging to the nest, turning its head this way
and that, waiting for the exchange. If a nestling's pink rear
view showed in the entrance hole the parent leant forward to
meet it and took the white sac as it swelled. It was a careful,
gentle transfer, unlike the rough stuffing of food into the
nestlings ; and devoid of any kind of nastiness, as Martin said
of the St. Kilda graveyard.

Sunlight never reached the nest itself but in the evening
touched the north-facing cleit wall in which it was built.
During calm evening shifts in the hide I watched the line of
shadow advance across the village, climb up the cleit wall, leave
it dark, and move on up the slope of Oiseval. In a few days the
young were ready to fly. Several times one of them came
half-way out of the nest and leant adventurously farther,
perched on the sill. Otherwise they lay with their heads half
outside, with the peculiarly unintelligent look of young birds
—blinking eyes and mouths half open. By the next evening
one of the young had flown and was calling from the cleit
wall ; its crescendo was warning of a parent's approach. Once
it reappeared a yard from the nest. Its tiny tail stump was
cocked up and it carried itself in a grown-up way in spite of
callow bill, absurd tailpiece, and youthful down still straying
amongst sleek feathers. Next evening the nest was empty.

St. Kilda wrens left the nest for a world without natural
enemies. Their only mortality was accidental. I retrieved one
tiny corpse from Mrs. Gillies's washtub and boiled it in a bully
beef tin to clean the skeleton. (What did you do on St. Kilda ?
Oh, I boiled a wren.) The village wrens spent most of their
lives in mousy creepings under some sort of cover, safe from
hawks, had there been any. The 1931 ornithologists said that
the wrens were only in the air for twenty-odd minutes in the
day, flying was only 2 per cent of the day's work. When they

did fly the wrens burred along like bumble-bees—at 12 m.p.h., said the ornithologists.

Unfortunately my apparatus could not have been more unsuitable for the indoor nest. Between the parents' visits I nursed it and read the mouldy native copy of *The Swiss Family Robinson*. At each visit a good beakful of squirming green caterpillars was delivered to the young, which were still only a few days hatched and had not flown by the time I left the island. From a little distance the noise of a parent's wings was like a moth's. Coming nearer, it was a harsher sound from the short stiff feathers : the old thrill of a bird's wings past the hide. When starlings flew over, each wing-beat was separable, but wrens' wings buzzed so fast they went with an insect's whirr. The wrens hung to the stones with tit-like acrobatics, they slipped as mice between the chinks on the way to the nest. I got glimpses which disappeared and reappeared at a range of one foot, of bright black eyes and clusters of green caterpillars ; then—clip—the bird was clinging to the nest. The camera lens was but two feet from the nest, far too close, but it could only get a sight of it from that one point.

Once both birds came together. One greeted the other by spreading and vibrating its wings and making queer little chipping noises. I flashed as they hung side by side—tremendous stroke of luck—I was quite fluttering with excitement—a double of St. Kilda wrens ! They looked wonderful in the instantaneous brilliance of the flash. Changing the slide afterwards, I saw that the focus had slipped ; the negative, when developed weeks later, was merely a fuzzy might-have-been.

When no more flash-bulbs were left I still lay to watch the wrens. They were so near it was like examining a bird in the hand ; their St. Kildan characteristics of larger size and stronger, greyer markings, robuster bills and legs, were plain. Pleasant to watch the stealthy bright-eyed approach to the nest, the gabbled transfer of caterpillars, the gentle receipt of the white sac ; and to hear the invisible whirr of wings amplified within the dark hollow of the cleit.

XXI

Natives and Visitors

IN St. Kilda the Past was always at hand, pressing so nearly upon Now. I almost expected Neil to turn and translate : " Finlay says he remembers being told of the time when Martin was here and they named that well o' water after him."

Elsewhere, " rich in historical associations " had never meant much to me. That Haymarket, S.W.1, had once been hayfields served only to remove still further the unsubstantial haymakers. In half a century's time the inhabited past of St. Kilda might become as unreachable as Rona's ; now the press of it was inescapable, two or three hundred years were as yesterday. The reason must be that the island had been familiarised, that everything had been seen so many times before ; a sameness, and so, a timelessness. The changing visitors from outside emphasised the constancy within. The somewhat puny monuments of old natives had little to do with it, the reason was rather with a climate that kept the look of the land stable. What counted was that people of centuries had been familiar with the island's daily phenomena, recorded again and again—its named landmarks, its weather signs, its corncrake, its treacherous squalls in the bay, its darkening sea-fowl—which were here and now. The natives' way of life was set by the island, so that as in Rona the passage of centuries outside made little mark. The natives themselves, here in the village, were the last of the line. Changelessness of the ocean, fixed by landmarks and people !

There was the flight of sea-fowl towards the island, which, " being compar'd, did exactly quadrate with our Compass," said Martin. The Keartons, of course, had noted it and so must have any one else who had ever steered or sailed or steamed towards the island.

257

The Inhabitants rely so much upon this Observation, that they prefer it to the surest Compass. . . .

" At the Head of the Bay there's a plain Sand," said Martin ; it was where the natives of 1697 had played their version of beach cricket. I bathed from it, and saw a dunlin there once, as the Keartons had " a very prim little fellow as he ran up and down the narrow spit of golden sand."

When I told the time by shadows on the factor's house—

They know the time of the Day by the Motion of the Sun from one Hill or Rock to another.

When I looked along the silent village street—

The distance between their Houses is by them called the High-street.

When I looked to the skyline broken by silhouetted cleits, Martin's pyramids—

Their little Stone Houses, of which there are some hundreds for preserving their Fowls, Eggs, etc.

When I saw a layer of cloud below Conachair that left the summit clear and Neil said that that meant heat, or the usual cap of mist that meant rain—

The Hills are often covered with ambient White Mists . . . in Summer, if only on the Tops of the Hills, they prognosticate Rain ; and when they descend to the Valleys it is a Prognostick of excessive Heat.

It was always so : under St. Kilda's sun there was no new thing.

I had begun with the shock of the *Dunara Castle*, already twenty-one years old when the Keartons came out in '96 ; to me the same swaying deck in 1938. Was forty-two years as

short a time as that? As a child I had used to think of
remotest time as long, long ago, before there were any motor
cars. Finlay MacQueen was a young chap in his thirties then,
the champion cragsman of the island. Of course he remembered the Keartons, he'd taken them fowling, one of them had
a game leg. And when he went on one of his fowling expeditions now, I took the same sort of photographs as Cherry
Kearton had taken of him in the days of his prime.

Mrs. Gillies had gone on up the hill on a field-day for
crotal. (Crotal—Martin called it the " scurf upon the stones,"
the grey lichen which, then as now, was boiled to produce the
standard reddish-brown of Harris tweed. Nowadays St.
Kildans got sixpence a pound for it. Crotal-dyed wool was
variegated by tying strings tightly round the hanks before
dyeing, so that the ties left undyed bands.) I found Mrs. Gillies
busy scraping the hoary stuff off the rocks with an old hoe.
Down below in the village Neil was a tiny black beetle outside
Number 11, moving to and fro to a saw ; he was making me
a St. Kilda mailboat. We saw Finlay start up towards us.
Mrs. Gillies screeched down to him and he screeched back ;
he was only a little dot five or six hundred feet below, but they
appeared to make each other understand, Gaelic being that
sort of language. Finlay came up on his broad bare feet with
the well-spread toes ; he carried a fowling rod, a hoe, opera
glasses, a sack and a coil of rope. He walked slightly bow-
legged with a long swinging stride, as sure-footed as the sheep.
He and Mrs. Gillies were both nearer eighty than seventy ;
they climbed a thousand feet from the village, spent all day at
the crotal, descended, and thought nothing of it.

Finlay was quite insensitive to heights. He perched on the
Lover's Stone, a slice of rock sticking up into thin air from the
cliff top. He liked to roll boulders over the edge and to watch
their frightful plunge and bounce. When I followed him down
to the scree called Carn Mor, in the western cliffs, he insisted
on roping us together, which was alarming. " Come on," he
kept shouting fiercely, tugging at the rope and jerking his head.
We got down among the piled boulders where the flying dots

of puffins made the air buzz, and their shadows flickered over the rock. The language common between us was, " good " (as in " good boy puffin "), " bad," " go " (home ?), " come " (on), " good-bye." His usual exclamation was " vary khood," and his expression for any misfortune, " on the rrocks."

Finlay made ready his fowling rod, an immemorial type of instrument. It was a long tapering pole with a curve of bamboo lashed to the thin end, carrying a running noose. The noose was of horse-hair with a split gannet's quill pleated in to stiffen it. Finlay chewed this for a time to make the noose stay put. The method was to creep within rod range of a group of puffins and gently to approach the noose, held verti-cally, to one of the birds, then with a quick twist to drop it over the bird's head. The puffin was hauled in flapping and kicking like a fish. Finlay so smoothly advanced the rod that it seemed to pay itself out. The puffins seeing it coming shuffled their feet—uneasy—and turned their heads about—curious. Most of them flew away in time. The noose hung with hardly a quiver in front of a puffin's breast, then—flip—one bird was struggling wildly and the rest were off in a panic. A pretty skill. Finlay playfully advanced his first puffin to the seat of my trousers, so I was pleased when it turned and got a good hold on the back of his hand and drew blood. He let that one go, perhaps it wasn't plump enough, but wrung the next one's neck and, as Martin would have said, instantly fell to plucking it. Finlay had his small purchase of sea-fowl for breakfast next morning.

I left Finlay and Mrs. Gillies scraping away at the rocks. " I saw you coming down the hill and put on the kettle," said Neil. The mailboat was complete, no amateurish tin can as of Rona, but the authentic St. Kildan design. It was a block of wood pointed at one end and hollowed out. The message went inside a bottle sealed with candle grease and the bottle went inside the boat, whose lid was nailed down and inscribed by penknife and red-hot poker : Please Open. The boat was wired to the float—a sheepskin bladder tacked round a staff, found complete in one of the houses. We nailed a flag to the

staff and sent off the whole issue from the jetty on the last day
of July. Finlay had sent mailboats in the old days ; once one
of his had been picked up on the coast of Norway. After their
visit the Keartons had received a letter by mailboat via the
south coast of Uist. A facsimile of part of the letter was printed
in their book :

> this is to be sent in a toy boat by the first north west wind of
> which Finly McQueen is Captain, with best wishes, remember
> me to your brother, I remain yours Faithfuly Neil Ferguson

(who had been in residence in Number 5 this summer).

I enclosed a self-addressed postcard in mine and got it
back a month later :

> found 24 Miles West of the Butt of Lewis on August 24 1938
> yours truly A Morrison 27 Borve Stornoway Lewis.

Neil obviously suffered from the lighthouse malaise, the
loss of purpose from long sameness and no outside stimulus.
Nothing to do but kill time, smoke too much, sit in front of
the fire, saw wood when it was wanted and not before. He
mowed the graveyard weeds or the grass along the street and
said that it passed the time. One year he had been completely
alone in the island for three weeks.

As for myself, at first I had momentarily wondered if island
occupations had lost their savour, exploring and housekeeping
all alone. I was soon too busy to think about it or I might
have been sitting in front of the fire, occasionally spitting at it
and saying " Aye " to myself like the Monach crofters. Instead
the days were too short.

Finlay went his own way ; his housekeeping, bird-snaring
and crotal hoeing kept him occupied ; he leavened these
activities with a little daytime sleep and with Bible reading.
On a fine day he put out his dried fish to air and to gather
the bluebottles, or he looked through his uninviting stock of
fulmars—birds snared earlier in the year, plucked, split, and
preserved in brine. Mrs. Gillies was always busy, carding and

spinning, knitting socks and gloves, baking oatcakes and scones, scrubbing the floor while the three of us watched.

I was given innumerable cups of tea in Number 11. Phonetically the Gaelic for " cup of tea " sounded like " coop-ah-tay " ; at first I thought this was English and wondered how on earth Mrs. Gillies could have picked up a Lancashire accent. " Coop-ah-tay ? " said Mrs. Gillies. " Have a sit," said Neil. Sometimes Neil and Finlay came for a drink at the factor's house. However large the tot of whisky, Finlay took it neat all at one go and then shuddered all over : " Oh dear me, oh dear me." I had only the one bottle. My sweeties also went down well and Finlay was always glad to add a couple of inches of the black twist to the secret hoard of tobacco which he invariably denied. This was a well-known phenomenon to St. Kilda visitors because he played his cards so badly ; he was apt to drop a coil of twist on the jetty while he gestured empty pockets. When Mrs. Gillies harangued her son I understood one word, but the trend was only too clear : great big man sitting there all day and puffing at that everlasting peep, peep, peep. Finlay used to clean out his ears exhaustively with a match-stick. Neil would make a " sap " (native boyhood dish ?), a slush of tea, sugar, and broken-up scone in a bowl. Sometimes I found it in myself to wish that he would not say " Okay chief " and " What's fresh ? " so frequently.

The three of them met every evening at Number 11. When I walked up the street I always looked in through the door of Number 2. Usually Finlay's deal chair stood empty and the fire was red embers. I would find them all at Number 11 : the sooted kettle being hurried with slivers of matchboarding ; Finlay carving and rubbing down slices of the black twist, a familiar coil warm and polished from long residence in his trouser pocket ; Mrs. Gillies padding silently in black felt slippers, putting out sugar and scones. Finlay sat wrapped in his beard within spitting range of the fire, Neil within range of the door. They took their tea nearly strong and syrupy enough to hold up the spoon. Mrs. Gillies's and Finlay's Gaelic interchanges were sometimes understandable because of the wealth of emphasis and gesture, but leading questions had to go via Neil. Sometimes we touched on Questions of the Day. " Finlay says he'd put Mussolini on Levenish "—vehement nodding from Finlay, bad, bad. " Or in Dugan's Cave on Soay."

After tea Mrs. Gillies would treadle away at the spinning-wheel, spinning thread from a pile of the fluffy wool, a thin cloud lighter than feathers, which she had carded out from stray tufts left about by the wild sheep. Neil said of such occupation, " It passes the time," but I was sure Mrs. Gillies or Finlay didn't so think of it ; the island had been their lives.

Sundays were strictly marked off from the rest of the week. Each morning and evening on Sundays the three St. Kildans in Sunday best walked slowly past the factor's house on their way to the church. I attended one service which, because it was so strange and unintelligible, I saw detachedly : a ritual carried out by a tribe of three, twice a day but on only one day in seven, in a particular house reserved for the purpose and not otherwise used. I cleared a space in the debris of a seat at the back and sat down. Finlay in spectacles conducted the service : prayers, psalms read and then sung, Bible reading, a twenty-minute sermon. Finlay read with fearful histrionic emphasis. They all sang the psalms in a soaring and swooping dirge, often nasally out of tune or out of time with each other, but they made a loud unselfconscious noise. The prayers were said fervently in an almost agonised hoarse whisper. Finlay's sermon echoed round the dust-deep room. " Change and decay in all around I see " . . . perhaps.

The large dirty room and the congregation of three—or four—put a strangeness on the performance which the St. Kildans evidently did not feel ; and why indeed should they ? But I was overtaken by the queerness of it ; the circumstances bizarre to me of fallen plaster and tattered books were irrelevant to them. They had been reared from birth to this religion so it came as naturally and essentially to them as eating or drinking (though it was a little odd that they didn't clear up their sacred house). For myself, from a southern orthodoxy of ignorance of anything to do with the Church, the oddness was not so much in the circumstances of the service as in the fact that it happened at all. I was reminded of a story in *Sunday at Home*—in the Free Library—the 1876 volume, I think—a story of the sameness of Australian outback sheep farmers' days and of their godless Sabbaths, until an itinerant parson turned up at one station and held an impromptu worship, and the farmers were *fed*.

After the service the male St. Kildans took a nip in the factor's house.

* * *

The centuries in St. Kilda were already so nearly telescoped; push a little harder and surely there should be resurrection: Martin himself to be carried ashore by the natives after his desperate boat voyage, to walk up the street —" all of us walking together to the little Village. . . ." Martin to meet in this village his fellow voyagers of the centuries. . . .

You may have heard of Sir Donald, Mr. Martin? Sir Donald Monro—Mr. Martin Martin.

Ane maine laiche ile—

I beg your pardon?

Ane maine laiche ile [I said], sa far as is manurit of it. . . . M'Cloyd of Herray, his stewart . . . as he himself tauld me, uses to take ane maske of malt ther with a masking fatt, and makes his malt, and ere the fatt be ready, the comons of the town, baith men, weemin, and bairns, puts their hands in the fatt, and findis it sweeit, and eets the greyns after the sweeitness thereof, quhilk they leave nather wirt nor draffe unsuppit out ther, quharwith baith men, women, and bairns, were deid drunken, sua that they could not stand upon their feet.

Thank you, Sir Donald. You may even have met Sir George M'Kenzie, the Lord Register, Mr. Martin? As a fellow informant of Sibbald the antiquary?—though rather your senior. I hardly know whether Sir George speaks from his own experience or from hearsay :

> The exercise they affect most, is climbing of steep rocks ; he is the prettiest man who ventures upon the most inaccessible, though all they gain is the eggs of the fowls, and the honour to dye, as many of their ancestors, by breaking of their necks. . . .

Mr. Martin, you won't have heard of the Rev. Mr. Kenneth Macaulay—since your time ; he is ashore for only a short visit, you understand; he has to make a report to the Society for Propagating Chriſtian Knowledge.

> It will be readily expected that a race of men and women, bred in *St. Kilda*, muſt be a very flovenly generation, and every way inelegant.—I confeſs it is impoſſible to defend them from this imputation.—Their method of preparing a fort of manure, to them indeed of vaſt uſe, proves that they are very indelicate. . . .

Mr. Martin, I thought it better not to introduce to you the Rev. Mr. Alexander Buchan ; he was the first resident minister, came in 1705, died here in the island in 1730—but perhaps you knew of him ?[1] Because I fear he spent his time pirating your book, often without acknowledgment, and one of his daughters published the notes after his death, under his own name ; she said your book was " dear, and out of date." Nor Mr. James Thomson ; of course he never visited the island—learnt of it from your own and other works, no doubt —but you might like to hear a little of his *Seasons* :

> *Here the plain harmless native his small flock,*
> *And herd diminutive of many hues,*
> *Tends on the little island's verdant swell,*
> *The shepherd's sea-girt reign ; or, to the rocks*
> *Dire-clinging, gathers his ovarious food. . . .*

Nor the Rev. Mr. J. L. Buchanan ; these clergymen from the

[1] Martin died in 1719.

Society are much of a muchness and anyway this one borrowed from his friend Mr. Macaulay.

Mr. Martin might care to meet one or two of a superior early type of tourist? We might annoy Dr. Macculloch by so describing him.

> He that has no other means of clambering up to the temple of fame, may come to St. Kilda : he will assuredly be remembered in its archives ; and some future Martin or Macaulay shall record him in calf well bound, as I myself trust to be recorded. . . . I placed the mountain barometer on the top of Conachan, splendid in all its polished brass . . . could not have excited more astonishment . . . found the height to be 1380 feet.

Mr. Macaulay :

> I made a fhift to take its height with fome degree of exactnefs, and found it no lefs than nine hundred fathoms.

Dr. Macculloch :

> Macaulay . . . appears to have determined to write a book without materials, calls it the " Teneriffe of Britain," and makes it 5400 feet.

You were pretty near yourself, Mr. Martin, with your " about two hundred fathom height " (1200 feet).

Mr. Martin—Mr. James Wilson, the yachtsman :

> We have already given expression to some of our sentiments regarding St. Kilda, its people, and their pastor, in a letter addressed to the Secretary of the Society for Propagating Christian Knowledge, and published in the *Appendix to Report* of that Society's proceedings for 1841.

Mr. Martin—Mr. T. S. Muir, the ecclesiologist.

> Visited the burying-ground—a small disordered spot full of nettles.

Mr. Martin—Mr. J. A. Harvie-Brown.

> Recommend our readers to scan the well-worn pages of in-numerable other writers, from Martin downwards.

Mr. Martin—Messrs. Richard and Cherry Kearton.

> I doubt not we shall be accused of adventurous foolhardiness. I must plead that we are English.

Mr. Martin—Scientists of Oxford and Cambridge Universities.

> The whole ecological experiment has already been damaged by allowing the islanders to go back each summer since the evacuation. . . .

Allowing the islanders. . . . Evacuation? Yes, Mr. Martin.

*   *   *

The Lover's Stone and the Well of Virtue were typical show-pieces of St. Kilda, the sort of guide-book features which St. Kilda visitors had always seized upon. Martin's (quaint) words about the well water were unfailingly quoted, its efficacy against windy-chollicks, its diuretick properties. But Martin had his proportions right, he was the independent gentleman who had read papers to the Royal Society, his writings were whole. Martin stood head and shoulders above the rest and by no means only because he got in first. Oddments of topography had no more than a just share in his all-seeing reports of country and natives, their customs and their crops, the fauna and flora, the weather. It was the tourist mind, heir of the Picturesque, which later on abetted the natives' often lop-sided ideas of what was special and encouraged the tiresome claptrap of devil's footprints, outlaws' caves, sacred wells, rocking stones, pigmies' isles and the rest —a lump of rock here, a hole in a rock there. Meanwhile I had a good look at the Well of Virtues and the Lover's Stone.

The visitors from Martin to Macculloch were manageable,

but thereafter, not.[1] The nineteenth century yachtsmen alone would have made a useful fleet. The first steamboat was as soon as 1834 (the natives rushed to tell the minister : a ship on fire was approaching the island). And once *Dunara Castle* had inaugurated the tourist trip there was no end to the stream of clergy, journalists, ladies, naturalists, and plain tourists.

The since famous spread of the fulmar began to be noticed about this time. Later on it was thought to be a result of the steamship service : more imported foodstuffs, and so less fowling—" the St. Kilda theory "—but the facts that fowling continued unabated for many more years and that fulmars had long been expanding in Iceland and elsewhere in the face of large-scale fowling, have since discredited the theory ; the fulmar's colonial effort remains unexplained.

Meanwhile as early as the seventies there was talk and newspaper correspondence about the possibility of a human withdrawal from St. Kilda ; life there, as viewed from Glasgow, was perhaps already an anomaly. The natives were being victimised by the proprietor, they were suffering famine —no, they were very well off, nothing could surpass the pro- prietor's benevolence ; rival subscription lists for their relief were opened to the public. All this was a good thing for the newspapers, and from then onwards the affairs of the island were an unfailing source to them, the hardiest of hardy annuals. Intermittently the papers invented Kings and Queens of St. Kilda and they were always pleased with the so-called St. Kilda Parliament—that is to say, the voluble gatherings of the men in the village street to decide whether to mend the boat, or not to mend the boat, or whether after all it mightn't be better to go and catch Tulmers to-day ? The natives were presented with boats, and livestock, and seeds ; a pier was built, a post-office. Sometimes a ship was wrecked and Admiralty vessels and special correspondents hurried out. Each year *Dunara Castle* and her sister ships returned with

---

[1] A remarkable bibliography was compiled by Malcolm Stewart in 1937 and included in *St. Kilda Papers, 1931.*

provisions and with loads of passengers. However, it all ended in falling roofs and Yorkshire fog.

St. Kildans were usually pretty well off. They were always better off than their contemporaries in Harris and Uist, even discounting the latter day perquisites of publicity. The cottages built in the early eighteen-sixties were fifty and more years ahead of the common crofts (black houses) of the main islands. Long before *Dunara Castle*, all sorts of improvements had been wished on to the natives by proprietor or minister or well-meaning visitor. A clergyman of 1850 brought an assortment of crockery : elsewhere, coal in the bath ; in St. Kilda, " certain articles, to which I cannot more particularly allude, freely used as porridge-dishes ! " How far-flung was the British lavatory joke !

The outspoken Dr. Macculloch, who was usually rude about Islanders and Highlanders and who was no sort of sentimentalist, had been enthusiastic about the natives' circumstances of 1815. " If this island is not the Utopia so long sought, where will it be found ? " he had asked. But education came, the young men began to leave their island Utopia to better themselves, and gradually man-power became insufficient to manage the traditional work of the island. The last Clearance of all was voluntary and by urgent request of the remaining forty-odd natives.

There were other, and not Gaelic native, aspects : of the uncompleted saga of *Dunara Castle*, for instance, or of a period piece in tourism. Mr. George Seton, Advocate, had lectured about St. Kilda for years before he even saw his subject. But when he did, it was on that historic occasion, the first cruise to St. Kilda of s.s. *Dunara Castle*. Some forty passengers were aboard, the brave and the fair ; the ship anchored in Village Bay, the morning of July 2nd, 1877.

After breakfasting on board the " Dunara," the passengers began to land in detachments about half-past nine. Heavy rain fell during breakfast ; but the weather speedily improved, and the sun shone forth most auspiciously.

The natives put on a show of cliff work.

> Uttering a shrill Gaelic cry, he descended barefoot, skipping and singing as he went, and occasionally standing out nearly at a right angle from the beetling cliff !

(Mr. Macaulay had been unable to watch his show, " fuch diftrefs of mind . . . could not for my life run over half the fcene with my eyes.") Then, back to the ship, and so— Farewell ! South-about, once round the island, across to Boreray and the Stacs, a view of the milling gannets—

> the vast variety of form and colour which delighted the party on board the " Dunara Castle " on the afternoon of the 2d of July will not soon be forgotten. . . .

Uncounted magic-lantern lectures to Free Church congregations alone ! And all the lectures and articles, variations on the theme of " A Visit to St. Kilda," made their pick from items of a standardised catalogue : Of sea-fowl and fowling, the fulmar, how caught and eaten ; of Lover's Stone—Well of Virtue—House of the Amazon or Female Warrior, etc. ; of the Parliament ; of the fluctuating population, the smallpox epidemic of 1724, the stranger's or boat cold ; of the incarceration of Lady Grange by her husband in the eighteenth century, her time spent in weeping, her house but lately demolished, etc. ; of the natives' extortionism, accused or denied, their passion for sweets and tobacco, their dress, appearance, physique, diet, devotions, folklore, legends, etc., etc. ; of Conachair, Conager, Conagra, Conachan, of Village Bay, village, cleits, church and so on, and so on : the grandeur and the quaintness, " from Martin downwards."

XXII

St. Kilda Evacuated

WHEN an evening was warm enough to sit on the bench outside Number 11, the midges prevented it. But in daytime somebody was always keeping an unconscious look-out, somebody's eyes always straying to the bay. It used to be said that a ship could never get into Village Bay without being seen—and all the dogs would break out yelping.

One day I was crossing the flank of Conachair and looked down to the calm bay water and beyond to—a ship ! For no known reason of my own this was suddenly exciting. I made out ESJA painted in big white letters along her side. She blew ; the plume of steam drifted and had disappeared by the time the sound came. I waited for her to turn, thinking what a full berth she was giving to the northern arm of the bay, but she steamed straight on past Dùn, met the swell again and bobbed like a cork. She was only a cruise ship from Glasgow, Neil told me ; she passed once a fortnight but she never came in.

Another day a trawler put in to the bay. The coming of a ship was a romance, some seaborne meeting in a far-off place ! This rusty old iron tank stopped engines, she lost way, her bow wave dropped, and she glided in the still water under Dùn. Then she blew, the white plume started out, the harsh blare echoed round the empty grass bowl of the island. Some tiny white fluttering from the village. She waited, but no boat put out to her. She turned and made out again, giving a final blow as she went.

A dream of romance, to stand in to Village Bay in one's own command, in steam ? To ease her off and lose way in the quiet water, and blare the siren round the hills to echo and re-echo—puffins swarming out like flies from the crags of

271

Dùn—wild sheep scampering over the skyline—the last forgotten inhabitants running out of the houses—a ship, a ship !

F.R.S. *Explorer* was marked before she had even cleared the point of the bay. The " F.R.S." was " Fishery Research Ship." Neil recognised her ; she had last put in to Village Bay two years before. She trawled up and marked white fish, working out their movements and migrations; fishermen who afterwards caught marked fish got half a crown for them from the Fishery Board. I watched her steaming dead slow round the bay, with her trawl down ; and then went off for a hot field-day to the other end of the island.

In the evening I came back and sat on the roof of a cleit on the hillside above the village. The *Explorer* lay stationary over her reflection. At this moment Neil was leading a ship's party up the street a few hundred feet below . . . branch off here to the graveyard, file in through the gate. One usually flushed a snipe or two from the disordered spot. Read the inscriptions. File out again. Now this erection is Mr.—er— Aitchison's hide. This is the chair he sits on, there's the wren's nest up between the stones. Move on again. This hole over here is the underground dwelling. No, it doesn't look much like a house. I think it's time we got indoors, the midges are bloody awful.

Explorer had been at Rona four days before, so one of her shore party told me. They had found all well with Dr. Fraser Darling and his household, and yes, he had got his hutment inside the sheep fank. (Lucky for him that the Rona Annual was missing a year ; but I wondered if, down there at the fank, the spray from a full-sized gale would not carry right over the neck of Fianuis ?)

Neil and Finlay had dressed up and been aboard for high tea, and Finlay wished me to understand that he had been requested to ask a blessing both before and after, and had so done. The kind company left us newspapers and fish in quantity. Neil sold them a few postcards but no socks or gloves, and Finlay had been up to his tobacco tricks again, said Neil, disappointed in the old man—shoving an empty pipe under the captain's nose the moment he stepped ashore, and all the time his pockets full of assorted tobaccos.

Explorer weighed anchor about nine o'clock in the evening and gave a final blow as she steamed away. I watched Finlay in his best black returning slowly along the street, thumbs hooked in his waistcoat; a formidable elder, the ghost of Sundays past.

Finlay went early to bed. He always shook hands before he left Number 11 to go back to his own house. After a social evening I would walk home alone along the street. I should expect to flush three or four snipe on the way. Footsteps ringing on the flagstones or muffled in the grass between. The line of houses from Number 16 to Number 1 : Finlay's as silent as the rest at this time of night: only the tin shack of the post-office to break the symmetry of deserted houses. Usually there would be light enough to read the card in the post-office window: " Views of St. Kilda. Also Socks, gloves and scarfs." I would see the snipe slanting across the sky as they drummed ; they became invisible as soon as they dipped below the skyline and were backed by dark hillside. Always the night air, still or breezy, was noisy with their chik-chikking calls.

I stood in the doorway of the factor's house late on my last night in the island. Indoors the mice scuffled and squeaked, and moths blundered round the storm lantern. The snipe were all about, the craker was sawing somewhere in the long grass. Martin's prognostic of excessive heat—clouds below clear summits—had been in force all day. Now the sky was clear and the skyline sharp and dark, knobbled with cleits. A warm breeze came from the back of the house, down the side of Oiseval, and rustled the pale grass heads. A glimmer at the head of the bay showed where the tide was uncovering the sand ; oystercatchers' cries sounded with the surf. The black enormous curve of hills and the broken crest of Dùn, they were the same and yet different from that similar time of night when I had first seen them, just ashore then, leaning over the garden wall of the manse and full of thankfulness and excited anticipation. To-night the moon was high over Dùn and nearly full, the glittering moon-track lay across the bay. At midnight the snipe used to quieten but the corncrake sawed on and on. In this calm he was echoed by the wall of Dùn. I don't believe he ever shut off.

*   *   *

The day before the ship was due was like a last day of term, the same loafing and desultory packing. The *Hebrides* it should be, sometime the next morning, and all four of us were going. Finlay crated up his fish and his fulmars. I packed my mice. Neil went round nailing shut the doors of the better houses to keep out the sheep which would soon discover when the village was deserted again.

Next morning, the 9th of August, was like that other August morning when John and I had been leaving Rona. There was the same flat mazy calm and fresh dew-drenched dawn, opening to hot glare from a sky of unbroken lightest blue, hardly coloured. We carted all our gear down to the jetty and sat about. It was like waiting for a train. Neil had sighted the ship early on but had lost her in haze. She showed again only a few minutes before she blew. The St. Kildans were in their Sunday clothes, though Finlay had a floppy white shirt and his ribboned Balmoral ; he looked the professor on holiday.

The *Hebrides* sent off two boatloads of passengers. As they landed they instantly rounded and pointed their cameras at the ship, and the sun. I realised the extent of my privilege—at a cost of ten shillings steerage each way and twenty-five shillings-worth of food. The factor's house looked unfamiliar with no domestic litter ; the herbaceous border was rather wilted. Neil and I brought up the rear of the last returning straggle of passengers. Post-office, factor's house, manse, schoolroom and church were locked up one by one. Neil collected the visitors' book from the manse and the unsold postcards, socks and gloves. The precious rose bush blooming against the wall

outside—there would be no one to see it—we went away with
a rosebud in our buttonholes. On board every one was
chivvied round the stern rail and the entire company photographed. *Hebrides* herself was a comparative youngster of
1898.

The ship headed for Boreray. After that she would steam
back to the Sound of Harris, straight through it, and on
non-stop to Coll and Tiree. I consulted the wireless operator.
For about half a crown he made some sort of wireless message
to " Ferryman Rodel Leverburgh Meet Hebrides Eight To-
night," but I did not suppose that anything would come of it.
However, the purser caused a radio to be sent off to the owners
(whereby, as it afterwards appeared, St. Kilda was still good
for a paragraph in the papers), which ended :

. . . again been evacuated and left to the undisturbed possession
of the seabirds. . . .

Over at Boreray the ship passed close under Stac Lee and
Stac an Armin. Close to, their white tops resolved into sitting
gannets and gannets' whitewash. The Stacs reared above the
ship, unbelievable lumps of rock heaved up from the ocean.
The ship's siren blew again and again, deafening blares of
noise, to send each time company upon company of gannets
out into the air : a swarm of thousands, a snowstorm of
gannets falling from the cliff. They rose and circled at high
level until all the sky was milling with black crosses.

Hebrides soon left the islands in a thick greyish haze through
which the sun struck with power diminished to cast only a
faintest shadow. At another season it would have done for
a snow sky. Nothing was left of the swell but the lowest of
long-drawn heaves, the ocean was all but at rest. The pavement of current tracks and cat's-paws carried as far as the eye
could see, until water and air coalesced in haze. Some faint
offlying rocks to the southward—the Haskeir isles ; a small
green island with black guillemots about it—Shillay, pointing
the way into the Sound. The ship seemed nearly to rub her

sides against the litter of seaweed-covered rocks as she followed
the zigzag track through ; about to pile up on the Harris shore
at one moment, then another pair of beacons walked into line
and she sheered off boldly again to run down the next seamark.
At half-past eight in the evening she rounded Renish Point,
opened Loch Rodel and all the stretch of the Minch ; and
sure enough there was Ferryman Rodel in a motor-boat. She
blew, the beat of engines stopped and she glided silently in the
glassy pond. I was interested to know how much it cost to
stop a steamship (cf. railway communication cord) and found
that it was five shillings. The motor-boat barged alongside.
I shook hands hastily with the St. Kildans and tumbled down
with all my goods and mice into the well of the boat. The calm
water churned under the steamer's stern, the rail was fluttering
with handkerchiefs ; Mrs. Gillies I could see, and old Finlay
farther along. By the time the motor-boat came into Rodel
harbour the steamer was diminished in haze.

*   *   *

Before leaving Lewis once more a quite new possibility was
made manifest. The idea of a boat of one's own was perhaps
inevitable. On the day of starting out from Stornoway to
join *Dunara Castle* I had happened to ask Kennie MacIver if he
knew of anything—some smallish seaworthy sort of fishing
boat, sail and motor, very low price ? No, nothing locally—
but wait a minute, come to think of it, yes. The old *Heather*
lying at Carloway over on the other side of the island, she was
up for sale. Of her size she was as good a seaboat as he knew.
In her time she had been used as pilot boat in Stornoway, but
he had no idea what state she might be in now. He would find
out who was the present owner.

Now, back from St. Kilda, I was serious enough to drive
across Lewis to investigate the boat *Heather*. Her owner was
a mainland doctor, now on holiday in Carloway. He had just
had the boat beached, he told me ; for several seasons she
had been fishing locally, but for the last year she had been

lying unused at moorings. We walked down to the sea loch.

Well, there she was : a bulky fishing boat lying half-dry on her side on the seaweed and shingle. SY 104 looked fairly derelict. The dirty dark-red paint was flaking off. She was a sort of improved *Rhoda*—of Bernera and the Flannans—but bigger and less loggish. A minute wheelhouse, open fish-hold, box-bunks in the cramped dark quarters forward ; hold full of stone ballast and rubbish, mast like a telegraph pole. This pole was lowered to rest on the wheelhouse ; it was stepped in the forward quarters, which it nearly filled up, and worked in a slot cut in the deck. The twin cylinder Kelvin looked dulled and elderly and not readily understandable, surrounded by a small dark space called engine-room. Wheel and chain steering ; a heap of damp sail ; a little ornamental mizzen ; about eight tons, about thirty-five feet by twelve beam. She was something to think about all right, but the price was quite out of my reach.

The hot calm weather held, the car was veiled in Lewis road dust. Regretfully I drove it alongside the *Lochness* to be, as they say, "uplifted." The mice had had two nights in the hotel and now they were travelling again. " Mr. Atkinson has taken some live mice with him from St. Kilda," noted the *Stornoway Gazette*. " These St. Kildan mice differ in structure from their mainland cousins, and are of interest to naturalists on that account." The circulation of the *Gazette* was world-wide, it went wherever there were Lewismen. One of the three Europeans on Easter Island, a Lewisman and a subscriber, might be interested to read about the mice in six months' time.

The usual anxious few motorists watched their cars swung on board in the black-and-white glare of the ship's floodlights ; another summer's long light evenings were gone. The ropes splashed into the gap of black water, the ship began to slide out astern. Cheerio Murdo, ta-ta Chrissy, all the best, boys.

The bow wave built up its sound of surf. The water was so calm within the harbour that the mirror image of the moon was whole and flawless. Stornoway Castle withdrew, Scottish baronial against the steely night sky. The surprising skyline of real trees growing from the Castle grounds was tinged above with orange, the last of the west.

The moon was still full-sized ; it was only four nights since I had seen its track across Village Bay and itself in levitation over Dùn. At first the ship steamed plumb along the moon-track as she might have been a car driving down a straight road. She cut through a school of porpoises whose wet hides glistened with moonlight, and whose revolutions swirled up phosphorescence in the shadow side.

The *Lochness* got to Mallaig at eight o'clock in the morning, as usual.

Island of Hirta, St. Kilda, July 23–August 9, 1938

FIFTH YEAR

SULA SGEIR

*

1939

XXIII

Ultima Thule

Sula Sgeir !—the sea-rock of the *sulaire* or solan goose,
I should fancy it means—what can be said of it ?—more
than it is a high, horrent, and nearly herbless strip of
gneiss, or other such-like adamantine matter, scarcely
one-third of a mile in extent, and so narrowed in many
places that, in the winter-time, the strepent wave must
be evermore lashing over from side to side, and cutting
up the whole mass into so many the merest of particles.

T S. MUIR again ! His visit had been in the luck of a flat
. calm, for of all the outliers the landing at Sula Sgeir was
the most precarious and immediately weather controlled. Dr.
Macculloch had failed on his day ; the swell ran too high for
even an attempt at landing. The Commissioners of Ancient
and Historical Monuments and Constructions had failed. The
Duchess of Bedford had failed. H.M.S. *Iron Duke* came and
indulged in target practice against the rock a hundred years
after Macculloch's sight of it. The naturalists Swinburne and
Harvie-Brown each achieved a run ashore in the eighties.

Latest in the series came Malcolm Stewart, landed by a
Grimsby trawler in July, 1932. The trawler was going on to
fish farther west, but the weather looked nasty and she came
back and plucked him off again next morning. During his
night on the rock " cries and considerable commotion " issued
from the walls of some rude bothies there, and he was at once
reminded of nights in the Rona village. Strong circumstantial
evidence of another, a fourth British breeding station of Leach's
petrels—Mother Carey's chicken-run, Muir might have said.

In each of our three seasons so far, 1936-7-8, John Ainslie
and I had been looking for the chance of a landing and a
night on Sula Sgeir.

Sula Sgeir

In 1936, to us in Rona, the rock was sometimes startlingly clear, sitting black and well below the horizon, with a stir of gannet specks about its cap : as unattainable as if one had seen it as a wholly imagined speck from the Butt lighthouse. In that year the Ness crew which made the traditional annual voyage to the rock to harvest the summer's crop of young gannets or *gugas*, had started out in mid-August, " on Wednesday, 12th inst.," as Mrs. Macleod reported in the *Gazette* ; the same day that steam drifter *Alert* removed ourselves from Rona. The Nessmen were on the rock while John and I were getting hungry in the Shiant Isles, and when we got back to Stornoway we tried, without success, to find a drifter willing to go and see them. " BACK FROM SULISGEIR," wrote Mrs. Macleod a fortnight later, and this was how she reported the Nessmen's return :

> Just as I am about to finish these notes, I am told that the Skegirsta boat has just arrived in Skegirsta, with over 2000 " gugas." I cannot give details to my interested readers but (D.V.) next week, after I see the Skipper. Hello, hello, here comes Sandy, flying stick in hand. " Are you in ? " " Yes, I am upstairs." " Well, will I come up, or will you come down ? " " I'm coming down, Sandy." " I called to tell you the boat returned from Sulisgeir with over 2000 " gugas." " " So I heard, Sandy, but we cannot give our readers the news in full till we have seen Norman Maclean, the skipper." (*Stornoway Gazette*, 4.9.1936.)

In 1937,. during the Rona Annual, the faint chance of getting across to the rock in the *Provider* while the sheep business was going on, had never looked like coming off.

In 1938, in the few days' interval between Monach Isles and starting for St. Kilda, we had got quite far on in negotiations with the *Ocean Rambler* of Yarmouth, until her company's agent had disapproved. Local skippers would not look at the idea. We went up to Ness to find Mr. Norman Maclean, the skipper of the Skigersta boat. Mr. Maclean was a spectacled elderly man who had spent part of his life in America : Yes, sir. He was one of the share owners of the Sula Sgeir boat, whose usual crew was nine or ten men. The passage in the open, unengined sailing boat used to take anything from ten hours to a couple of days, he said. This boat, the *Peaceful*, was a Ness *sco*, a shallow draft double-ender of 19-foot keel, in the lineage of Norse galleys. She was very nearly the last of her sort left in the Hebrides and had been built in Port of Ness in about 1913 by the Macleods, the only boatbuilders in the Outer Isles. In some years, such as 1935, weather prevented the boat from starting at all, said Mr. Maclean. When they did get to the rock they hauled the boat up high and dry, sixty feet up the cliff. They cleared the shags and the muck out of the old bothies and lived in them for up to three weeks. In that time they would expect to kill, pluck and salt down round about two thousand gugas, about six tons of them. The meat of the guga was black and had a thick layer of white fat over it. When they got back to Ness they would be posting the gugas all over the world, U.S.A., New Zealand, Australia, Canada, pretty well wherever there were Lewismen ; the guga's circulation, like the *Stornoway Gazette's*, was world-wide. The selling price of a guga, carriage extra, was one shilling. The crew took a barrel of water with them in the boat but relied on catching rain water while they were on the rock. One dry year they had run out and had had to boil and drink the stagnant brackish dregs of rock pools. It was a thick scum, said Mr. Maclean, " as green as any paint."

We asked after the petrels of Sula Sgeir. Mr. Maclean evidently did not separate fork-tails from stormies but there were some small birds right enough which came out at night and made a noise round the bothies : Yes sir. We asked him if he could catch a specimen for us when he should be out there this coming autumn, and he said he'd try. Also please could we have a guga each ?

Well, try again next year, we thought. Alec MacFarquhar had said he would definitely be going to Rona again then. We might be able to share a charter with him, be dropped off on the way to Rona and picked up again on the way back (though that wouldn't give us a night on the rock). Or possibly, if there were plenty of visiting drifters in Stornoway and the fishing was bad, one of them might be persuaded. I found that the Sgeir had become like a mountaineer's peak which must be achieved : unattained Ultima Thule.

In this autumn and winter of 1938 both Sula Sgeir and Rona were having quite a turn in the news. Bird protectionists viewed disapprovingly the annual plunder of the gannetry. After the Nessmen's return from the rock in September with another year's haul of two thousand gugas, a correspondence worked up in both *The Times* and the *Stornoway Gazette*. A question was asked in the House. Bird protectionists wished to stop the voyages altogether ; others, traditionalists, admired the Nessmen's immemorial enterprise and would rather have protected that than the gannets. After all, the gannetry had survived the Nessmen's farming for centuries and if the numbers were diminishing now there was the huge undisturbed gannet reservoir of St. Kilda. There was not much of commercial greed in gannet farming, it was far more of a traditional adventure. Two thousand gugas was a good average haul : at a shilling each, £100 ; £10 a head for ten men after two or three weeks of a toughness and privation unknown anywhere else in the country, and all expenses to be found. This brave remnant of all the old-time open-boat sailing voyages for seals and sea-birds might at least be allowed to survive while it could. This was the middle, modern, conservationist view, balancing natural resources against human interests. What seemed the most likely end—distaste for rank gannet flesh because of modern imported foods, the common disuse of seals and sea-birds as elsewhere in the islands—showed no signs of happening ; rather the reverse ; emigration and the post-office between them had made the guga a global delicacy, and a link with home.

To myself one day in the autumn the postman brought a heavy biscuit tin : gugas. John came to attend a ceremonial opening. Layers of sodden newspaper reeking with sea-bird oil : the *Scottish Daily Express* headlined CZECHS WILL ACCEPT and THERE WILL BE NO WAR. Two gugas

were squashed tightly inside, lead-heavy corpses like large
lumps of putty—specimens of course, not poultry. There was
also a syrup tin packed with more newspaper, fish-curing salt
and a little sodden black body, made smaller by its matted
feathers. It gave off the authentic petrel smell, this sometime
bird. We spread it out into a sorry likeness of a Leach's fork-
tailed petrel. So one at least of the petrels of the far-off Sgeir
had been a fork-tail. Proof of their breeding now wanted only
the sight of an egg or a chick. Next summer !

When, back in August, the *Explorer* had brought news from
Rona to St. Kilda, Dr. Fraser Darling was only at the beginning
of his island season, but when the September crisis came the
authorities removed him and his household in something of a
panic. It had been six weeks before the weather had allowed
them to return. They had come off again just before Christmas,
leaving the island capped with sunlit snow. And now Dr.
Darling was lecturing in London ; the newspapers reported
him. What should they make of Muir's " Rona—Beloved ! ",
of Monro's " ane little ile " ? " WEIRD BIRD DANCE ON
' LONELIEST ISLE.' . . ."

St. Kilda had also reached out to London. The field mice
George and Bessie, labelled in English and Latin, were living
in the Rodent House at the Zoo ; open to the public ; to be
mentioned in the Society's Annual Report. I was thankful
when they had been safely delivered, for by time I got them
home they were unique. The rest of the mice in a second cage
had gnawed their way to freedom in Mallaig, perhaps to upset
the purity of the mainland breed, perhaps even to confuse and
anger some future mammalogist.

*   *   *

The antiquity of the Nessmen's voyages to Sula Sgeir
became almost fabulous when Sir Donald Monro's note of 1549
was thought of as merely the first written record. Nowadays
the Ness district of Lewis preserved a stronger Norse tradition
in place-names and in the people's blood than anywhere else

in the Hebrides. Ness was as nearly wholly Norse as Orkney and Shetland, and in open-boat design and seamanship Ness belonged to the Northern Isles, not to the Hebrides ; the *sco Peaceful* was of straight Norse descent. It was not, then, an unfounded stretch of imagination, having gone back four centuries to Sir Donald Monro, to go some centuries farther and to derive the Sula Sgeir gannet hunt from Norsemen already well settled in Lewis by the ninth and tenth centuries.

The smaller the island the more Sir Donald Monro was interested. He dealt circumstantially with all the outliers, and Sula Sgeir was no exception :

> Be sexteen myle of sea to this ile, towards the west [ie. from Rona], lyes ane ile callit Suilskeray, ane myle lang, without grasse or hedder, with highe blacke craigs, and black fouge thereupon part of them. This ile is full of wylde foulis, and quhen foulis hes ther birdes, men out of the parochin of Nesse in Lewis use to sail ther, and to stay ther seven or aught dayes, and to fetch hame with them their boitt full of dray wild foulis, with wyld foulis fedders.

With a little alteration in spelling this could have gone straight into a September issue of the *Stornoway Gazette*. Sir Donald continued :

> In this ile ther haunts ane kynd of foule callit the colk, little less nor a guise, quha comes in the *ver* to the land to lay hir eggis, and to clecke hir birds quhill she bring them to perfytness, and at that time her fleiche of fedderis falleth of her hailly, and she sayles to the mayne sea againe, and comes never to land quhyll the zeir end againe, and then she comes with her new fleiche of fedderis. This fleiche that she leaves zierly upon her nest hes nae pens in the fedderis, nor nae kynd of hard thinge in them that they may be felt or graipit, bot utter fyne downes.

The colk ? " The Fowl called the Colk is found here," said Martin a hundred and fifty years later.

> The *Colk* is a Fowl somewhat less than a *Goose*, hath Feathers of divers colours, as White, Gray, Green and Black, and is

beautiful to the Eye ; it hath a Tuft on the Crown of its Head like that of a *Peacock*, and a Train longer than that of *House-Cock*. This Fowl looseth its Feathers in time of Hatching, and lives mostly in the remotest Islands. . . .

Unfortunately the colk was no fabulous rarity but merely the common eider, the drake showy and parti-coloured, the duck drab and lining her nest with her own " utter fyne downes."

In the usual procession of Monro—Martin—Macculloch—Muir—The Naturalists—The Moderns—it was now Macculloch's turn, but he had failed ; so, another jump and—"Sula Sgeir !—the sea-rock of the *sulaire* or solan goose I should fancy it means " . . . and so on. Personally I had become fond of ambagious old Muir. Nowadays he was to be classed, I suppose, as a minor Victorian rediscovery, long forgotten by all but a few remote specialists in ecclesiastical archæology, and they no doubt impatient and critical. To judge from his books Muir must have been somewhat tiresome in the flesh. I imagined him and John Wilson Dougal as kindred. (Wilson Dougal—Rona Annual, 1927—was the amateur geologist and faithful summer migrant to the Hebrides who discovered, to the tardy admiration of the professionals, the belt of Flinty Crush rock running the length of the Outer Isles.) Muir's writing was in the circumscription of his time yet was over-blown into originality, a brand of verbiage all his own ; Dougal relied on many adjectives to make his image. They were to be pictured (I thought) as kind, fussy, rather twinkling old gentlemen, both finding congenial company with elderly women and cups of tea round a peat fire, both living in a world where all was, without doubt, for the best, both much loved throughout Lewis, both notably tough and courageous. But however Muir may have walked in life there was no doubt that parts of his writings of Sula Sgeir in 1860 were, to an admirer, of his finest vintage.

He said good-bye to the Rona Annual on the evening of July 11th, and then found that the wonderful weather was " perhaps just a trifle or so *too much* of a good thing for our bit of seafaring business between Rona and Sula Sgeir."

Instead of the three or four hours that had been thought enough and to spare for the run, it was well upon the fifth hour of morning, or, in other words, very little short of a whole round of the dial, ere we were oaring ourselves into the *Geodh a Bhun Mhòr*, in the eastern side of the Sgeir.

They landed easily, " ascended to a convenient nook in the crag," lit a fire and had breakfast.

Breakfast over, and the talk, we rambled a little way into the island, diverting ourselves with the physical aspect of the place, and the no less extraordinary aspect of the ceaseless and curiously-diversified motions of the pinioned inhabitants who multitudinously thronged us around, and so familiarly, that often we might have taken hold of them with our hands. To me, however, it was, after a time, still more interesting occupation, to look for, and to find, traces of an inhabitant, who in an age long since gone by, had shared the solitude of the Sgeir with the puffin and goose—feeding as precariously as them, in all likelihood, and housing himself far less comfortably, perhaps.

Even the Sgeir, it appeared, was a holy isle with a teampull and a sometime hermit. St. Flann of the Flannans was sufficiently incredible but a resident monk in Sula Sgeir was really beyond all bounds. Muir named his teampull " *Tigh Beannaichte* (Blessed House)" and distinguished it from the huddled bothies, from which it stood apart. Certainly the six-inch ordnance map called a projection of the rock *Sgeir an Teampuill* and one of the bothies *Tigh Mhaoldonuich* (House of the Bald Saint, or Tonsured One), but Muir could not bring up even a legend to support his nameless hermit. No one else mentioned such a man. No, surely here at last the hermit must be a fabrication and the chapel built by some long gone, holier generation of fowlers.

"With a long day before us," said Muir, " we took our full of the Sgeir very deliberately "—a different matter from the wild leap and hasty run ashore of his successor, John Swinburne, first of the naturalists, on a June evening twenty-three years later. Swinburne's birds'-nesting was rather hampered by the jealous attentions of his Ness pilot, who looked on the gannets as private property. He saw the bothies —" indeed curious-looking erections "—got back to his yacht *Medina*, and stood away for Rona.

It was Muir's weather again for Harvie-Brown and party, who landed from *Shiantelle* " with perfect ease, and scrambled up the tilted strata of the old-world gneiss." This was on the evening of June 19th, 1887, three years to the day and hour after Swinburne's visit. " Quite a number of Fulmars were circling round and even resting on the rock," said Harvie-Brown, " but I searched vainly for eggs or young." He saw one " wretched-looking half-or wholly-starved sheep." As for the gannets, said H.-B., " *they swarm*," and his note of the local water supply, as sometimes sipped by the Nessmen, was :

> Foetid hollows and dark-green spray pools . . . usually covered with green slime and feathers, and surrounded by dead young birds, rotten or highly incubated eggs, and old saturated nests. . . .

Shiantelle drew away. Later on came the mind's-eye view of recollection :

> Our visit to Sulisgeir in 1887 will ever be remembered as one of the most remarkable incidents of our Hebridean peregrinations during many years, more especially if we look to the ghastly lonesomeness and geologically disintegrated nature of the whole place ; almost pathetically sad in its collection of rough stone huts, the solitary wretched sheep, and the remains of another, and the heads of defunct Gannets strewn all over the surface.

Then—a forty-three years' silence, with that picture left for any would-be follower.

The silence was broken by John Wilson Dougal, who was taken out to the rock in a small motor-boat in September, 1930, and who wrote one of his long gentle accounts about it, printed in his collected *Island Memories* (1937) after his death. He does seem to have been the first stranger to have landed ever since *Shiantelle* sailed away in '87.

Sula Sgeir

Four crofter-fishermen of Ness left the harvest fields to man the converted *sco Pride of Lionel* (the last of the standard 21-foot keel *scos*, since broken up). " Their pluck is splendid in fitting up a scow with a seven horse-power petrol engine," said their passenger, " and thus maintaining with their kith and kin of Ness and Skegirsta, the continuity of a famous race of seamen, in the Viking remnant of the Butt of Lewis." All honour to them, but not forgetting that their passenger was an elderly Glasgow manufacturing chemist, on holiday, setting sail in an open boat at midnight, into the North Atlantic.

> Steadily the boat made its weird passage through the heavy swelling currents. . . . In mid-boat the flicker of light from the hand lamp showed the steersman and the crew discussing the course in Gaelic. . . . At this stage of night dreaming, when still spelled by the scintillating panorama of the heavens, the boat was dipping and rising from basin to basin, with sometimes a rending slap on the bow that made more than one of us look involuntarily, to see if the bare planks had sprung. There was no pretence that our scow had a trail boat, or even a life-belt.
> Forsaking the damp night air, rest was sought for a few hours on a plank and a restless bag of straw, till the grey glimmer of a chilly, sunless morning brought us to look around on the still tossing currents, with early solan geese already alive to the day's necessities. . . . Soon we heard with sympathy and interest the skipper's shout, " Rona, Rona ahead ! Sulisgeir ! Sulisgeir ! Starboard there ! " and shaking his fist at the elements of sea and sky, he cried " Have I not the eye of a hawk ? "

Porpoises escorted them to the rock ; *Pride of Lionel* was kedged in, and, by Wilson Dougal : " A jump was made to a six-inch ledge." . . .

> We were fortunate within ten minutes of landing to discover the abundant presence of Flinty Crush rock. . . . The elation of reaching the island—the desire of many years—helped to sustain us against the soaking showers of rain which beset us as we ranged, hammer in hand, over the rough rocks. . . .

" We viewed the chief prominences " . . . and the gannets,

the bothies, Muir's teampull, and *Suidhe Brianuille*, the Seat of Brenhilda, on which she had pined for her possible brother St. Ronan.

We should mention that a trial was once made with two sheep placed in the island for a year, but they did not survive.

They had " four sodden hours " on the rock and another six at sea before they made their Lewis landfall.

When we reached the peaceful haven of Ness, friendly hands welcomed us home to some comfort after our adventure in lonely northern seas.

Two years later, in 1932, came Malcolm Stewart for his lonely, petrel-disturbed night on the rock. He was back again himself in 1937, with trawler exchanged for steam yacht, to count the gannets (4418 breeding pairs). Another two years and here was the threshold of another island summer, a fifth, 1939. To see Rona from the Sgeir instead of the Sgeir from Rona? To sit of an evening in Teampull Sula Sgeir with the fork-tails fluttering round?

XXIV

Attempting Ultima Thule

ANOTHER old motor car and freedom from July 1st—it was a start. John Ainslie could not get away then ; probably he would be able to later on, but he was showing a certain resistance to much more voyaging amongst the Hebrides. Since last autumn Hugh LeLacheur and I had been keeping common household in his Thames sailing barge moored in London. He had another old car, a free week which might be stretched, and he was very ready for an introduction to the Outer Isles. He was determined that the fishing boat *Heather* should be bought, an idea I had been toying with a good deal on my own account. I knew she was still unused and unsold. The price asked should have come down a bit in the interval. As far as Hugh was concerned I could do what I liked with my unpronounceable Sula Sgeir, but he was going to make sure I didn't shy off from actually putting in an offer for the *Heather*.

Our barge household had recently acquired a nestling barn owl which we were hand-rearing and to which one or other of us was perpetually tied ; so the owl had to come along too, in a tea-chest. After some difficult arranging, and then parting and starting again individually a few days later from widely different sources, we successfully met in our respective motors one afternoon early in July on the north road somewhere near Penrith. Hugh was loaded with tea-chest and owl, I with box of flash-bulbs and the rest of the island goods. We proceeded in company all night and arrived alongside the *Lochness* with the customary five minutes to spare, having done the fifty miles of Mallaig road in the unprecedented time of two hours exactly. Hugh's car we put up in Mallaig ; mine was uplifted for the Outer Isles, but I bought only a single ticket for it, thinking to sell it out there when it should have

292

done whatever might be required of it. We arrived in Stornoway and set up in the hotel with the owl. Thereafter our Hebridean affairs went forward with ever-increasing speed and complication for the rest of the summer.

*   *   *

As for Sula Sgeir—" how to get to it, and upon it—that is a question ! " It was the perennial question, ever since originally postulated of North Rona by Muir. This year when one had got to the only place to ask it, it seemed unusually rhetorical.

Every small boy in Stornoway was going about carrying a string of some sort of fish, as usual, but no doubt the fishing was a washout. The fishing—what there was of it—was south-wards, Kennie MacIver said ; there were few visiting drifters in the port and no Englishmen. But well, he would ask one or two skippers. One skipper we asked did not know where Sula Sgeir was, and he was quite promising until he found out. For the rest, no, the fishing may have been bad but it certainly was not bad enough to tempt a crew to go on the hundred and forty-mile trip to Sula Sgeir and back for expenses and a few pounds over.

We drove across the moors to Carloway. The fishing boat *Heather* was still there, deserted, lying at her moorings in the loch.

We drove up to Ness and saw Alec MacFarquhar. He was trying to fix up with a Stornoway drifter for the Rona Annual in about three weeks' time, but he could not find a skipper to say yes ; just now he was waiting to hear from the *Ellen and Irene*. He would be glad to arrange a joint charter (but that still would not yield a night on the rock). When I went to see the skipper of the *Ellen and Irene* I found that he had just posted his refusal. Och, it was a dirty chob, the mess the sheep made, and they might wash off in a beam sea. There was also the usual rider about insurance which only covered a ship for fishing, and the common unwillingness to forgo the gambler's chance of a night's fishing.

John wired that he would be free at the end of the month ; I replied that I would try again then. There might be some visiting boats in Stornoway by then ; if not, we should have to go along with the Rona Annual and chance to luck.

Meanwhile we did some more looking at the abandoned *Heather.* Kennie MacIver wired off my embarrassingly low offer and next morning said : " Well, you're the owner of the cheapest boat in Scotland." We drove over to Carloway and looked at her, rowed out and stood on her deck ; it was difficult to believe. Where to make a start ? Hugh had two days before he must start south again. We brushed some of the rubbish off the deck, took off the magneto and brought it back to Stornoway for overhaul. I left my ill-used car behind and we went off together in the *Lochness.*

* * *

At the end of the month John and I came north to our traditional schedule, in his same bottom-scraping vehicle of last summer. It rained all night long and all the way across the Minch.

We sat in the bay window of the hotel watching the life of Stornoway, and, as at every other return, "we might never have been away." The *Lochness* came in or went out. The bruised buses gathered from their townships to park along the waterfront ; the small boys ran about with their gleanings of fish ; the gulls squawked and splashed on the fish-market ; the fish-curers' lorries and drays charged to and fro ; our friends of the hotel said successively : " So you got back." There was no influx of visiting drifters.

Lewis was dripping wet. The moors and the roadside grass stood in puddles of water, temporary streams had started up, and the burns proper were in roaring dark brown spate, piling up brown froth along their banks. Curtains of the horizontal sort of rain swept across the Ness road when we drove out the thirty miles for news of the Rona Annual.

He had fixed up with a Stornoway drifter, the *Comrade,*

said Alec MacFarquhar. He should have gone by now ; he
had wired the skipper when he was ready a day or two ago,
but the skipper had replied that he was waiting for the English
boys. Indeed ! For a moment the skipper appeared as an
unknown philanthropist. Go without them, Alec had wired.
Not for your offer, replied the skipper.

We found the *Comrade* in Stornoway harbour, one of the
fleet of massive, paraffin-engined boats which looked as if they
had been hewn from the solid. It was Saturday afternoon and
the skipper had gone home. We ran him down at Tolsta, a
dozen miles out, and it being the week-end, he was rather
bloodshot. It appeared that the English boys were going to
stump up £25 for the extra steaming between Rona and Sula
Sgeir ; no wonder he'd waited. The true origin of this Gaelic
fantasy was irretrievable ; we had not even a language fully
in common. We had a long unprofitable discussion about the
high cost of paraffin and the great distance of Sula Sgeir. The
loss of a night's fishing was mentioned many times. (This
morning twenty-four drifters had landed a total catch of ten
crans : at ninety shillings a cran, an average taking of a bit
over thirty shillings a ship.) Drifter skippers must be like press
photographers, going around in a flock and treading on each
other's heels in case one should find something and the others
miss it. After some silent reflection, the skipper said haltingly
that if he put us down for a night on the rock he would miss
not one night's fishing, but two ; one could not deny it. I
put forward other and more complicated schedules whereby
he would find himself shooting his nets at all sorts of unlikely
times and places.

Alec MacFarquhar had asked us to come to an agreement
on his and our own behalf, and to try to fix up to start on
Monday morning. We didn't seem to be getting on very well.
After more inconclusiveness we went away, leaving an offer
which obviously wasn't going to be accepted ; and the skipper to
his usquebaugh. The next day was Sunday, so nothing happened.

On Monday morning, on board the drifter, we tried again
and went through a similar catalogue of times and distances,

consumption of paraffin, wear and tear of the presumably ageless engine. The skipper had little to say himself except : " It's no a canny chob," several times, with head-shaking ; he seemed to be in the hands of his crew. We thought we were keeping our end up quite well, though the Gaelic asides had us beat, but the revised conditions laid down were now obviously not going to be accepted by Mr. MacFarquhar. We bore them thirty miles to him. Mr. MacFarquhar snorted and said, Och, it was a try on. But he lifted his offer a cautious pound or two and threw in a sheep for good measure. He sent back with us his young joint-tenant, Murdo, for direct negotiation. We awaited a spectacle of Gaelic argument, but the affair went off quietly—suspiciously quietly. In the end we lost badly ; Murdo got his charter for very nearly the customary amount, and now it made no difference whether we came or not. If we decided to, then our extension to the trip would cost us half as much again as our agreed top limit ; take it or leave it ; they would be sailing in an hour or two.

This was the one chance, as we very well knew. And the night ashore was promised. We retired feeling unhappy and frustrated. But it was yes or no, so it had to be yes, and we went back and reluctantly closed the deal. (Another time one would have one's own boat.)

We bought a few provisions, loaded up the gear, and drove back to Ness with Murdo, who was sympathetic and appreciated that it was unhappy to have to pay more than it was worth for something one must have. An ancient, ancient motor-lorry hobbled up to Mr. MacFarquhar and was loaded with the Rona apparatus. We branched off to Port Skegirsta to thank Mr. Norman Maclean for his gugas and for the salt-cured fork-tail of last autumn. We found him on the jetty, just in with a boatload of white fish. He was the elderly white-haired man who had been much in America ; he now seemed to be very happy, which was also nice for us after our prolonged dose of Gaelic dourness. Plenty of fish now, he said, but none in the summer ; that elusive Hebridean summer again—this was the last day of July. Was the wee bird he'd sent still alive ?

—benevolent twinkle. The landing at the rock was easy, in the right weather. There were not very many of the small birds there ; they came out of the stones of the bothies, nowhere else. On a calm night they were all ashore, especially on a dark foggy sort of night. It was pleasant to hear this familiar note of our old friends, the remembered Dull Calm Night of Maximum Activity, particularly from one who did not know the birds' name. The one he had caught had shuffled out of a wall into his shoe.

Back at Port of Ness the ancient lorry was waiting, and groups of men and dogs were waiting. We all went on waiting. This endless Monday was at last ending. At midnight the headland round which the drifter must appear was a dim silhouette and the quiet sky began to rain. It was gentle weather with a fitful night breeze. There were still lights in some of the scattered crofts and a corncrake or two were sawing. In daylight the bare district had an unfinished and backyard look, scattered anyhow with houses and peat stacks, rubbish and old tins.

The personnel began to disperse. The ancient lorry set up its inward shuddering again ; it crawled off into the darkness with someone walking ahead, because long years had passed since its lights had worked. We took Mr. MacFarquhar back to his house and more or less slept on his sofa until four o'clock. At half-past four and in daylight again we drove to Port of Ness, looked at the empty bay, and returned to the sofa.

When we got back to Stornoway the *Comrade* had just returned. She had got half-way to Ness and then had broken down. A wee wheel had broken in the water pump. Another drifter had towed her in.

Stornoway, August 1, 10 a.m. Atkinson to MacFarquhar :

comrade towed back to stornoway last night still disabled possibly okay tonight will communicate afternoon.

Stornoway, August 1, 5.30 p.m. Same address :

comrade still disabled possibly ready tomorrow.

The *Comrade's* poor driver—as a motor-drifter's engineman is called—worked on until three o'clock next morning. The weather turned to wind and rain. *Comrade* sailed about half-past one in the afternoon. We saw her go.

Once more we jarred the thirty miles to Mr. MacFarquhar's house, where he himself was waiting until firm news should be brought to him. So we did the same. The car needed a rest because it easily became overheated—the water ran so fast from its radiator. Also the self-starter was having a mood of remaining engaged with the engine, which helped progress but was rather a drain on the battery; and there were other things; the car was finding the island standard. The weather cleared again to a fine evening, blue sky and warm sun. The hayfield in front of the house had just been mown for all but a solitary tuft in the middle; a kindly thought for the corn-crake which continued to sit there on her ten eggs.

News came of the approaching drifter. We filled up the radiator from the millstream and drove Mr. MacFarquhar to the Port. The *Comrade* lay at anchor in the bay and was being loaded, a long noisy process but at last done, the men, the dogs, the posts and rolls of wire, a new ram or two for the island flock. The small boat was heaved inboard and urged back to its chocks.

We got off about half-past eight and steamed out in the fine evening towards the straight sharp horizon.

*   *   *

The moon came up in a clear sky, the swell gradually increased. Near to, gannets flew pitch-black. The only light was the bright square of the open engine-room hatch. In this sort of boat the engine-room was forward and the propeller shaft ran the length of the ship. Peering down into the oily racket one saw the glow where the naked flame burners played on the vaporiser. We were all variously curled and huddled about the encumbrances of the deck. Out of the darkness a cryptic Gael remarked : " If the reward is good, the news is good." Translated from the Gaelic, he explained ; he was one of the usual Sula Sgeir gannet crew, come to lend a hand at Rona. The sky clouded over at midnight and the moon was lost. Some rain fell. It was bitterly chill for all of us sleepless bundles on deck. The drifter went rolling and labouring on, puffing her whiff of paraffin smoke and choking out dirty water.

At half-past two we were close up to the familiar shape of Rona. The drifter turned west towards the Sgeir, yet barely visible. It seemed a long way between the two. The drifter was rolling more now and the swell seemed to be coming straight from the north-east, the worst possible quarter. Rona became dim in mist astern while the two black lumps of the Sgeir increased.

There was white water all along the cliff foot. Apparently the swell was driving straight on to the only landing place, the low saddle in the middle ; the spray was throwing up white. There was a half and half drab daylight. The place looked utterly inhuman.

The skipper began to be feared. We had been afraid of that ; he didn't know the ground. Gannets flew out to meet us ; the south part of the black sea-rock was gannet-white. The skipper wanted to turn back, then he said that if we did get ashore he would come and fetch us in the evening ; he didn't like the look of the weather. " Aren't you feared to lose your lives in that place ? " he said. We argued, but he was adamant about the evening.

The Sgeir was two great lumps of rock lying end to end and nearly disjoined in the middle. The drifter stopped and rolled, a long way out. The anchor was bent on to some endless length of sticky black net rope and let go into what, to me, was bottomless ocean. The anchor found bottom and bit ; the drifter sluggishly came round, nagging at the rope and slopping about in the swell. The small boat took the plunge, a boat's crew jumped down, and reached for the long poles of oars, rowlocks, something to bail with. We threw down our gear and tumbled after it, cast off, and set out on a long spidery bobbing towards the middle of the Sgeir.

We passed an outlying rock and began to be a little enclosed by cliffs on either hand. The left-hand block, to southward, stuck out a good boss of cliff to the eastward, and the right-hand block shut off the north. Ahead and in between the water looked quieter ; this side of the saddle was quite embayed. Seals were dropping thick and fast from shelves and sloping rocks, dropping into the water like big slugs. The swell swilling up dark bare rocks—streaming seaweed—it was exciting ! The crew worked the boat in stern first to a low place in the rock. Seals' heads were bobbing all around in the hectic moments. I jumped as the boat lifted and turned about to catch the gear. John proffered it piecemeal from the stern, waiting for swell and boat's crew to bring us momentarily within safe throwing range. It took some time for our few items, across the ever-shifting gap of sea. John jumped and landed, the swell sluiced and caught one leg before he could get it out of the way. We called subversive last words as the boat pulled away : try to persuade the skipper—must have the night !

Now we were standing on Sula Sgeir and it was about five o'clock in the morning.

Harvie-Brown used to quote from his journals. I scribbled down later on in the day : " Walked up from landing place into southern block, stone bothies, pillars and slabs. Young fulmars thick, impossible avoid wasting their substance. Bothies noisome, wet slime and dead shags. Old boots, etc. Centre part green but not with grass. Stood and looked, exhilarated, the last of all. North part dour, central encampment ancient and queer, mayweed edge of gannetry just seen —white guano beyond still unknown. Grey and a fierce squall. Spread rickcloth over bothy. Food."

XXV

"What can be said of it?"

THE day in retrospect was one long rush. We took our full of the Sgeir, like Muir, but far from deliberately. Now and then we plumped down of exhaustion for a few minutes. We clambered over pretty well every foot of accessible rock.

Neither of us had been in a gannetry before. We stood a few yards from the edge and watched : extraordinary shouting squalor. In the air the crossing and recrossing birds were chalky white against a stormy sky, the whole air was moving, it filled the sight, and even when you were not looking the stir impinged at the corner of your eye. It was not a native, British effect at all : some unknown guano rock of the farthest south, an ancient mariner landed and standing amazed before the deafening city of the nameless white birds, each as big as a goose and squawking and jabbing with pickaxe bill.

Sula Sgeir had no sort of inland. You could nowhere be more than about fifty yards from the sea, but always you were elevated a hundred or two feet above it, except at the saddle, where only about twenty-five yards separated ocean from ocean and seaweed was fastened half-way across. No need for any of Muir's strepent winter waves to split the rock into two ; it looked as if high water springs would swill right over. Beyond this divide rose the bare northern ridge, Lunndastoth of the six-inch map, bent in a little from the straight line of the island and so sheltering the landing-place rocks from the north. Southwards from the landing the rock rose and broadened into the main block of the island, where the bothies were squatted on a slope of loose stones and mayweed. Beyond the bothies the rock split into two arms with a cavernous geo in between, south-east to Sgeir an Teampuill, south-west to Creag Trithaiga. The gannetry was from the cliff brinks of these two arms, downwards.

Sula Sgeir

We started with Lunndastoth. The high quarter-mile ridge of broken-up rock seemed the limit of barrenness. The stone was covered with slippery yellow lichen ; there was no particle of soil, only an occasional tuft of thrift or orache or scurvy grass rooted in a cleft ; the downward view showed only precipitous knobbled rock to the surf. There was hardly any life about it : a shag or two, a few aukeries now deserted, seals' heads in the surf. We covered the whole of it and counted only seven young fulmars. Birds did not even perch on it. It was an extraordinary change to come back, down to the saddleback bridge and up again into the southern block, and into one unceasing hive of birds. From the landing place onwards we were in the midst of it : littered puffin carcases, clumsy young black-backs splashing away through the rock-pools, their parents complaining overhead, nestling fulmars always at our feet, feathers, corpses and castings, splashed rocks —the casual untidy mess of a sea-bird island. How many times would one have to walk past a young fulmar to teach it not to waste its oily insides ? The film of fulmar oil on the pools had a rainbow iridescence. The nestlings sat wet and bedraggled, jerking with their coughs ; they were mostly half-grown and thus of an age not to be attended by their parents except for the occasional retching regurgitation. From the landing rocks to the bothies, 59 young fulmars ; about the bothies, 161. In Harvie-Brown's day, not one.

We looked down into the geo called Geodha Blatha Mor in the west cliff, over from the bothies. Down there on dank walls never sunlit the tiers of white kittiwakes shouted their echoing noise. The far greeny water at the bottom heaved and boiled into surf. Seals' heads were dotted thickly ; the animals paddled to lift themselves, they showed their speckled chests as they craned to get a view of ourselves on the skyline. The rocks were lined with stinking snaky-necked shags ever twisting and peering.

At eight o'clock in the morning the sun struck through. The lovely flood of sunlight was warm. We had hardly noticed the lifting of the sky ; almost suddenly there was no cloud at all, nothing but the bowl of palest blue. The sun climbed, hotter and hotter. The day was set. It was the final, ultimate stroke of luck.

Rona over there in the east was hazy all day, showing an unfamiliar view of its reddish western wall. The white surf at the cliff foot ten miles away was as fixed as the land. All around the deep-blue empty ocean, glittering to southward and sunward, a breeze from the east, our own local outlying rocks collared with a swirl of surf. Pale, palest blue sky, blazing sun, the rock hot to touch. We went in nothing but shorts and gym shoes, slipping in the spread of slimy gannet dung. The seals showed deep under water greeny cool, pale distorted swimmers. I lay on my back and watched the gannets streaming over, not turning to follow them but letting the stream go by, wings creamy translucent against the sky. Sula Sgeir, August the 3rd, 1939 !

All day as we clambered about the thought kept recurring, it is true, we really are on Sula Sgeir. I kept stopping to look about to believe it—illimitable ocean, gannets, the heaped bothies, underfoot the iron-hard gneiss—" or other such-like adamantine matter." Of course, it was Muir's weather again —" ' Och, and what a glorious weathers ! ' was the joyous exsufflation that slipped out of the mouth of Iain Mackay. . . ." Here they had come, the ghostly visitors, who could leave no mark on the rock. They had marked themselves somewhere far else, in the human way, on a page of writing ; transferable to another age, to a different mind and fashion, to be brought back to the same unchanging rock ! Their phantom vessels could lie off the Sgeir together : *Shiantelle,* Muir's little *Hawk,* the *Pride of Lionel,* Swinburne's *Medina,* Stewart's Grimsby trawler, the steam yacht *Golden Eagle.* Here was Muir's oval-shaped teampull, and here rose the stench of fœtid rock-pools smelt by Harvie-Brown. Gentle Dougal came tapping his geologist's hammer in the streaming rain, and found the Flinty Crush !

*   *   *

The bothies looked like heaps of flat stones from outside, which in fact they were, but inside the huge flat slabs showed in a cunning architecture ; the slabs rose overlapping inwards and inwards until they met in a vaulted roof complete except for a smoke-hole. All the bothies stank of shag. The floors were deep in a hardly negotiable wet black slime which incorporated putrefying birds, feathers and straw ; it was as if a cartload of gannetry had been brought and spread indoors. Evidence of Man was strewn about, bottles and old boots, disintegrating tins, a broom head, a rotted curtain of sacking. The largest and best-preserved building revealed itself as the main living bothy and contained a barrel and a heap of rotten straw ; a chain with a hook on one end hung from the roof. The manurc was as deep here as in the others. The seats and beds were stone slabs round the walls. Looking into the bothies some picture emerged of wild men—crouched, barefoot, shock-headed—gnawing the thigh bone of a gannet ; but when you met the gannet men in the flesh in their homes in Ness, you found quiet bespectacled readers of the *Scottish Daily Express*.

These bothies were of the traditional type called " beehive shielings," once common in the Hebrides but now hardly to be found ; their characteristic was the overlapping of drystone flags to make a " false arch." A protective covering of turf was usual, and the Royal Commissioners of Ancient Monuments said that once that was gone the rest usually fell rapidly into a heap of stones. They never saw the Sula Sgeir bothies, which looked unique to my eyes because of these huge flat building slabs stepped inwards course by course in a rough circle, and because of the absence of any sort of vegetative help or footing in earth. The cleits of St. Kilda were quite different, being built of random-shaped stones rising in more or less vertical walls, spanned transversely across the top with long stone flags, and then heaped with earth and turf. That was the type of construction of the chapel on the Flannans, for instance, though there the cap of turf was replaced by a pile of loose stones. The old Hebridean black houses, the St.

Kilda byres, and island stone huts in general were all of this massive vertical wall type, but were finished with pitched timber rafters and some sort of thatch. The Royal Commissioners had found only one or two proper and entire beehive shielings throughout Lewis and Harris, and none at all in the Uists and Barra. The point here on Sula Sgeir was that of the Rona village over again, not absolute age but ancient usage hanging on long after its time. Here beehive shielings were maintained and lived in when elsewhere they were listed as archæological monuments. Admittedly I was always ready to stretch island features into the unique, but the Sula Sgeir bothies did seem worth a look from a modern archæologist.

Teampull Sula Sgeir was rather more ordinary and recognisable. It was something like a larger Flannans chapel with the doorway in the side instead of the end. Certainly the eaves were stepped inwards a little in the beehive manner but the finish was of stone flags laid across, with a heap of loose stones on top. The walls began vertically, a massive pack of masonry. From outside, the teampull's straight walls made it look more like a house than the sprawling domed bothies. There was no sign of use about it though the window of Muir's day had since been filled up with stones. Inside squatted two nestling fulmars.

Besides the bothies and the teampull there were various slabs stuck up on end and some square piles of stone. One of these was the Seat of Brenhilda, *Suidhe Brianuille,* the draughty perch of St. Ronan's sister, where she " spent most of her time " until she ended up with a shag's nest in her skeleton. On the six-inch map the cavernous inlet nearby was suitably named *Bealach an t-Suidhe (bealach,* a breach, a gap). Captain Burnaby the sapper must have had a Nessman with him ! His own remains were more anonymous and businesslike than those of other visitors : the careful outline, the named geos, spurs and rocks ; triangulation marks for clues.

The half-dozen bothies, the village of Sula Sgeir, were the topographical as well as the human centre of the island. A bright turf of mayweed grew around them. It was almost

homely, the fœtid green mat with big flowers and the loose
scattered stones—a transported patch from some far southern
freestone district, a bit of Cotswold rickyard perhaps. The rock
was clothed only patchily by the thin black hide of peaty
guano, which plants kept fixed. The best of the vegetation was
about the village—mayweed, orache, thrift and chickweed ;
these four, with scurvy grass to be found rooted in bare clefts,
made the total listed by Malcolm Stewart. We added sea
spurrey and the little weed grass *Poa annua*. Finding the *Poa*
was like coming upon house sparrows in the eaves of the
shepherds' hut on Handa years ago.

Away from the village the plant cover thinned out until
only orache and thrift were left, and then thrift alone. Thrift
was evidently first colonist of the gannet guano, and along the
ridge of Creag Trithaiga it grew fantastically. " To the very
edge of the precipice the island is covered with wonderful tree-
like tussocks of seapink," wrote Harvie-Brown, " often
developing single stems like tree ferns, and their roots and
gathered earth binding together the great, loose, weathered
slabs and boulders, which strew the whole upper surface, and
rattle beneath our footsteps as we pass along " . . . on the
19th of June, 1887. The columns of the thrift rose a foot and
more high, these years later. They were mushroom-shaped
and nearly touching each other, a nitrogenous overgrowth
which hardly flowered. It was a fearful job getting about in
this area ; you had either to frisk on the wobbly stilts or plough
along the stony bottom with your feet out of sight. Like the
first sight of the gannetry the tree-fern thrift did not look
native. It covered patches of the slab-strewn top of Creag
Trithaiga, which we thus called the badlands.

A pretty and elementary succession of bird and plant life
was in progress. It was plain that the boundaries of the
gannetry were retreating southwards away from the centre of
the rock. The inland limits of gannets which we marked on
the map were well south of the line mapped by Malcolm
Stewart in 1932 and slightly south of his 1937 line. No green
blade could exist in the gannetry itself, but retreating gannets

left a bed of manure which was at once colonised by thrift and orache. The area which had been gannetry seven years before was now green and dotted with nestling fulmars. After his 1932 visit Stewart wrote that the number of fulmars " probably does not exceed 150 pairs " ; our total for the whole rock was 610 nestlings, of which 226 were on Creag Trithaiga south of the village and 157 on Sgeir an Teampuill. The overriding gannets kept at bay the push against the gannetry from each other sort of life ; but when they gave way the others instantly moved forward. Some young fulmars were parked to the very margin of the gannetry, whose edge was a tide-line for green stuff.

The emptiness of northern Lunndastoth was a nice demonstration that fulmars must have some earth or greenery to nest on. In the southern block they were confined to the crests and slopes, the cliffs being either bare or gannet-ridden. Lunndastoth took off a good third of the rock so that less than twenty acres were left for some 9000 head of gannets, 1200 of fulmars and uncounted kittiwakes, auks and shags ; thus the hive. Some late guillemots were nesting quite on the cliff top " where any child could scramble with ease and safety," as Harvie-Brown remarked. Most of the auks were already away to sea, their places empty and whitened. The Sgeir was not a big puffin rock, to judge from the few still about ; underneath boulders was about the only nesting place for them. We saw a curlew, a whimbrel, an oystercatcher, one pair of arctic terns, rock pipits, but no colk.

The gannetry became familiar and lost some of the wonder and alien-seeming of first sight. All day the shadows of winging birds continually flickered across the rock. The volume of noise on the breeze was of a great gathering of agricultural machinery, a concourse of ill-lubricated iron. The stench in the hot sun was ammoniacal.

There was still plenty of accessible gannetry on the crests and top slopes of the Creag Trithaiga cliffs, where we slid about. The sun had dried a crust on parts of the black slime. It was like negotiating some filthy bog. Bluebottles rose in clouds. The gannets themselves were clean except for black-slimed tails. Fish lay everywhere, in stages of putrefaction. Herring gulls waited about in the midst of the gannets and made opportunist snatches at regurgitated herring and mackerel. The gannets kept on sicking up fish all day long. Some of the young birds were in an awful state, floundering in the filthy slush. All stages of nestlings were represented, though most were about three-parts grown and spent the time fighting amongst themselves.

It was pretty extraordinary all the same—all those big white birds sitting there packed together by the acre—the noise, the stench, the milling white curtains in the air. Again and again, we really were on Sula Sgeir !

* * *

The Sgeir had not quite the look of a place for a colony of fork-tails—not enough soil. There was a complete absence of any clue, no sign of a burrow entrance, no stray corpse, no smell, not even a feather, but then the Flannans colony had been similarly unmarked in daytime. At ground level the pungency of mayweed swamped any other scent.

Nothing could be done with the monumental bothies, though petrels were known to be there. We began urging at flat boulders in the village mayweed, but most were immovable: our two selves half-naked in the sun and the sea-birds' hive, heaving and passing on from rock to rock, immovable, nothing, immovable, movable by both, nothing, nothing. " You heave and I'll grunt." Then, under a " movable " sat the familiar fragile ball of grey fluff. The black beady eye peeped out of the fluff ; the chick scrabbled with its tiny black webbed feet. We lowered the slab and returned it to darkness. John kept on heaving and found two more.

The sun was finishing his course. We searched more often towards Rona for the speck of the drifter. Fulmars began their evening circlings. It was going to be a race between petrels and drifter. The breeze fell away to a quiet warm evening.

The skipper had been so emphatic at dawn, yet we began to wonder, were we going to get the night after all ? Rona was still just visible as we stumbled up once more through the tree-fern thrift, the badlands, to the southern summit of Creag Trithaiga. The gannetry had quietened.

An hour and a half after sunset we sat back restfully against a bothy wall. We knew now that we had the night. Mayweed flowers glimmered in the warm dusk. The moon was climbing up from the sea, a few days past full and beginning to be lop-sided. Now the island was nearly quiet up here above the perpetual undertone of the ocean. Only gulls still gave an occasional short call. We sat waiting.

There was one ! The first bird was in, a dim bat-like flicker across the dusk in front. In five minutes three or four fork-tails were dashing in the air, intermittently seen, a fast brushing of wings. Six minutes from the first bird, the first call. The jerked-out cry came faintly from up the hill towards the gannets. We waited on against the bothy but activity seemed to be slow in working up. We went to have a look round the teampull mayweed ground. A fork-tail's burrow call came churring from beneath a big slab. We propped the torch, got a good purchase on the slab and, both together, heaved. The slab came up on edge ; another smaller slab underneath ; the churring continued. We prised again, a bird scuttled away, was grabbed before it could take off : feathers angrily raised on the head of Leach's fork-tailed petrel ! The musky flavour and queer hooked bill, the neat pushing webbed feet and spindly shanks—we had last met fork-tails at the Flannans two years before so this was quite a reunion ; here at the last of the outliers, at the fourth and final British breeding station (so far !). This important petrel now in the hand had come from an egg, which was addled. Chicks, adult, egg—there was no need to disturb any more burrows. I crawled into the teampull and caught a petrel fluttering inside.

At this stage we thought, just a small colony centred round the buildings. The birds brushed close past our faces ; John was twice touched by a bird on a very localised circuit before it plumped down and scuttled into the bothy wall a foot from where he sat.

Still the sky was clear. All night the high shining moon was up there, slowly travelling the firmament. The sea was silver, the old rock bathed with moonlight, cast shadows pitch-black. The night was as perfect as the day.

The village was getting livelier. We set out stumbling to find how far the activity stretched. We soon walked out of it going down towards the landing place, where the soil ended, but going up and along into Creag Trithaiga petrels were with us all the way. The new green fulmar ground taken over from the gannets was a hotbed of fork-tails. The tree-fern thrift was full of them. The petrels' range extended right up to the summit cairn (229 feet) near the end of the Creag ; here petrels and vegetation ended and the cap of gannets began. The very ground churred with petrels, they scuttled under-foot, they were headlong in the air. There was evidently a better depth under the thrift columns than we had realised, good burrowing room under the loose slabs and amongst a peat of thrift roots. Along the flanks of Creag Trithaiga fork-tails and gannets abutted, another pressure against the gannetry. Part, at any rate, of the fork-tails' colony must have been of recent increase, because some of the ground now churring with them had been gannetry seven years before. It showed that the fork-tails, whose economies in Rona we had thought so haphazard, had it in them to increase and spread at the opportunity.

The gannets were stilled until we came stumbling along with our torches and disturbed them. The complete change-over of life from day to night was remarkable : all day the sky full of gannets and their unceasing cacophony ; a brief no-man's-land of silence at dusk and dawn ; all night the wild dashing and outcry of petrels, flying out over the heads of sleeping gannets.

Back in the village the petrel night was in full swing. The bothy walls talked with petrels, we could smell petrel musk in the air. The burrow-calls, the flight-calls, the purrs and exclamations fell thick and fast, close and loud or faint with distance, here, there, and everywhere. The total effect was of a colony at least as big as Rona's.

I had brought some bulky and otherwise unnecessary gear all this way because I wanted to get a flashlight photograph of a nearly black petrel in flight in the middle of the night. Even if a bird should be in the way when the flash went off, and the flash carried to it and the focus chanced to be right, the fiftieth of a second of stabbing brilliance had no hope of stopping sharply the movement of flight ; but even a streak would be Leach's petrel flighting over remote, exclusive ground. I set up the camera pointing at the top of a bothy and opened the shutter. It was an exciting game. One watched for the faintly seen dash of a petrel, then jabbed hopefully at the flashlight button. The instantaneous brilliance seemed to mask what it illuminated ; the ground and bothies were so starkly bright that it was difficult to see what the flash had found in the air above. Two or three times there was nothing, we were too slow. Of course the petrels seemed thickest not here but just over there. There was a drench of dew ; the moonlight cast long shadows of rock over the wet mayweed. We stumbled and slipped, and our activities became slower and clumsier of sheer weariness. I felt myself some slow automaton going about in an aura of hot tiredness. John kept falling asleep as he sat holding the torch.

One flash did arrest several birds, bright streaks just to be registered before the total blackness of after-flash. The birds' activity began to thin out as the first appreciable daylight came again. We transferred to the teampull and set up opposite the doorway. One bird anyway seemed to have a fairly settled flight-track over the roof ; it showed quite clearly against the sky. A second flash seemed to catch it well after a complete miss the first time. Our weary reactions must have been gluey slow.

John fell finally asleep, heaped like a sack of potatoes against a bothy wall, while petrels fluttered about his head. I waited a little longer and then threw down the rickcloth on the stony mayweed and crept between its folds (we had brought it against a day and night of rain). I was lying for a few minutes hearing the last few calls. The rustle of unseen birds' wings as they came out of the ground and set away to sea added a final whisper. When I closed my eyes they felt burning hot; a moment of absolute bliss before I went off.

Some of the shepherds woke us up about an hour and a half later. They said that the drifter was waiting, but they were going to get some gugas. It was a quiet, dim morning, five o'clock; the swell was down and the landing easy. The gannetry was already in its daytime turmoil before the shepherds entered upon it. We left the rest of our provisions in a water-can hooked on to the chain inside the main living bothy; Mr. Maclean and his boys would find them later on. Four man-loads of gugas came back from the gannetry and were thrown into the boat.

We found out how we had come to have the night after all. The shepherds had found too much of a swell at Rona for the usual east bay landing. It seemed that they had had a trying day. They had not been able to start embarking sheep until nine o'clock in the evening, when the swell had gone down enough to let the small boat use the eastern landing, and then they did not finish until well after dark. Our luck was to have got ashore at all at Sula Sgeir in easterly weather, and then the same easterly weather which had brought us the wonderful day delayed the shepherds over in Rona long enough to give us the night; very fluky. The skipper looked back to the rock and said indeed what one had expected— that he would never go to that place again.

Again the sun climbed hotter and hotter over the North Atlantic, and we slept in heaps on the slow-rolling deck.

The poor driver was in trouble once more when it came to anchoring at Port of Ness. Apparently he missed some Gaelic instruction—he was not a Gael himself—and he either left her in " ahead " too long or put her " full-ahead " at the wrong moment. There was a sudden babel of shouting—seamen

312

being men of few words except at moments of emergency—
and the unfortunate loss of an anchor.

We dealt with another flat tyre and returned to Stornoway.
Next morning we asked some of the driftermen to come for a
drink (another week-end was starting). Now you see, I said
to John, the skipper will tell us that he would not go to that
place again for a hundred pounds. And it was so, the exact
sum ; " no, I would not." We could afford to be more
sympathetic now, having been out in his ship ; his dislike of
strange places far from the help of other drifters was most
understandable. The ancient engine seemed likely to break
down at any moment and the whole affair liable to burst into
flames. I remembered the local marine engineer saying how
he had been in one of those engine-rooms when the paraffin
waste in the bilge had been afire, and the flames came up
first one side and then the other as the ship rolled.

The skipper had once landed at St. Kilda. He gave us
some legendary ornithology of stormy petrels which included
their hatching upon the face of the waters, with their eggs
tucked under their wings.

Island of Sula Sgeir, August 3–4, 1939

XXVI

The Fishing Boat "Heather"

YESTERDAY we had landed from Sula Sgeir. Now after baths
and a twelve-hour sleep we felt quite spruce in clean
clothes, and rather pleased with ourselves, sitting in the bay
window of the hotel and waiting for the mailboat to come in.

Each season John and I had come back to these kind headquarters, to issue forth and to return dirty and highly
unrespectable, for baths, sleep and a refit ; keeping no sort of
hours, hastening down in the morning to capture breakfast
before it became lunch, trying to get in long after the doors
were closed and long before they were opened. And each year
and each time : " So you got back." The hotel's material
appointments had yearly increased in circumstance. Once
there had been a drinking-room downstairs with chairs and
tables where English skippers held court, very loud and
irreverent, dirty old trilbies on the backs of their heads, chairs
tilted back. Shy young Gaels watched with a sort of giggling
admiration at the Rabelaisian show. All that had been swept
away. The new bar was furnished in a décor of roadhouse-
marine, portholes in the walls, a ship's bell for closing time,
coloured lights, painted galleons. The barmen wore white
coats ; it might indeed have been a roadhouse but for the
same dour and thirsty press of herring fishers. The touchy
plumbing which had required local knowledge was gone, the
bathrooms were sexed. Each year we had greeted the castor-
oil plant in its tub half-way up the stairs, but at last it had
grown too big ; now it cast a gracious umbrage in the entrance
hall.

Sula Sgeir being achieved, John was about to go south
again. My next commitment was somehow to get the *Heather*
the fifty or sixty miles round the Butt from Carloway to

314

Stornoway, to be laid up for the winter. Kennie MacIver had splendidly said that he would pull her up when he beached his own *Sulaire*. Hugh was coming north again for the boating expedition ; he and the owl were due in the *Lochness* just now.

We had quite a social evening. The owl had become a confident flier and was much admired in the hotel. Long-suffering Mr. and Mrs. Chisholm !—last year it had been mice, this year first a nestling and now a nearly grown-up owl.

The weather held yet another day, it was a heat-wave now. We had the unprecedented experience of spending a Sunday bathing pleasurably and of lying in the sun on the golf course sands. We did not like to risk losing Carloway goodwill by going over to work on the *Heather*.

On the Bank Holiday Monday we beached the boat at high water. John went off in the evening, but not before he had done a good turn of scraping with a piece of iron barrel hoop at the encrustation of barnacles and weed. Hugh and I returned and set up camp on the grass-grown Carloway jetty, a few yards from the boat. The fine weather came to an end. Six days now remained before Hugh in turn must catch the mailboat, to join the very first batch of conscripts under the new Act.

We scraped at the hull for two days. The engine's gearbox and crankcase were both full of water and the gearbox was solidly rusted in "ahead." We removed the gear-box bodily to Stornoway and presented it to Mr. Scott, the large and deliberate marine engineer. He stood over us while we dismantled it, uttering an occasional wise and tolerant word (already we were collecting his oracles). He wired to Glasgow for a new bearing. We went back to Carlo-way and attacked the engine. Some bits, such as the at-first rather esoteric governor, were so well rusted up that one could not tell which were the alleged moving parts. We unblocked and blew through the fuel pipes and did many such-like things which called for no great engineering knowledge. The bilge pump was about the one item in working order, as found ; the hull made water only very slowly and had been kept pumped out at intervals ; it was mostly rain water.

A problem always with us was that of victualling the owl. Butcher's meat alone was no good, he had to have fur or feather as well to form the unattractive pellets he brought up with deliberation from time to time. Our only weapon was a .22 pistol, which was usually unsuccessful, though it made a lucky bag of a herring gull feeding on a dead rabbit in the roadway, during one of our frequent dashes across the island to Stornoway. The hotel set mouse-traps, Margaret MacIver set mouse-traps ; the owl was an endearing character. At Carloway there was conveniently a large stone warehouse on the jetty ; he sat up in the rafters all day and came out and flew about at night.

The new bearing came promptly from Glasgow, the gear-box was reassembled. We persuaded Mr. Scott to come back with us and it to Carloway. We rowed it out—the *Heather* was back at her moorings again—and getting it aboard only just did not drop it once and for all into the loch. Mr. Scott had brought a pocketful of springs and washers and so on to replace the more corrupted pieces ; also a heavier hammer than we had. After several hours' work, the engine was ready for a try and we introduced ourselves to the novelty of swinging over its iron guts. The thing started ! It clattered and shook within its dim compartment ; water and smoke spat from its exhaust pipe.

In a trial run round Loch Carloway the engine stopped only once, but gave us an exhausting struggle to get it going again. We returned Mr. Scott to Stornoway by midnight, knocked up Anglo-Oil for a drum of paraffin, and were back in Carloway by two o'clock. At eight o'clock we struck the tent, embarked all our goods and the owl in his tea-chest, left the car standing on the jetty, and sailed.

> *A ship I bought, and, yet undaunted, cast*
> *Once more my fortune to th' Atlantic waste.*

The morning was unprepossessing, windy, rainy, grey and

unwarm. We chugged slowly out of Loch Roag ; gradually felt the outside swell. We left the last islets well behind before we turned northwards along the coast, keeping well offshore. Wind and sea were astern, a biggish swell which carried the boat forward by surge and sag ; we hoisted the hefty lugsail to help along. The engine kept plugging away hour after hour, occasionally with an added loud hammering noise. " Sometimes a heavy knock comes on her as if the fuel is only so-so," Mr. Scott had said, with his customary sigh.

We got to the Butt, worked slowly round it and turned southwards. Half-way, and the tricky part done. There was good shelter at first, close inshore down the east side of Lewis, past Port of Ness and Cellar Head and Tolsta Head. But off Tolsta the bilge pump came apart in my hands—with the plunger part stuck at the bottom of the shaft, and nothing would retrieve it. If only we had had a length of stiff wire to hook it up with—but we hadn't. A brisk leak had developed somewhere, and the failure of the bilge pump set other events in train. We couldn't keep the bilge water below the flywheel by bailing ; water reached the flywheel which flung spray all over the engine-room ; the engine gradually drowned, one cylinder first ; the other continued for a little while until the magneto gave up under the steady shower of spray; the engine expired in a last puff-puff—puff : silence and swilling water. The gearbox was again immovably jammed in ahead so that even if we could have kept the water down we probably should never have been able to restart the engine.

We went on very slowly by sail in a short, uncomfortable cross sea and made another four or five miles before darkness and a night at sea, for which, as Martin remarked when the storm caught him at Boreray, we were no ways fitted. We sailed and bailed to and fro off Tiumpan Lighthouse all night. The owl took up his perch on the defunct engine. For ourselves it was a very trying and exhausting night. Bailing in the engine-room was the worst part, dipping with a little tin and filling an iron cauldron which had been left on board, crouching and pushing the cauldron up above one's head through the hatch, tipping it out and getting some of it back down one's neck and arms : repeated to exhaustion. The engine-room and ourselves were one smear of black oily water.

We sailed to and fro between the lighthouse and a line of drifters whose lights had appeared. Stornoway was only about another ten miles, and we thought we would keep in the same place until dawn and then get a tow in. But when a dirty half-light did come the drifters had all disappeared. Although we had lost no ground during the night we had become exhausted. We set on down the coast, but terribly slowly ; Stornoway was in the eye of the wind. Luckily a solitary steam drifter came our way ; we waved to her ; she closed and threw us a line. After that the speed seemed like an express train ; the old boat had probably never been so fast in her life. We crouched on top of each other in the minute wheel-house and let the bailing go hang. Heading into the short tumbling sea at ten knots the boat bucked and bumped and drenched herself in spray that flung against the wheelhouse. The joy of that tow ! We were in Stornoway in an hour. By then bilge water was half-way up the engine, but with the essential piece of wire borrowed from the drifter's engineman, we had the pump plunger retrieved and the pump reassembled and working in a couple of minutes. All night we had racked our weary brains for something wherewith to hook up that plunger ; I had even taken off a fuel pipe and bent it straight and tried to use the nipple on the end as a hook. When we got in we realised that the drifter was no stranger but the MacIver Company's own beautifully kept *Windfall*. We left the boat dry for the moment, went up to the hotel for a long bathroom session with household cleanser, then another breakfast to follow the drifter's herrings and back to the boat for another pump-out and more work. To-morrow evening's mailboat was the last possible sailing and we had to leave the *Heather's* engine in some sort of condition for over-wintering. We sponged the water out of the engine again for a start, but the gearbox would have to remain in ahead until next year.

Now : to get to Carloway, collect the car and sell it. For

the last few days we had been driving about with " For Sale
£5 Ask Driver " chalked across the back, and there had been
a bite or two. To-day was some sort of carnival day in
Stornoway, which added to the general dream unreality. We
found a bus going to Carloway and went in it. The bus driver
suggested that he might buy the car, but at Carloway there
was a client with his five pounds ready counted out. We
showed him the certain subtle knack of how to start up, left
him with the engine running and returned to Stornoway in
the same bus. We fell asleep and woke up every time our
heads banged against the windows. Then, at last, to bed.

An irremediable misfortune happened while we were
having our fill of sleep : the owl escaped. We looked vaguely
at Stornoway rooftops during the day and told the police. We
worked on the *Heather* again, took off the magneto for winter
storage, smeared the whole of the rusty iron box with grease,
and all the so-called moving parts, and poured oil into the
cylinders. The boat was making water reasonably slowly now
that she was stationary in calm water. Half an hour before
the *Lochness* sailed we did a final pump-out. Happily Kennie
MacIver would beach the boat in a day or two—we weren't
to worry about her—and that was a great relief ; but we sailed
sadly without the owl.

Next summer, when Hugh's naval service would be over,
we should fit out the *Heather* and go almost anywhere.

On the evening of the day I got home, a telegram came :
" =OWL RETURNS PHONE=CHISHOLM++." He
caught the *Lochness* and started off on his seven-hundred-mile
journey. Two days later I collected the tea-chest at the
station. The floor of the box was strewn with his pellets and
with food in variety from red meat to apple cores. As for the
owl himself upon his perch—not a feather out of place ; really
he looked rather pleased with himself.

LONG INTERVAL

LEWIS REMEMBERED

XXVII

Lewis Remembered

"ROUND many western islands have I been"; and the Butt of Lewis, the cold northern headland of habitation, was the place for imagination to return to, to call them over.

From the Butt, the imagined line of the outliers lay over the horizon. North and a little east to Rona and the Sgeir, forty miles; south-west to the Flannans, forty-five miles; and another forty miles beyond them, St. Kilda. There was no sameness even among these lonely lumps in the sameness of the ocean, though all were made of gneiss or other such-like adamantine matter. Rona—a hide of sour grass and sedge, the unique village, the seals, the low peninsulas north and south. The black horrent Sgeir white with gannets, the bothies, the rocky desolation. The Flannans—a lighthouse, pasture close and sweet, the barest skin of all, elevated within the total wall of cliffs, a warren of rabbits and puffins. The sea continent of St. Kilda—the one and only beach, wrens and mice and *mouflon*, thousand-foot cliffs, the human survival. And common to each different mountain top risen into the air from the ocean bed, were some ancient holy remains, and a colony of fork-tails. Then the others, less withdrawn: the Monach Isles, a sand-dune, different in kind; the basalt of the Shiants and their vegetative profusion, the rats and cats; Handa, landward and first, heather, lochans, the first impact of cliff colonists and seals. They were all vignetted now. I should never regret the devotion of the precious first five summers of my twenties!

The gap widened; the look of the date "September, 1939," in print began to fall in with imagined hot days of "August, 1914." The thirties with their so-talked-of moral failures became days as of solid Edwardian plenty, pre-war.

Already the thirties, yesterday, were a closed and labelled period, another little packet of time past, so promptly placed because continuity at personal levels was broken. The strangeness and bewilderment of autumn 1939 were ancient; we were beginners; war had long since become normal, year in, year out.

Would any one ever be able to pick up again in his own small affairs where he had left off? The Hebrides anyway would not change? But looking through the fat back numbers of the *Stornoway Gazette* was looking into another world.

> —Callum Sheorais and his crew of four, as is their annual custom, paid two visits to the Flannan Islands last week with motor boat " Rhoda,"

reported Our Bernera Correspondent in the issue of August 4th, 1939. Two years later old Mr. Malcolm Macleod, Callum Sheorais, spent three days at sea in the *Rhoda* looking for a reported ship's boat; he had passed his eightieth birthday then. One day after that he picked up his newspaper at the Bernera post-office and went home and he died in his chair.

In 1939 the Nessmen had set out for the Sgeir in the usual way, Norman Maclean and his nine companions in the *sco Peaceful*.

> All those who have been anxiously asking whether a crew was going to Sulisgeir this year will be relieved to know that the " Discovery II " set out on her voyage of exploration a week ago,

reported Our Ness Correspondent. But next week:

> On Sunday no less than six special buses were required to take the reservists into town. Ness has the distinction of having the only 10 persons in Europe, possibly, who are quite unconcerned by the crisis—they are on Sulisgeir for the guga. . . .

A month later, the editorial:

> Even the outbreak of war has failed to stem the flood of corre-

spondence in the Press on the Nessmen's annual visit to Sula Sgeir for the guga.

But, said the editor, weighty and factual,

> it is doubtful if, value for value, there is a better food bargain on the market today than a guga for 2s.

War news was thin during the winter of 1939-40 though the disproportionate sacrifice of young Hebrideans was already repeating the other war. Most of the men were naval reservists, and the islands were drained. There were soon heavy losses in the reservist crews of the armed merchant cruisers which U-boats sank so freely early on in the war.

One day I found myself transported to a Polish troopship sailing from the Clyde, round the Mull of Kintyre—to Skerryvore and Barra Head—up the Minch—past the Shiants plain and close—past Tiumpan and Tolsta where Hugh and I had spent our night of bailing—past the Butt—to the Faroes, to Norway. And I was just too dog-tired to wait up for a sight of Rona and the Sgeir. It was in the log afterwards : " 2100. Fix on N. Rona."

Clyde to Forth, and Forth to Clyde : the coastal convoys rounded closely on Cape Wrath on the east-bound run, and kept out towards the Butt coming the other way ; then southwards between Shiants and the Lewis coast. It was thought to be a soft job for the trawler escort though uncomfortable in the winter. We were transferred to ocean convoys.

One summer day in 1941 our convoy was late in forming up from one of the mainland west coast lochs. We were allowed to run across to Stornoway for a few hours if we wanted to, " for provisions and water " ; so we did, streaming an urgent trail of thick black smoke across the Minch. There was time for a quick run ashore; there was Kennie MacIver, saying that his own *Sulaire* had been commandeered, that he was commissioning the *Heather* for harbour work ; and there was *Heather* herself up on the beach, with a gentle white-haired shipwright caulking and hammering ! I wrote off to Hugh, full of drawings and plans : the telegraph pole of a mast done away with, the noisome fo'castle made habitable, given standing room with a raised combing and portholes ; planks refastened (copper fastened) and ribs recapped ; a four-cylinder Kelvin to replace the old twin—still stuck in ahead ? Hugh replied with an equal enthusiasm from the Mediterranean. Some day, in 194?, we would take up where we had left off. But Hugh was left behind in 1941.

*   *   *

In his book on the *Islands of Scotland* (1939) Hugh Mac-Diarmid wrote :

> Apart from economic, political or literary matters, the Hebrides come into the newspapers nowadays mainly through one or other of a small set of recurring circumstances—either because of an aeroplane flight to convey a patient from one of the isles to a Glasgow hospital . . . or because of some trouble of the sea—shipwreck or the marooning by wild weather of lighthouse-keepers taken ill on duty and unable to be reached by medical attention.

Anything to do with difficult childbirth without a doctor's help was another one ; and for economics and politics, the state of the roads and lack of piers, the romantic crofters' disputes, grievances, petitions and evacuations, were perennial.

The scraps of print were different now. " Plane Crash on St. Kilda." A Sunderland flying-boat had flown into the side of Conachair ; long afterwards the crash was found ; a minister went out from Stornoway to conduct a burial service.

> —Reykjavik, Thursday. A British warship on Tuesday stopped the coastal passenger steamer Esja off the south coast of Iceland.

ESJA—painted in big white letters on her side—she passed once a fortnight, but she never came in !

In 1940, in a wireless programme, " Scrapbook for 1930,"

the stray-heard voice—gentle, husky, Hebridean—of Neil Ferguson, sometime postmaster of St. Kilda :

" That was old Finlay, he hasn't a word of English, he was saying he wished he'd never left the island."

In Stornoway the *Heather* was in use by the Home Guard, so I heard, for evening fishing trips, " coastal exercises."

A Whitley aircraft of Coastal Command, Wick station, crash-landed on Rona. The crew survived and were fetched by naval trawler.

There was room in 1943 for a note of one more island withdrawal, a newspaper snippet which said that the last inhabitants had been evacuated from some remote islands off the coast of North Uist in the Outer Hebrides, the Monach Islands.

When Dr. Fraser Darling's island books came out, the reading was as much between the lines as in them, for any one with local knowledge. He had found the bracket razorbill ! —that most particular of the myriad sea-fowl which John and I found nesting on a clump of thrift growing out like a fungus from the three-hundred-foot wall of the west cliff of Rona. We had admired and photographed it in 1936 ; Dr. Darling had found it in 1938 and again when he had been back for ten days in June, 1939 ; and here was its latest portrait in *Island Farm* (1944).

During his 1938 residence Dr. Darling had been restoring the chapel. He had built up the south wall, working to Mr. Norrie's photograph of 1887 when the wall was not yet fallen. In our time the entrance from chapel to St. Ronan's cell had been so silted up that a fulmar could hardly get through ; in Muir's time it had just been negotiable—" I had to draggle myself forward "—and even in days of habitation the doorway had been " such a hinder." The ground was too holy then for improvement, or had a certain Hebridean *laissez-faire* been content to leave things as they were ? Dr. Darling had dug down in the chapel to uncover a doorway over four feet high, floored with stone paving and leading into the older cell.

There were so many things to go back for. The month of Chune ! I had never seen the islands then, when the sea-fowl's landward season would be at its highest pitch and there would be no darkness in the shortest summer nights—the flower of the northern seasons. And still there were more islands— Gasker, long in mind, the forgotten islet eight miles off the Harris coast, was outstanding for a visit ; so were Mingulay and the rest of the tail-end isles of the Hebridean chain ; so were the sea-rocks of Haskeir off the coast of North Uist—in 1939 R. B. Freeman had found a single Leach's petrel, no egg, in a hole there. Possibly fork-tails were founding new colonies, all unbeknownst ?

John Ainslie came to be billeted in the house of one Dr. Leach, and what should he discover there but a stuffed Leach's petrel in a glass case. However, the bird was purely coincidental and had been bought for five and sixpence.

*   *   *

Early Bronze Age Food Vessel (slightly restored) *c.* 500 B.C. This pottery food vessel originally contained food for the buried man in case he should need a little sustenance before his recognition and final acclimatization in the next world. . . .

The descriptive card in the West Highland Museum, Fort William, was waggishly propped against a tin of anti-gas ointment. The upstairs had become a naval officers' club. Deep in dust in the entrance hall was a St. Kilda mailboat— sheepskin bladder, staff and boat—just as the outfit Neil Gillies and I had sent off five years ago. Fort William had become a naval training base. The Grand Hotel which I remembered once entering with John on some journey north, to fall asleep in the arm-chairs at five o'clock in the morning, was now the officers' mess ; the same arm-chairs, still intermittently slept in. I found myself north again.

One day the security policeman on the pier passed me his

paper, have a read of the *Oban Times* for July 24, 1943.
" Primitive Norse Mill in Lewis." Quite so, that was the old
mill at Shawbost, the only one of the sort left, another case
of immemorial design hanging on. The type, whose water-
wheel was a vertically mounted tree trunk, set with a bristle
of paddles below and crowned above with the upper mill-
stone, was supposed to have come into Lewis with the Norsemen in the ninth century. We found the mill, John and I,
during one of our tours in the £3 Singer. And up at Ness
Alec MacFarquhar was sometimes to be found grinding barley
at his own more orthodox water-mill. The banks of the streams
up there were a blaze of musk in the month of July. Harris
tweed was like musk, it had lost its smell ; the traditional
reek was supposed to come from the crotal, but no doubt peat
smoke and other domestic flavours had to do with it, such as
the steeping of tweed in a mordant of soot and urine (so one
heard). The washing and dyeing of the wool, the teasing and
carding and spinning, was now done in the Stornoway mills,
which sent out thread to the crofter-weavers and received
back the tweed for finishing ; thus was preserved the valu-
able descriptive " hand-woven."

The looms in the moorland country townships were tucked
away in the various crofts and bothies, byres, buts and bens.
Tweed and wool were the cash crops, so to speak, but they
were hidden. That was always the first feature and puzzle of
the houses ; they stood about anyhow beside the track over
the moor, without visible means of livelihood, seeming to have
nothing to do with the land or with each other. They had
no idea of nestling, as in an English village, nor yet of standing
four-square to the weather ; they just straggled. The moor
came up unfenced to each wall and, in the case of black houses,
continued underneath as floor. Commonly there was nothing
to look like a farm building, no enclosure or yard or garden
of any sort, just peat stacks, some hens, a cow, a few haphazard
sheep, the telegraph poles. Yet the economy was of cash, with
buses and lorries, shops, post-offices, even the telephone.
Crofting was merest subsistence, or less—

small irregular patches of cultivation visible among the rocks
. . . rather what a cock with a little harem of hens might
scratch up any fine morning, than a winter's sustenance for
human beings.[1]

The few remaining black houses, the low barrows of drystone and thatch, grew out of the ground and gave a clue to
earlier subsistence living, with little or no cash. They had
been all but replaced by white houses in the twenty years
between the wars. It was the white houses which looked so
foreign and unsupported by the moor, perched, grey, cement-
faced boxes, lined with matchboarding, roofed with slate or
corrugated iron, and ugly as sin. The frequent churches were
larger versions of them.

Dr. Johnson's declaration to a Scotsman did well enough for
Lewis :

" Your country consists of two things, stone and water. There
is, indeed, a little earth above the stone in some places, but a
very little ; and the stone is always appearing. It is like a
man in rags ; the naked skin is always peeping out."

There was shell-sand behind some of the seaside and boulder
clay in places, but the rest was rock and water and a blanket
of peat up to nearly twenty feet deep, usually being rained on.
The Macaulay Experimental Farm outside Stornoway was on
one of the deepest peat bogs, but this did look like a farm.
There were concrete cowsheds and thousand-gallon cows, a
tall silo, fenced field crops. A caterpillar tractor crawled over
the peat dragging a wooden sledge. The farm manager said
he had seen it sunk in the peat until the top of its radiator
was at ground level. A block of breast-high oats looked queer
enough in the middle of the moor. It was done by draining,
liming with shell-sand and dressing with artificials, at a price.
The crofters were not noticeably interested, being unable to
afford a caterpillar tractor perhaps. They continued to
scratch like their hens.

[1] James Wilson, 1842.

The moors were always busy in August ; however far and wide stretched the heather and the bog, there was usually somebody in sight. The peats which had been cut and stacked to dry earlier in the season were being carted home in carts and decrepit motor lorries ; the roads were scattered with peats as if a troop of elephants had passed along. The cattle were still at summer pasture on the moors, in the traditional practice. Sheep after all were newcomers, Highlanders and Islanders were originally cattlemen, and the surviving habit of taking the stock to the moors in summer and of living meantime in a shieling was presently paralleled by the peasants of European mountain country, with their seasonal upward migration of themselves and their cattle. Contemporary shielings were anything from a wooden hut to the rudest heap of turf and stone with a tarpaulin thrown over and dangled with stones. A drift of peat smoke eddied from the ground, the black women padded to and from the burn.

On a fine day in August the pollen rose as dust as one walked the heather—August, the moorland and seaside month, when inland south was having its worst fly-blown season of dusty greens and thistles and concrete earth. The moors went on and on, criss-crossed with rivers and burns ; lochs or lochans stood in every hollow, like potholes in the road. Flawless white water-lilies floated on some lochs ; bogbean grew as fluffy-blossomed thickets ; delicate flowers of water lobelia rose clear where shallow water lapped a pebble shore. The wet walls of peat cuttings oozed into black malariae-looking drains where nothing grew. The evening of a fine day was hellish with midges.

Most of the roads were grit and pothole, the less important routes a pair of wheel-tracks with a line of grass and rushes down the middle, but each year new tar extended a bit farther from Stornoway. By 1938 Macadam was well on the way to Harris. Mainland contractors came over with heavy machinery, foreign road rollers trundled far into the moors ; there were hutment barracks miles from anywhere, like logging camps, where the crowd of rough men lived. By 1939 the first enamelled road-signs had been placed by the Royal Automobile Club, and stoned by the youth of the country. Internal communication was all by buses, which Lewismen urged along regardless, hooter instead of brakes. This Jehu manner was quite in keeping with the custom of any European peasant country where roads were bad and cars imported ; the common features a complete disregard for machinery, and continuous use of the horn. Sheep continued to sleep in the roadway, the occasional corpse was thrown to one side. The buses were mostly modern but were soon bruised and flogged to death. The Lewis bus driver was a figure of romance ; children wanted to be bus drivers when they grew up.

Except for one or two choice stretches the roads were all single-track with passing places every few hundred yards. In dry weather a bus was marked from miles away by its dust-cloud. One soon fell in with the island customs, when to push on and when to give way, but occasionally one would be bluffed into reversing by some unstoppable bus charge to Ness or Carloway or Uig. Hardly a motor cycle was to be seen ; sufficient evidence of the younger men's lack of cash ? Just as corrugated iron for human dwellings was always an index of poverty—or merely of a Celtic region ?—or were poverty, Celts and corrugated iron always conjoined ?

The £3 Singer of our first island motoring found its proper level in Lewis ; there were plenty of contemporaries. Its mudguards flapped like wings, its bonnet jittered between radiator and body. Wherever there was habitation the road was parcelled out into the territories of furiously barking dogs, where one had no sooner dropped behind than the next took up. This was very fraying to the tourism of the Singer, abetted by the engine's own intermittent splutterings and stoppages, and Lewismen were sometimes very bad indeed at watching with detached interest any one cranking and cranking at an engine which would not start. Urbanity sometimes failed. Gaeldom !—a shack-town litter, yapping curs, a straggle of hideous houses problematically maintained, full of black ministers and elders and peathags all gabbling away in Erse and knocking back the usquebaugh. Calvinism, and worse, folk-lore, red rags to a bull. In these parts you could not have so much as a stone with a hole in it without its gathering some infantile mossy legend, smugly trotted out by fatuous guide-books—between the advertisements—and gaped at by feeble-minded tourists.

This was the country Lord Leverhulme had wished to develop after the 1914 war with his ideas of a fish cannery, a big dairy farm to supply the whole island (milk was and still is imported by sea), white houses for black, and the rest. One of his projects was an east-coast route to Ness, and beyond the red corrugated iron post-office and the bedstead fences of Tolsta a large, completed, ferro-concrete bridge dwarfed the burn below it. Two miles farther on the new road petered out into a heap of stones on the moor, where no sign of habitation was in sight. The iron marking-pegs were still in the ground, their tops burred over by the sledge hammer. It was as if the workmen had gone on strike. By now the pegs were nearly rusted through.

Lord Leverhulme had soon given up Lewis as a bad job, had presented Stornoway Castle to the borough and trans-ferred to Harris, where he raised a storm by getting the name of the village of Obbe changed to " Leverburgh." He had died when his ambitious fish-curing and harbour works there were half finished. They remained half finished thereafter ; " a millionaire's dream," as the Stornoway guide-book remarked, but " Leverburgh " endured.

For its own part the *Official Guide* named Stornoway " Queen of the Hebrides."

> Its handsome buildings, busy streets, modern shops and hotels, its stately Municipal Pile, its comfortable Playhouse, its several large churches, all suggest that this is no different from any other progressive seaport and market town.

No doubt that the Municipal Pile was stately, the churches large and numerous, but the catalogue was misleading. Stornoway was herring and tweed, but it was also the front between Glasgow and hinterland Lewis, partaking of both—a frontier town. So naturally sheep wandered into the town and hens scratched in the potholed back streets ; and naturally had come Woolworth's and cinema.

Wireless and ceilidh of course, petrol pump and peat stalk, all-black women and peroxide blondes, Woolworth's, ship chandler, Burton's Tailoring, flesher, twopenny library, wool merchant. But there was much more to it than, say, the common ancient-and-modern antithesis of a publicity photograph, airliner over the Pyramids or shiny motor car in a show-piece village. Lewis (so I thought) was like a larger St. Kilda. Things kept on coming into the island, and once there, stayed. Things wore out and were thrown away ; they lay as they fell. (That might even be a master clue to the Hebrides : Things lie as they fall.) It seemed that nothing was ever actually destroyed. On the mainland there was some rotation, obsolete goods became scrap and were burnt or squashed flat or buried or melted down and turned into something else. What remains would future archæologists find of motor cars in England ? Even now where were the cars of twenty and thirty years ago ? But in Lewis they might find the skeleton of an early motor lorry beautifully pickled in a peat bog. The moorland alongside the roads was an occasional though increasing museum of old abandoned cars ; very interesting. These were early days yet, but where else could one still find Model T Fords ? Not that Model T's weren't still running in the island. One old motor bus which had been tipped into a loch had initiated a subsequent dump of cows' and horses' heads ; elsewhere the curious mixture would have been separated, reduced to the respective raw materials of steel and bonemeal and put into circulation again.

There was no neat archæologist's sandwich of century layered upon century. The usages of all times were jumbled together in the advancing present. Gugas and Glasgow wrapped bread. Summer shielings one way, caterpillar tractors the other. Spinning-wheels and fifty-shilling tailoring. There would be a wireless aerial among the tepees of tinkers' encampments, and in with the stock of horseflesh, a shaggéd motor-car or two. The Stornoway cinema's young audience would go home by bus to box-beds and bundling—or had that been given up? Anyway, they would have spent part of the evening sitting patiently in darkness while the breaks in the film were mended. Of course the whole railway era had been missed out, which produced the publicised sort of circumstance whereby old bodies who had never seen a train sailed blithely in aeroplanes.

The products of industrial advertising became interesting at their geographical limits, in the Celtic island environment: a familiar brand on a bag of cement in St. Kilda, the dance-band tunes universal to the farthest bothy, the unavoidably known makes of soap, razor blades, cigarettes, tinned food. Much of the stuff was of Scottish origin, but sometimes English goods in some remote shack-shop would strike as patriotically as if chanced upon abroad.

The human attraction of Lewis (to me) was always the mix-up, the half-and-half look: The rusty petrol pump sprouting lonely from the turf, the trumpet wireless sets speaking the single universal voice of the News, the standardised interiors of matchboarding and mantle lamps; most of all, always the lonely line of telegraph poles, bleached and leaning, carrying over the moor. The Islands' own telephone book was a splendid pamphlet, as thick as a newspaper; who could one ring up?

Down in Tarbert, Harris, the agent of Highland Airways had a window full of leaflets in the slick lay-out of Commercial Art—faded, curled and dusty. Stornoway herself had no air-port, the nearest landing ground was a strip of beach fifty miles away in Harris. A perpetual battle was carried on for the convenient golf course. (A golf course was inescapable even in the Outer Hebrides, though the only other one was that sporting 5-hole links in the Flannans.) And boating, tennis, bowling, fishing and bathing, added the *Guide*. Bathing dresses at the windows of the Caledonian, the County and the Royal? They would seem as appropriate, hung from the windows of the Bank of England. However, one picture postcard of the town had had a foreign foreground of bathing beach rather crudely painted in. Certainly urchins sometimes splashed in the genuine foreground. It was where the drifters tipped their rubbish and where they came ashore to careen, or for some patient driver to see what had happened to the propeller.

The *Stornoway Gazette* was the only local paper I ever came across which was readable. It dated from 1917, was printed on the mainland[1] and went to Lewismen all over the world. The district notes particularly were written in a humane and human way quite foreign to the common run of reported parish affairs elsewhere. Even obituaries and weddings were without syncophancy ; best wishes for a wildish young man and hopes that he might now settle down, regret that some prominent native had omitted to return to Lewis to die. (Remote crofts were very normal birthplaces for successful ministers, doctors, schoolmasters and business men.) The best and raciest of the *Gazette's* team of correspondents was the unlettered driver of a drifter who reported Tolsta. Some others were a girl driver of a grocer's van, an unschooled butcher's assistant, an Elder of the Free Kirk. Mrs. Macleod, who was Ness correspondent for many years until she was eighty-eight years old, had previously been a schoolmistress ; she was an exception.

*   *   *

Stornoway was the melting-pot of the islands. The two camps met there—but halt ! When it came to trying to generalise about people in their own country—indeed that was something to give pause to an English summer tourist who was anyway happier with " things " and to whom Gaeldom, unless personalised, was but an ignorance of black-dressed religion, incomprehensible language, and peaty folklore.

Were there even two camps ? The elder old fashioned, the younger emancipated or new fangled ? That division hardly

---

[1] The first Stornoway-printed issues came off the press in 1949.

served when one heard that many of the girls who went away to service in Glasgow would never enter a cinema. But undoubtedly Calvinism was one extreme and it set the tone of the country. The cinema was an evil house, a view with which any one might feel sympathy, considering the films apt to reach the Hebrides. The harmless-looking gramophone was an engine of wickedness, dancing was wicked. Government summer-time on the clocks was called new time as against old or God's time. Of course Sunday observance was cast-iron ; the curtains drawn—the two services interminable—the piano in the house, if any, draped—the Bible much read—the food cooked beforehand. What might and what might not be done on The Day was subject to the nicest regulations; black serge and misery, to be met with a sort of prep schoolboy's remembered hate. The Bible told them to rest, so rest they did, though in this rather circumscribed manner.

Out in the country the only smooth flat surface was the concrete of new bridges. Young men and girls, rebels, would gather there in the evenings and dance to a concertina ; Elders would come and harangue them. Fantastic scene ? The headlights of any tourist's car might illuminate it, common island controversy. The Elders were said to disapprove even football, but this seemed unbelievable. Football was very keen in Lewis. The *Gazette* was always printing long reports of the matches, Back *v.* Gress, Tong *v.* Point, Eye *v.* Knock. Reformers within the island, trying for village halls and similar amenities, would say that the first battle was always anti-church, anti- that religious attitude of unbending acquiescence to the strait and very narrow. Certainly Calvinism was one citadel, and always being undermined; "Ring out the false, ring in the true"; the circulation of the *Scottish Daily Express* was as successfully pushed up in the country districts of Lewis as anywhere else.

Drink was the one licence allowed by the Church, but then plenty of the men would be extremely strict teetotallers. In spite of the Hebrides being a depressed area there always seemed to be plenty of money to slap down in the surf of Stornoway bars. A Lewisman at closing time on Saturday evening might buy a bottle of whisky and a few quart bottles of beer to take home for the week-end. There were no bars out in the country ; Stornoway in fact was the fount for the whole of Lewis, so Saturday evenings were brisk. On Sunday mornings broken bottles would be lying about the pavements, the streets would be empty under a grey and drizzling sky, the town withdrawn into the full rigour of the Sabbath.

To upstairs visitors in the hotels the turmoil of the bars below swelled and faded like the tumult of a sea-fowl colony. " The Lambeth Walk " one year—old Gaelic lament ; another year, " Red Sails in the Sunset," island boat song, traditional. Upstairs there might be a few English salmon fishers, impatient with Hebrideans and complaining about the roads. Glasgow commercial travellers would be loathing Stornoway, dead-alive place, just the single one-horse cinema. The Gaelic summer school would have attracted some elderly Scots and English schoolmistresses—ha, very peculiar indeed, the English ladies. Gaelic culture was as raffia-work nowadays. " Fond memory brings the light Of other days around me " ; the evening when John and I got back to the hotel from our residence in Rona, civilisation so novel ; we had baths, and when we came down in clean clothes to the dining-room for supper, over in the corner was a helpless gentleman earnestly spreading butter with his fork. Stornoway—uncaring ! As a young Lewisman in the *Lochness* once apostrophised : " Storrn-o-way—here I come ! " The hotel plumbing had used to be an original. " Hot " then was always scalding, " Cold " would deliver only a peaty trickle. John and I used to have to go round the empty bedrooms collecting water-jugs and pouring them into the boiling bath. That was in the days of the down-stairs drinking-room ; since the redecoration H and C had gushed from chromium plate.

When the men were away in the 1914 war the women voted for prohibition. The men came back and had to club together to buy whisky by the gallon from the grocers. They went camping out with it. The timeless, lugubrious-quarrel-some, dirgeful parties were so easily imagined. Like the old account of a Highland funeral perhaps : " They lay drinking on the ground : it was like a field of battle ! " That episode was a microcosm of the Hebrides ?—a certain tortuous slyness of dealing, no compromise or discussion but the decision secretly arrived at and suddenly sprung, *fait accompli*. No doubt there was much to be said on both sides in this case and no doubt it was, afterwards. You could make all sorts of denunciations of your fellows and yet remain very affable to them.   As English tourists of course we never really knew what was going on ; we met instead a kindness and hospitality remarkably different from anywhere else.   The common English layering of class and money was missing in Lewis.

Among Stornoway people was to be discovered a kind of humane tolerance, lofty and careless, whether directed towards the interior or towards Glasgow.   Frontier wisdom ?   A careless disregard for Calvinist dogma one way, and for all the sorts of pretentiousness and newspaper excitement the other.   This atmosphere was extremely refreshing, but it could hardly have been expected to enter much into the civic official affairs of the town.

Even in our few years the push of progress or change was obvious, though in the country it seemed to come desultorily and in spite of itself. (Even in 1935, in mainland Kinloch Bervie, the police were requiring that motor bikes be licensed.) In Stornoway a new pier was built and all the hotels were redecorated throughout.   The policemen were cheerful and understanding—Stornoway people said that they knew better than to interfere with their own little ways—but the behaviour of traffic was tightened up all the same.   The tweed mills were still fairly new, though herring-curing had been a capitalised industry for generations.   Fish-curers spoke affectionately of the days before the mainland telephone, when they couldn't be got at for the whole week-end ; older people remembered the sight of several hundred sail of drifters all beating to and fro on their inch-by-inch return to harbour.

Something had always been coming into the islands : Christianity— Norsemen —potatoes —tea —steamships —the telephone—motor cars—wireless—aeroplanes; what next? The Hebrides to be Glasgow's lung? A national park—a military training ground—afforestation—a refuge for English simple-lifers? The two big resources of tweed and herring were industries, while the lesser resources of subsistence but not of trading value went on falling into disuse. The inshore fishing was spoilt by trawlers, corrugated iron replaced thatch, concrete replaced drystone, food was bought instead of won. If the tendencies of the thirties carried on, land would go out of cultivation rather than come in, coal might even replace peat in the fireplaces. The trend would be to get money so that everything should be imported—a revolution long completed throughout England, where the whole farmhouse economy was gone, replaced by cash purchases from shops. Nowadays the only thoroughgoing counter-revolutionaries were a few crankish communities aiming at self-sufficiency. Monasteries in the Hebrides had once made a precedent. Would English neo-peasants, renouncing the twentieth century, be coming to wrest sufficiency from the Outer Isles, more croft-like than the crofters? It was surprising, when one totted them up, how complete were the elemental resources of the Hebrides, how-ever far and barren they seemed. The crofter's life looked not a bad one, from outside, for a quietist—" Happy the man whose wish and care A few paternal acres bound," and so on —and I did hear born Lewismen claim that in fact the crofters were pretty well off. They could build a house for next to nothing with all the Government grants, and the old resources of what used to be called good wholesome fare— fish, oatmeal, eggs, potatoes, dairy stuff, sheep—remained. Even St. Kilda and Rona had been one-time exporters of food. Shell-sand and seaweed were at the ocean-side for the carting, peat was for the cutting, homespun for the spinning. Timber was the one thing missing ; precious roof rafters had used to be handed down from generation to generation.

But no, it would never do for the alien English. It might be all very well in theory but a look at the simple values on North Uist was enough. The treelessness, the climate, the religion—one would have to be reared to it from birth. The young men of the islands might go away and make a living in the world, but many of them would come back to their native strand to die.

So there they all were, the Hebrideans, doing something to the peat or to the sheep, to the herring or to the tweed ; the spirited young men, the old men—some dour and unconversable, some gentle and twinkling—dressed young and old in the island uniform of blue boiler suits. The all-black, uncountrified-looking women were fetching and carrying, seeming like black spiders scurrying on the moor. The moor dwarfed townships and crofts, where the human litter was not unlike the scattered mess made by a gullery. Peat, stone and water—and throughout the winter months at the Butt the wind was blowing at gale force more often than on one day in three. All the year round rain was beating down on two days out of three, the grey clouds for ever renewed from the west. There they all were, and perhaps all that a visitor might safely comment was that the amount of outsiders' good advice which had been offered to them was by now immeasurable. But :

> *Oh that the peats might cut themselves*
> *And the fish chump on the shore*
> *That I might lie upon my bed*
> *And sleep for evermore !*

THE
HEBRIDES REGAINED

★

1946

XVIII

A View of the Shiant Islands

THE Mallaig road was novel, to be seen from a train, a
fifty-mile stretch of smooth black tar now. One had known
it in its frontier days.

Mallaig ; the third-class quarters of the *Lochness* ; the
Minch suitably grey and heaving under a uniform grey sky,
the sea-fowl, the bone-seeking breeze after a usual unslept day
and night of travel from the south. We were a party of three
coming to try a little first, unambitious cruising in the old
fishing boat *Heather* : John Naish, with whom I had been
associated in many outings but not so far to the Outer Isles,
and Christopher Harley, associate of war-time motor boating,
a Scotsman but also new to the ground. (John Ainslie doubted
his own return to the Isles.) Kennie MacIver had sent one
of his letter-length telegrams, like others of happy memory,
saying that the *Heather* would be all ready.

The cliffs of Shiant showed faint in the south, then, ahead
and all on one bow, the grey teeth of Lewis appeared like some
uncharted archipelago where a ship could enter and be lost
in rocks and seaweed and northern birds. It was ten years
to the day since John Ainslie's and my first landing on North
Rona.

The crowd to meet the steamer, the fish-market, the waterfront hotel, the line of bruised buses ! The fishing was a
complete washout and Kennie was saying so ! We put up in
the hotel and later on, in the midnight dusk of July, he took
us up to the head of the quiet harbour. Old *Muirneag* lay
derelict against the wall (*Paradigm* and *Muirneag*, the last two
Stornoway sailing drifters, had been still in commission in
1939 ; *Paradigm* had since been broken up, for fencing posts ;
here was the survivor). The trim little motor-cruiser lying

alongside her was hardly recognisable, which could not be
and yet was, the sometime fishing boat *Heather*. The two
freshly varnished masts in tabernacles and the new standing
rigging, as against the telegraph pole Hugh and I had left
felled into its chocks on the matchbox wheelhouse ; a raised
combing of fore-cabin where once one had peered down
through a slot in the deck into a black hole ; wheelhouse
replaced by a new dodger and screen, engine controls brought
up through the deck, the coconut matting new and untrodden,
cordage new throughout, a little anchor winch ; from one
end to the other fresh paint and varnish hardly dry ! The
motor-cruiser *Heather*, the single-screw motor-yacht *Heather*,
8 tons. It was as if one had been lent Aladdin's wonderful
lamp and had given it a brisk rub ; and *Heather* rode gently
in the dim, lopping harbour.

Everything found, when we moved aboard in the morning :
crockery, bedding, a Primus galley, wireless set, compasses
standard and steering, electric light from a car battery. When
Kennie MacIver's own *Sulaire* had been commandeered early
on in the war he had taken in hand the reclamation and
conversion of the *Heather*, the start of which I had seen for
half an hour in 1941. She had been in use about the harbour
on and off ever since, graced with many of *Sulaire's* fittings.
And as for the poor abused *Sulaire* in Admiralty care, twice
she had dragged her moorings, the second time finally ; her
poor bones lay up in the rocks on the far side of the harbour.
Her owner had had to stand by and watch the story of pro-
gressive, uncared-for decline and careless end.

War-time fishing trips in the *Heather* (the Home Guard
exercises ?) seemed well remembered in Stornoway. Her
blithe crews seemed to have been in frequent trouble with
the authorities : what, us ? There was a boom across the
harbour entrance then, with the usual array of signals for port
closed, port open, and the rest, which had evidently made little
impression on holiday parties busy outside with a good evening
bite, and then trying to come home after hours. " Surely to
goodness the boat was well enough known to slip in and out

without all that palaver," etc., etc. It was Mr. Scott who was saying so. I had called to resume his oracle, and he stood as heretofore, holding somebody's urgently wanted fragment of engine, while occasional fishermen arrived bringing broken bits to be joined. All about the *Heather* of 1939 was to be recalled, the later engine he had since fitted, the weather's past, present and probable future, the war—a large unhurried indulgence for the ways of authority (considering that common sense wasn't to be expected) for the whole of foolish humanity, viewed from the midst of his litter of engines and motor cars (each lacking some one essential part). Here, anyway, 1939 might have been yesterday.

The *Heather's* present engine was the standard fisherman's four-cylinder Kelvin—start on petrol, run on paraffin, like her original Kelvin with two more cylinders added on, and some fifteen years taken off. The engine-room was recognisable, with the same benches at either side when one crouched to the iron altar. A couple of fire extinguishers replaced a remembered biscuit tin of damp sand. An extra fuel tank put range and endurance up to about 150 miles or twenty-four hours' steaming. The bilge pump now discharged through the side instead of in an oily smear all over the deck. The ballast was pig-iron instead of a substantial part of Carloway beach. The new floor-boards were covered with cortecine, not old engine oil. The original loose planks covering the fish-hold had been raised to a fixed ridge and done over with canvas to make a watertight job. Two bunks and the Primus galley lined the sides of the sometime fish-bay. The fore-cabin was the luxury compartment with its yacht furniture, cupboards and lockers, settees and cushions, two built-in bunks, wireless set and barometer.

The boat had been laid up for a few months for all the painting and rigging, and we ran into a little initial engine trouble, a persistent oiling-up of plugs, leaks past shrunken pump leathers to fill the crankcase with water. I appointed myself engineman, or more properly, driver, and began to relearn the elements of Kelvinism from young Johnnie, who had been running the boat. Altogether familiar, to be mopping out the crankcase, wringing out cotton waste into a bucketful of black oil and water. Johnnie worked like a slave, lifted off the great iron pots and fitted new piston rings, though unnecessarily. Finally, in a difficulty of tact, we persuaded Mr. Scott to attend. He lowered himself into the engine-room and there rested once again, spinning his Kelvin wisdom of unruffled common sense and saying to ourselves straining at the handle : " Och, it's just a knack, give her another touch." He went away saying that there would be no more trouble, and it was so. Thereafter the iron castanets clanked away hour after hour, the required parts remained hand-hot, the dirty warm water spat into the sea, the wisp of paraffin smoke blew down to leeward. Once or twice the gearbox stuck familiarly in ahead, though remediably. Bear on the lever and strike with a heavy hammer, the book said. One struck, sparks sizzled into the black bilge and the lever hastened into neutral. Putting oil in the clutch made it stick, the book said so ; " some wee pig-headed b—— who thinks he knows better than The Company," as Mr. Scott would have said, and in fact did. The makers were sacrosanct to Mr. Scott ; he was never, never one of those engineers, to be found in all walks of engineering, who airily knows better than The Company.

At first the swinging over of the engine to start seemed a knack of impossible strength but it was soon thoughtless ; even as John Naish, commissariat, soon came to understand ration books from cover to cover, including the new bread rationing.

The enormously heavy lugsail, which Hugh's and my manpower had been quite inadequate to haul taut enough to sail anywhere near the wind, had been saved by tanning and cut down to make the present mainsail. Kennie lent us a dinghy and a flounder net. We provisioned, topped up with water, and sailed on a grey evening. A preliminary run down the coast, an excursion to the Shiant Isles, weather and circumstances permitting.

* * *

A View of the Shiant Isles

Loch Shell was full of fish, sea-fowl splashed among patches of fry, porpoises went revolving as far as the shoal water at the head of the loch, where shoreward herons stood fishing. The first haul of the flounder net yielded sixteen flounders, a skate and a couple of large crayfish.

The north-west had had a miraculous spring though the summer of 1946 had long become universally disastrous. The forecast received by ship's wireless on our second evening in Loch Shell was unpromising, but next morning brought a flood of sharp sunlight on the sea and the hills, a chill early breeze. We steamed out of Loch Shell and headed across to the Shiants with the dinghy bouncing astern on the glittering chop of water. The sun had some power of warmth, the sky was the huge Hebridean bowl of blue and white.

We took a turn right round the islands and went in by the northern gap ; down along the puffin-buzzing eastern side of the Garbh to nose in towards the shingle strip between Garbh and an Tigh and anchor in sight of the bottom. Ten years ago the tide had been running like a river past the *Sulaire*. To-day the bay was bland, the stationary sea water an extra-ordinary pellucid green. *Heather's* underwater red of anti-fouling was brighter than if she had been hauled up ; the whole carriage of a boat in water so plain and magical as we idled round her in the dinghy. The imagined propeller now gleamed plain, lock-nut and split-pin, the seat of the rudder, the straight line of iron-shod keel curving upwards into forefoot, breaking surface at the stem. The patterns of sun and water shifted along her side, the anchor cable led away into depths and seemed to dance because of the surface ripple ; a sight of pale boulders on the bottom five or six fathoms down.

Wrens' songs carried out from the shore. Fulmars' farm-yard noises came down from grassy places in the cliffs of Eilean an Tigh, whose columns were in shadow, footed down here sheer into quiet dark water. We went rubbing against the cliff foot in the dinghy, in the chill of shadow, because the water was so quiet and greeny dark against the wall. The stretch of Eilean Mhuire shut in the bay from the east, a broad pavement of bay. A place to be, the Shiant Isles, with a boat on a summer's day !

We landed at the shingle strip, Muir's narrow shingly stripe, and pulled up the dinghy on the boulders. Then round the rocky corner into Eilean an Tigh, " without a particle of climbing," and there stood the house again on its coastal plat of silverweed. The attendant bothies had fallen into a bed of nettles, but for the house itself—recent habitation ! The remains of the window woodwork had been freshly painted blue. We pushed open the door. Repairs to some of the matchboard lining, a kettle on the hob, a roll of bedding on the floor, some volumes of Tonybee's *A Study of History* on a shelf. Afterwards, over in Harris, we met one of the Shiants' sheep tenants ; a chentleman had come in the month of Chune and he had lived in the house. ("A delicious solitude, if suns would always shine and seas were always calm," Dr. Macculloch had said.) The gentleman—having finished the *A Study of History*?—had lit a fire on the hill and the people in the island of Scalpay had sent and fetched him off.

The Shiants were still just in use. Five hundred sheep grazed the three islands, said the shepherd in Harris. We saw lobster pots piled in the old sheep fank on the shingle strip. A new fank had been fenced in beyond the snipe bog. The shepherds' house remained, but no shepherds, only a chentleman in Chune. No sign of cats nor this time even a possible eagle, but the mushrooms were better than before. I looked down from the cliff top of Eilean an Tigh. " View of *Heather* lying in the Bay of the Shiants, July 22nd, 1946." It was so !

The *Heather* lay quietly all day under the beetling cliffs ; we let her out of our sight. The west had been sending out fingers of cloud until now in early evening all the sky was grey again. The breeze dropped altogether and the sky began to look nasty. Eilean Mhuire was still to be landed on and explored, another visit, another year, for, like Muir, warned by the waning of our day, and certain murky-looking gatherings over head, we were obliged to take our departure out of the place without setting foot on the island.

The lobster boat *Speedwell II* of Oban, which had been picking up pots outside, came into the bay as we went out. The rain began again and the wind stirred. The big red buoy in the channel between Shiants and Lewis—it had marked the war-time convoy route—was still there, with the tide piling against it. But this time Loch Shell plaice and Shiant mushrooms were sizzling in the civilian galley. By the time we were snugged into the little basin of Loch Maaruig half-way up Loch Seaforth the rain was pelting and the gusts from the mountains blew breakers against the inland shore. All snug below while the boat yawed and tugged at her cable and the rain hammered on the deck.

There was a stiff breeze and a green-and-white sea outside when after another night's anchorage at Tarbert we set back for Stornoway. We gave the engine a rest and blew along famously. We crowded into Stornoway harbour entrance under sail and power, doing perhaps eight or nine knots. " By-God-man-she-came-in-like-a-torpedo-boat," said one of Kennie's henchmen, the famous Bob who always spoke like a machine-gun. Speed was the thing !

Shiant Islands, July 22, 1946

XXIX

A View of North Rona

" **B**UT still on RONA dwells th' impatient mind." If only
the weather would settle. There was no point in going
all that way in risky weather and then not being able to land.
But as Mr. Scott remarked as he looked out at the curtains of
rain blowing across his garage doorway, the weather wasn't
just so very patent.

We were berthed in the press of native and visiting drifters,
whose fishing continued scanty. The Stornoway boats looked
no older—*Comrade* and *Corona*, *Home Rule* and *Harvest*, *Ellen &*
Irene, *Lews*, *Verbena*, *Dove*, *Speedwell*, *Provider*, *Cailleach Oidhche*.
Before we left there was suddenly a big fishing; almost at once
a glut and restrictions on the number of nets to be shot.
The last time we entered harbour, in evening sunshine,
we stemmed the whole fleet as it came tumbling out,
each various ship thrusting at her best speed. First came the
steamers, fastest and farthest-going, then all the old black-
hulled, loggish, paraffin-engined double-enders and the
smaller, newer, standardised boats of the visitors, typed by
their varnished finish, diesel engines and canoe sterns. Last
of all came the smallest and slowest, most local and decrepit
of motor-boats, bare of wheelhouses and with only the
sketchiest accommodation, that black hole forward of the
fish-hold. And one night's best haul was made by a smallest
and slowest : a dreadful old local whose best speed was a
quivering amble of four knots.

The hotel bars of Stornoway had forgotten their pre-war
pretensions. The crowd soon sniffed out which bar had
something left, and there swarmed, bulging the doors. No
more conversational barmen in short white coats. The
managers rolled up their sleeves and came to help ; the sweat

dripped off them. The tills swam with wet money, every single glass was out, not a moment even to mop up the surf on the counter. The dirty concrete floor was out of sight, the have-not customers seethed among the haves, searching for empty glasses. The fumes of battle filled the air, the noise sounded from afar. Next day the bar would be locked and silent.

Stornoway had got an airport out of the war, now that the Americans were away. The newspapers came by air. The endearing telephone book of the Isles had been replaced by a page or two in the Aberdeen directory. The individual vying bus services had been rationalised. The town had been divided into one-way streets, though sheep still used them. A housing estate was going up on the outskirts, as it might have been any churned plot outside any town in the kingdom. Squatters had taken over the naval Nissen huts in the castle grounds, long before the rest of Britain had thought of squatting. It was an old game to Hebrideans ; years ago they had squatted all over Lord Leverhulme's proposed island dairy farm ; evictions and squatting were naturally mutual. Victoriana remained in the fantastic greenhouses at the back of the castle, now fast decaying into heaps of broken glass and skeleton iron.

Bouts of wind and rain continued from the west ; very kindly Margaret MacIver lent us her car. After the arrest of the war years the new tar was fast extending again and by now it was well on the way to Ness. The occasional dead sheep lay thrown to one side ; a few more motor cars had retired to the roadside museum. The moors were busy with seasonable activities of peat-carting and shieling life, but the activity of building along the roadsides was unprecedented. The surviving young men were home again and they were building themselves houses. These were commonly tiny concrete boxes dotted upon the waste, seeming more than ever without possible means of livelihood. They had a sawn-off appearance ; it seemed to be an accepted understanding to leave the walls at one end unfinished, as if a second room might be added later on. Did the builders ask any one first—permits ? housing grants ? Did the moor really *belong* to any one or did the builders, bred in the district, just cast their concrete walls as and where they thought fit ? A few bags of cement, some local pebbles and sand, a few planks and rafters, rolls of felt or sheets of corrugated iron, one door, one window, and there was a one-box house ; and absolutely nothing else. The road was the obvious surface for mixing a heap of concrete—och, the traffic could go round it. Some sizable two-storey houses were also going up, with solid walls of stone ; local resources were being found again in the days of mainland shortages. Some of the crofts were topped off with little windmill generators of home-made electric light ; that was something quite new ; there was more money about nowadays.

" Man alive, but I'm glad to see you," said Alec Mac-Farquhar—and I to see our old friend ; but the Committee had taken over most of his land, the mill had fallen into disrepair, his partner Murdo—the quiet, likeable Murdo, whom we had once carried to Stornoway to argue with the *Comrade*—had been killed in the war. Mr. MacFarquhar, Himself, the tenant of Rona, now spoke of the pension and of a mainland croft. Would any one take on the tenancy for the sentiment of it, for a sanctuary for birds and seals and the like o' that ? If we did get a landing on the island we would not forget to count the sheep ? He would have to go again himself next year anyway ; the sheep didn't throw their own fleeces and the Inspector would be after him if he let them go another year. (Once in another island there had been a prosecution by the Inspector in the matter of neglected sheep ; sheep left too long unshorn, and thus, cruelty to animals. As for the dipping regulations, they were understood to be waived for remote island flocks so long as any sheep brought back were dipped immediately after landing. But, said Mr. MacFarquhar, sheep brought from Rona were awful homesick, they never did well, no, not unless they were killed within two or three days.)

Mr. MacFarquhar was now a lay preacher whose unworldly interests took him ever more closely into the bosom of the Church. I remembered the sitting-room text ; after making

354

some vapid remark one caught it staring : " Christ is the silent Listener to every conversation." And " You tell Kennie MacIver not to go curing the herring on the Sabbath," said Mr. MacFarquhar; " aye, you tell him that from me, and see what he says." There were many stories of the tenant of Rona in Stornoway ; in the episode of the herring he had taken exception to the overworked curers working against time, on a Sunday. He had been referred to the forthright Bob, that well-known Stornoway character who spoke like a machine-gun, and who had then fired words which had lasted.

Mr. MacFarquhar had been three times to Rona during the war. He had been to the Committee and had told them that he would be prosecuted by the Inspector if he didn't go ; the Committee had seen the Authorities and he had been fixed up with a naval trawler from Stornoway. That trawler ! —man, it was a luxury after those Stornoway drifters. The captain had never been to the island before, but he knew just the course to steer. They had been given blankets for the night and life chackets, told what to do if anything should happen ; and the guns had been fired off, some practice or the like o' that. The lowliest naval auxiliary had been a glimpse of the great world to the tenant of Rona.

The speed of the trawler ! They were there in no time and the captain anchored so close in it was no trouble at all with the small boat. The first time they had found Dr. Darling's hut in the sheep fank—" and what a chob we had with it before we could even start " (the eaves had been well dangled with boulders). As for the aeroplane that was supposed to have crashed on Rona, there wasn't a sign of it ; he shouldn't be surprised if it weren't all a story. And there was another story of some airmen landing in the little dinghy they had, but och, he didn't think there was anything in it.

Seafaring had ever been a closed magic to Mr. Mac-Farquhar. He recalled a pre-war time when the returning drifter had " lost the course " and in an hour or two " we might have been anywhere on the face of the earth " ; and, as I had heard him do before, he recalled his first visit of all

355

when he had vowed he would never go there again, not for
all the sheep in creation. And now the last traditional link
with Rona was to be broken? It was a shame, as Mr.
MacFarquhar said; he had a sentiment for the island, all the
times he'd been there, but there it was. Further, and somewhat overtly, he seemed a good deal exercised about losing
the acclimatisation value of the Rona flock. This property
acquired by sheep was a substantial item in the ingoings of a
Highlands or Islands sheep farmer taking over his predecessor's
acclimatised stock, whether to be kept or cleared; but if
there were no successor?

One of the wholesale strokes of the war had found Miss
Daisy Macleod. Middle-aged Miss Macleod, who had started
her tea-room in Port of Ness while she was yet wearing black
for her mother, who had told John and I in her confiding
whisper that really she ought to have gone on the films because
of her Glasgow accent, had been, in brutal incongruity, " lost
at sea."

I ran into Mr. MacFarquhar again in the Stornoway
barber's. Sabbath-keeping was the theme. The voice of
conscience the only guide. The only permitted work was the
work o' necessity. This was the general theorem; discussion
was minutely pursued into what was and what was not the
work o' necessity. Surely the curing of highly perishable
herring which a big fishing left over into Sunday—while the
weary local driftermen slept red-eyed [*sic*] at home—surely
that was the work o' necessity? No?

The barber told a story for an example. The lassie
who was helping in the minister's house. " You heard of
that, Alec?" Mentioning no names, but " you'll know
who I mean." " Aye, aye," from Mr. MacFarquhar, who
evidently didn't. He incidentally was on his way to some
important convocation at Leverburgh—sixty-mile bus ride
from Stornoway, longest route in the islands. He was dressed
the part : bowler hat, wing collar, black tie, shiny black boots,
blue serge suit. He mustn't miss the car. " Och no, Alec,
you'll catch it right enough."

"Well then he had a lassie to help in the house, the minister I'm telling you of," said the barber. "She wass a dab hand at setting the table and the like o' that. And one day the minister had some friends to see him." Snip, snip. "On a Sunday. To dinner you understand. Well, they all sat down. The lassie brought in the supe. That was all right." Snip, snip. "She cleared away the supe and she brought in the meat and the spuds. And the minister looked at the spuds, they'd been peeled you understand? And he asked the lassie, had she peeled the spuds on the Sabbath—only he wouldn't call them that, you understand. And she said yes, she had." Snip, snip. "He bawled her oot for it, aye, and before strangers, he bawled her oot." Snip, snip, snip, snip. "Well, the next Sunday the lassie didn't peel the spuds, she brought them in in their chackets, you understand, and she stood back to see what he would du. Well, the minister he started to peel the spuds at the table. And the lassie came forward and she said what wass the difference between what he wass doing at the table now and what she wass doing last week when he bawled her oot, and before strangers?" Snip, snip. "Och, the minister had nothing to say, he hadn't a leg to stand on. And the lassie said to him she wished the strangers that were here last week were here to-day." Snip, snip, snip.

"Aye, aye," said Mr. MacFarquhar, and reflectively: "aye." A difficult point. The conversation turned to sin. The R.A.F. lad hurried out looking glad to escape, and it was now Mr. MacFarquhar's turn for the chair. He stood up saying sadly, "Aye, I'm covered in sin from head to foot" —but no, this is hardly fair, it's best left between him and the barber; but he would brook no denial, no, he would not.

*   *   *

One day the wind blew near gale force, driving dazzling cumuli borrowed from April across the moors; it slackened at evening when a gale warning was broadcast. The next day, sheets of blowing rain, but a fine evening. Some of the fisher-

men even committed themselves to a forecast of fair weather,
though perhaps only because out of kindness they wished to
please. We couldn't hang about any longer ; time was getting
short, we'd better have a shot at it anyway.

Next morning's shipping forecast was indifferent but early
sunlight was flooding, the breeze felt summerly. We sailed at
seven-thirty a.m. on the seventy-mile voyage to Rona. The
last few drifters were hurrying in.

Outside, visibility carried forty miles and more across the
Minch to the mainland mountains. Coasting up the Eye
peninsula, we cut inside the sea-bird rock Eilean a Chrotaich,
a glassy-watered floor to the cleft between it and the cliffs. I
knew it was clear enough because seven years before and
coming the other way the steam drifter *Windfall* had surged
through the gap, towing the old half-drowned fishing boat
Heather. The firmament had all the look of a bland summer's
day. The breeze was northerly, light ; the sunshine warm in
the shelter aft of the dodger ; the horizon far and hard, deep
slate-blue sea, glittering sun track, light wispy cloud. Porpoises
revolved alongside, pale shapes weaving under water, coming
up, coming up—glistening cetaceous hides when they broke
surface. Tiumpan Light, " Chump'n," walked out from behind
the near cliffs. The smooth face of the down at the back of the
lighthouse was scribbled with the black hieroglyphics of peat
cuttings, the lawn-like grass of sunlight was really sour bog
growth. Chump'n's white pillar was side lit by the sun ;
abeam and full lit ; astern and side lit. Cellar Head, distant,
then Tolsta Head, nearer, opened beyond.

Cloud shadows were blotched over the hinterland moors ;
the shadowed patches on the cliffs looked as if pots of dark
paint had been splashed there. The clots of cumulus kept
forming and dissolving. Now low cloud grew all along the
north-east.

Tolsta abeam : Tiumpan a low blue hump astern with a
tiny needle on top : Cellar abeam. We found we were making
only five and a half knots over the ground, and tide in favour ;
there was enough of a little chop from the north to take the

speed off her. Braga rock off the next headland was low and brown in the blue sea. Hugh and I had not seen the rock until it was abeam to seaward in a grey and white smother. We had kept close in down the coast from the Butt then, had been glad of the shelter ; we had no chart, only a map of Scotland, and did not know if the channel between the rock and the land was clear, but hoped so.

Braga rock was our departure for the northern ocean. We turned on it just before midday, set north-north-eastwards on the forty-mile leg, and began to relinquish the land. The course laid off on the chart would deliver us at a point midway between Rona and Sula Sgeir, perhaps. We drew the Butt abeam and its jagged northward teeth ; it became no longer a silhouetted corner ; there was a view low and faint down the Atlantic coast of Lewis, astern.

The best of the day was already gone. We had hardly started into the ocean when the cloud cover became overall, and the weather began to look not just so very patent. All the summer colour had gone, the ocean was the usual heaving slaty waste. Squalls, thunderstorms, said the faint one o'clock News. In a couple of hours the land was gone.

" Och, you don't want to worry about the enchine. Unless she'll take a block in the chet "—Johnnie's homespun advice. She had now been thumping away for half a day without a falter, a beat as rhythmic as a train's. As with any self-governed engine, I found it more remarkable that it should continue to go on and on quite on its own, rather than that it should get upset and cough and stop. With all our delight in the boat I had become particularly attached to the engine ; it was pleasant to sit beside it and enjoy the warm aura while it beat its oily guts. We counted on it ; a ship under power, not a wayward sailing boat. Minister an occasional squirt of oil into holes provided by The Company, see that the water-and-exhaust pipe remained hand-hot, that the oil drippers dripped not too fast and not too slow and she would keep going for as long as there was paraffin in the tank. The Kelvin driver's commonest check was to open the compression tap of each cylinder in turn, to see that each plug was firing. This was the very voice of a Kelvin : the hoarse wet puff through the hole when the plug was not firing ; the stab of flame when it was, breaking out from the inner furnace with a sharp bark ; the jog-trot of bangs and puffs when the plug was and wasn't. The tappets jumped up and down, the enormous flywheel spun in the cut-away floor-boards. The hull was making a little water under way, you had to keep an eye on the bilge and pump out occasionally lest the flywheel should dip.

We took our turns at the wheel. Chris, navigator, had laid off course and tide allowance as meticulously as if he were conducting a battleship. West-going stream sets in direction so and so from x hours before H.W. Dover until y hours after at a rate of z knots at springs; east-going stream, this, that and the other. The engine-room hatch was the best cockpit ; you were warmed from below and could see what was going on on top. Porpoises were jumping clear, showing their horizontal flukes and the scars on their hides. Steady hot pulse of the engine ; the short punch and pitch of a chubby, driven boat ; uneventful, uncomfortable, lurching plod at brisk walking pace ; the usual ocean unwarmth. It was quite like a war-time sea-going—an engine beat aft, the crash of water against the hull, the creak and quiver, a faint pit of worry ; and an hour in one's warm bunk !

Visibility came steadily down and down and now there was misty rain. At something over four hours out from the Butt came the rather derisive cry : " Land Ahoy ! " It was right ahead, and recognised as the hump of Sula Sgeir. We threw off a bit to the eastward (which the navigator was just about to require for tide allowance). Where Rona should be was a squally-looking patch ; it lifted and Rona was plain to see. After that it was a matter of patience while the island grew from the sea.

The weather forecast between Children's Hour and News made out a general inference of rain spreading from the west, thunderstorms, moderate to fresh westerly winds. Hebrides : north-west, fresh, backing west to south-west. Sula Sgeir

disappeared in dank mist, the breeze was shifting about, the
sky was a grey pall. Rona nearly disappeared in turn, while
the Sgeir stood out again, stark this time against a band of
yellow on the western horizon. We were right up to Rona
before the island grass was green and the dark mark of the
village could be made out on the hill. We came up outside
the skerry of Gealldruig Mhor and along the eastern cliffs ;
village and chapel showed on the skyline. There was a bit of
a tumble of wind against tide off the eastern hill ; Fianuis
opened ; we rounded the corner into the bay. Arrived !

There was no hope of landing. The northerly swell was
slapping straight on to the cliff foot of Toa Rona. The bay
was all a short chop of broken water. And what a wild place
it did look, the cliffs leading up into the high bare ridge, the
bare rock sprawl of Fianuis. All the shouting sea-fowl were
breaking out from the cliffs, the seals' heads were bobbing
everywhere—swarming, entirely extra-human metropolis !
One couldn't but come as a foreigner to this place, nothing
found, no snug anchorage, only the bare mound fringed with
warning surf ; the mound swarmed upon and burrowed in
by countless sea-birds. It was all the more obvious when
conducting one's own small vessel ; arrival meant no change to
security.

We took a turn round the bay, then hauled off to the
eastward for half a mile, out of the way of the land ; stopped,
cut the engine, and rolled. Stornoway to Rona had taken
exactly twelve hours.

Landing was impossible now ; the breeze was nothing, but
it was northerly and so was the swell. We considered : according to the six o'clock shipping forecast the wind should back
and freshen during the night ; if it did, the bay would at once
be sheltered. The wind could freshen quite a lot but so long
as it was westerly a landing might be managed—unless the
northerly swell persisted. We decided to lie off overnight and
to try to land at dawn, counting on a backing of the wind. So
we just rolled unattached in the ocean with nothing to do
except wait and see what the weather would do. Paradoxically

we counted on its worsening ; the wind was unlikely to back right round without unpleasantness.

The boat rolled and rolled and rolled, an aimless derelict. Neither a lash-up sea-anchor nor the tightly sheeted mizzen made any noticeable difference. She just got herself broadside on to the sea and rolled her guts out ; and we were either sick or wondering when to be sick. As Mr. Scott had said of a war-time fishing trip in this boat : " You couldn't sit stand or lie in the b——". John managed to cook some fish, which we ate on deck without enthusiasm. With more difficulty we transferred the paraffin from two extra ten-gallon drums into the tanks. We were going to be close for fuel, at five and a half knots instead of the expected seven. There was nothing of an anchorage between Rona and Stornoway, seventy miles ; probably we had better make for the mainland Loch Inchard, fifty miles. No doubt we could get fuel there and then cross the Minch at leisure. For me anyway it would be intriguing to come to Kinloch Bervie again, to the Sailors' Home—and from seaward.

Birds and seals came out from Rona to look at us—close to, seals' breathing was an asthmatic blowing through their so-controllable nostrils. The evening made a tremendous display of angry coloured cloud and flame over the pitch-black base of Fianuis. We were carrying away very slowly eastwards.

Once again the inhuman sea chill of the small hours ! At half-past two it was my turn to huddle inside the watchman's blanket. The north-east was a range of black mountainous cloud whose crags and peaks were already backed with a tinge of yellow dawn. There was a cold sheen upon the shifting face of the waters, the Northern Ocean, the bosom of the deep ! The sky overhead had cleared, and was pale and starlit. The black hump of Rona was still well in sight. The shiveringly chill wind had indeed done the necessary backing and was now full westerly. So far so good.

Three-fifteen and one might have seen to read. At three-thirty a momentary fluttering of a bird against the dawn—a

fork-tail going to sea ? Some large half-seen cetaceous creature
broke alongside, blew with a hoarse wet blast like one of the
engine's compression taps, and returned to the deep. Nothing
else but the sounds of the boat abandoned to wind and sea,
the slop and slap of water and the slacking to and fro of her
rudder. The war-time reclamation of the boat had included
the fitting of large pinch-bolts along her beams from one side
to the other : tighten by one turn a year ; they'd take a turn
or two after this planktonic night ! At four o'clock it was a
relief to start up and put some purpose into her—and ourselves—after eight hours of abandoned rolling.

The bay was splendidly changed. The wind was even
south of west and the bay seemed calm and inshore after the
the outer ocean. The last of the northerly swell was only a
low, slow heave. We anchored carefully in ten or eleven
fathoms, letting out all the cable we had.

The sky was fast clouding over again from the west, but
at five-thirty a sudden flood of yellow sunshine broke over the
island. Everything was instantly sharp and clear, the puffins
and black-backs dotted all over the green northern slope, the
sheep fank and the wall across the neck of Fianuis, the customary flock of young shags in the bay, the seals' heads, the
family-cruising eiders. The sunshine lasted five minutes. We
did not see it again for a day or two.

A gannet plumped into the sea right alongside and came
up with a mackerel, got it down, washed vigorously, and took
off again in a long taxi-ing round the bay. We, too, had a
quick breakfast while we waited to see how the boat would
settle. She took away some of her cable and then seemed to
lie quite reasonably, though the anchor could only have been
resting on the rock bottom. Soon after six o'clock John and
Chris went away in the dinghy. They landed and pulled up
the boat, obviously without difficulty. They went off, one
into Fianuis, the other up the northern hill ; two more new
visitors to Rona, and an uprising of the natives !

The seals' breathing was so noisy ! The heads popped up
to stare and turn about—large curious eyes, working nostrils

—and sank silently down again. The sea-fowl were shouting and echoing in the caverns of Toa Rona. It was exciting! This surely was the ultimate of native remoteness, to old Macculloch the completion of solitude and desertion. Brood after tended brood of alien puffins and black-backs and shags and seals, each after its own kind, self-contained ; a careless see-saw regulation of accident and untidy killing ; a sprawling camp made up of discrete units where yet each unit counted for nothing. How many individuals the same identities now as ten years ago ?

The *Heather* lay first one way and then another and rolled at her tether. Nearly time for the weather forecast. I switched on the set, but it remained silent. What was the matter with the thing ? We had received at this range last night—surely the near cliffs couldn't be cutting us off ? Oh of course, Sunday. It wouldn't be for another hour yet. A rain squall broke over the island. I retired to my bunk and listened to the rain. They would be getting wet.

The wireless came alive at five to eight. Rain spreading from the west (it had done that already) . . . moderate westerly winds (yes, now) backing to south and freshening to strong. Southerly and strong ; oh dear, that would mean a wretched day-long punching to get back to the Minch.

I saw the others coming back down the hill. They rowed out and reported that they had counted scruffy-looking sheep up to a hundred and forty (which Mr. MacFarquhar afterwards thought satisfactory). This time Chris stayed on board. John and I landed and pulled up the dinghy—easy.

The island was so large and solid as soon as one stepped into it, and the boat very small. That was the way with landing at any small island.

Of course everything was just the same, even the grey weather mixed of rain and mist was fully typical. Here were the same rough beds of salt-bitten orache, the bright green *Poa* grass, the gulls aroused from splashed and littered rocks. Interesting remains of Dr. Darling's hut were spread around the sheep fank. A single section containing a window was

still in one piece, propped or blown against the fank wall.
We climbed the northern hill and looked down to rimmed
Fianuis and to our own wee boatie in the bay. A rain squall
swept over as we topped the ridge and opened the southern-
ward ocean. It looked unpleasant, a grey and white welter
and the spray throwing up in bursts on Gealldruig Mhor. The
wind was ever freshening, it was south-west now and backing
all the time towards south. We knew well enough we were in
for an uncomfortable time ; an hour ashore would make no
difference.

In Lewis we had met a party of botanists who asked us to
collect anything we could from outlying islands for the South
Kensington Museum. So far we had delivered one wilted load
from the Shiants ; now we snatched up handfuls of the wet
rank herbage of Rona. I picked up the rusty remains of a
smoke-float and that was the only sign of the famous crashed
aircraft.

The old lazy-beds above the village still grew wild white
clover. The shepherds' gravestone leant over more than ever ;
it had weathered to the status of an Ancient Monument. The
manse—no change—starling-splashed stones and a floor of
sopping wet chickweed. The village reeked of fork-tails, young
fulmars were parked in their accustomed nooks. The deep,
weedy grass was laid over by wind and rain. Coming like this,
insecure, wetted, in a hurry, and once again the village made
its impress : this was once home to generations of humans.

The chapel looked quite reformed with its south wall high
and entire, and a doorway in it. Within at one end, which
Dr. Darling had said would do for an island museum, was his
collected heap of quern stones. And, just as he had described,
you could now stoop and enter St. Ronan's cell by the excavated
doorway. The floor of the cell was an upheaval of black earthworks, as left by the excavator when he had gone so far and
then stopped for fear of unsupporting the walls. Young fulmars
still squatted about the dim interior and the streams of sick
showed that they had already received a visit to-day. There
would be fewer bones left now that the fledglings could shuffle

straight into the chapel and thence out through the southern doorway—without a particle of climbing.

I was relieved to cross the ridge and bring the *Heather* in sight again. She had gone to the opposite scope of her cable and we could see that a new swell was already feeling round the eastern hill from the south. The anchorage would soon be untenable.

Back on board we all felt pleased that the weather had gone so exactly to forecast and that in plan and execution we had been neatly opportunist ; though now we felt no great urge to start into the ocean. We secured the dinghy very firmly inboard, looked over the boat, and had something to eat before the new swell should force us out of the bay. Chris laid off his course to the southward. We should make for Loch Inchard, for its most landward recess ; nine or ten hours perhaps. It would be a strange entrance for not good weather, but we ought to be there just before dark. We should have the sea a bit on one bow to start with, though the wind was obviously going to go on backing and freshening ; we were bound to end up by punching pretty well straight into it.

For myself it would be a return to Kinloch Bervie, where eleven years ago the youths Ainslie and Atkinson had arrived on their first cast of island-going. The engine was putt-putting, the anchor coming up. We steamed out round Toa Rona and into the ocean : the *Heather*, she sayles to the mayne sea againe.

North Rona Island, July 28, 1946

EPILOGUE

A Bird's-Eye View

THIS was a proper use for an aeroplane, to be drawn on its invisible string over sunlit Hebridean seas : the flying omnibus, the R.A.F. Sunderland, its guns and bombs left at home. James Fisher had borrowed it for a day, for a survey of bird cliffs under the ægis of Airborne Research Facilities. He was continuing an enthusiasm for the outliers begun in 1939 when he had organised a yachting trip that had taken in St. Kilda and Sula Sgeir. To-day it was by his grace that mine was one of six uniquely privileged bodies now being flown from Stranraer—to Mull of Kintyre—to Skerryvore—to Barra Head, the bastion cliff of the Outer Isles.

One by one every single outlier of the Hebrides was to pass below the flying boat's wing ; so easy ; in one day each different island I had struggled to at sea level was to be brightly mapped from above. My twelve years were telescoped into one day.

The sea was shallowing, sand-floored, the astonishing sea colour about the Monach Isles. The islanders were back ! Corn marigolds coloured the arable patches, a boat was drawn up. Tide was low on this wonderful morning of July 30th, 1947, the fords between the Monach Isles were dry, the sand dazzling in the sunlight ; and the solitary cottage of Ceann Iar still stood lonely by its crescent bay.

Black Haskeir rocks—you could have landed there easily in this settled calm. The *Heather* had yet to get there. By air, Haskeir to St. Kilda, fifteen minutes ; by sea, Leverburgh to St. Kilda, eight and a half hours. Only a few weeks before had *Heather* (John Naish, James Fisher and myself) steamed into Village Bay at dawn, in the rain, to anchor under the lowering mist pall : the first post-war visitors. (In the battered

367

village more roofs were gone, hinges rusted away and doors blown in, the rooms sheep-dunged ; the old migrant villagers had been spared the sight. Soay sheep had increased to something like a swarm. Change from the deep grass of 1938 was *gaunt* ; there was no cover, the village grass was a closely-grazed sward littered with stones ; stunted bracken was beginning to creep ; the snipe had gone ; most of the cleits contained dead sheep. But in a cleit by the manse was a St. Kilda wren's nest, once more to face the flash-bulbs.)

The Stacs were a sun dazzle of gannets from above, Boreray a spectacle even more incredible than that given to the little cork *Heather* when she was chugging round the bottom. Rockall next, the rare speck, chief objective of the flight ; and there it was, the ultimate haystack of rock, with a cloud of kittiwakes flying off it. A hundred and eighty-five miles back to St. Kilda, quite a long wait, over an hour. At the Flannans —Relief Day ! *Pole Star*, or another, was in the act of steaming away while the dot of red flag still fluttered at the flagstaff.

Loch Roag was an inner maze of islands as far as the eye could see. *Heather* must get in there and explore, some year. The western seaboard of Lewis : crofters' toy animals, their dolls' houses. The Butt Lighthouse was ahead, abeam, astern.

At Sula Sgeir sunlight was lower for another dazzle of gannets ; Rona lay waiting in the east. (In a few weeks the men of Ness would be out at the Sgeir ; would go back with a first post-war haul of over two thousand gugas, to be sold in a rush at six shillings a head.)

Rona was bright green in the blue sea. The slant of sunlight made the south slope stereoscopic—of course, the archæologist's aerial view ; how unknown detail was revealed ! Now old enclosures and walls and more lazy-beds were traced over nearly all the slope, which one would never have guessed from the ground. Round the eastern hill, and the shadow of the flying boat was running over Fianuis. No time, it went too fast ! There was the sheep fank, sheep were streaming up the north slope of the ridge. They looked so brilliantly white ; had they just been sheared ? (So they had, and only a day or

two before : Mr. MacFarquhar had a new partner, Rona
Annuals a new lease of life. The sheep were highly profitable,
and old ways were set for a few years yet.) The flying boat
finished its single circuit, and Rona lay astern once more.

Cape Wrath led on to Sandwood Bay, to Bulgie Island—
not, after all, to be landed upon in 1935. Loch Inchard led
deep into the mainland and there was that seaward rock spur
with the swell breaking white on it, the spur *Heather* had been
careful to give a wide berth last year on her travels about the
loch—between Kinloch Bervie and her anchorage in the loch's
most landward recess. There were the sandstone tiers of
Handa Island, the evening-quiet Bay of the Shiants. Fifteen
hundred miles, a little over nine hours up, and the flying boat
was back at Stranraer ; time to make a dash for the harbour
station and catch the London train.

Select Bibliography

MARTIN MARTIN will always come first. His very readable *Description of the Western Islands of Scotland* (1703) was last reprinted by Eneas Mackay (Stirling, 1934) ; an edition which includes his *Late Voyage to St. Kilda* (1698) and also Sir Donald Monro's *Description* of 1549.

J. A. Harvie-Brown's pioneering voyages are described in his and T. E. Buckley's *Vertebrate Fauna of the Outer Hebrides* (Edinburgh, 1889), which covers birds, mammals and fish—anything with a backbone ; a unique sort of natural history *cum* guide book illustrated with reduced six-inch maps and the first photographs taken in the smaller islands. There is no Hebridean *Flora* but Miss M. S. Campbell's *Flora of Uig* (Buncle, Arbroath, 1945) is a start towards one. Dr. F. Fraser Darling's wide review of *Natural History in the Highlands and Islands* (New Naturalist, Collins, 1947) does the Islands' share handsomely ; the essays he wrote during his residence in Rona in 1938 make up *A Naturalist on Rona* (O.U.P., 1939) ; life in Rona also comes into his *Island Years* (Bell, 1940) and *Island Farm* (Bell, 1944). The handbook of Rona, Sula Sgeir and the Flannans is Malcolm Stewart's *Ronay* (O.U.P., 1933)—his own visits thither, a resumé of their histories and a bibliography. All the outliers, even Rockall, are described in the Scottish Mountaineering Club Guide, *The Islands of Scotland (excluding Skye)* (S.M.C., Edinburgh, 1934), and all Hebridean hills are appraised ; a complete cover of reduced Bartholomew's maps is included. The Biblical English of the Admiralty *Pilots* is well represented in the *West Coast of Scotland Pilot* (Admiralty, 1934), a mine of information.

Island Memories (Moray Press, 1937) is the collection of John Wilson Dougal's gentle essays. T. S. Muir's *Ecclesiological Notes* on *Some of the Islands of Scotland* (Edinburgh, 1885) are largely Hebridean ; but for a full archæological review there is nothing less than the Royal Commission on Ancient and Historical Monuments and Constructions of Scotland's *Ninth Report with Inventory of Monuments and Constructions in the Outer Hebrides, Skye and the Small Isles* (H.M.S.O., Edinburgh, 1928, £1 12s. 6d.)

George Seton's *St. Kilda* (Blackwood, 1878) reviews the island's history up to 1877 and is a steady item in second-hand bookshops. J. Sands' forlorn *Out of the World ; or, Life in St. Kilda* (Edinburgh, revised edn., 1878) is a pleasant curtain-raiser to the many other visitors' books published during the next thirty years, which include the Kearton brothers' *With Nature and a Camera* (Cassell, popular edn., 1902). Twenty-five copies of *St. Kilda Papers, 1931*, various authors, are distributed among the chief libraries of Britain ; this collection, with Malcolm Stewart's included *Bibliography of the Island of St. Kilda*, is of first interest to any one concerned with the island's natural history.

Louis Macneice's *I Crossed the Minch* (Longmans, 1938), " the book of an outsider who has treated frivolously what he could not assess on its merits," says the author, is very entertaining to others in like case. Compton Mackenzie's comedy fictions of Great and Little Todday, *Keep the Home Guard Turning* (Chatto, 1943) and *Whisky Galore* (Chatto, 1947), with Gaelic glossary, are exceedingly lifelike. Finally, no visitor to Lewis should be without—as the compiler might himself have put it—the *Official Guide to Stornoway* (Simmath Press, Dundee).

Events and Dates—North Rona

[with acknowledgment
to Malcolm Stewart]

VIITH, VIIITH OR IXTH CENTURY
   (Dark Ages)   Building of St. Ronan's Cell and residence of St. Ronan (?).

MIDDLE AGES

                     Building of chapel. Roman Catholics' later Teampull nam Manach still survived in part in 1800, disappeared sometime later.

XVITH CENTURY
   1549   Sir Donald Monro collecting information about the island. (His MS., *A Description of the Western Isles of Scotland called Hybrides*, was not published until 1774.)

XVIITH CENTURY
   (Pre-disaster)   Note on island included in a " *Description of the Lews* by John Morisone, Indueller there."
Parochial visit of Mr. Daniel Morison, minister of Barvas.
Sir George M'Kenzie of Tarbat gave *An Account of Hirta and Rona* (probably hearsay) to Sir Robert Sibbald.

   (Disaster) c. 1680   Extinction of the Ancient Race. New colonists later sent out.

   (Post-disaster) c. 1695   Martin Martin collecting information from Mr. Daniel Morison and others for inclusion in his *Description of the Western Islands of Scotland* (1703). Men of new colony probably lost in boating accident, women later brought back to Lewis. (Next in-

habitant a female whose fire was relighted by divine agency ?)

XVIIITH CENTURY

Island in hands of tacksman (? Murrays of Ness). Shepherds in residence. Potatoes introduced.

c. 1773

Publication of ode *A Maid of Rona* by Rev. Dr. Dalgleish.

1777

Publication of narrative poem *Rona* by Dr. John Ogilvie.

1797

Publication of report of island by Rev. Mr. Donald Macdonald, minister of Barvas, in *Statistical Account*. One shepherd family in residence (? Finlay Mackay).

XIXTH CENTURY
1813, July 25

Boat's crew landed from H.M.S. *Fortunée*.

c. 1815

Visit of Dr. John Macculloch in revenue cutter. Kenneth MacCagie, shepherd, and family in residence.

c. 1820-1840

Various shepherd families in residence.

c. 1844

Last inhabitant, Donald M'Leod, King of Rona, left the island.

c. 1850

Ordnance Survey of island by Captain Burnaby and party. Island offered to Government for penal settlement by Sir James Matheson, proprietor.

1857, July

Visit of T. S. Muir and Iain Mackay in trading sloop *Ada*.

1860, July 10-11

Rona Annual with Daniel Murray (tenant), T. S. Muir, Iain Mackay and a Stornoway schoolmaster.

1883, June 20

Visit of John Swinburne and Norman Macleod (pilot) in sailing yacht *Medina*.

1884, May 20

Murdoch Mackay and Malcolm MacDonald, shepherds, landed and

374

set up in manse. Visited by friends from Ness in August and September.

1885, February April 22	Deaths of Mackay and MacDonald. Their bodies discovered and buried. Later exhumed for post-mortem and reinterred.
June 16	Short visit by J. A. Harvie-Brown, H. G. Barclay and Norman Macleod (pilot) in steam yacht *Eunice*.
1886, June 29—July 1	Residence of R. M. Barrington in village.
1887, June 18, 19	2nd visit of Harvie-Brown, with Prof. R. F. Heddle and W. Norrie in sailing yacht *Shiantelle*.
1894	Visits of Sir Archibald Geikie in steam yacht *Aster* and of D. L. Popham, yachtsman returning from Faroes.

XXth Century

1907	1st visit of Duchess of Bedford.
1910, July 19 and August 25	2nd and 3rd visits of Duchess of Bedford.
Pre-war	Visit of Dr. Francis Ward (Scottish Fisheries Board).
1914, June	Residence of two unknown gentlemen in manse.
June 21 August 23	4th visit of Duchess of Bedford. H.M.S. *Sappho* searched island for enemy aircraft base.
1924	Island included in purchase of lands in Lewis by Barvas Estates Ltd., from the late Lord Leverhulme.
July 14	Visit of staff of Royal Commission on Ancient and Historical Monuments, etc.
1927, July 29	Visit of John Wilson Dougal with Rona Annual in steam drifter *Pisces*.
1928, October	Visit of Prof. James Ritchie and W. L. Calderwood (Scottish Fisheries Board).

375

1929, July 13	Visit of ketch *Dalga* (A. B. Duncan) with Rev. J. A. McWilliam and J. B. Duncan. (July 14-15, hove to off Rona in westerly gale.)
1930, July 31—August 4	Residence of Malcolm Stewart and D. M. Reid in manse. Landed and retrieved by steam trawler *Sophos*.
1931, August 28—September 3	Residence of Malcolm Stewart and T. H. Harrisson in manse. Landed and retrieved by steam trawler *Sophos*.
1936, July 16—August 12	Residence of J. A. Ainslie and R. Atkinson in manse. Landed by steam drifter *Rose*, retrieved by steam drifter *Alert*.
July 30	3rd visit of Malcolm Stewart, with Mrs. Stewart, by Rona Annual (A. MacFarquhar, tenant), in motor drifter *Cailleach Oidhche*.
1937, July 28	A. A. Macgregor and R. Atkinson with Rona Annual in motor drifter *Provider*.
August 1	4th visit of Malcolm Stewart, in steam yacht *Golden Eagle*.
1938, July 12—September 30 and November 15—December 22	Residence of Dr. F. Fraser Darling and family in hut in sheep fank. Landed and retrieved by fishery cruiser *Vigilant*.
1939, June 18-29	Residence of Dr. and Mrs. Fraser Darling in hut in sheep fank. Landed and retrieved by fishery cruiser *Vigilant*.
1941, April	Emergency landing of R.A.F. Whitley aircraft. Aircrew unhurt, retrieved by naval trawler; aircraft recovered in remarkable salvage operation (Fl. Sgt. D. C. F. Waller).
1946, July 27-28	Visit of *Heather* (R. Atkinson) with Dr. J. M. Naish and C. J. Harley.

INDEX